A Shift in Fate

Lost Legacies
Book 2

Maddox Grey

GREYMALKIN
PRESS

The Lost Legacies Series

A Shift in Darkness*

A Shift in Shadows

A Shift in Fate

A Shift in Fortune

A Shift in Ashes

A Shift in Wings

A Shift in Death

A Shift in Tides

*A Shift in Darkness is available for free download at maddoxgreyauthor.com.

Published by Greymalkin Press
www.greymalkinpress.com

Cover Design by Seventhstar Art

eBook ISBN: 978-1-7375381-0-3
Paperback ISBN: 978-1-7375381-6-5

Note from Author on Language & Content

I am a strange, strange person, and I've lived a bit of an odd life. I was born and raised in California, but was mostly raised by my Canadian grandmother and was then unofficially adopted by an Irish family in my late teens. You might be wondering why I'm mentioning this, and the reason is that I have a bit of a magpie approach when it comes to the English language.

Sometimes I like the American English spelling... sometimes I'm really attached to that extra "u" and go for the Irish version (yes I'm specifically choosing to say Irish and not UK because I don't want my family to smother me in my sleep).

Bless the soul of my copy-editor because she just sighs heavily at the start of each manuscript and deals with my eccentricities. So if you're an American and looking at a word and thinking it's not spelt right... it is most likely the non-American version of the word.

Okay. We got that out of the way. Let's chat real quick about what to expect in this book. This is a fantasy novel that contains adult content and situations. If it was a movie, it would probably be rated "R" for violence and language. If you want to go into this book completely blind and prefer not to read content warnings, you can skip on ahead, my friend.

If there are certain topics that you need to avoid for the sake of your own mental health, or that you simply don't like, please take a look at the list below for some things you will find in this book.

- References to emotional child abuse/neglect
- Drinking alcohol as a coping mechanism
- Depression related to grief related trauma
- Consensual explicit sex scene (there is no dub-con or non-con)

To Abbott, Chrissy, and Lindsay. My three ride or die besties. Thanks for putting up with my antisocial grumpy ass.

Chapter One

My back slammed into the mat for what felt like the hundredth time. Rather than get up, I just lay there panting. It seemed like the smarter move.

"Nice technique you got there."

"Shut it, vampire," I growled.

As usual, Mikhail did no such thing. "There are two vampires in this room," he smoothly stated. "And I'm not even the one who's been kicking your shifter ass for the past thirty minutes. Why does he get to be called by his name but I just get 'vampire'?"

"Because I like him more than you. Obviously." I winced as I pushed off the ground and leaned on my elbows. That last kick had probably fractured my ribs. My shifter healing was already fixing the damage, but it still hurt to breathe. A second later, a hand appeared in front of me, and I grabbed it, allowing Magos to pull me to my feet.

"All good?" Magos asked, not appearing the least bit remorseful about delivering that bone-shattering kick.

I scowled up at him. At just under six feet, I was tall, but

Magos still had several inches on me. Tall and broad shouldered, Magos looked every inch the warrior he was.

"I'm fine," I grumbled and rubbed my side. "Wasn't expecting that last kick."

"Obviously," Mikhail chimed in, echoing my tone from earlier.

"It's not like you fared that much better," I snapped.

Before kicking my ass, Magos had sparred with his nephew. Magos didn't believe in holding back in fighting practice. Which was why Mikhail was laid up on our couch healing from his sparring session, giving him the perfect view to provide commentary on my sparring session. If I'd had a knife on me, I would have thrown it at him, but Magos had instituted a rule months ago that all weapons had to be put away when we entered the apartment. Apparently, Mikhail and I constantly trying to stab each other wore on Magos's nerves.

The three of us were still figuring out our dynamic. Even though Mikhail had retired from the vampire Council, it was still hard not to think of him as their notorious assassin. Magos enjoyed having his nephew around, even if their relationship was a bit strained. That was mostly why I tolerated Mikhail staying with us. He was the only family Magos had left, and I didn't want to take that away from him.

Even if Mikhail had the audacity to declare he should move into the empty apartment on the second floor. I'd flat out laughed in his face when he'd made his little declaration. In truth, I had been thinking about offering that to him, but because he got pushy about it, I changed my mind. We'd been bickering about it ever since, but I was holding fast in my refusal. So Mikhail remained on our couch and I had to listen to him heckle me while I got my ass kicked by Magos.

I stretched to test how my ribs were doing. Still sore, but another few minutes and they'd be good as new.

"We should leave soon," Magos said.

We were planning on taking the vampire kids out around the town. Mikhail had never confirmed their whereabouts to the Council before he split ties with them, but just to be safe, we made sure one of us was always with them when they left the apartment. It had taken some time for the vampire kids to get comfortable around Mikhail; they'd grown up hearing stories of the infamous vampire assassin, so he had set them on edge at first. But they had gradually accepted him over the past few months. Mikhail grunted in agreement and swung his feet off the couch. A grimace of pain spread across his face, and I smirked. Before I could ask him how those ribs of his were doing, our front door flew open and Pele strolled in.

"Vampires. Out," she announced and dropped the black duffel bag in the living room.

Magos and Mikhail stiffened slightly and looked at the daemon warily.

"Pele, remember how we talked about you being slightly nicer to my vampire roommates? Well, Magos anyway," I reminded her.

"I remember you whining to me about it. But I never agreed to anything."

I huffed a laugh. Given that Pele owned this building and was allowing the vampire kids to live on the first floor and two other vampires to live on this floor, we should probably all be happy with that. I was pretty sure she was warming up to Magos, but she wasn't a fan of Mikhail.

"What brings your beautiful self to our apartment this evening?" I asked.

Pele's bright turquoise eyes focused on me, and a wicked smile spread across her face. "Jinx mentioned that while your panic attacks have gotten better, you still have issues with being bound. The warlocks almost captured you last time because of it." She flicked a hand at the bag and ropes sprang out of it, looping themselves over the steel beams that ran across the ceiling. "You've been sulking these past few months since your werewolf boyfriend ran off. I'm tired of it. So I thought we'd play some games and see if we can help prevent you from immediately panicking while bound." Pele sauntered over to me. The tailored dark blue suit played perfectly with her bright red skin and showcased all her curves. She stood in front of me and ran one of her sharp nails down my neck. "I figured it would help with the whole sulking thing, too."

I shivered as her nail went back up my neck. "Right," I breathed. "Magos? Are you . . . umm . . . good with taking the vamp kids out?"

Magos looked at me, amusement flickering in his copper-colored eyes. "Yes. I think we can manage."

I glanced at Mikhail and jerked my head towards the door. He rolled his eyes and followed his uncle.

We'll join the vampires, a voice grumbled in my head. Magos and Mikhail paused by the front door. A moment later, two cats trotted out from the hallway that led to the bedrooms, one black and one silver. Jinx and Luna.

Jinx glared at me as he walked by. Magos opened the door for him and followed him out. Mikhail waited for Luna. The silver grimalkin paused and looked up at me. I met her lilac eyes and gave her a soft smile. *Will you be okay?* I pushed the thought to her.

Yes. Thank you, a soft voice said in my head. When Jinx had found Luna in the woods of a fae realm years ago, she'd been seriously injured. He'd managed to get her to some fae who healed her body, but her magic had been completely depleted. When I first met her, she hadn't been able to speak telepathically. The past few months, her magic had started to come back and so had her voice. Unlike Jinx, she was pleasant to talk to, so I enjoyed our conversations. She still had no memory of what had happened to her before ending up in those woods with a nearly fatal wound.

4

Mikhail knelt slightly and held his arm out. Luna trotted over to him and smoothly leapt up his arm and settled on his shoulders. To everyone's surprise, they'd become quite close over the past few months. It was probably the only reason Jinx tolerated Mikhail. Jinx would do anything to make Luna happy and feel safe.

Mikhail walked towards the door and called over his shoulder, "Don't break any of the furniture." He hastily closed the door behind him.

The ropes moved slowly and wrapped themselves around my wrists, tugging my arms up. Panic immediately seized me, but the ropes loosened until they were gently supporting me rather than binding me. The panic was still there, but it had eased a bit. Pele was one of the few beings I trusted completely. She ran her fingers through my long ash blond hair, undoing it from the braid I usually kept it in, and leaned in to whisper in my ear, "Now then, what games shall we play first?"

A FEW HOURS LATER, I lay stretched across my bed. I lifted myself up slightly and reached out to trace a pattern across Pele's sweat-soaked skin. She'd been right. I had needed this. While I was far from being free of having panic attacks while bound, a significant weight had been lifted off me. Pele had always been able to do that for me just as I could for her. We'd had no interest in turning this into anything serious. Kaysea had learned that humans referred to this situation as "friends with benefits" and found the term hilarious. But it summed up my relationship with Pele accurately enough.

"How are you doing? Really?" Pele asked.

I started to lie and say I was doing fine but stopped myself. This was Pele, she would understand. "I'm waiting for the other shoe to drop," I admitted. "The warlocks have backed off for now, but they know my secret. I just want to be done with all of it and live my life in peace without worrying about the fae and daemons finding out about my magic and killing me. Or figuring out a way to use me. I'm not sure what I fear more."

I looked at the drawing on my dresser of the fae tree in the woods nearby. Andrei had given it to me shortly before he left town. "I've never had a normal life, Pele. First it was my parents dying, then it was meeting Sebastian and hunting witches and warlocks, and then . . . everything else." Thinking about Myrna still hurt; killing Sebastian had helped with that pain, but it still lingered. "I just want to be free from everything and have a chance to figure out who I can be without all of my baggage."

"And play house with a nice werewolf, perhaps?" Pele turned her head and arched an eyebrow at me.

"Maybe." I flicked her nose in reproach. "I'd like to be able to try."

She slapped my hand away. "You seem to have a better handle on your magic. Kaysea's suggestion helped, I take it?"

"Yes." I raised my hand, and blue flames danced across my fingers. "Apparently keeping a stranglehold on it like I'd been doing my entire life is what made it so difficult to control. After that fight in the woods with the warlocks, I never put the chains back on it. It's calmer now. Kaysea says it's similar to fae magic in that it's almost sentient." I let the flames fade away, and my magic hummed across my skin as if pleased with my assessment.

I went back to tracing patterns on her skin, and we lay there for a few more minutes in silence until Pele shifted onto her side, propped up on her elbow. Her sharp eyes focused on me, and I knew without a doubt that she was plotting. And that I wouldn't like it.

"Out with it," I said, bracing myself for whatever bomb she was about to drop on me.

"I have a favor to ask of you."

"Seriously?" I flopped back down on the bed and stared at the ceiling. "It must be one hell of a favor if you felt you had to sleep with me first."

"Don't be ridiculous. I slept with you first because I wanted to get laid and I figured you would be irrational after this conversation," she explained calmly, her lips tilted up in a slight smile.

I glared at her. "What, pray tell, is this favor?"

"About a year ago, a fae child stumbled into a small mountain village in Tír na mBeo." The mention of the realm where the fae capital was located immediately set me on alert. "He was young and badly injured. No one recognized him, and he either wouldn't or couldn't answer any questions about where he had come from and who he was. The only thing the villagers knew was that the child was sidhe and that he already possessed great power. Far more than any young child should have. He understood and spoke the language of the fae but in an old dialect, and he didn't have a translation mark."

"Odd." My brows rose. "Those are typically given in the first year of life. Even in the most remote villages I've been to across the fae realms, I've never encountered anyone who didn't have a translation mark."

Translation marks were practically a universal staple across all the realms. Originally designed by the daemons, the fae had created their own version, but they both worked effectively the same way. The mark was applied behind the ear with a magic branding device. It didn't hurt but left a permanent mark behind the ear which would warm slightly when in use. The design of the mark changed periodically. The current one for the daemons was a fish they called the "babel fish". The fae one had been the same for the past few hundred years, a mockingbird. The mark allowed someone to understand any spoken language, but some nuances were lost in translation, which is why most of us spoke at least two or three languages along with some different dialects. Given how many languages were spoken across the realms, it was a basic necessity and probably the most commonly used magic spell in existence.

"He didn't have one," Pele continued. "They gave him one so he could better understand them. Those who choose to live in the mountains like their privacy. The child was odd but didn't cause any harm and no one came asking about him, so they let him stay in the village and hoped that as he grew to trust them more, he could tell him where he came from."

Pele paused as she rolled out of bed and swiped one of my T-shirts off the ground. She pulled it on and proceeded to pace in front of the large window that overlooked the rocky coastline. When leading meetings or negotiations, Pele always presented a calm and collected appearance. But when she was with her friends and family, Pele was a pacer. If she couldn't pace, she would fidget nonstop. I'd gotten her a bag full of exquisite and well-crafted fidget spinners for her birthday years ago.

I remained on the bed but sat up and rested against the headboard. "I've been to fae villages like that. They definitely like to be left alone." I pondered the information a bit more and slowly said, "Still . . . I would have expected them to at least report the child's appearance to the nearest city."

"Mirrors don't work in that mountain range once you get above a certain elevation. There are a few fae mountain ranges where that happens. No one knows why exactly." Pele shrugged. "One of my cousins is obsessed with studying it and trying to figure out what causes the interference. Most magic works fine in the region, but apparently mirrors don't. That only adds to the appeal for the fae who choose to live there."

"Can't blame them," I said with a huff. "There have been

times in my life where I've shed my human skin and lived in my feline form for years. Solitude is nice sometimes."

"These villages are remote and communication is limited, but they do get regular deliveries of supplies. Two months ago, a supply train arrived in the village and found it decimated."

I looked sharply at Pele. Words failed me. The fae would fight amongst themselves, but no one else messed with them, and I couldn't think of any reason internal fae politics would have resulted in a random mountain village being destroyed. Even more surprising was that they'd kept this quiet enough to stop any rumors from spreading.

"They killed almost everyone in the village," Pele continued, her tone even. "The only reason some children survived is because some of the adults quickly realized they were outmatched and sacrificed themselves to create one hell of a ward around the basement where the children were hiding." Pele paused her pacing and looked at me, her words soft and serious as she spoke. "The beings that attacked the village . . . they were devourers, Nemain."

"Impossible," I breathed.

Devourers were the bogeyman across all the realms. They appeared seemingly out of nowhere thousands of years ago and poured into multiple realms as gateways opened at random, linking our realms to theirs. That event and the others that followed were known as Cataclysms. The devourers were composed of many species, but they all had three things in common: They were always a predator species, they were immune to any form of magical attack, and they consumed magic. Hence their name. As far as I knew, no devourer had set foot in a fae realm for at least a thousand years.

"What type of devourers were they?" I asked.

"We don't know," Pele growled in frustration and resumed her pacing.

"What do you mean? No one recognized the species?" I

asked in confusion. "Describe them. I might know what kind they are."

"The devourers were gone by the time the supply wagon got there. No one who is still alive saw them. We only know they were devourers because of the bodies left behind. All drained of magic." Pele stopped pacing and looked at me before pacing again. She paused after a few steps, clearly unsure how to proceed. Unease ran through me. Pele was never this rattled.

"What else? Might as well keep this fun train moving along," I said lightly.

"We're pretty sure the devourers were fae-like. Or at least able to take that shape."

Every part of me stilled. "How? How do you know that?"

"There were tracks leading out of the village. They walked on two feet. And they wore shoes. The children never saw them because there were no windows in the basement they were hiding in, but they heard them talking. Arguing about something. The language they spoke was fae."

"Are you sure?"

Pele nodded. "Translation marks react differently when it's the same language but a different dialect. It was an older dialect of fae but definitely fae."

"Like the boy," I murmured as I thought through the implications. "Did they find the child?"

"We're not sure. He wasn't with the other children in the basement, and they did not find his body anywhere else. Based on the argument the devourers were having when the children overheard them, it seems like they didn't find him, at least at the time of the attack. It's been over two months since the village was destroyed, and there have been no further sightings of the devourers.

"All travel out of that fae realm has been severely restricted. We don't know how the devourers got into that realm, but the

10

most likely way is that they used an existing gateway. Assuming that is how they entered, it stands to reason that's how they planned to leave."

"Devourers don't plan. At least nothing like this. Many of them are skilled hunters and they'll plan attacks and ambushes, but this is well beyond that. They don't plan how to travel between realms while posing as fae. And none of them speak."

"We both know that's not exactly true."

My eyes locked onto Pele's as her words hit me. "I'm not one of them," I growled.

"I'm not saying you are. But you do have devourer magic," Pele pushed. "Maybe whatever these things are is something similar to what you are."

I rolled off the bed and grabbed my robe off the back of the bedroom door and stalked out into the living room. I pulled the silk robe on and lashed the belt across my waist as I stood in front of the windows and watched the waves crash ashore.

Pele came to stand beside me but said nothing. I'd hidden my magic from almost everyone my entire life, including Pele. But I'd told her everything recently. About my ability to tear open gateways in any realm despite that fancy spell crafted by the fae and daemons to protect their realms against Cataclysms. And I told her about my devourer magic that manifested as pale blue flames and allowed me to consume the magic of others. At first, Pele had been both shocked and scared. Not of me, but for me and what would happen if my secrets were to get out. Devourers were killed on sight by the daemons and fae.

I glanced at Pele. "Any ideas why they were after the child? This all seems odd. A powerful sidhe child appearing out of nowhere and then being attacked by a band of fae-like devourers that no one has ever encountered before? I feel bad for the kid and I'm pretty curious about these devourers, but should I get involved in this? The sidhe must be crawling all over this. I'll have run-ins with them, and every time I encounter them is just another chance they'll figure out what I am."

"I told you I needed a favor," Pele murmured.

I snorted. "This is a bit more than a favor."

"The sidhe are hiding something. My father's always suspected the fae knew more about the devourers than they've ever let on. Honestly, I always thought he was just paranoid. But I've uncovered some odd things over the years, and a lot of shit has been going on in the fae realms recently. Something big is coming. And I think this child might be at the center of all of it."

Pele reached out and gripped my shoulder. "You need to find the child, Nemain. And you need to hide him from the fae when you do."

"Are you insane?" I stared at her in disbelief. "That is a death sentence. I thought we were trying to figure out how to keep me alive. Not get me killed faster!"

"Hear me out." Pele held her hands up in a calming motion. "You just need to keep him safe until we figure out exactly what is going on. If the devourers made it into the fae realm through one of the existing gateways, they likely had help from a fae. There might be some shift taking place in fae politics right now that we don't know about. If we deliver the child to the wrong party, we'd be helping them do whatever the hell it is they're trying to do. I need time to figure this out. And in the meantime, I need someone I can trust who is good at finding lost things to locate the damn kid. Once we figure out what's going on, we can barter for your freedom with the fae and daemons. If we can tell them about your magic and get them to agree to never come after you, the warlocks will no longer have this hold over you. This could be your chance at having a truly free life."

Tentative hope rose within me as I rubbed my forehead. Jinx and Magos would not like this. Although it would be kind of funny to watch their expressions as I explained all this to them. Their heads might literally explode. "Is one of the Queens making a play against the other?" I asked.

"I don't think so." Pele pursed her lips, and her eyes grew somewhat distant, as they always did when she was thinking through possibilities. "They rarely agree and occasionally take swipes at each other, but they are sisters and love each other. That's not to say they're not involved, though. This could be a coup against the both of them."

"Great," I said dryly.

"Figure out who is coming with you and bring them to my office, and I'll give you the rest of the information, plus any leads I have. Make sure someone stays behind to watch the vampire brats. I don't want them left alone here."

I rolled my eyes, and Pele swatted my arm. "Oww," I said and rubbed the spot she'd hit. Blood welled over a few scratches from her claws. They'd heal in seconds, but still. "When are we leaving?"

"Tomorrow. You leave tomorrow."

Chapter Two

I LOOKED around the living room, making sure I had cleaned up everything after my play time with Pele. Wouldn't want to scandalize poor Magos. If Pele hadn't asked me for that damn favor, I probably would have done so just to provide some entertainment. But now all I could think about was what Pele had asked of me and how I would explain it to Magos. Specifically, the part where he couldn't come with me.

Unlike Mikhail, Magos didn't exactly get along with sunlight. It wouldn't kill him right away, but it was incredibly painful for him to be in it and it would weaken him greatly as his magic tried to heal the constantly burning skin. Besides, someone had to stay behind to monitor the vamp kids.

I sighed and glanced at the clock. Just past midnight. It could be hours before Magos and Mikhail returned. Mikhail would come with me, whether I wanted him to or not. Jinx would come as well. I didn't know about Luna. Her magic was coming back, but it was still unpredictable, and she still couldn't remember her past. For all we knew, she had pissed off someone powerful in the fae realms and would be in danger there. I was reasonably sure we could convince her to stay and help watch over the kids. So far that left me traveling with a grumpy grimalkin and an annoying vampire. Ugh.

"Who else could I bring?" I wondered aloud as I absently tapped my fingers on the granite countertop of the kitchen island. We would need to move fast and be able to defend ourselves if the devourers found us. Or if we had a run-in with any fae who might have a bone to pick with me for any number of reasons. When you've been around for a few centuries, you gather some enemies along the way. I certainly did at any rate.

A thought came to me, and I walked over to the large mirror that hung in the living room next to the hallway. One large body length pane of glass made up the center of the mirror with another piece on top and two narrow pieces running down the sides. Thick wood carved with glyphs framed all of it. The glass piece on the right side had several glyphs running down it, each a dull blue. I tapped the third one down, and it glowed brightly. The piece of glass in the center darkened slightly as it became cloudy. I waited for a few minutes. He probably wasn't home. If he was, he'd either be in his shop downstairs or in his office, and it would take him a few minutes to answer.

I was about to reach out and tap the glyph once more to cut the connection, when the mirror cleared and revealed Eddie.

Swiping his long, dark blond hair out of his face, Eddie grinned at me. "Hey, bestie. What's up?"

"Bestie?" I grinned back at him. "That's a new one."

Eddie's odd amber eyes looked over my shoulder as he surveyed the room behind me. "Eh. I was hoping Mikhail was there. Seemed like the kind of thing that would annoy him."

"Probably." I snickered. "You busy? I got something to ask you, and it'd be better if I explained in person."

He refocused on me with a curious look. "Just finished up a sale and don't have anything else planned. Come on by."

"Be there in ten minutes," I said and tapped the glyph.

Eddie faded away, and the mirror returned to its normal state. After strapping my favorite short swords onto my back and loading up with a few other weapons, I scribbled a note to let Magos know where'd I'd gone and left it on the counter.

Eight minutes later, I parked my Yamaha on the street outside Eddie's shop. Eddie had keyed the ward to me months ago, so I could pass through easily, and he'd left the door unlocked, as usual. I passed by the small kitchen and the living room, heading down the hallway. Ignoring the door on the left that led to his bedroom, I went through the doorway on the right into the office. That was where I always found Eddie.

I carefully stepped around the piles of books and papers stacked haphazardly on the floor. "Still trying to find something from your realm?" I paused by the desk and peered around him to see what he was studying. It looked like a ledger of some sort. I didn't recognize the language and couldn't read any of it.

Leaning back in his chair, Eddie rubbed his face. "Yeah. Pretty sure it's another dead end."

"Sorry," I said quietly and tried very hard not to glance at the painting that hung behind his desk.

Of the woman with fiery red hair and bright emerald green eyes. Eddie had helped me when the warlocks had been in town trying to capture me. During that time, he'd learned about my ability to open gateways to any realm and had sworn a blood oath to never tell another soul in exchange for one thing—opening a gateway to his home realm so he could rescue his love. Under normal circumstances, I'd be able to open a gateway there even though I'd never been there before by using his connection to it.

But Eddie had been exiled, and whatever spell they had

cast to exile him had cut off his connection to his home realm. Without some connection to it, I had no way to open a gateway there. Usually it wasn't that hard to find something from a realm, but whatever realm Eddie was from was locked down tight and he was having a hard time finding something from there. Since he hadn't told me anything about where he was from, I couldn't help him in his search.

If he didn't find something soon, I was pretty sure I was going to die of curiosity.

I had no idea what Eddie was. No one did. He'd shown up in town a few months before me and opened up a shop of rare books and artifacts. He'd built up enough of a reputation that Pele vouched for him as someone who could find your ingredients and other spell casting supplies on short notice, which is how we'd met and eventually become friends. But even after hanging out with Eddie these past few months, I still knew little about him. Emerald Bay was a small town, and I wasn't the only one curious about him. New theories and rumors were swirling around constantly.

"Have you heard the latest rumor about yourself?"

Eddie cocked his head and looked at me with a crooked grin. "I think I'd make a fantastic half-daemon prince."

"The daemons have no princes," I said wryly.

"I know." Eddie laughed. "I'm pretty sure it was a bunch of young daemons who started the rumor."

"Wouldn't surprise me." I straightened a pile of papers on his desk that was close to joining another less fortunate stack on the floor. "So . . . not a half-daemon then?" I asked casually.

Eddie snorted.

"Oh, come on! Give me something," I complained. "Do you have any idea how hard it is to hang out with you when you smell so freaky?"

He quirked an eyebrow at me. "What do you mean?"

"You smell of fire and ash."

"I burn a lot of incense in the shop. It clings to the skin," he said smoothly.

"I don't speak of your body. Your soul. Your soul burns." I looked at him.

Eddie went still, and something swirled in his eyes for a moment and then was gone. "You can read souls?"

"Family gift from my mother's side. I only got a drop of her power. She could tell everything about a person. What they were. If they were good or bad or somewhere in between. Their deepest and darkest secrets were always laid bare to her. It was one of the reasons we always lived far away from others. She didn't like most people. Unlike her, I only get a taste."

Eddie said nothing and remained utterly still. Most of the time, Eddie looked harmless. He liked to crack jokes. His hair was shaved on the sides, and he wore black jeans and punk band T-shirts. But sometimes I saw a glimpse of what was underneath. Whatever the hell Eddie was, he was a predator, and he packed some weird powerful magic. In all my years and all my travels, I had never come across anything like him. I looked at the woman in the painting. "Does her soul smell of fire and ash, too?"

"Yes," he breathed and then stood up and left the office.

I watched him go and turned back to the painting, studying the woman's features once more. "I'll help him find you again," I promised her and left the office.

Eddie was slumped at the kitchen table, a bottle of cheap whiskey in front of him. I thunked down in the chair beside him, turning so I could sit comfortably with the swords still on my back.

"Good," I said and grabbed the bottle of whiskey. "We're going to need this as I tell you about my upcoming adventure."

The whiskey burned my throat as I slammed a shot back after filling in Eddie on what Pele had told me. His face had grown more serious the longer I spoke, and he was staring at the table. I poured two more generous shots and slid a glass to him. He grabbed it without looking and raised the glass to his lips, drinking it down in one swallow.

"I think it's time I came clean with you about something."

"That sounds ominous," I replied.

"I never told you how I found you exactly."

"You said you heard rumors about someone who was good at finding things in other realms who worked through a daemon contact." Tension swept through me and bled into my tone. Eddie and I had become close friends these past few months, and I had trusted him with a lot, even though he had kept some secrets from me.

"I did, and that was true enough. You've built a solid reputation over the years as someone who is good at finding lost things. With Pele managing your gigs, no one was ever in a position to ask questions about how you accomplished what you did."

I kept my mouth shut as my heartbeat sped up.

"I knew of you before I ever heard the rumors of the work you do through Pele."

A muscle ticked in my cheek. "How?" The word was more a command than a question.

Eddie poured each of us another shot of whiskey. "When I was first exiled and thrown into the human realm, I traveled around trying to find a way back. At first, I hoped I could find a fae or daemon I could bribe to open a gateway for me. When it became clear that wasn't going to happen, I looked for other options. My magic allows me to pull memory echoes from objects that have magic or have been used by strong magic users."

"That explains why you run a shop full of rare artifacts and books," I observed. "I've heard of others who can tell what type of magic something has by touch. I've never heard of someone being able to pull memories from an object, though."

"It's a common talent among my kind. Sometimes artifacts have enough magic themselves to store memories. Excalibur, for example, was wielded by humans who had little magic, but the sword itself had so much magic that I can see almost its entire history. Even during times when it wasn't wielded by anyone."

My eyes lit up. "Do you have Excalibur?"

"No, but I know who currently does." He gave me a sly grin.

"Meh. That's not as cool."

"Whatever. During my time traveling around, I came across a dagger that contained some intense memories from the person who wielded it."

"Who wielded it?"

"Did your mother ever speak of her sisters?" Eddie asked.

"They died before I was born." I shook my head. "I was named after her older sister, Nemain. Her younger sister was Badb."

Eddie nodded. "I know little about the sister from which you get your name. She died not long after they fled their home realm. But Badb isn't dead, Nemain. She's very much alive in the fae realms."

"Not possible." I said firmly and crossed my arms over my chest. "My parents would not have lied to me about this."

"Sorry." Eddie shrugged. "But they did. I swear to you that Badb is alive."

I stared at the center of the table and processed this information. Once I got past the shock of Eddie's declaration, denial immediately rose up. But as much as I wanted to believe Eddie was wrong, he never was when it came to stuff like this. Did my parents lie to me and Cian? Or did they not know my mother's sister was still alive? Eddie was staring at me from across the table, patiently waiting for me to accept what he'd just told me.

I met his gaze. "Keep talking."

"Your mother was a powerful necromancer. Her older sister, Nemain, was a strong telepath. The younger sister, Badb . . . could open gateways. To any realm. At any time."

The world slipped out from under me. My mother knew. And she never told me. Even if she hadn't known her sister was still alive, she knew someone in our family had magic similar to mine. She watched me struggle all those years with my magic and never uttered a word.

Not one. Damn. Word.

My magic flowed out, wrapping itself around my skin, trying to comfort me as my emotions raged. I had long suspected my parents knew more about my magic than they had let on but never something like this. If they were still alive, I would rage at them and demand an explanation. But they had died protecting me and Cian, which made me feel guilty about being angry at them. I was so confused about how I should feel. I wished Cian were here so we could talk it out. My brother was always the rational one. I closed my eyes and sank into my magic, letting it soothe me as I took a couple of deep breaths. When I opened my eyes a few minutes later, Eddie was staring at me in amazement. Something swirled in his amber eyes, almost like smoke; he must be using his magic to see mine.

"Your magic is a wonder, Nemain," he breathed. "I know why you have to hide it. But know that you never have to hide it around me. I swear on my soul I will tell no one." Magic emanated from him, and I knew without a doubt Eddie would never betray me.

I cleared my throat but left my magic out. "Did my parents know my aunt was still alive? Did my aunt know about us?"

"Yes, to both. I don't know how much they communicated with each other, but each sister definitely knew the other one was alive."

"What exactly has my dear aunt been up to all this time?"

Instead of answering my question, Eddie asked, "Did your mother tell you about what happened when their realm fell?"

"Yes," I said slowly and thought over what I'd been told. "She claimed they fought their way to a gateway the daemons held open. I'm going to take a wild guess and say that's not how it happened." The realization of what must have happened hit me. "My aunt opened a gateway, didn't she? She's the reason they escaped."

"Yep. That's not all she did, though. Apparently your Aunt Badb was so pissed off at the fae for closing their gateway, and thus dooming all the shifters, that she tore open several gateways directly into the fae realm. Including one directly into one of the fae Queen's strongholds."

I whistled. "Holy shit. I'm surprised she's still alive."

"It's not for lack of trying on the Queen's part," Eddie said, the corner of his mouth quirking up into a grin.

"Which Queen? Seelie or Unseelie?" Most of my experience with the fae was with the Seelie court. I tried to avoid interacting with anyone who was politically relevant. Fae politics were bloodthirsty and complicated, and I wanted nothing to do with them.

"Seelie," Eddie replied. "It took a couple years, but eventually the Seelie Queen figured out who your aunt was and sent some sidhe warriors to retrieve her. She and her sisters were living in Ireland at the time and slaughtered all the warriors. The Seelie Queen responded by unleashing the Fomóire on Ireland. It wasn't the best political move by the Seelie Queen. The Unseelie Queen stepped in and political power amongst the fae shifted in favor of the Unseelie, but the Seelie Queen didn't seem to care. She just wanted Badb dead. Badb, your mother, and your Aunt Nemain were quite ferocious on the battlefield."

"I wish I had known them," I whispered.

"Do you want to see?" Eddie asked tentatively.

My brows rose and bunched together in confusion. "What do you mean?"

"When I was piecing all this together, I went to Ireland. I figured out where the last battle took place and where your Aunt Nemain died. The magic seeped into the earth there, and I was able to use it to see part of the battle." He held his hand out towards me. "I can share it with you."

I was pretty sure I had stopped breathing as I looked at his outstretched hand. After a few seconds, I reached out, fingers trembling, and took his hand.

"Ready?" he asked.

I nodded.

Magic punched me. I gasped and squeezed my eyes shut, trying to come to terms with it. When I opened them, I saw a battlefield. The sound came crashing in a moment later. Metal clanging against metal. People screaming in pain and rage. I whirled around, studying the battle taking place in front of me. The Fomóire were easy to spot. Their telltale grey skin was covered in armor, but their eight foot tall, bulky forms stood out across the battlefield. All of them wielded battle axes I would struggle to lift, let alone fight with. They clashed with an army made of humans, feline shifters, and beings who might be druids.

The battle was going in favor of the Fomóire. Shifters in both feline and human form lay dying around me. The humans were also dying in massive numbers. They'd shown up to this fight, even though they had to know they were physically and magically outmatched. I'd seen a lot of death in my life, but I'd never seen a battle like this before. I hoped I never would.

A huge Fomóire, over ten feet tall, howled and charged across the field. At that size, it must be a female. They were considerably larger than the males. She wore a long cloak made of black feathers. The battalion leader. She aimed towards the druids, who were barely holding a line against the Fomóire. She was twenty yards away when a gateway opened in front of her and three beings leapt out. Two leapt over the large Fomóire with a familiar feline grace and tore into the line of Fomóire who had charged after their leader. The third landed directly in front of the Fomóire leader and brandished a sword.

I froze.

I knew that sword. Growing up, it had hung over our mantle, I'd watched my mother wield it on more than one occasion. I moved to the right to get a better look, and my jaw dropped. Black armor coated my mother like a second skin. I'd never seen armor like it before. It looked light and flexible, but I could see hits she'd taken from arrows and swords the armor had deflected. It was torn in some sections, where blades had finally managed to cut through it. Her sword was coated with blood, and her green eyes were bright against her golden brown skin. Holy shit, my mother was enjoying the hell out of this.

I glanced at the two sisters who were tearing into the Fomóire. They wore the same black armor. One was using a sword like my mother and the other a spear. They laughed as they dodged and slashed their way through the Fomóire ranks.

"I told you," Eddie said from beside me. "Surely you've heard the tales of The Morrigan."

"But I thought The Morrigan was one of the Tuatha Dé Danann?" I frowned. Not a lot was known of The Morrigan, other than they served the Unseelie Queen. Because of that, most assumed they were sidhe and belonged to one of the elite families known as the Tuatha Dé Danann.

"Everyone does. The Tuatha Dé Danann have done nothing to dissuade people of that notion. But now you know the truth."

24

The Fomóire leader swung her axe at my mother, who gracefully leaned back, letting the axe pass over her. She used the motion to thrust her sword up into the Fomóire's armpit, the weakest point of the armor. The blade bit into flesh, and the Fomóire growled in rage. My mother tore the blade free, and it glowed with a soft blue light. She hacked at the arm just below the shoulder. A piece of the armor broke off, and she hacked again. The Fomóire's arm fell to the ground along with the battle axe, and the Fomóire fell back, screaming in pain.

"I'd forgotten her sword did that," I murmured. My brother still had the sword. He'd asked me once if I wanted it, but I told him to keep it. I couldn't bear the thought of wielding her sword.

My mother walked towards the Fomóire leader, who pushed herself to her feet again. Blood poured from her shoulder; she would bleed out in less than a minute. My mother knew this, and a cruel smile spread across her lips. A chill ran through me. I'd never seen that smile on my mother before. She took her time walking towards the Fomóire. The Fomóire looked behind her; almost all of her battalion was dead. Her eyes flicked to the ground several feet to her right. I followed her gaze and saw what my mother did not.

"No!" I cried and started to leap forward.

Eddie grabbed me. "I'm sorry. This has already come to pass. There's no changing what comes next."

I watched helplessly as the Fomóire dove to the right and picked up the spear with their remaining arm and hurled it. My mother was fast and her sword burst through the Fomóire's chest, but not before the spear found its mark. A scream tore across the battlefield, and Nemain grasped the spear that had gone through her chest.

Through her heart.

A few Fomóire were still alive. They wouldn't make it, so they followed their leader's example and focused their attention on the wounded shifter. They leapt towards her and bit down, tearing at the armor until they were finally able to get to the flesh underneath. Shifters had incredible healing abilities, but a wound to the heart was taxing and her magic couldn't keep up with the damage being dealt to her body. My mother and my remaining aunt ran towards their fallen sister and tore the Fomóire off her. My mother cradled her sister's head in her lap and wept.

Badb fell to her knees on the other side and tore the helmet off her head. Tears streaked down her face. Every part of me went still. Twins. She wasn't my mother's younger sister. She was my mother's *twin* sister. Nemain reached her hands out and clasped each of her sisters. She took one more shuddering breath and her hands fell. My mother and Badb screamed, and I clamped my hands over my ears.

More Fomóire approached from over the hill and sprinted towards the battlefield. My mother and Badb rose and, after one last look at their fallen sister, charged to meet the enemy.

My sight went dark for a few moments, and Eddie's magic left me. We were once again sitting at his kitchen table. He handed me the whiskey. We sat there for a few minutes as I drank.

"My mother and Badb were identical twins." I put the bottle down and propped my elbows on the table, leaning my forehead against my hands. I understood the implications of that but didn't want to face it just yet.

"The story isn't over," Eddie said softly. "After your mother and Badb defeated the Fomóire, the Seelie Queen took a different approach. She'd lost too much politically, so she had to be more subtle. She sent the Erlking."

"The Erlking? As in the Wild Hunt?" I asked, surprised.

"Yes, but this is where my information dries up." Eddie lifted his hands. "From what I can piece together, the Erlking went after Badb. She walked away. He didn't. Badb joined the court of the Unseelie and became untouchable to the Seelie Queen. Her sister, your mother, remained in the human realm."

"Did she kill the Erlking?" I asked as I thought about what I knew of the Erlking and the Wild Hunt. Not much. They hadn't been active for centuries. Paintings of them were common throughout the fae realms; he was always portrayed wearing black armor and a helmet that obscured his features. His eyes weren't hidden, though, and they were always painted the same way. Obsidian black, with no emotion. As if he had no soul.

"I don't know. There have been no sightings of the Wild Hunt since that encounter, but I can't say for sure he's dead. Not much was known about him other than he served the Seelie Queen."

"Badb still serves the Unseelie Queen?"

"Yes," Eddie said. "And given what you've told me about this boy, it seems unlikely the fae Queens aren't already involved in this, which puts you on a collision course with them. I don't know what your aunt does for the Queen, but you need to be prepared to meet her."

I grabbed the bottle and took a long swig. "Why didn't they tell me, Eddie? Why didn't my parents tell me my aunt was still alive?"

"I wish I knew. But we should be careful while we're looking for the boy in the fae realm. It seems odd she didn't come to you sooner. She had to have known about you and Cian. We do not know what her agreement is with the Unseelie Queen."

"So you're coming with us, then?"

"Absolutely. First, I need to make sure you stay alive so you can help me out with my problem."

"Thanks," I said dryly. "And second? I'm assuming there's a second here?"

27

Eddie's grin turned into a full-fledged smile. "And second, think of all the shit I can steal from the fae while we're there."

I helped myself to another shot of whiskey as the image of Badb pulling off her helmet played over and over in my mind. Eddie was right to tell me this now since it was possible for me to encounter my long-lost aunt at some point of this adventure. But I didn't even know where to begin processing this, and I couldn't let it distract me from our immediate concern of finding the boy. The whiskey burned down my throat as I did my best not to let my thoughts run wild at what it meant that my aunt was my mother's identical twin. And that my magic was nothing like my mother's and very much like my aunt's.

If my parents had held this truth from me, what else had they lied about? If I met Badb, would she tell me the truth? Or would she lie to me more? *Do you even want to know the truth?* The accusation rose up past all my other questions, and I didn't know the answer.

Chapter Three

"I'm coming with you," Magos said, his expression hard and determined.

I sighed. We'd been having this argument for the past hour and weren't making much progress. I'd temporarily given up and was snacking on a block of cheese while Magos continued to make his case for why he should come.

Mikhail glanced at me briefly and faced Magos. "She's right, Uncle. You're restricted to traveling at night. If the group decides to stay together at all times, that will significantly slow the progress down and lower the chances of us finding the child. And increase the chances of someone we don't want finding him. If the group decides to separate and travel without you during the day, they would be down one fighter while traveling and you would be on your own, making you a prime target."

Magos clenched his jaw but said nothing.

"Besides," Mikhail continued. "Someone has to stay with the brats. And while they've gotten more comfortable around me, they don't trust me as much as they trust you."

"For obvious reasons," I added around a mouthful of cheddar. Magos gave me a disapproving look. "What? He's the former assassin of the vampire Council. They have every reason to be wary of him."

"I don't like this," Magos said, defeat clear in his voice.

"I don't like it either," I admitted. "But this makes the most sense. Mikhail, Eddie, and Jinx will come with me. Luna will stay with you and the kids. I'll let my brother know what's going on. If anything happens while we're gone and you need to get out of here, you can reach him through the mirror. Dante can open a gateway to the death realm, and all of you can hide at their place until we return."

Dante won't like that, Jinx said to me.

Dante can blow me, I thought back at Jinx, and he snickered. Dante was my brother's lover. Given they'd been together for quite some time, mate was probably the more accurate term. I just didn't like him, so saying "lover" made it sound more short-term in my mind. Dante's true name was Hades, but Jinx, Kaysea, and I were the only beings who knew the truth. And my brother, of course.

"Now that we're all in agreement, we should get some sleep. Pele wants us to leave later today, and it'll likely be awhile before we have the opportunity to rest for a long time in a safe place. But first, Magos and I should go check in with Elisa and let her know the plan." I glanced at the clock. Sunrise was fast approaching. "She'll probably still be awake."

"She will not like this plan either," Magos said, disapproval clear in his tone.

I grunted in agreement as we walked to the downstairs apartment. Elisa was the de facto leader of the vampire kids, and she worried about everyone. She was incredibly smart and resilient for someone who had only celebrated their twentieth birthday last week.

I let myself into the apartment without knocking. Closed bedroom doors were respected, but otherwise we'd all gotten used to breezing in and out of each other's apartments. Misha sat at the kitchen counter, nibbling on some leftover pizza. The vampire Council had confined the four vamp kids for their entire lives because they all came from special bloodlines known as the Apex bloodlines. Apex vampires had additional magical abilities that other vampires did not. The Council had been trying over the past century to add more Apex vampires to their ranks by having anyone with an Apex bloodline reproduce. The parents were not involved in the lives of the children, they brought them into existence and then handed them over to the Council to raise as they saw fit. This resulted in a very limited and strict childhood, one that definitely didn't include things like pizza.

Now I was pretty sure the two teenage boys, Misha and Damon, sustained themselves almost completely on pizza and junk food. And blood, of course. I grinned at pale skinned, dark-haired Misha, and he raised his hand in greeting as he shoved another slice into his mouth.

"Elisa still up?" I asked.

Before Misha could respond, a crash sounded from down the hallway where the bedrooms were, and Elisa shouted, "Isabeau! Get your butt back in here right now!"

A second later, a small girl with riotous brown curls burst into the living room and leapt onto the couch. Elisa came rushing into the room after her, and I felt a push of magic from Misha. I glanced at where he had been sitting and found the stool empty, the half-eaten slice of pizza discarded.

Elisa saw us and the now-empty kitchen stool and whirled back around to the hallway. "Coward!"

"We dealt with her all night! We have a barricade set up in our room. You can't make us come out!" Misha yelled back.

I smirked and shook my head. Isabeau had been quiet at first, but the six-year-old vampire child was rapidly becoming a terror. The three older vampires adored her and took turns watching her, but apparently Misha and Damon felt they had done their duties for the night.

Elisa turned back to face the couch, crossing her arms and scowling at Isabeau. In response, the vampire child giggled, crossed her arms, and declared, "I'm not tired!" Probably true. We were rapidly learning that Isabeau had two modes, nonstop rampage and passed out face first into a pillow. Nothing in between.

Magos touched my shoulder and gave me an "I've got this" look before walking over to the couch. He crouched in front of Isabeau and smiled softly at her. "Would you like to continue our story? I believe where we left off, I was only halfway through the tale of Anne Bonny and Mary Read."

Before Magos had even finished speaking, Isabeau squealed and leapt at him. He caught her and carried her down to her room while she pretended to be wielding a sword.

I looked blankly at Elisa. "Are they talking about pirates?"

"Yes." Elisa chuckled and straightened up the cushions on the couch before sitting down herself. I sat on the other end of the couch and propped my leg, turning slightly so I could face her. "I'm pretty sure it's Eddie's fault. We were in his shop a couple weeks ago, and Isabeau saw some random map Eddie claimed was a treasure map that led to pirate treasure. Isabeau got really excited about it and wanted to know what pirates were and if she could be one when she grew up. Magos found a book on pirates and has been telling her stories ever since."

"Ummm. . ." I raised my hands in the air. "I don't really know what to say about any of that other than she can't get a parrot."

Elisa smiled. "No parrots, noted." She brushed a strand of long black hair back. "I'm guessing you didn't stop by to chat about pirates, though?"

"I truly wish that was the case," I said, proceeding to tell Elisa everything we knew so far. "Mikhail, Eddie, Jinx, and I are leaving later today. We're going to get a few hours of sleep and then meet Pele at The Inferno in the afternoon. Magos is staying behind to watch over all of you."

"I could go with you," Elisa offered. "If I shift into my wolf form, the sunlight won't bother me. I don't have a lot of experience tracking, but my sense of smell is quite good in that shape. I might be able to help track the boy."

I looked past her at the heavy curtains we'd installed to cover the floor to ceiling windows that took up most of the wall in the living room area. We'd done the same in all the apartments. I was working on a more permanent solution, but the curtains allowed the vampires to freely move about the apartments during daylight as long as they were careful. They usually went to sleep around sunrise and woke in the early afternoon.

Elisa's striking blue eyes met mine as I focused on her once more and thought about her offer. My sense of smell was excellent in my feline form but not as good as a wolf's, but Elisa not only had little experience tracking in her wolf form she didn't know much about the fae in general. And she'd never been in a real fight before. I hoped we'd be able to sneak in and out of the fae realm with no one the wiser, but that seemed unlikely. Elisa was willing to take the risk, but I wasn't willing to risk her. If we got into a fight with whatever these devourers were and Elisa was hurt or killed, I'd never forgive myself.

"I appreciate the offer, I really do. But you would be trapped in that form during the day, which could cause problems. Between Eddie and myself, I think we'll be able to find the boy. Besides, Misha and Damon would riot if they learned you were leaving them alone with Isabeau."

Elisa snorted. "I'm pretty sure Damon was about to cry earlier. He went and hid in his room as soon as we got home."

I laughed as I rose from the couch. "I'm heading back upstairs to sleep for a bit. Our communication will probably be limited while we're in the fae realm, but I'll ask Pele to keep you informed."

"Be careful, Nemain." Elisa looked down the hallway to where Magos was reading bedtime stories of pirates to Isabeau. "I hope the lost boy gets a happy ending, too."

JINX WOKE me by pouncing on my stomach in the early afternoon. I screamed and swore at him as he darted out of the room. Luna rose from the corner of the bed she'd been sleeping on.

Sorry.

"You could have warned me," I grumbled.

I know. Her lilac eyes flickered deviously, and she jumped off the bed following Jinx. While I was happy she was feeling better and more comfortable around us, living with two grimalkin was starting to become a lesson in frustration. I rolled out of bed, showered, and dressed quickly. I packed a small bag with a change of clothes, a bottle of water, and some dried fruit and meat. The bag had plenty of room to stuff my weapons in case I wanted to shift into my feline form and carry the bag with me. Or better yet, I could get Eddie to carry it. I grabbed a short leather cloak with slits allowing my short swords to poke through. The hood would be helpful if we had to pass through any towns. Even if I kept my magic hidden, my golden skin with its lighter rosettes made me the person who stood out most in our group. Satisfied, I headed to the living room and found Mikhail already waiting with a similar small backpack. I blinked as I took in his appearance.

Since moving in with us, he'd added a lot of daemon style clothes to his collection, but most days he wore loose pants and a sweatshirt. No casual clothes were in sight today. The daemon-crafted black pants were made from a material similar to leather but more flexible and breathable and were practically molded to him. A cloak similar to mine hung across his shoulders over a black shirt just tight enough to show off his muscles when he moved, and the dark hair he usually wore loose was pulled back away from his face. Between the clothes and the hair, he looked dangerous. I'd forgotten this about him the past few months as we traded barbs back and forth, and I was unsettled by how it affected me.

"Ready?" Mikhail asked.

I snapped out of my stupor and nodded. "Yes."

Turning back down the hallway, I rapped on Magos's door. He opened it immediately, standing slightly back.

"We're heading out."

"Be careful, Nemain," he replied and purposely looked towards the living room.

I glanced to where Mikhail waited, and my eyes widened in understanding. "Eww. Yeah, no, that's not going to be a problem. You should probably be more concerned with me not cutting out his tongue at some point when he annoys me. How long do you think that'd take to grow back, by the way?"

Magos rubbed his forehead. He did that a lot around me. "Just be careful. And come back. Bring all of them back."

"I will. I promise." He nodded, and I headed back towards the living room, my steps heavy. It felt weird doing this without Magos. I'd lived most of my life without him by my side, but I'd gotten so used to it these past couple of years that it had quickly become normal. Leaving him behind felt wrong, but it was the right decision.

Jinx and Mikhail followed me out of the apartment and down the stairs.

"Meet you guys at the bar," I called over my shoulder. By the time I got on my bike and headed out of the parking lot, both of them were gone. The only thing that remained was some mist still swirling in the air from where Mikhail had been.

Given that I didn't know how long we'd be gone, I didn't want to leave my bike on the street, so I slowly drove down an alley next to Pele's bar, The Inferno. The alley opened to a small paved area used for storage. I parked the Yamaha out of the way and walked in through the back door. I spotted Mikhail, Eddie, and Jinx at the bar. My eyes narrowed at the person sitting with them, currently chatting up the bartender. I knew with every fiber of my being I wasn't going to like this.

"Kaysea? What are you doing here?" I leaned against the dark wood bar and stared suspiciously at my best friend.

Kaysea spun on the stool to face me, sending her dark green hair whirling. Her lighter green eyes looked at me, wide and innocent. "Can't a mermaid just meet up with her friends at the bar and chat up lovely bartenders?" She blinked a few times and smiled at me.

Out of the corner of my eye, I could just make out the lovely bartender in question, Zareen. Most beings would probably describe Zareen as fierce or terrifying, at least when it came to appearances. With her jet-black eyes and red skin, plus the horns growing out of her curly black hair, there was no mistaking Zareen as anything but a daemon. Her fearsome image took a bit of a hit when she started speaking and you realized she was cheerful, to an annoying degree at times, and she made the absolutely most delicious pies and cakes in any realm.

I turned my attention back to Kaysea. "Cut the bullshit."

The mermaid sat up straighter on the stool, steeling her back and shoulders. "I'm coming with you. And before you argue, Pele agrees it's a good idea."

Mikhail and Eddie didn't say anything as they glanced back and forth between me and Kaysea. I stared at her for a few seconds before I shoved off the stool, stomping towards Pele's office at the end of the bar. The dark purple curtain parted for me, and I entered her office. The others followed me, and Kaysea called out, "It was nice meeting you, Zareen!"

Pele was leaning against the front of her desk, wearing a black pantsuit that made her red skin and turquoise eyes stand out even more. "Hear us out, Nemain," Pele said calmly.

"Hear you out?" I gestured at Kaysea. "She is a freaking fae princess! And one of the most powerful seers in the past thousand years. And last time I checked, we weren't going to be swimming through the fae realms, which means the small amount of defense magic she has won't be available to her! We have no idea who these devourers are or what else we might run into. It's too dangerous."

Kaysea glared at me. "I'll be—"

"No," I cut in, fear gripping me at the idea of my best friend coming along on this quite possibly insane task. "You're not coming, Kaysea!"

She and I stood there squared off against each other, glaring.

Eddie let out a dramatic whistle, and we both turned our glare to him. "Sorry." He held up his hands. "Just felt like this needed a whistle to really underline the whole standoff thing." Mikhail and Jinx were slightly wiser, and both of them posted up in the corner of the office and kept their mouths shut.

"I need to come, Nemain," Kaysea tried again. "First, it's too dangerous for all of you to be traveling in the fae realms without a fae with you. I'll provide a certain amount of political protection should you need it. And as you pointed out, I'm one of the most powerful seers currently alive. And what's going on is definitely related to all the visions I've been having lately. I might very well get another vision that could help you or warn you of something. And since you'll be difficult to contact during all of this, it makes sense for me to come with you."

"You think this is related to the vision you had a few

months ago?" I frowned, annoyed at myself for not considering that sooner.

What vision? Jinx asked in annoyance. Mikhail shifted slightly, which was how I knew Jinx had allowed everyone to hear that. Mikhail still wasn't comfortable with Jinx talking in his head.

I flinched. "Kaysea might have had a vision a few months ago that involved me. And I might not have mentioned it to you. In my defense," I said hastily, "it happened when everything was going down with the vampire Council and the warlock Circle and it had nothing to do with that problem, so I decided to list it as a 'future problem to deal with' and let it go."

It would seem the future problem is now very much the current problem.

"Seems that way," I begrudgingly agreed.

What exactly was the vision? Jinx's golden eyes focused on Kaysea.

"At first it was just a flash of gold over and over again and the words, 'A change is coming carried on wings of gold.' I couldn't get beyond that until I met with Nemain, which triggered the rest of the vision. I saw Nemain standing by a cliff with a young woman who was gravely injured and a small boy. Nemain told the girl, 'Some must fall in order to rise,' and then she shoved her off a cliff."

"Well, that's a lovely vision, ain't it?" Eddie said.

I snorted. "Kaysea also repeated that line—'Some must fall in order to rise'—in her creepy vision voice. I'm not exactly sure what it means. But the boy in the vision could very well be the same fae child we're looking for. I should have considered that sooner, but I'd forgotten about that part. Me shoving the girl off the cliff is what stood out more." My magic shifted uneasily. I wasn't a stranger to violence, but Kaysea's vision had made it seem like I shoved an innocent girl off a cliff and it had freaked me out. But the vision had seemed unrelated to everything else going on at the time, so I had just hoped it wouldn't come to pass. I looked at Pele. "Did anyone mention a young woman being with him?"

"No." Pele shook her head. "But only a few young children were left. Several adults in the village took care of the boy. One of them might have been the young woman Kaysea saw. Or she could be one of the devourers after the boy."

Kaysea shook her head. "I didn't get that impression from the vision. She was protecting him."

"If Kaysea has more visions about the child, it's important you know them. They might even help you find him," Pele said.

"Connor should come, too, then," I said reluctantly. To say Kaysea's brother and I didn't get along was a bit of an understatement, but Connor was extra protective of Kaysea. If he came with us, his priority would be to keep her safe, which would allow the rest of us to concentrate on finding the boy.

"He can't come," Kaysea said. She was trying to keep her expression calm, but sadness touched her features and my heart stumbled a bit.

"What's wrong?"

"Our father is fading."

"Shit." I closed my eyes. "I'm sorry, Kaysea. How much longer does he have?"

"A few years. Hopefully." A few years to beings that lived for thousands of years was nothing. The fae aged oddly. For the first few decades, they mostly aged the same as humans. But around their mid-twenties, sometimes early thirties, they stopped aging. Their lifespans varied based on how much magic they had. Some lived only a thousand years while others lived for several thousand. Eventually their magic faded, and when that happened, they started to age again. If Kaysea's father had only a few years left to live, his magic had been fading for at least a decade. I hadn't seen him in person for quite some time, so I hadn't known.

"Why didn't you tell me sooner?" I asked softly, feeling a little hurt that Kaysea hadn't come to me earlier with this.

"You were going through so much," Kaysea said. "And it's not like you could have done anything. My father has accepted it. My mother is still struggling, but Connor and I will be there to help her."

I nodded numbly, not exactly sure what to say. My parents had died in front of me, but it had happened quickly. Kaysea would spend the next few years watching her father slowly fade until death claimed him. I wanted to say something to help her, to support her somehow. But I really sucked at these kinds of conversations.

"I take it someone is being appointed?" A thought occurred to me, and I looked at her in panic. "Gods, it's not Connor, is it? Is that why he can't come?"

Kaysea let out a choked laugh. "No. It's not Connor. My brother has no interest in the throne; he never has. He's served all this time as a protector of the throne because he wanted to keep our family safe. I'm not sure what he'll do when the new Queen takes over."

"Queen?" Pele asked. She looked at Kaysea with sudden interest, like a shark sensing blood in the water. Pele lived and breathed politics. Everyone knew her father was preparing her to one day take his place as the leader of the Assembly. In the meantime, she would have to prove she was worthy of such a position, so she schemed and plotted with the best of them. Daemon and fae politics often overlapped, so Pele snapped up every political rumor she could find. The Seelie and Unseelie Queens were at the top of the political food chain when it came to the fae. But the ruler of Tír fo Thuinn, the territory of the sea fae, was close behind. Tír fo Thuinn territory extended across multiple realms, both Seelie and Unseelie. I didn't know enough about fae politics to really understand how the balance of power worked, but Pele certainly would. A new leader of Tír fo Thuinn could shake things up politically.

"Oh shit, it's Ashling, isn't it?" Pele asked.

Kaysea's lips twitched. "I can neither confirm nor deny that."

I glanced at Pele and back at Kaysea. "Why does that name sound familiar?"

"Ashling climbed up the ranks in the royal guards quickly over the past century and has been in charge of handling security threats for Tír fo Thuinn for the past five decades. She's young with sharp wits and an even sharper tongue."

"Sounds like your type, Pele," Eddie offered.

"Ashling does nothing without purpose, including her choice of lovers," Pele said in distaste. "I don't fault her for it, but sleeping with her, even once just for fun, would be perceived as a political move. Regardless of how I felt about it, she would have found a way to use it to her advantage. I won't be used by anyone."

I recognized the light dancing in Eddie's eyes as trouble and interrupted whatever he was about to say next. "Getting us back on track. Is what's currently happening in Tír fo Thuinn going to cause problems for us? What's Connor's involvement in all this?"

"There's no way to know for sure. The timing of all this is inconvenient, but I don't think it's directly connected to whatever is going on. My father has been fading for the past decade, but there was no way to know when exactly he'd be stepping down. Connor is staying behind to help make sure the power transition goes smoothly. My father has ruled for over a thousand years, and he has made enemies along the way. And Ashling isn't universally loved."

"So Tír fo Thuinn might turn into a shit show," Eddie said. "Great."

Kaysea winced. "I wouldn't phrase it like that exactly, but you're not far off."

"That could work out in our favor," I mused. "Obviously, I want your family to be safe, Kaysea. But if things get turbulent in Tír fo Thuinn, it might draw some of the fae Queens' attention away from this lost child business."

"Possible," Pele mused. "Or whoever these devourers are, they have been waiting for this transition and will use it for their own advantage. The devourers after the boy aren't working alone. They can't be, given that they got into the fae realm undetected and have stayed hidden since. They must have alliances within the fae realms and possibly outside it as well. We can't trust anyone or anything until we know more."

"Are you including the daemons in that?" I asked. I was biased towards liking the daemons more than the fae, but that didn't mean all the daemons were good guys. Pele would know better than any of us what role the daemons could play in this.

"Yes. I don't suspect anyone, specifically, and I doubt any daemons are involved in this. But several high-ranking officials will want to use this to take the fae down a peg. I'm not opposed to that, but I think whatever is going on with this fae child is the key to learning everything else, and I don't want their political maneuvering to ruin that."

"Why?" Mikhail asked. "What makes you think the boy is the key?"

"I've noticed things over the years," Pele said slowly. "A number of species have grievances against the fae and daemons. Usually, they just complain loudly and occasionally stir up trouble. But lately they've been more reserved, as if they don't want attention drawn to them. I think they're working together or with some outside party I'm not aware of yet. My father has long suspected the fae Queens know more about the devourers than they've admitted. And here we are, an unknown fae child being hunted by devourers. Devourers who might be fae and are almost certainly being helped by someone in the fae realms."

"You think the warlocks are involved in this?" I thought about how the warlocks who had gone after me months ago seemed to be more powerful than any warlocks I'd encountered before. At the time we'd dismissed the idea they could be working with the fae or daemons because neither of those groups had ever bothered with witches or warlocks before. But perhaps we'd been mistaken in that assumption.

"Possibly." Pele nodded. "They're on my list of groups to monitor."

"This is *so* not going to end well," I grumbled and looked at Eddie. "Your job is to watch over Kaysea. Whatever it takes. If that means grabbing her and running from a fight, you do that. Do you understand?"

"Absolutely not!" Kaysea said at the same time Eddie said, "Agreed."

"Deal with it, Kaysea. I'm not exactly happy about you joining our party, and this is the only way I will allow it." Kaysea crossed her arms and shot daggers at me but didn't argue. "Anything else we need to know before heading out, Pele?"

"I already gave Eddie some maps of the region. The immediate area around what's left of the village has been searched thoroughly, so I doubt the child is anywhere in that area. I'd still recommend you start your search there. It's possible something was missed. Not to mention with both Eddie and Kaysea with you, something there could trigger their magic."

"Good a place to start as any. Do you have something from that area? I can open a gateway."

"Actually, we're going to use the fae gateway in the forest here to get to the fae realm. We can travel to the gateway in the city at the base of the mountains and hike up. It will only take us two days if we move quickly," Kaysea said.

"We could be there in one minute if I open a gateway to the village. There's no one left there, right? So there's no one to see me opening a gateway on that end," I argued.

"There probably isn't anyone there, but we can't know that for sure," Kaysea said. "Things are really tense in all the fae realms right now, but Tír na mBeo in particular. Extra attention has been paid to everyone coming and going out of that realm. Everything is recorded. If we go there through one of your gateways and for some reason we are stopped, they're going to ask which gateway we entered through and they'll check the logs. When they see no record of us coming through that gateway, all kinds of questions will be asked."

"Okay, but they might very well ask a bunch of questions about us if we go through one of the official gateways," I countered. "Our party consists of a fae princess, a vampire who can walk in the sun, a shifter with weird-looking magic, an asshole grimalkin, and whatever the fuck Eddie is."

I'm only an asshole because I hang out with you lot, Jinx grumbled.

"I have a contact at the gateway," Kaysea explained. "We need to leave soon because it's a relatively small window. She'll make note of us entering, so it's in the records, but no one will be there to question us."

"Oh," I said sheepishly.

"You're not the only one who can come up with sneaky plans, Nemain," Kaysea said dryly.

"Off to the woods we go, then?" Eddie asked.

"Yep," I responded and gave a wave towards the exit. "I'll meet you guys outside. I have a favor to ask of Pele."

"Given the favors you guys seem to ask each other, I can only imagine what it is." Eddie snickered, and everyone left the office.

Pele quirked an eyebrow at me. "Am I going to get laid before you ask for this favor? We don't really have time for that, unfortunately."

"That's your MO, not mine." I pulled out a vial of blood and handed it to her. "This is Mikhail's blood. I'd like you to ask around and see if any daemons would be willing to make a spell that would allow Magos and the vamp kids to walk in daylight."

"That's a hell of a favor." Both her eyebrows shot up.

"Considering the last favor you asked of me was to locate a mystery sidhe child with obscene levels of power who is being chased by fae devourer assassins, all while staying unnoticed by everyone else who is also looking for said child, I think my request is fair." I crossed my arms and looked at her.

"Fine," Pele replied. "Next time I want to get laid before the asking of favors, though."

"Duly noted."

Chapter Four

WHILE THE DAEMONS typically constructed their gateways indoors, like at Pele's bar, the fae preferred to create more natural gateways. The section of the forest outside Emerald Bay was legally owned by the fae, and in the center of it stood a gigantic tree with only a passing resemblance to the other trees of the forest. The glamour on it made sure no humans who stumbled across it would see it for what it was.

As we approached the clearing where the fae tree sat, I glanced at Mikhail. "You've been awfully quiet."

"Are you complaining?"

"Not at all. It's just not like you. Regretting coming on this journey?"

His dark twilight eyes flicked towards me and looked ahead once again. "No. It's just different, is all."

"Because it has nothing to do with vampires and werewolves?"

"That's all my life has been for six hundred years. I've met some fae and daemons along the way, but I've never really felt like I was a part of their world. A year ago, I understand my place and my role in things even if I didn't enjoy or want it. Now . . . I don't know."

"This has always been my world. For better or worse," I said. Mikhail didn't respond, and I called over my shoulder to where Kaysea and Eddie were chatting. "How are we doing on time, Kaysea?"

"We should be fine," she replied and smiled when Jinx leapt down from the trees and rubbed his head against her leg, purring away. Jinx was never an asshole to Kaysea, and she doted on him. It wasn't fair. I'd been feeding and housing the ungrateful asshole for *centuries*, and I didn't get the same treatment. "We shouldn't dally when we get to the tree. Our window is closing, and soon others will join my contact at the gateway who will likely ask questions we don't have answers for."

A few minutes later, we reached the clearing and stood at the edge, looking at the fae tree with its branches stretching far and wide. The leaves on it shimmered between shades of green, blue, and purple. Kaysea could activate the gateway by touching the wide trunk and then navigate us to the correct gateway on the other side. Just one problem. A lone figure stood between us and the tree.

"Huh," Eddie said. "Didn't see this coming."

Everyone's eyes fell on me, but I stared at the person standing in front of the clearing. My heart beat rapidly, and I couldn't begin to understand all the emotions churning through me.

"Hello, wolf," I breathed, stepping into the clearing. "Didn't think you were coming back."

"I told you I would," Andrei said.

"That was six months ago," I said, trying very hard to keep my expression and voice even. "I assumed you changed your mind."

"Your assumptions were wrong, kitty cat." He grinned.

My heart did a few flips at that grin. Ugh. Stupid heart.

"I'm happy to let you tell me why my assumptions were wrong, wolf. But not now. We've got places to be. I can explain when I get back." I started walking towards the fae tree, but he stepped to the side to block my way.

"No worries," he said lightly. "I'm coming with you."

"Like hell," I growled.

"I do believe y'all are on a bit of a schedule." Andrei looked behind me where my friends still waited to see how this would play out. "So unless you want to be late, I suggest you just accept that I'll be joining your group of misfits."

Mikhail started moving forward. "I'll deal with this."

Andrei's eyes flashed yellow. "Try me, vampire."

I slid between them and put my hands on Mikhail's chest. Andrei growled behind me. "Don't," I said. Andrei was no match for Mikhail, and I didn't trust Mikhail not to seriously injure or possibly kill him.

"Ah, come on. Let them fight. It'll be funny to see the pup face off against the vampire," Eddie drawled.

Agreed, Jinx said.

"Not. Helping." I growled and shoved Mikhail away. He took a step back, but remained there.

"Nemain. . ." Kaysea said worriedly. I took that to mean we were running out of time.

"Andrei, I don't have time to explain now. This really isn't a good time and you cannot come. It's too dangerous, and there's too much at stake."

"I may not be the strongest fighter, but I'm a better tracker than all of you. Even before I became a werewolf, I was good at tracking. I've been following all of you for the last two miles, and none of you had any idea I was there. Given the conversation I was able to pick up, I know you're looking for a lost child and you're starting in a mountain village." Andrei's hazel eyes focused on me. "You have a better chance of finding the child with me helping you."

I studied Andrei as I thought through my options. I had no doubt we could get past Andrei and make it through the gateway. But based on the stubborn expression on his face, we'd have to hurt him to do it. Something had changed with him, too. Before he left, Andrei had been struggling to keep his wolf nature under control. He didn't seem out of control at the moment, but the wolf part of him was pretty close to the surface. Maybe he was finally coming to terms with it instead of trying to keep it locked away.

Want me to take him out? Jinx asked.

"The wolf comes with us," I said in answer. "The tracking skills will be useful."

"Plus, we can always make him carry our shit," Eddie said as he walked past us, followed by Kaysea and Jinx.

Mikhail stopped next to me and said quietly, "This is a bad idea. He's going to get himself into trouble, and you're going to get yourself killed trying to save him."

"It's not like you'd shed any tears over that," I snapped. "If I'm out of the picture, you and Magos will be considerably safer since you'll only have to worry about your enemies and not mine. My death would simplify your life."

Mikhail's jaw clenched as anger sparked in his eyes. "Nothing about you is simple. I very much doubt your death would be." Before I could respond, he stalked off after the others, leaving me with Andrei.

"You're getting quite the vampire following since I've been gone," Andrei said flatly.

My eyes snapped back to Andrei, annoyance flickering through me. "Don't start. I will knock your ass out and leave you here."

"I've missed the sweet things you say to me." He laughed softly, there was a raspy quality to it that wasn't there before.

"I've missed you, too." He took a step forward until he was standing in front of me and brushed a loose strand of hair behind my ear. "Did you miss me, Nemain?"

I was acutely aware of his finger trailing down my neck and under my jawline. Heat spread through me, and every part of me wanted to explore that touch more. To explore him more. Instead, I gave him a disinterested look. "Not really. It took a couple weeks for the wet dog smell to get out of my apartment." I stepped around him and moved towards the fae tree. "Try to keep up, wolf."

"Thought you were always happy with how I paced things?"

I tripped at his words and tried to carry on like nothing had happened. Kaysea and Eddie smirked. Mikhail just stood there, his usual bored expression back in place.

Smooth move, Jinx said, as he laughed at me.

"I hate all of you," I said. "Are we ready to go?"

"Yes," Kaysea replied. She laid her hand flat against the massive trunk of the tree, and her magic pulsed. Daemons relied on glyphs in their gateways to control them and designate which gateway opened on the other side. I wasn't exactly sure how the fae did it, but I was pretty sure it relied on intentions and them feeding their own magic into the gateway. It was actually pretty similar to how I opened gateways, only I didn't need a gateway to exist first. I could create them on the fly and close them afterwards.

A section of the trunk shimmered, and the bark glowed a dark blue and faded to black. Within a few seconds, we could see through the trunk to another clearing where a fae in silver armor waited for us.

"All right, let's go." Kaysea stepped through the gateway to the clearing on the other side.

I waited until everyone was through the gateway before moving to step through myself. Before passing through, I patted the tree. "Thank you," I said, and then took the few remaining steps to the fae realm.

As the portal closed behind us, I felt a brush of the tree's magic, gentle and inquisitive. Almost like it was saying, "You're welcome."

———

WE WAITED a short distance from the gateway while Kaysea spoke quietly with her contact. I looked around to get my bearings. The gateway was located just outside the city, which we'd be avoiding. I was pretty sure we needed to travel north and head up the mountain to get to the remains of the village. Once we looked around there, we'd decide where to go next.

"How long will it take us to reach the village?" I looked at Eddie since he'd been the one to review the maps with Pele. "Could we reach it by tomorrow night?"

"Yeah, I think so," he said, as Kaysea joined us. "Depends on how much ground we cover today. We'll probably want to make camp at night since not all of us can see in the dark."

Kaysea stiffened slightly. "We don't have to stop because of me. I won't be a burden on anyone, and I can pick my way carefully at night."

"I was actually talking about myself," Eddie said. "As soon as night truly falls, I can't see much, even if it's a full moon."

"Oh," Kaysea said, studying Eddie carefully.

I let out a sigh. "I know. We all want to know what the hell he is, too." Eddie laughed and Kaysea smiled.

"Eddie, you lead the group towards the village. I'm going to shift and explore the area a bit and keep a lookout for unexpected visitors." I glanced at Andrei. "You should do the same. If we see or smell anything, we'll alert the group. Once it starts getting dark, we'll pick a place to make camp for the night."

Everyone nodded, and I slipped my backpack off and set it

on the ground. I took my swords off first, followed by the daggers that fit in my bracers and the ones strapped to my thighs. I slid those into specially designed sleeves inside the bag and pulled my clothes off and tucked those into the bag. My boots got tied to the outside. Once I was done, I handed the bag to Kaysea. That was when I noticed both Eddie and Mikhail were carefully studying the trees ahead of us.

Kaysea laughed. "The boys are shy."

I snickered and glanced at Andrei, who was also stripping off his clothes and shoving them into a bag. The snicker died in my throat as he stood and handed the bag to Kaysea. "Thank you for loaning me the bag," he said kindly as I valiantly tried to keep my eyes above his waist. I failed. *Get a grip, Nemain,* I scolded myself. Then I thought of some things that would be fun to grip and heat spread through me.

Andrei's head whipped towards me and his eyes flickered yellow. "What are you thinking about, kitty cat?" A knowing smile spread across his face.

"I'm thinking about all the tasty game we can hunt in these woods," I lied and quickly pushed my shifter magic into action. I fell to all fours as the magic swept through me, rearranging my bones and muscles and sprouting fur across my skin. Despite all that, I still heard his response. "Liar."

I shook to loosen my muscles and trotted over to the others. Andrei had started his shift, but werewolves usually took longer. Eddie looked me over as I approached them, and I realized this was his first time seeing me in my feline form.

"Huh," he said as he circled around me. "Your coloring is the same in this shape as your other one."

I raised a golden paw and admired how the sun reflected off it. My coat was a deep gold color with lighter rosettes throughout it. Slightly longer fur started at the base of my neck and ran down my shoulders before fading back in with the rest of my coat which was the same light color as the rosettes. My coloring was the same in my human form. Usually, though, I had my glamour activated, which made my skin look tanned and flat, no rosette patterns. I hated it even though I knew most of the people I cared about could see through it anyway. If I lived in a realm besides the human one, I wouldn't have to worry about wearing a glamour. But then I'd have to worry about whatever politics came with that realm.

"I can carry those bags," Eddie offered.

Kaysea shook her head. "It's fine. I'm used to carrying Nemain's stuff. She used to shift all the time when we'd travel around."

"I didn't know you two did that," Mikhail said. "Traveled around, I mean."

Kaysea's eyes lit up. "Oh, yes. We traveled around for a few years after meeting. I had spent little time outside Tír fo Thuinn at that point and wanted to see more of, well, everything."

Eddie glanced at me slyly. "And how much trouble did our dear Nemain get you into during that time?"

I swiped at him, but he jumped back and avoided my claws. Kaysea laughed. "A lot of trouble."

Mikhail chuckled. "Was Jinx with you?"

Of course I was. Someone had to bail Nemain out of the trouble she always gets herself into.

I glowered at him. *Kaysea got us into just as much trouble.*

Jinx sniffed. *Not the way I remember it.*

I was just about to tackle him when Andrei finished shifting and trotted over to us. Andrei was on the larger size for were-wolf at around 800 pounds, which made him several hundred pounds heavier than me. I didn't like the feeling of a larger predator standing next to me, so I hissed at him and laid my ears back. He snapped his teeth at me playfully, and I got to see the two rows of teeth lining his jaws up close. Getting bit by a werewolf was not fun.

Kaysea flicked her fingers in our direction and I felt a distinct bop on the nose. Andrei jerked his head back slightly at the same time. Kaysea just smiled at both of us. "Don't make me separate you two."

I chuffed and moved off to the side. *I'll take this side. Andrei, watch the other side. Jinx, stay with them.*

Andrei dipped his head in a nod and bounded off through the trees. I waited until the others had started walking and trotted off to the side. We were still at the base of the mountain, and the terrain was mostly flat, but that would change quickly. A road led to the village, but we'd decided to avoid that since anyone traveling to or from that area would likely be taking the road. It would make our trek slightly harder, but at least no snow lay on the ground.

The trees and fauna grew wildly throughout the forest. This temperate climate in some ways resembled the forests that grew along the Washington coast like those around Emerald Bay. But everything was larger and more colorful. Many of the bushes growing around the trees had bright, shiny gold leaves. Others had blossoming flowers of orange, purple, and yellow. I inhaled deeply as I weaved through the plants, being careful to avoid some of the more suspicious-looking ones. Carnivorous plants were common throughout the fae realms. I was too large a creature for most of them, but that wouldn't stop them from trying. Most of the scents I picked up were of rodents and a few large grazers. Some older scent trails came from predators that roamed these woods, but nothing recent. That would become more of a concern the further as we traveled into the mountains.

I kept a steady pace for the next few hours, listening to the group as they made their way up the mountainside. We started out at a pretty good pace, but as the terrain got steeper and more rough, our progress slowed. I studied some trees ahead and selected one that looked to be the tallest. Breaking into a run, my long legs ate up the distance. As I neared the tree, I leapt, claws digging into the bark, and climbed to a thick branch midway up. I surveyed the branches that extended above me. The leaves were a bright green with orange highlights and glistened in the fading sun. The branch I was on seemed sturdy enough, and the tree looked healthy. *Nothing ventured, nothing gained.*

I leapt the fifteen feet to the nearest branch. It groaned slightly under my weight but held, and I leapt to the next one. Exhilaration flowed through me as I climbed higher and higher until finally making it to the top of the tree.

A few miles ahead of us, the terrain flattened for a bit before rising back up again. That would be a good place for us to make camp. We were still too far away to make out the village, but the main road carved a path through the forest. It would make sense that they wouldn't have clear cut the forest to build this village. I looked back down the mountain and calculated how far we had traveled in the past few hours. Assuming we kept the same pace tomorrow, we'd probably make it to the village by mid-afternoon.

After climbing back down the tree, I headed towards the others. *Andrei?* I pushed the thought out as I made my approach, trusting that he heard me. *I'm regrouping with the others. We're almost at a good place to camp.* Werewolves could hear telepathic thoughts perfectly fine, but I'd never encountered any that could push thoughts back. When in their wolf form, the wolf side superseded the human side, and speech was beyond them.

"Our fearless leader has returned!" Eddie announced as I rejoined the group.

You've been talking the entire time, haven't you? I asked.

"Yes, he has," Mikhail said before Eddie could respond.

If I kill him, we could dissect him and then find out what he is, Jinx grumbled.

"They're very grouchy," Eddie complained.

The terrain levels out ahead, I told everyone. *Probably less than an hour away. We can make camp there for the night. We should be able to reach the village by mid-afternoon tomorrow.*

Eddie looked up at the sky. "Good. The sun is setting fast. We'll likely be making camp in the dark." Eddie stiffened slightly as Andrei glided out of the woods, silent as a ghost. "Freaking werewolves," he muttered and jogged ahead to help Kaysea navigate a particularly rocky section.

Mikhail and Jinx glanced back and narrowed their eyes at Andrei before returning their focus on the path ahead. No one had sensed Andrei's approach, and it unnerved everyone, myself included. Something that large shouldn't be able to move that silently through the woods.

The werewolf moved to walk next to me, bumping me slightly with his shoulder. I hissed and snapped my teeth at him. He swung his head towards me, flattening his ears and propping them forward again, giving me an innocent look. I glared at him again and trotted after the others, leaving the wolf to follow.

Chapter Five

THE FLAMES CRACKED and flickered in the night. We'd all eaten our fair share of the game Andrei and I had caught and brought back to cook over the campfire. Kaysea had located an underground spring and used her magic to bring some of the water to the surface for us. I could almost pretend to be enjoying a night out in the woods with some friends and ignore the rest of it. Almost.

Light from the fire reflected off Andrei's eyes as he watched Mikhail sharpen his sword. His eyes remained hazel but he'd gone predatory still and I didn't think he realized it. I gently thumped my leg against his and he blinked before looking at me. The wolf side of him was definitely closer to the surface these days. "You good?" I asked.

"Yeah." He looked curiously at the swords on my back and then once again at Mikhail's swords. "Why no guns? Some of the werewolves train with them but I've never seen you use them before."

Mikhail snorted and Andrei narrowed his eyes at him. "They don't do enough damage and they're not fast enough," I explained before Andrei could pick a fight with Mikhail.

Andrei refocused on me, amusement lighting up his eyes. "Are you telling me that you're faster than a speeding bullet? Can you also leap over tall buildings in a single bound?"

I frowned at him, not seeing what tall buildings had to do with this. "I'm usually faster than whoever is wielding the gun. Vampires are generally faster than werewolves so any wolves you know who train with guns are foolish." Mikhail grunted in agreement. "Moving on to a more relevant topic, who do you think the child is, Kaysea?" I asked.

Her pale green eyes studied the flames as she pursed her lips. "I don't know. I've been trying to think of possibilities, but nothing makes sense. The children who survived the massacre weren't able to say much about the boy. They did say they overheard their parents claim the child's power rivaled that of the Queens."

"Could he be the son of one of the Queens?" Eddie speculated.

Kaysea shook her head. "Neither of the Queens has bonded with anyone. There's no way they would be able to keep something like that hidden. I don't see how it's possible either of them could have a child."

"Why?" Andrei asked. "Love isn't exactly a requirement for having a child. Maybe they just had a lover for a short time that no one knew about and the affair resulted in a child."

Eddie looked at him and laughed. "You are a newbie, aren't ya?"

Andrei bristled, and I reached out, placing a hand on his arm.

Mikhail glanced around the group and settled his gaze on me. "So it's true then?" he asked. "The fae reproduce by magic?"

"Only the sidhe," Kaysea cut in. "The rest of us still do it the old-fashioned way." She winked.

"You're not sidhe?" Andrei asked. The tension eased out of

him as curiosity settled in once more. He might be quick to anger, but his curious nature usually overrode everything else. A small smile played across my lips. I had missed him.

"Gods, no," Kaysea answered, distaste spreading across her features. "The merfolk are closely related to the sidhe, but we're not the same."

"Oh . . . sorry?" Andrei offered.

I laughed softly. "You'll find that while many acknowledge the magic and political power of the sidhe, they are generally not well liked. All fae tend to be arrogant assholes"—I held up a hand towards Kaysea—"present company excluded, of course, but the sidhe are on a whole other level."

"And they reproduce by magic?" Andrei asked. I could practically see the next thought that popped into his head. "So they don't have sex?"

"Oh, they fuck," Eddie said with a grin. Jinx's raspy laugh sounded through my head.

"Eddie's right," I confirmed. "They fuck. A lot. But they no longer reproduce that way. Haven't for thousands of years. They reproduce when they find someone they are magically compatible with. There's a little more to it than that." I frowned and looked at Kaysea. "I don't really know how to explain it. Saying they have to 'find their one true love' sounds sappy and gross."

Kaysea snorted. "Also not entirely accurate. It may be true for a lot of sidhe, but it's not a requirement. Plenty have a child with someone they're not romantically involved with. The sidhe relationship with magic is strange and hard to define. They can choose to bond with another being, usually sidhe, but it's possible across species. The bonding does exactly what it sounds like. It binds them together. Magic to magic. Soul to soul. Being bonded doesn't guarantee they will have a child, but it is the first step."

I waited, knowing Andrei wasn't done asking questions.

Kaysea glanced at me, humor lighting up her eyes. She knew Andrei well enough to anticipate more questions. Jinx was clearly bored with the conversation; he'd moved over to lie next to Mikhail who was absently stroking the grimalkin's fur.

"What if the sidhe's mate is the same sex? Can they still have a child?" Andrei frowned. "Do they even have different sexes?"

"Technically yes. But they've always been a sexually monomorphic species, so there are few differences between females and males aside from their reproductive organs. All the sidhe have the same build, tall and slender with angular features," I explained.

"Boring," Kaysea said in a singsong voice and tapped her fingers across the top of her generous thighs. "The merfolk have more variety. And more fun."

"I don't think anyone would dispute that," I agreed. "Only a female sidhe can carry a child to term and give birth. However, all sidhe are capable of holding the embryo inside them when it's first created by magic, and they can pass it to another. So if the pair whose magic created the child are both male, they can find a surrogate. Females can do this as well if they neither want nor are capable of carrying the child to term."

"How long can they hold the embryo before the pregnancy has to proceed?" Mikhail asked, still stroking Jinx's fur.

I looked at Kaysea. "Indefinitely?"

She nodded. "I don't think we know for sure, but I've heard of some sidhe waiting centuries, essentially putting the pregnancy on pause during that time. That's unusual though as most proceed with the pregnancy immediately or at most delay it only for a few years."

"So how can we be sure this child doesn't belong to one of the Queens?" Mikhail asked. "Maybe they've been holding onto the embryo for centuries and recently passed it to a surrogate."

"The sidhe don't reproduce often," Kaysea explained. "When this occurs, their magic builds up for months. It's plain for everyone to see. Someone would have noticed if this had ever happened with either Queen. I have no doubt they have secrets. But they are too closely watched to have hidden this from everyone. This child is not theirs."

"Is there any chance his parents are alive and looking for him?" Andrei asked. I heard the ache in his voice. His parents had died when he was young, and he barely remembered them. I brushed my leg against his, and he leaned into my touch.

Nobody spoke to answer Andrei's question. We all knew it was likely the parents, whoever they were, were no longer among the living.

It's unlikely the parents are still alive, Jinx said in a gentle tone he rarely used. *The only scenario I see with them still being alive is if someone wanted to capture the family and the child escaped. But if a sidhe family with a child who possessed strong magic was attacked, we'd know about it. And no one knows who this child is.*

I glanced at Jinx. He was lying against the side of a fallen tree that blocked the light from the fire, and his black coat made him almost invisible in the darkness. His golden eyes practically glowed in the night. A suspicious thought stirred to life in my mind. I concentrated and pushed a thought to only Jinx. *When you were looking for me after the vampires captured me, you traveled through the Seelie realms, correct? That's when you encountered Luna?*

Jinx turned his golden eyes on me but said nothing.

Which realm did you find her in, Jinx? I pressed him. Now was so not the time for his stubbornness. Especially if I was right about this.

61

Jinx stared at me another moment and rose from where he was lying and stalked away from the campfire. *This one. I found her about two days from here.* He disappeared into the darkness. I heard his claws dig into bark as he climbed up a tree. Given everything at stake, he wouldn't go far. He must have been thinking about this since he saw the map of where the village was located. Annoyance and frustration surged through me but also concern. Grimalkins mated for life. And Jinx was head over tails in love with Luna.

Well . . . that's an unexpected development. Eddie's voice rumbled through my mind. I froze and slowly turned my head to face him. I'd forgotten Eddie could eavesdrop on telepathic conversations.

Mikhail glanced at where Jinx had disappeared and then back and forth between me and Eddie. "Care to share with the group?"

"After I was captured by Sebastian and his vampires, Jinx looked all over for me. Including the fae realms . . . including this realm," I said. "He found Luna here, two days from here, to be exact. She was badly wounded and her magic was practically non-existent. And she had no memories of who she was or where she'd come from. A short time later, the boy turned up in the village."

"There's no way that's a coincidence," Eddie said.

"No," I agreed. "Luna is likely involved in this somehow. If the devourers aren't able to find the boy on their own and they learn about Luna, they might go after her in hopes of using her to find the boy." My stomach twisted as I thought of another option. "Or use Luna to draw the boy out from wherever he's hiding."

All of us stared into the night where Jinx was perched in a tree somewhere. We didn't have absolute proof Luna was involved, but my instincts told me she was. The grimalkins usually stayed within their clans, but sometimes they would bond with another being and leave the clan. Jinx had been bonded with me since birth. If Luna was bonded with this boy, she would have done everything in her power to protect him just like Jinx would do for me. That would explain why she'd been so gravely injured, but I had no idea what had happened to wipe away her memories and knock her magic offline for so long. So far, the more we learned about this child, the greater the mystery grew. Hopefully this trend wouldn't continue when we reached the village the next day.

"Get some sleep. I'll keep watch tonight." I stood and walked away from the dying fire to a large tree with branches stretching unbelievably wide. I stripped off my weapons, clothes, and boots and left them at the base of the tree and then shifted. A few leaps took me midway up the tree, and I padded out on a branch that had to be at least six feet wide. I settled on the branch and looked out over the group as they bedded down for the night, Jinx curled tightly by my side.

Everyone woke shortly after dawn, and we continued to the village. We followed the same pattern as the day before, with me and Andrei flanking the group and watching out for any potential threats. No such threats appeared, and we arrived at the village shortly after noon. I'd been right about them building the village amongst the trees. They'd cleared just enough land for the buildings and left the trees to weave amongst them. A few small houses had even been built up in the trees.

"Am I the only one who finds this super creepy?" Eddie asked as we studied what remained of the village.

Most of the buildings were still intact. A few had holes in the walls. They were fairly large, and I suspected a body being thrown had made them. It took a hell of a lot of force to throw a body hard enough for it to go through a wall. Some buildings had thick trails of dried blood on them. The village was empty. I'd been keeping my magic tucked away in case we encountered any fae while here, but it slowly unwound itself and spread out in front of me as if tasting what was left behind.

"It's all kinds of creepy." I shuddered. "Those of you who can see magic, what do you see?"

Kaysea and Eddie looked over the village, and Jinx cautiously walked through the buildings. *It looks like devourer magic. And fae magic,* Jinx announced.

"It looks like your magic, Nemain," Kaysea said as she studied a particular building with a gaping hole in one of its walls. "Yours is slightly different because of the shifter blood in you. But until today, I've never encountered any magic that looked like yours."

"Great," I muttered and started exploring the buildings.

Part of me had been hoping that when Kaysea or Eddie examined the magic traces left behind they would decide it didn't look anything like my magic. If I tried to look at this from a positive viewpoint, it meant if we managed to capture one of these devourers, they might be able to shed some light on where exactly my magic had come from. But I didn't know if I would like the answer. Recently I'd brought Kaysea with me to visit Cian, and she examined his magic; my brother's magic was nothing like mine and didn't resemble fae magic at all. Add all of this to what Eddie had revealed about my aunt still being alive and having magic exactly like mine. I couldn't ignore the possibility of my parents not being my biological parents much longer, and it was weighing on me.

"Let's look around and see if we can find any clues," I told the others and forced myself to focus on the task at hand. "Anything that might tell us who these devourers are or what might have happened to the boy."

Everyone split up and started scouting around the village. Jinx and Mikhail focused on the buildings in the trees and the perimeter of the village, and the rest of us searched the buildings on the ground. It didn't take long for us all to meet back in the center of the village. Perhaps the only blessing in all of this was that the village was small so the deaths were relatively few. If the boy had been taken to the city at the base of the mountain, the death toll would have been in the hundreds, if not thousands. Although, maybe they would have been able to fight off the devourers.

"We didn't find much, but this was well coordinated," Mikhail said. "Some tracks outside the village are likely from the devourers. They surrounded the village and moved in as a unit, making sure no one could escape. The damage around the village is minimal, but what was damaged was likely done to cause terror. They moved in, seemingly out of nowhere, forcing everyone to the center of the village. The residents would have been able to see their magic, which would have only further terrified them. Then the devourers brutally killed a few of them." Mikhail gestured towards some of the damaged buildings where blood still streaked the wood. "They either did this to get the villagers to talk or to terrorize them. Or both."

Kaysea and Eddie looked at Mikhail like they didn't know him. Andrei was watching him warily with wolf-yellow eyes.

"I take it that's what you would have done?" I asked.

Mikhail met my gaze, unflinching. "It's what I have done."

"We found nothing useful in our search," Kaysea said after a few beats of silence. "I was hoping at least something here would trigger a vision, but nothing so far."

I scanned the buildings we'd searched. "Where did the children hide? Did anyone find that?"

"No . . . it was a basement, though." Kaysea furrowed her brows slightly. "It might not actually be under a building. Sometimes in villages like this, they build a basement for food storage at the base of a tree. We were looking in and around the buildings, so we might have missed it."

We split up again, each checking the trees that wove throughout the village. Andrei called out, "Found it!" We all converged on his location and examined the wooden doors that almost blended in with the base of the tree.

"Let's see if there is anything." I pulled the doors open and slowly made my way down the stairs.

The others followed close behind me until we found ourselves in a small room with barrels of grain stashed against the wall and some root vegetables stored on shelves.

"Not really much to see, is there?" I frowned as the disappointment I'd been feeling grew. We'd been banking on finding something useful in this village, but so far we were coming up empty. Kaysea surveyed the room, slowly turning in a circle, taking everything in. She froze when she faced the stairs we'd come down.

"Eddie, can you close the doors?" she asked.

"Sure." Eddie hopped up the stairs and pulled the doors shut once more. The soft fae lanterns that lined the walls blazed brighter to make up for the lost sunlight. "Oh, shit," Eddie said as he stepped back down the stairs and studied the dark wood of the door.

"What?" I squinted at the doors as if that would help me see whatever they were looking at.

"I don't really know how to explain it," Kaysea started. "I've never seen anything like this before. I can still see the magical echo left behind from the ward the sidhe placed around this basement. But there's another echo on top of it. I think. . . I think someone cut a hole in the ward that allowed them to pass through."

I glanced at Eddie. "Is this what it would look like if you passed through a ward?"

Kaysea looked away from the door to stare at Eddie, who shot me an annoyed look. I gave him a sweet smile.

"You can pass through wards?" Kaysea asked. "How?"

He mimics the magic, Jinx responded. *He was able to pass through a standard perimeter ward and bring Nemain through as well a few months ago.*

"I don't recall giving you permission to share my secrets." Eddie's expression hardened, and he glared at Jinx. His amber eyes glowing slightly.

"Given what's at stake, perhaps you could overlook the sharing of your secrets and answer the question," Mikhail cut in. "I'm assuming the child we're looking for was locked down here with the rest. But he wasn't there when the children were rescued later. It stands to reason he's the one who worked magic on the ward to pass through and flee."

"It's not the same as my magic," Eddie said reluctantly. "The grimalkin is right. I can mimic other types of magic, at least on the surface level, and that allows me to pass through wards. It probably wouldn't have worked on a ward this strong. But even if it did, no magical echo is left behind. As far as the magic is concerned, my magic blends with that of the ward magic. Whatever the kid did allowed him to pass through the ward to escape but kept the ward intact, which is the only reason the other children survived."

"Why did he run, though?" Andrei asked. "He was safe here."

"Maybe he thought the ward wouldn't hold and took the opportunity to escape while the devourers were distracted with something else going on in the village. Or maybe he thought that if he ran, the devourers would follow him and leave the rest of the kids alone," I guessed. "We can ask him when we find him."

Kaysea took a few steps towards the stairs and paused, looking over her shoulder. "Can one of you catch me in case I fall?"

Andrei nodded and followed her up the steps. Taking a deep breath, Kaysea extended her hand until her palm was flat against the door. I could sense her magic expanding as it interacted with what was left behind from the magic the child had done.

Seconds after touching the door, Kaysea gasped, and her head rocked back. Andrei caught her, holding her upright, palm still flat against the door. "He's running. Gods, he's so scared, and I can feel the guilt radiating off him. He blames himself for what happened to the villagers. The devourers know he made it out of the basement. They're tracking him. He can't outrun them. A river. He reached a river, and he leapt in. Cold. I can't make anything out. Too much churning. He's falling. A waterfall? Cold. Darkness. I can't see anything else!" Kaysea screamed in frustration and thrust her other hand against the door. "Alive! He's on a river bank. Blood is running down his arm, but he's alive. A woman is there. She's found him. It's the young woman from the cliff! They've found each other."

Kaysea went rigid, and her head slammed back directly into Andrei's face. He swore as blood poured from his nose and half dragged, half carried her down the stairs. I jumped towards them and helped lower Kaysea to the ground.

Her pure white eyes latched onto me. "A child of both worlds with eyes of change. Born in darkness but pulled to the light."

"You know I hate it when you go full seer, Kaysea," I said as I cradled her against me.

After a few minutes, the tension left her body and she went boneless. Blinking a few times, she glanced around at everyone and turned her now pale green eyes up at me. "That was fun."

I snorted. "Tell that to Andrei's nose."

"Sorry," Kaysea said, her eyes tinged with remorse.

"Not your fault." Andrei waved her off as he wiped the blood from his face with a towel he'd found. "Already good as new."

"Well, at least we know where to head from here. And the boy has now linked up with the woman from your last vision." I was glad the kid had found someone to help him, but this meant we were that much closer to Kaysea's vision of me shoving the young woman off the cliff. There had to be more to the vision, a reason I would do such a thing. "And we have even more fun riddles to obsess over and figure out their meaning. Yay."

Kaysea gave me a small smile. "Previous visions gave us, 'A change is coming carried on wings of gold. Some must fall in order to rise.' We can now add 'A child of both worlds with eyes of change. Born in darkness but pulled to the light.'"

"Does the kid have wings?" Eddie asked. "I feel like someone would have noticed if he had golden wings."

"Maybe he can hide them," Mikhail suggested.

"Wouldn't he have flown away then instead of falling or jumping into a river?" Andrei said.

"We can think about this while we search for the river. Any idea where to head, Eddie?"

Eddie pulled the map out of his bag. After glancing around, he walked over to the wall and extended the map. "Hold this," he told Andrei, who held the map spread open.

"We're here." Eddie pointed to a spot on the map. "A couple of rivers are nearby, but I'm pretty sure this is the one. I don't know if it has a waterfall, but it's the closest one to the village, and I doubt the kid would have been able to make it to the other ones before the devourers caught him."

"Looks like it's maybe fifteen minutes from here. We still have a few hours of sunlight left. Let's head there and follow it downstream and see if we can find the waterfall. We'll find somewhere to camp along the way."

Andrei rolled the map up and handed it to Eddie, who tucked it in his bag. Sunlight filtered into the basement as Mikhail opened the doors and helped Kaysea up the stairs. I paused next to Eddie. "Kaysea won't admit it, but using her magic like that weakens her for a while."

"I'll watch over her," Eddie promised.

I nodded and followed the others out. It was good we'd started our search in this village, but I was looking forward to leaving it and the empty homes behind us. I hoped we wouldn't be finding another massacred village in our future.

Chapter Six

"Yep," Eddie announced from where we all stood on a rocky outcropping looking several hundred feet below. "That's a waterfall."

Andrei laughed next to me. I was pondering shoving Eddie over the edge when I saw Jinx slowly creeping up behind him. Great minds think alike. The boy had survived the drop, so Eddie would most likely be fine. Plus, we'd find out whether he had the ability to fly. Kaysea looked over her shoulder and smoothly took a step back and to the side so she was blocking Jinx's path.

Spoilsport, Jinx announced and turned back to the trees lining the river.

Eddie turned and looked suspiciously at Jinx. "He was thinking about pushing me over the edge, wasn't he?"

"Raise your hand if you were thinking about shoving Eddie," I said and held up my hand. Both Mikhail and Andrei raised their hands. An amused smile spread across Kaysea's face, and she shook her head and followed Jinx.

"Rude." Eddie glanced up the river. "I'm going to catch us some fish for dinner."

"I'll keep an eye on Kaysea," Mikhail said, and they both walked off, leaving me and Andrei alone.

I took a few steps closer to the edge of the large boulder and sat down, dangling my feet. Andrei plopped next to me, his leg brushing against mine.

"Looks like a nice swimming hole."

"It does," I agreed. "So . . . gonna tell me what you've been up to the past few months?"

"Was wondering when you would ask." He shifted so he was facing me, still leaving his right leg dangling off the cliff. "I told Stela about the warlocks and what happened when they were after you a few months ago. About Sebastian. Not all of it, obviously."

Even though it'd been six months, I still felt a rush of emotions at Sebastian's name. At one point in my life, I'd loved him more than anything. Part of that was based on a lie, but not all of it. He'd stalked and tortured me for decades before eventually telling the Circle about me in a bid for power. He'd died by my hand, and I was glad he was dead. But hearing his name still made me want to scream and rip his heart out of his chest. Again.

"She thinks the Circle killed her lover, doesn't she?" A flash of guilt hit me. Stela had been dating Jolie for months without knowing Jolie was not only a witch but Sebastian's niece. I'd killed Jolie for her involvement in Sebastian's scheming, but I hadn't really thought about how it would impact Stela.

"She does," Andrei confirmed. "It's true in a way."

I snapped my head towards him. "It's not and you know it."

Andrei met my irritated stare. "If the Circle hadn't been involved, Jolie never would have come to town and met my sister. Therefore, she wouldn't have died."

"I don't need you to justify my kill," I said harshly.

"I'm not," he growled. I went back to looking over the

forest, and we sat there for a few minutes. Finally, Andrei continued. "Stela wanted to go back to the pack that found us. The one my parents had led. We didn't leave them on the best of terms before. Most of what's left of that pack want to go after the vampires, and at the time, we'd wanted no part of that."

My blood went cold at his words. *At the time.* The war between the vampire and werewolves had raged for centuries. The wolves had lost. Only a fraction of their population remained scattered across the world. Going after the vampires was a suicide mission. Even more so now that they were working with the warlock Circle.

"When we came back, they could tell Stela was out for blood, so they were more forthcoming with information." Andrei sighed and rubbed his face.

I glanced over at him and saw what I hadn't seen before. He carried a tension he hadn't when he left.

"Are you going to rejoin that pack? Start up the war again?" I kept my voice flat even as my heart beat faster.

"Honestly, I don't know. I don't want to. But Stela . . . she's all in. I convinced her to come back to Emerald Bay for a while and check in with the wolves living there. I'm hoping if she takes a break from the other pack and thinks about this more, she'll back off."

"I'm sorry this happened to you. To both of you," I said, still not looking at him. "I know this is the exact opposite of what you wanted. You both moved to Emerald Bay to not get involved with the war between the werewolves and the vampires and to avoid getting caught up in magical bullshit altogether. I really wanted to keep you out of it. I thought I could, but I should have known better. I'm sorry, Andrei."

Andrei's warm fingers brushed against my chin, and he gently guided my face towards him. "You have nothing to be sorry for. I'm perfectly capable of making my own decisions

73

and standing by them. I admit the past few months have been tough and this isn't what I wanted for my sister. But I don't regret meeting you, Nemain. I've missed the hell out of you the past few months."

His thumb trailed over my bottom lip and traced my jawline. "I missed you, too, wolf," I breathed, and his eyes flashed yellow for a second before his mouth was on mine. Our kiss deepened as he ran his fingers through my hair, pulling me closer to him. My hand slipped under his shirt as I gripped him to me.

If you two fall off the cliff, none of us are going down there to fish you out, Jinx grumbled.

Andrei and I broke apart and stared at each other. Andrei's expression was a mixture of lust and amusement. "Jinx probably has a point. This isn't exactly the best make-out location."

I became a little more aware of my surroundings and realized I'd inched closer to the ledge. I'd been moments away from moving to sit in Andrei's lap, and that move most likely would have resulted in one or both of us tumbling down to the water below.

"Every once in a while Jinx makes a good point," I said wryly.

Rude.

Andrei laughed and helped me up. "I'm going to go check on the others."

"Go ahead. I'll be there in a few minutes."

I watched him walk back to the woods where the others were setting up camp for the night, which really just meant starting a campfire and cooking dinner. None of us had packed bedrolls or tents because we'd be moving fast. Half of the group shifted into fur or already was furry in the case of Jinx. Being a mermaid Kaysea didn't really get cold, even in this form. I figured if Eddie or Mikhail wanted something warmer at night, they would have packed it.

Jinx?

A few seconds later, a dark shape dropped out the trees and slunk over to me. *Wasting no time getting back with the dog, I see.*

I let that comment slide. *There's something I need to tell you that the others don't know yet. Eddie told me when I went to tell him about this trip. Did my parents . . . did they ever talk to you about my mother's sisters?*

Jinx leapt up onto a higher portion of the rock ledge, putting him almost eye level with me. *Nothing more than what she told you, that both of them had died. Why?*

According to Eddie, that's not true. One of them is still alive, Badb. It's a bit of a long story, but basically when the shifter realm fell, she was pissed about the fae doing nothing to help them so she opened a gateway to the Seelie Queen's personal chamber. A lot of devourers made it through and wreaked havoc in her home and the capital city before they were killed. That kicked off a war between the Seelie Queen and my mother and her sisters, who became known as The Morrigan.

Jinx went absolutely still at my words. *She opened a gateway?*

Yes. I swallowed. I'd kept our communications telepathic because I wasn't ready for the others to know this. I wasn't ready to say the words out loud. *Also, she was my mother's twin sister. Do you think . . . Do you think Badb is my birth mother? Even though I didn't have my mother's magic, I always assumed I had to be her daughter because we look so much alike. But Badb is her twin. Her identical twin. And I have her magic.*

It's possible, I suppose. But if that was the case, why didn't Badb raise you? And who is your father?

My father is Nevin. I voiced the thought firmly. *Whatever we learn, Nevin and Macha raised me. They're my parents.*

They were your parents in every way that mattered, Jinx reassured me. *But Nevin and Macha were completely devoted to each other. I don't see either of them having an affair with someone else. Which means if Badb is your birth mother, there is no way Nevin is your father by blood.*

I know. Should we try to contact your mother? I asked carefully.

Jinx loved his mother. But their relationship was strained. She'd given him over to my parents to bond with me when I'd been born and he'd been only a few years old. For grimalkins, that was the equivalent of just barely being a teenager. He'd seen her occasionally over the years, but it was usually brief and decades would go by between meetings. The last time we'd seen her, she'd delivered a cryptic warning about it not being wise for me to be in the fae realms and had told me to leave quickly.

I think we should, but it would take me a while to track down a way to send her a message, and we don't really have time to do that. Plus, there is no guarantee she would respond. His words held a slight bitterness, and I reached out and rubbed him behind the ears.

Once we find the kid and get him stashed somewhere safe, how about you and me track down your mother? I think she owes us some answers. I smiled wickedly at him.

Jinx's eyes glowed brighter. *I think that's a brilliant plan.*

WE SET out early the next morning and made our way downstream. We couldn't climb down near the waterfall, and none of us were willing to try jumping. So we had to backtrack a bit. We walked a few hours following the river downstream, and Kaysea stopped and studied the surrounding area.

"I think this is where he got out of the river," she announced. Eddie shrugged his backpack off and pulled the map out. He stretched it across the ground, and we all crouched around. "He could have gone anywhere," Kaysea murmured.

"Well, we know the girl found him when he got out of the river, right?" I asked, and Kaysea nodded. "He was wounded, so if there is a town nearby, she might have taken him there to get him healed or for supplies."

"Here." Eddie pointed at the map. "It's only an hour away. It's off the main road that leads up the mountain. Most of the towns are built around that road, but that one is the closest."

"Let's head there." I stood up, waiting for Eddie to tuck the map away. "Maybe we'll get lucky and they'll still be there. If not, at least we can ask the people in town who the girl is and if they saw the boy."

"Assuming everyone in town hasn't been massacred," Mikhail said.

"If that town had been hit too, Pele would have known about it. Unless it happened in the past few days," I said. "Nobody has seen the devourers who wiped out the town. I have no doubt they're still searching for the boy, but they must have decided to keep a low profile."

We started heading in the direction of the town, and I moved to walk by Mikhail. "I forgot to ask before," I said. "Is this your first time in a fae realm?"

"Yes," he responded and smoothly dodged a dark purple vine with large hooked thorns that were reaching out from a nearby tree.

"You don't seem all that impressed."

"Why? Because I'm not stopping to stare at everything wide-eyed like the pup?"

I laughed softly. "I had to stop him from touching a flower. He thought it was pretty and 'friendly looking'."

Mikhail shook his head. I pursed my lips and looked at him out of the corner of my eyes. It was none of my business, and I shouldn't ask. But at the end of the day, I was a cat and curiosity always got the better of me. "Why can't you summon a sword out of the mist like Magos?"

He hid it well, but I saw the slight hitch in his stride at my words and the tightening of the muscles across his shoulders. Magos could summon his sword at any time. I knew it was part of the magic both Magos and Mikhail had before they were transformed into vampires. In their home realm, elemental magic was common amongst their people. Magos had an affinity for water; Mikhail had an affinity for both water and sunlight. While most of the others like them used their gifts for peaceful things like growing crops, Magos and eventually Mikhail had trained to become warriors so they could protect their people. The magic that ran in their blood was honed for different purposes, and one of them was to summon a sword out the mist. Magos still did. But I'd never seen Mikhail do it, and the last time I'd asked him about it he'd just stared at me and then vanished into the mist himself.

The silence stretched between us, and I thought he wouldn't answer.

"In our home realm, before it fell, a lot of training came with becoming a warrior. Our people were peaceful, and while we knew sometimes violence couldn't be avoided, we wanted to ensure we never strayed too far down that path. When we trained to become a warrior, we made a lot of vows. About when to use magic. And when not to. The end of the training included a ritual to bind our sword to us. That's what allowed us to summon the sword anywhere. But we had to make a vow to ourselves that we would only raise our sword when it was right to do so."

I frowned slightly. "Seems vague. What determines what is right?"

"That is something everyone must decide for themselves."

The pieces clicked together in my head. "You can't summon your sword because you don't believe you have the right to wield it any longer."

"The werewolves killed my family. They slaughtered half of what was left of my people. Had I just hunted down those responsible and ended them, I would have been justified in my acts. But I helped wage a war against their species for the past few centuries. I allowed myself to be consumed by rage and grief. That village we passed through that the devourers destroyed? I've done that. Dozens of times. I've slaughtered innocents along with the guilty. That sword is no longer mine. I have no right to it, after all I've done."

An uncomfortable feeling went through me at his words. Words that could just as easily apply to me and what I'd done to witches and warlocks over the past few centuries. The warlocks orchestrated my parents' death. Until recently, I didn't know which one specifically played a role in their death. Part of what had drawn me to Sebastian originally was that even though he was a warlock, he seemed to hate them just as much as I did. He'd used my hate and directed me at witches and warlocks who were blocking his bid to power. I'd never allowed myself to feel guilty before, but when I discovered the truth about Sebastian using me for his benefit, I couldn't help but rethink what I'd done.

I had no problem killing. If someone posed a threat to me or mine, I would end them and sleep soundly at night. But killing innocent people was a whole other matter. "Having a conscience sucks sometimes," I muttered.

Mikhail laughed softly, and we walked the rest of the way to the town in a companionable silence.

The town turned out to be twice the size of the last one and thankfully, everyone was still alive. This area of the mountain wasn't as heavily forested, and small plains stretched here and there. The town was built right on the edge of the forest and onto one of those plains. Smooth stone pathways wound between colorful houses and shops, all of which had vines growing along their walls. We were still on the outskirts of town but were already getting curious glances.

"I vote we start at the pub," Eddie announced and immediately started walking down the pathway towards the center of town.

"You don't even know where the pub is!" I called after him.

He spun around, so he was facing us, and continued walking backwards. "I always know where the pub is." He winked and spun back around.

Andrei and Kaysea laughed. Jinx sighed and Mikhail just looked amused. We followed Eddie, who did indeed find the town pub right away. We stepped into a large open building with tables scattered around. Skylights allowed sunlight to filter in, and vines similar to what grew on the outside of the building grew across the ceiling around the skylights.

Andrei looked around in wonder. "It's beautiful." Only a few of the tables were occupied, a young dark-haired sidhe wearing an apron cleaning up a recently vacated one while an older sidhe managed the bar. The barkeep. Hopefully, they'd be willing to talk to us. They were the most likely to have the information we needed.

"Let's sit at the bar," I said. "Let me and Kaysea handle the talking. You three will attract attention just because of what you are. Vampires and werewolves aren't exactly a common sight around here. Eddie, you're just annoying, and Jinx is an asshole." Everyone grunted in agreement.

We settled at the bar, and the sidhe working behind the bar made her way over to us. Her dark skin practically glowed against the deep purple tunic she was wearing. She gracefully slid to a stop in front of us and scrutinized us with sharp, light brown eyes. "What an interesting group to come wandering into our town."

Neither her expression nor her tone gave me any idea whether she meant us harm. No matter their standing, all sidhe loved to play mind games. Talking to them was like walking through a minefield with a sword dangling over your head. And it was never the minefield or the sword that was the true threat. So many hidden dangers in every conversation. Annoyance and impatience flooded through me, but I did my best to keep it and my magic in check. The last thing I needed was for my magic to erupt and be on full display here.

"We're actually looking for someone to add to our *interesting* group," I replied evenly. "We believe a girl, a young woman actually, who lives in town recently came across a young boy. Do you know of them?" Awareness flickered through her eyes. I smiled at her and did my best to appear non-threatening and concerned. "Someone is after the boy. He's in danger and so is anyone traveling with him. If they're still in town, everyone is in danger here, too."

"And you're just looking for him out of the goodness of your own heart, of course," she said with that same even tone that was really irritating the crap out of me.

Clearly sensing how close I was to grabbing the sidhe and introducing her face to the top of the bar, Kaysea smoothly cut in, placing a hand on top of my arm. "As you noted, we are an interesting group. I'm a seer, and this boy has been haunting my visions for quite some time now. I can't let this go, and my friends were kind enough to come with me. As you can imagine, this path is not a safe one."

"Especially for one so far from her element."

"Indeed," Kaysea agreed.

"Who is after the child?" the barkeep asked, still studying Kaysea.

"Killers," Kaysea said. "Assassins of some kind. We don't know what they are exactly." Truth and lies. Kaysea was much better at these conversations than me.

The barkeep gave our group a once-over, lingering the longest on me, Mikhail, and Eddie. "Almost everyone in your group is a killer," she noted.

My magic churned under my skin, my growing irritation setting it off. I took a deep breath in and out, and it calmed down slightly. "You're not wrong," I said. "But given the things that are after this child and what they are willing to do to those who stand in their way, killers of a different sort are called for."

"And you're all killers of a different sort." She gave me a sly smile. "I imagine those after the child wouldn't have stood here answering my questions. So perhaps you are more than a killer," she said, more to herself than to us. "The young woman grew up in a nearby town. Her name is Bryn. She's not fae. That town has a reputation for taking in refugees from other realms. She was left there as a baby and raised by one of the local families. She's never demonstrated any strong magic, so no one has any idea what she is. Definitely not human, or at least not completely human. Probably a mutt." The barkeep shrugged. "Pretty enough though. She caught the eye of one of the local sidhe girls here. My niece, actually. They had a brief tryst for a while that didn't amount to anything, but Bryn stayed in this town instead of going back to hers. She worked here occasionally and also made supply runs to other villages."

"Worked?" Kaysea asked. "Does she no longer work here?"

"No." The sidhe shook her head. "Left town a while back. Shortly after finding that boy. She said he'd gotten lost in the woods and she was going to take him back to his family and then head back to her town."

"Did you see the boy?" Kaysea asked. "Can you tell us anything about him? Was he injured?"

"Honestly, I didn't get a good look at him. We had a festival in town that day, and the bar was really busy. Bryn came in to let me know she was leaving, and he waited for her by the door. He was wearing a cloak with the hood up, so I couldn't tell anything about him. And the bar was full of sidhe from out of town. So much new magic was floating around I couldn't get a sense for him."

"Thank you for the information," Kaysea said. "Any guesses on where they might have headed? Where his family was located?"

"No. But I'm pretty sure she was lying about that. Bryn is a nice, honest girl. Lying doesn't come easy to her, and she's not particularly good at it."

"Unlike the fae," I muttered and then instantly winced. One of these days, I'd learn to keep my mouth shut.

The barkeep tilted her head back and laughed. "You're not wrong," she said in between laughs. "The only reason I didn't question Bryn further is because while she may be a terrible liar, she has a protective streak a mile wide. I didn't doubt her intentions to get the boy somewhere safe, wherever that may be. Even if she'd just met the boy, Bryn would protect him with her life and do whatever she needed to in order to keep him safe. That's just who she is." That sly smile appeared on her face once more. "She's a killer of a different sort, I suppose. Or will be soon enough."

Chapter Seven

"So what now?" Andrei asked from where we were all gathered in the forest.

We'd decided it was best to not spend any more time than necessary in town where we could draw unwanted attention, so we left after finishing our conversation with the barkeep. We'd been meandering around the forest just outside the town on the off-chance it would trigger one of Kaysea's visions. None of us actually believed that would happen, but it gave us something to do while we thought about our next move. It had been over an hour and no visions had come to Kaysea, so it was time to move on.

"Now you earn your keep, wolf." I raised an eyebrow at him. "You said you were a good tracker. See if you can find us a scent trail."

"What do I get if I find one?" Andrei gave me a heated look that made it clear what he wanted as a prize.

"You get me, lover boy," Eddie said in a breathy, dramatic tone and winked at Andrei.

I let out a low chuckle, and Andrei raised an eyebrow at me and pulled his shirt off. The chuckle died in my throat, and an entirely different feeling spread through me.

"Actually, I think Nemain is interested in being your prize after all," Eddie said with a laugh.

I elbowed him in the stomach, he grunted, and I set to picking up Andrei's clothes and stashing them in a bag. Andrei finished shifting and shook his grey coat once before bounding off into the woods.

I walked to a large tree and sat on the ground, leaning against it. "Let's wait here and see if he finds anything."

"Think he will?" Kaysea asked as she sat down next to me.

"It's possible. Parts of the scent trail will have washed away by now, but maybe some of it remains in an area more sheltered from the elements. We're not going to find a complete scent trail at this point, but maybe Andrei can find enough of one to at least point us in a direction. Werewolves do have an insanely good sense of smell."

All of us, except Kaysea, turned to look at the woods behind us. A few moments later, Andrei appeared. He stopped in front of us and backed up a few steps and turned back the way he came, trotting off at a steady pace.

"I think that means we're supposed to follow," I said.

We all started off a brisk pace after Andrei. After a few miles, Mikhail stopped suddenly in front of me at the same time Eddie stopped and reached for Kaysea, moving her behind him. I spun around so my back was against Mikhail's.

"How many?" I asked quietly. I'd heard the branches snap a second after the other two did. Jinx had already disappeared into the trees.

"At least four," Mikhail answered.

My eyes scanned the forest trying to locate them; movement to my right caught my attention. "We need to get Kaysea behind some cover."

"Over here." Eddie grabbed Kaysea's hand and pulled her

towards some boulders piled up against each other with a fallen tree in front of them. Mikhail and I darted after them, ducking into the small space between the tree and the rocks just as a strong amount of magic rose and a large chunk of rock slammed into the boulders above us. A wide crack formed in the boulder. They didn't bother throwing another rock; instead, another wave of magic rose and crashed into the weakened spot of the boulder, causing it to split even further. The magic that had thrown the boulder was earth based and common among fae. But this latest attack had been a pure concentration of magic. My magic reached out to taste it, but I knew what it would be even before my magic confirmed it. Fae magic. And devourer magic. We'd found our bad guys.

"They're trying to keep us pinned so they can flank us," I growled.

"We can't stay here," Mikhail said from where he crouched with a dagger.

I quickly thought about our options. We didn't know where Andrei was, but I hadn't heard him. If they'd attacked him, there was no way it would have been a quiet fight. He was likely hunkered down somewhere, biding his time. I had no doubt Jinx was already in a good position to attack as soon as I gave the signal. We needed to make sure Kaysea was safe. Decision made, I faced the others.

"Eddie, you distract them. Mikhail will get Kaysea out of here. Jinx and I will start cutting through them." I pulled one of the daggers out of my bracer and shifted my weight so I was on the balls of my feet, ready to run.

"Why do I have to distract them?" Eddie asked.

"Because your magic can mimic theirs! You don't have to worry about being skewered with magic and pinned against a tree!" I hissed at him.

"That's not how my magic works!"

"How the fuck does it work then?" I hissed.

86

"I want you to know it literally pains me to tell you this." Eddie's expression was indeed pained as he placed a hand over his heart. "I absolutely adore my secrets like they were my children. In fact, I probably love my secrets more than I could love any spawn of mine."

"I'm going to slam your head into a tree if you don't get to the damn point," I ground out.

"My magic requires sustained contact with other magic in order to mimic it. That's why wards are so easy for me to get through. They're not going away or trying to kill me so my magic has all the time it needs to study them. But if you hit me with blasts of magic, there is fuck all I can do about it."

I filed this information away in case something ever happened and I had to fight Eddie or others like him. I went back over the first time I'd seen Eddie display some of his magic and narrowed my eyes at him. "Eddie, I watched you get hit with fire magic when we got jumped by those two sidhe guards six months ago. They tried to barbecue you, and you took their fire and freaking played with it."

Silence.

"That was different magic," he said begrudgingly.

"Great. Fantastic," I grumbled as magic slammed into the boulder above us again, causing a few decent size chunks to fall. Mikhail gracefully dodged one that landed where he'd been crouched seconds before. "New plan. Mikhail, you attack first. I'll follow a second behind. Once their attention is on us, Eddie gets Kaysea out of here."

"If I remember right from the map, there's another river less than a quarter mile from here," Kaysea said. "If Eddie can get me to that water, I can protect myself from there."

I nodded. Kaysea wasn't a warrior like her brother, but she was still a mermaid and water was her element. At the very least, she would be able to defend herself, and if any of the devourers tried to pursue her in water, it would be their death.

I glanced at Mikhail. "Ready when you are."

In a blink, Mikhail vanished, leaving nothing but swirling mist behind. No sounds came from wherever he landed, but the magic barrage that had been aimed our way shifted to somewhere else in the forest.

Now Jinx! I told him at the same time I leapt over the fallen log and sprinted in the direction of one of the attackers. Magic started to build up to my left, but I ignored it and out of the corner of my eye saw Jinx's dark form leap from the trees above onto the figure. The magic building abruptly died.

Ducking and weaving through the trees and the undergrowth, I saw my quarry. They had been in the trees but dropped down to face me. I slowed my pace as I approached them and stopped when I was still a safe distance away and out of striking range. They were likely waiting for others to join and surround me, but I wasn't going to pass up this chance to learn who they were. The taller of the figures pulled back his hood, confirming what we already knew. He was fae, specifically sidhe. Even though we had been expecting them to be fae, I was still a little surprised. Part of me thought they would look drastically different. His appearance was different from the average sidhe but not drastically so. My magic stretched from me and met his magic. It recoiled. Devourer.

Pele was right. They were like me. Devourer mixed with something else. Never in all my searching and traveling had I ever come across something like me before. How the hell had this happened? If he'd been the only one, I could have written him off as a freak of nature like me, but two others appeared to my right with their hoods drawn back. Both sidhe with devourer magic. I needed to get them talking; if I could find out how they came to have devourer magic, maybe it would shed some light on how I came to have it as well.

Mikhail snapped into existence at my side, mist rolling off him and blood dripping from his blade. The short one with their hood still up took a step back. Whoever it was, they recognized Mikhail. *Jinx? Take out shortie when you have an opening. Keep them alive if you can.* The sidhe were too dangerous to be kept alive for questioning. But I suspected whoever was under that hood wasn't sidhe.

I shifted my weight slightly and saw the muscles tense on the sidhe in front of me. It wasn't enough that these three had freaky fae devourer magic, but of course, they were also trained warriors. It wasn't uncommon to encounter sidhe who relied solely on their magic and were absolute shit at melee or sword fighting. The two sidhe to the right already had their blades out. The one in front of us didn't, but a handle was poking out over his shoulder. I had no idea if my magic would work on them or not. The way it had reacted when it tasted the magic of the one in front told me I wouldn't be able to devour their magic. It made sense. Magic was useless against most pure devourers.

"Well," I drawled. "This has certainly turned out to be a delightful stroll in the woods."

"Indeed, it has," the sidhe in front of me agreed. He had a deep, powerful voice that was rather pleasant. It fit with his appearance. No doubt he and the other two were sidhe, but they were a little taller than the typical six feet of most sidhe and considerably broader. I didn't know if that was because of the devourer blood in them or if they were from a line I'd simply never encountered before. Pale blue eyes looked me over as I looked him over. I trusted Mikhail to keep an eye on the other two in case they tried anything.

"I am Lir." He continued to stare at me, and his magic crept closer. "You seem . . . familiar somehow." His magic snapped at me, and mine rose to slap it back. Suspicion and something akin to awareness flashed across his face. "Impossible," he whispered.

"Why are you after the boy?" Mikhail asked.

"He belongs to us," Lir replied, his expression once again neutral. "We simply wish to bring him home."

"And where is home, exactly?" I asked.

"I can show you." Lir looked at me curiously. "You don't belong here. With *them*. Help us find the boy, and you can return with us. I'll answer all your questions. Come home with us." His words and the way he was looking at me sent me spinning off kilter. I didn't trust him, but why would he bother trying this approach if there wasn't at least some truth to it? He clearly recognized something about my magic, which meant he knew something about me. About what I was and where my magic came from. He might be able to answer the questions I'd had my whole life. I needed to find out who he was and how he knew me, which meant we couldn't kill him.

Nemain? Jinx asked, and I snapped back to myself. Finding out who Lir was would have to wait until later. No way in hell were we helping them, which meant we had to get out of this situation. Mikhail and I were both skilled killers, and we also had Jinx. But I had no doubt these three knew how to handle their weapons, and the fourth figure was unknown. Plus, they could have others waiting in the trees that we hadn't spotted. Still no sign of Andrei, which worried me slightly, but I couldn't afford to dwell on that now.

"Tell me something. If you'd been able to get through the ward at that village, would you have spared the children?" I asked calmly. Silence stretched between us. I already knew the answer, but I was curious if he would lie about it.

"No," he finally said.

"There's your answer." I slipped one of my blades free from my bracer and flung it at one of the sidhe to our right. He dodged to the right so my throw missed, but Mikhail vanished the second I threw the blade, appearing right where the sidhe had moved. He thrust his sword into the chest of the sidhe, who didn't have time to dodge. Mikhail's sword struck the heart, and the sidhe jerked on his blade. That was all I saw before Lir and the other sidhe unleashed themselves on me.

I barely had enough time to pull my swords free and parry both blows. Lir struck at my right side while the other struck at my legs. I spun aside and slashed, causing both to step back. The pair split apart to circle me, and I stepped back, knowing with absolute certainty Mikhail would be there. Mist curled around me, and I felt his back against mine. Lir stopped just to my right, and I assumed the other sidhe was positioned to strike at Mikhail. Jinx dropped from the branches on the other side of Lir, forcing him to split his attention between us. If Eddie made it back to us, the odds would be four against two. I liked those odds.

The smaller figure who'd been with the sidhe took a step back and fell over a raised tree root. My gaze flickered to him, and I stiffened when I saw his revealed face.

Warlock.

One of the warlocks who had been in the woods when I had met with the Circle months ago. I focused again on Lir because I couldn't afford to be distracted. The warlock scrambled back and took off, running behind Lir.

"Your friend is a bit of a coward." I smiled savagely at Lir. A flash of grey fur moved between the tree after the fleeing warlock. Andrei. My smile grew wider.

"Honestly, I didn't want him along for this anyway. My hand was forced." Lir grimaced. "We need her alive."

My eyes narrowed at his words, but I couldn't afford to take attention off him and I trusted Mikhail to watch the sidhe at my back. I got the impression Lir's command was to someone we weren't taking into account. Enough. I struck fast and Lir parried. We clashed across the opening, and Mikhail was doing the same behind me. Lir was fast and well trained, but I was better. He blocked a hair too slowly, and I cut deep across his ribs. I forced him to take another step back and opened another gash across his chest.

We moved across the clearing and until we were in the center. My instincts told me something wasn't right. I was a better fighter than Lir, but he didn't seem like the type of fighter to let me push him around like this. I glanced up at the clear blue sky above us. He'd maneuvered us so we were more in the open, and a sly grin spread across his face as I realized what he'd done.

Look out! Jinx screamed at me. A shadow fell over us and I tried to dive to the side, but I was too slow. Claws pierced my flesh, and I screamed as something yanked me off the ground. I managed to keep my grip on both swords, ignoring the pain as I twisted to get a better look at what had grabbed me. Between the creature jerking me around and the angle, I couldn't get a good look, but it resembled an odd mix between a bird and a dragon. Lir had given it a command, so whatever it was, it was sentient. The trees flew by beneath us. Falling from this height would not be fun.

A gasp escaped me as it shifted its claws, causing a fresh burst of pain. It had been commanded to keep me alive, which meant it probably wouldn't drop me unless it had no choice. Time to be a difficult passenger and test that theory. Its body was too far away for me to reach, so I lashed out at its legs. I couldn't get much strength behind my blows, but I still made some cuts. The creature shrieked in rage and dug its claws further into me. I screamed as blood poured out of my wounds. I steeled myself to make another round of cuts, but the creature careened to the side. The ground yawned up at us as its flying became unsteady, and it jerked in a different direction. The trees were rapidly approaching. After a couple of failed attempts, I got my swords back in their sheaths and then I braced myself. This was going to hurt.

We crashed through the trees, and I gripped onto its legs in case the creature let me go and drew my legs up the best I could. A large tree came up on our right side, and bones crunched as the creature's wing collided with it, causing us to veer sharply. The creature dropped straight down, and I let go of its legs. A second later, its claws released me and I kicked off a branch to get further away from it so I wouldn't end up crushed beneath its bulk. I smashed through a few branches, slowing my descent before slamming into the ground.

I lay there gasping for a minute, unable to do anything else. Mikhail appeared, standing over me. Blood was pouring from a wound in his head and his arm didn't look right. I squinted at it. Definitely broken. "What the hell happened?" I pushed out between gasps.

He crouched next to me, looking a little unsteady on his feet. "After that creature grabbed you, Jinx and I were left dealing with the other two. Fortunately, Eddie showed up and Jinx told me to go after you. So I misted and caught up to you and then dropped down on whatever the fuck that thing was and damaged its wings, forcing it to land."

We both looked at where the creature had fallen and lay still. Dark blue feathers with green tips covered its body. Despite the bird-like appearance, a long narrow muzzle protruded from its head, not a beak. Like the legs, the muzzle and most of the head were covered in dark scales before turning into feathers. The feathers trailing down the back of the neck were green and long, giving it a mane-like appearance. Even in death, it was beautiful, and I felt a twinge of guilt at its loss.

"Any idea what it is?" Mikhail asked.

"No." I shook my head. "I've never seen anything like it before. I'm pretty sure it was sentient. Lir gave it a command and seemed confident it would follow it. It never spoke to me though, and I didn't feel any magic off it."

Mikhail stood and helped me up. "We should get back to

the others. I don't think we're too far, and it flew mostly in a straight line."

I brushed the leaves and dirt off the best I could and studied Mikhail. "You're wounded." Blood coated his right side, and based on the way he was standing, I suspected he had multiple broken bones. "Bad enough that it has significantly slowed your healing down. You need blood."

"I'll be fine," Mikhail replied stiffly.

"I'm not carrying your ass back." I crossed my arms and glared at him. "You need to drink."

"I'm perfectly aware of my limits. I'll be fine." His dark eyes focused on me, and I arched an eyebrow at him. Annoyance flickered across his features, and I smirked because it would annoy him. "Fine," he ground out.

I moved towards him, pulling my hair away from my neck. His expression darkened slightly as he tracked my movement. "I'll drink from your wrist."

"I'm not taking the bracers off." I lifted my arms up and shook them slightly. "Don't be a baby, just drink from my neck."

Mikhail glared at me but said nothing.

"Just a warning though," I said, keeping my tone light. "My blood is . . . a bit intoxicating, and you might feel a little frisky. Do keep your hands to yourself."

"And how exactly do you know that? You make a habit of feeding vampires?"

"When Sebastian captured me, he let the vampires that worked with him drink from me. They liked to come in and have a drink and then play with each other." My expression and voice were flat even as memories of my time being held captive surfaced once more.

Mikhail stiffened. "Did they ever—"

"No," I said sharply, knowing where his mind was going. "Sebastian made that a rule, and they never crossed it. They kept their fun to breaking my bones and cutting me up. When they drank my blood, they'd get frisky with each other. Never me."

He nodded as he looked at my neck intensely and looked away. He stepped back until a tree blocked him from going any further. "My healing is already catching up. I'll be completely healed in the next thirty minutes."

"Or you could just drink from me now and we can be on our way in the next two minutes." I closed the distance between us, and Mikhail's body tensed as his eyes watched me. I didn't understand why he was being so stubborn about this, and I was out of patience. My hand shot out, slamming him back into the tree and holding him there. I leaned in to crowd his space further. "I mean this in both the literal and nonliteral sense. Fucking bite me."

One second I had Mikhail pinned against the tree and in the next my back was against it and his teeth were at my throat. I gasped as his fangs pierced my skin, and warmth spread through me as the mild venom vampires used took effect. Mikhail pinned my hands above my head with one hand as the other gripped my hip. He drank deeply from me and slowly pulled his fangs out. Instead of pulling away, his hot breath brushed against my neck. A different kind of heat spread through me as his lips left light kisses up my neck. Then my jawline.

"Mikhail," I breathed. His mouth covered mine and whatever thoughts I had melted away. His tongue slipped into my mouth and I kissed him back even as the small rational part of my brain was screaming, "What are you doing?!"

Mikhail groaned as he pressed his body against mine, and I felt every inch of how excited he was. He let go of my hands and buried one hand in my hair as his other ran up my ribs towards my chest. As he touched the underside of my breast, he froze, and then he was abruptly gone. I stumbled forward at the sudden loss of his body and tugged my shirt back down. Mikhail was staring at me with genuine alarm on his face from ten feet away.

"I warned you," I said and wanted to slap myself for how husky my voice sounded. I took in a couple of deep breaths, and once I was sure I could speak normally, I added, "My blood packs quite the punch."

"That's one way to put it," Mikhail grunted. The alarmed expression was already gone from his face, but his twilight eyes still held a hint of wildness.

"We don't mention this to Andrei," I said, keeping my tone casual. The last thing we needed was a fight between the two of them on this trip. It wasn't like the kiss had actually meant anything, and technically, Andrei and I weren't really involved at the moment anyway.

"Agreed," Mikhail replied, and then added, "We don't mention this to Magos."

"Agreed."

Chapter Eight

A FEW HOURS LATER, we tracked down the others. They were waiting in the same clearing where we'd fought the sidhe and I'd been carried off. Kaysea was pacing back and forth. Andrei and Eddie were standing a short distance away from her, guarding the warlock that had been with the sidhe. They'd tied him to a tree and gagged him. I let out a sigh of relief. I'd refused to give in to thoughts on the way back here that someone had not survived the encounter with the sidhe. That sense of relief quickly evaporated when I caught sight of Jinx. I recognized the dangerous glint in his golden eyes as he looked over me and Mikhail, and I narrowed my eyes at him. *Don't you dare.*

Did you enjoy your meal, vampire? Jinx said slyly.

You are such an asshole. I flipped him off as I stalked further into the clearing. Mikhail smoothly moved away from me, heading towards the warlock. Jinx just snickered and walked over to Kaysea, who lightly thumped him on the head.

"That wasn't very nice," Kaysea admonished him but didn't bother to hide the amusement that lit up her face. Cautiously, I snuck a peak at Andrei. He casually leaned against a tree, watching Mikhail walk across the clearing. Slowly, as if feeling my gaze on him, he turned his head. Intense yellow eyes bore into me, and my heart skipped a beat.

"Glad to see everyone is still in one piece," I said evenly. "What happened after my unexpected flight?"

"Jinx and Mikhail were holding their own against the two sidhe," Eddie said. "I returned after getting Kaysea safely to the river and told Mikhail to go after you. The devourers switched over to using magic. Jinx and I were able to block some of it, but they were just using it as a distraction to retreat. I'm guessing they were hoping to regroup wherever that flying pet of theirs was taking you."

"And him?" I gestured at the warlock.

"The wolf caught him." Eddie shrugged. "Figured we'd question him when you got back."

"That confident I'd be returning, huh?"

"I had no doubt the vampire would find you and between the two of you, you'd kill anything that stood in your way."

I very deliberately did not look at Mikhail. We hadn't spoken as we jogged back to this clearing, and things between us were a little awkward. It would pass in time, but I really didn't want to deal with Andrei losing his shit right then. The wolf was too close to the surface, and Andrei's control over it had never been strong.

"Did you do a sweep of the area to make sure they didn't leave anyone behind to spy on us or set a trap?" I asked.

"No. Between guarding our prisoner here and keeping a watch over Kaysea, none of us felt comfortable dividing our group more until you and Mikhail returned," Eddie explained.

"Fair enough." I started pulling my weapons and clothes off. "Andrei and I will do a quick sweep to make sure we're safe here and then we can have a fun little chat with the warlock." I bared my teeth at the warlock, and he shrank away slightly. Without waiting for an agreement from Andrei, I shifted. A few minutes later, we took off through the trees. I started with a small perimeter check and concentrated on looking in the tree canopy, leaving Andrei to detect any scents on the ground. Once I was confident no one was in our immediate area, I widened the search and we did another loop. Aside from Andrei almost becoming a meal for yet another fae plant, we didn't find anything. The entire time tension was building up in Andrei, and I wanted to address it before we headed back to the group.

We reached the area where we had started our wider sweep, and I stopped to shift back to my human form. Andrei shifted back as well and studied me intently with wolf-yellow eyes.

"I know you have questions—"

Andrei's mouth was on mine before I could finish. Warmth spread through me, and I kicked out, sweeping his feet from under him, and he fell to the ground. I moved with him and straddled his hips.

"I take it this is about Mikhail?" I asked dryly.

Andrei's hands moved across my skin, as if he couldn't feel enough of me. "I don't give a fuck about the vampire," he growled, and his eyes faded back to hazel. "I made it back to the clearing in time to see that flying thing grab you. I couldn't do anything. There was no scent for me to follow. You were just gone." The traces of the panic and rage he must have felt still echoed in his eyes, along with a desperate need.

"I'm not that easy to kill." I leaned down and nipped at his neck. His hands gripped my hips, and he hardened beneath me. A second later, he flipped us so he was on top, and I laughed as he kissed my neck and moved lower. I gasped and arched my back as he sucked on a nipple and continued his downward trajectory.

"Andrei," I breathed as he kissed the insides of my thighs and wrapped his arms underneath. My body was trembling in anticipation, and I screamed at his first lick. That was all the motivation he needed to dive in and devour me. My back arched as the tension inside me built until I was incapable of piecing together a single coherent thought. His finger rubbed my clit at the same time his tongue dove into me, and it was enough to push me over the edge.

I sagged to the ground, enjoying the lingering sensations, but Andrei wasted no time. He moved back up my body and kissed me hard. I kissed him back, enjoying the taste of myself on his lips and tongue. A scream tore out as he thrust into me. He swallowed my scream with another kiss as he thrust harder. I ran my claws down his back hard enough to draw blood, and he growled as he continued to push closer to another edge. I gripped him to me as my body shook in pleasure and then pushed up with my hips as I twisted. He landed on his back with me on top.

"My turn." I flashed my fangs at him, and he snapped the air back at me. Yellow flooded his eyes as the wolf came out for a moment and faded back to hazel. I rocked back and ground into him as he moaned and gripped my hips.

"Fuck," he growled.

I smiled and continued to ride him, gradually speeding up my rhythm. My breathing turned ragged, and his fingers dug into my flesh. When I threw my head back and screamed, Andrei came with me. I stayed on top of him but leaned down against his chest. "I missed that," I said with a satisfied sigh.

He laughed as he brushed some of the hair out of my face. "Same, kitty cat. Fucking same."

I moved so I was no longer on top of him, and he wrapped an arm around me, pulling me tight to his side. We needed to head back, but I wasn't ready to let this go just yet. Before Andrei had left town we'd been seeing each other for a few months. Being with Andrei had given me a break from the rest of my life. I loved Pele and Kaysea—they had both been my friends for a long time—but they were a part of the daemon and fae politics I tried to stay out of. Andrei didn't want anything to do with magic, supernatural politics, or the other realms. When we were together, I could forget about the rest of it too. We lay there for a while longer, neither of us saying anything, just enjoying the feel of each other's skin and companionship.

"It's time to head back," I said quietly.

"I know." Andrei sighed.

We shifted and made a beeline back to the others. Everyone knew exactly what we'd been up to, but I hoped they wouldn't make a big deal of it, given our other problems. I should have known better to expect that out of my friends. As soon as we entered the clearing, Eddie dramatically sniffed the air and started to slow clap. Mikhail and Kaysea rolled their eyes, and Jinx just snickered.

"I hate all of you," I said without any real heat and turned my attention to the warlock.

He was still bound to the tree, and fear and tension shone in his eyes at my approach. The vines that had been used to tie him to the tree rustled as he pulled against them, but they didn't give. He was average looking with pale skin, light brown hair, and forgettable brown eyes. What wasn't forgettable was the scar that ran from his temple to his jawline. He belonged to the warlock Circle, and he worked for their leader Emir.

"Hello, again." I crouched in front of him. "What's your name?"

"Nicholas," he answered and swallowed nervously.

"Last time I saw you, it was in a forest clearing with all of your other warlock buddies. Here are once again." I gestured around at our surroundings. "In a forest clearing, but you've got some new friends." I smiled at him. "How about you tell us all about these new friends of yours?"

"They'll kill me." He shook his head vehemently. "I can't tell you anything. You have no idea what they'll do to me."

Mikhail sauntered over and causally pulled a blade from its sheath. Color drained from the warlock's already pale face. My smile widened. The warlock had panicked at Mikhail's presence earlier. Given that the warlocks were working with the vampires, he must have known all about the famed vampire assassin. He might be scared of the beings he was working for, but they weren't the immediate threat. Mikhail crouched beside me, tapped the blade on the warlock's leg a few times, and paused. The warlock got the message.

"They needed someone who could move about the human realm unnoticed," the warlock said in haste. He trembled as Mikhail traced the blade up and down his leg light enough that it hadn't broken through the fabric. Yet.

"And why would they need that?" I asked, keeping my tone light.

"Most of them are trapped in a realm. They were trapped there by the fae Queens eons ago. We agreed to help them break free from this side, and they agreed to help us gain more power and to give us the human realm."

There was our confirmation that the fae Queens were heavily involved in this and knew more about the devourers than they had ever let on. I tilted my head in a purely feline gesture. "And who is 'we' exactly?"

"In the human realm, it's us and the vampires. But there are others!" He was practically tripping over the words to get them out as quickly as possible. "I don't know who. Emir does, and probably some of the vampires. In other realms, I don't know what type of deal they made with fae with devourer magic, but plenty of people out there aren't happy with the fae Queens and the daemons ruling over everything."

Mikhail glanced up at me and shook his head. The vampire Council had clearly been hiding things from him long before he defected. I reached out and grabbed the warlock's chin, forcing him to look at me. "Why is the boy so important? Why risk hunting him through fae lands?"

Nicholas swallowed and glanced back and forth between me and Mikhail, his lips forming a stubborn line. I sighed. Apparently, his cowardice only went so far. I nodded at Mikhail and didn't flinch as he slammed the knife into the warlock's thigh. The warlock screamed in agony, and I continued to watch him, keeping a patient expression on my face. Andrei moved behind me, but he said nothing. Eddie or Jinx likely blocked him from interfering.

"You start to utter a spell, and we'll cut out your tongue," I said. "If we need to heal you, we can do that. But we'll keep cutting on you until we get bored. Then we'll spice things up a bit by breaking bones." Mikhail slowly pulled the blade out, and the warlock cried at the movement. "I know you weren't directly involved in my time being held by the vampires. That was Sebastian's doing. They took great delight in torturing me and came up with all sorts of tricks." I forced the warlock to look at me again, and whatever he saw in my eyes made him whimper. "To say the warlocks and vampires aren't my favorite people is a bit of an understatement. Are you sure you want to give me even more of a reason to inflict harm on you?"

Mikhail dragged the blade down the warlock's arm, cutting away the fabric of his clothing but not breaking the skin. He dragged the blade back up the arm on the bare skin and blood swelled in the knife's wake. It was enough to break through the brief glimmer of loyalty the warlock had.

"We don't know!" he exclaimed and quickly rushed on. "We were told the boy was vital to the cause, and we had to help them in any way we could! Other groups are trying to run interference while we search the area. We're close to finding him. The girl who has been protecting him was captured a few days ago. It's only a matter of time until we find him now."

"Where is the girl being held?" She might already be dead, but if she was alive, we had to find her.

"I don't know!" the warlock cried in panic. "I've been with this group the past couple of days and I don't know where the others are! We heard about someone asking questions in a nearby village about the girl and came to investigate. Last I saw the others, they were twenty miles west of here, but I don't know if that's where they still are, I swear!"

"We need to move," Kaysea said from where she stood behind the others. Concern flickered across her face as she looked off into the woods. "We have to save her. I've seen her over and over in my visions. She's been trying so hard to protect the boy. We can't leave her to this fate." I didn't point out that in her visions, Kaysea had seen the girl die by my hand. It's possible the vision had changed and Kaysea just hadn't gotten a new one yet. Or we could go to rescue the girl and Kaysea's vision of me killing her could come true. I didn't see how that was possible, but Kaysea's visions were rarely wrong.

"Someone from the village we passed through must have sold us out," I murmured. "A local is working with them."

It was that young sidhe who worked in the bar. He overheard our conversation with the barkeep, Jinx replied. *He not only told the fae devourers about us but followed us and kept them updated on our position until they could get here.*

"Did you capture him?" I frowned at Jinx. "Where is he now?"

I captured him early on and told the wolf to guard him. Jinx turned his golden eyes on Andrei. *Apparently, the wolf saw fit to let him go.*

All of us turned to look at Andrei. "What?" I asked incredulously.

The muscles flexed across Andrei's jaw as he bore our scrutiny. "He was just a kid. He knows he made a mistake and regretted it. My options were to stay and guard him or help in the fight. I chose to help in the fight."

"You could have knocked him out or tied him to a tree," I said.

"He won't cause us any more harm. We're leaving the village behind anyway," Andrei argued.

I shook my head, frustration pouring out of me. "You let a local sidhe go who is clearly okay with helping these fae devourer things capture someone from his own village. Someone like that can't be trusted. And he clearly has some tracking skills because he followed us easily from a distance. You better hope we never see him again."

"We won't," Andrei promised with relief in his eyes.

Jinx scoffed in disgust and walked away. I couldn't really blame him. The local sidhe was a problem, one I hoped wouldn't come back to haunt us. But we couldn't do anything about it now. We didn't have time to track him down; rescuing the girl was more important.

"Let's go," I said and started to follow after Jinx. Mikhail drew his sword, and the warlock pleaded for his life. I blocked out his cries but heard Andrei move between Mikhail and the warlock, causing me to pause and turn back around.

"Wait," Andrei said, with his hands up. "We can't just kill him."

"Pretty sure we can," Eddie said. "I mean, Mikhail's sword looks pretty sharp. I think it'll do the job."

"We shouldn't," Andrei tried again and looked at me for help. Whatever he saw in my expression told him I wouldn't be any help in this. He looked at Kaysea. "We're the good guys. Good guys don't kill people that are bound and unarmed. This isn't right. He's been secured and isn't going anywhere. One of you can set a ward around him to secure him further, and we can come back for him later."

"And do what with him, exactly?" I asked softly. "You going to keep him locked away in the basement at the wolf lodge?"

"We can turn him over to the sidhe. They must have a prison they can lock him up in, right?" Andrei pleaded.

He's a warlock who has worked with their enemy. The sidhe will kill him and possibly us for bothering them with such a nuisance. Jinx growled. He was quickly losing his patience. I needed to end this conversation before Jinx took out his frustrations on Andrei.

Before I took a step towards the warlock, water shot out from a pouch Kaysea had tied at her waist. It thinned into a whip and slashed across the warlock's neck before he could even scream. His head tumbled to the ground a moment later. Andrei stared at Kaysea in horror and shock.

"They're hunting children," Kaysea spat. Her expression held no mercy. "People who hunt children don't get to live. I'll need to refill my pouches on the way. We can swing by the river." Kaysea walked off in the river's direction. Eddie and Mikhail followed her.

I looked at Andrei, who stood clenching his fists. "I'm sorry, Andrei. But we take no prisoners."

"How can you be okay with that?" Andrei looked at me with a stricken expression before directing his attention to the blood pooling in the dirt around the warlock's body. A familiar pain came back to me. When we'd been together before, I'd been worried about how Andrei would handle the more violent aspects of my world. I'd hoped I would be able to keep him apart from it, but it had been a growing problem back then, and now with him insisting on coming along with us . . . there would be no sheltering him from it.

"I don't know exactly what is going on yet. I don't know why these fae devourers are so hellbent on capturing this child. But nothing good will come of it. And he's out there right now. Scared and alone. The girl who has been protecting him has been captured and gods know what they're doing to her. My priority is rescuing her and finding the boy before they do. Anyone who stands between me and that goal will end up like that warlock."

"It can't be this black and white."

"Sometimes it's not. Often it isn't," I agreed. "But right now it is. Keep that in mind." I turned and left Andrei in the clearing as the tree roots moved to drink in the warlock's blood.

Chapter Nine

Hours later, we crouched behind some large rock outcroppings uphill of the enemy's camp. Night had fallen shortly before we'd tracked them down. They had moved from the last location the warlock had seen them but hadn't gone far. Andrei had picked up their scent, and we'd tracked them here and had been studying them for the past hour. I spotted Lir almost immediately.

Besides him, there were at least thirty others. It was a much larger group than we had expected, but I was fairly certain only a handful of them were devourers; the rest were just sidhe. I felt the unease pouring off Jinx and felt the same. The fae only helped the fae. And the sidhe, in particular, were very obtuse to outsiders. Even though these devourers were clearly part sidhe, that wouldn't matter. If anything, it should make the sidhe hate them more. And yet there were sidhe there. Working with them. And clearly other fae had helped them enter this realm. Pele's paranoia hadn't been misplaced. We couldn't trust anyone.

"There are too many for us to take on by ourselves,"

Mikhail said quietly. "I don't think Lir will fall for any type of trick to lure them away from the camp, either."

"Unlikely," I agreed and looked at Eddie suspiciously. "Awfully quiet over there, Eddie."

"I have an idea." Eddie's amber eyes lit up, and he gave me a mischievous smile. "We can't fight them. Nor can we lure them out of that camp. But I find panic makes for an excellent distraction. I can make everyone in the camp panic for at least a minute. We know the girl is in the tent at the center of the camp." Eddie pointed at the small grey tent we'd seen them drag the girl to half an hour ago. "As soon as the camp is in a panic, Mikhail will do his mist travel thing and free the girl. He tells her to run one way, and then he makes himself seen in a different part of the camp before disappearing again. Just to throw them off even further. The rest of us will go after the girl in whatever direction she goes, but not alert her to our presence."

"She'll lead us to the boy," I murmured.

"Probably not right away. My guess is she'll want to make sure she's not being followed," Eddie said. "We'll have to make sure no one else follows her. But once she's sure no one is after her, she'll almost certainly go wherever she stashed him last."

"All right. How do we make the camp panic?" I asked. "It'll have to be something big to make them not immediately see through it as a distraction and move to secure the girl."

"I find fire usually does the trick." Eddie pulled a lighter out from his pocket and flicked it open with a grin. Turning to Kaysea, he said, "For this to work, I'll need a minute to make the flame big enough. Can you cast a glamour strong enough to hide me and my magic?"

Kaysea pursed her lips as she thought about it. "Everyone in that camp is fae and sensitive to magic. It will only work if we keep the workings of your magic away from them and someplace they wouldn't naturally be looking, anyway. And even then, the most I'll be able to buy you is a couple of minutes."

"More than enough time," Eddie said confidently.

I looked over the camp below and all the sidhe moving around. "Are you sure? This won't go well for us if the distraction fails."

Eddie's entire face lit up with a smile, and something in his eyes flickered. "Of course I'm sure. I'm amazing, remember?"

Jinx scoffed, and a wry smile played on Mikhail's lips. I just shook my head. "Right. Of course."

We should move to the other side of the camp. That direction makes the most sense for the girl to run, Jinx said. *We can use the fire to wipe away the immediate scent trail so they won't know what direction to start looking in. Hopefully, we can find a river or something to lose them further. Between Kaysea and me, we should be able to block most forms of tracking via magic. Blood magic could be a problem, but those spells usually take a few hours to work.*

"Usually the sidhe don't do blood magic," I said.

True, but we have no idea what these sidhe are capable of. They might have another warlock stashed somewhere.

"Fair enough. Let's hope we can find the boy quickly afterwards and get the hell out of this realm." I made my way quietly to our agreed-upon position, and the others followed me. This side of the camp was heavily forested, which made for good cover but would hinder our escape later. Jinx leapt up into the trees, and I glanced at Andrei. "You should shift. You'll be faster that way."

He nodded but said nothing else. Just stepped back a few paces and pulled his clothes off and stuffed them in a bag. He'd been quiet since the warlock incident, and I wasn't sure what I could do about it. We'd have to talk about this more, but now wasn't the time.

"Everyone ready?" I asked.

Mikhail faced the camp. Mist rolled off him in wisps, and

he focused intensely. Eddie grinned, held one hand outstretched, and flicked the lighter with his other. The flame immediately leapt to the palm of his hand, and he tucked the lighter away. Kaysea concentrated on Eddie, her hands moving in graceful patterns as the flame he held between his hands grew larger.

Something stirred in Eddie's amber eyes that reminded me of smoke, and they seemed to glow brighter as the flame grew. Wonder and suspicion warred within me as I watched him work with the magic. There were several species known for fire magic, and I'd encountered all of them. Whatever Eddie's magic was, it felt significantly different. I was rapidly starting to believe he was something we'd all been told didn't exist anymore.

"Get ready, vampire," Eddie rumbled, and his hands shot up. The fireball raced towards the sky above the camp and stretched into a web over all the tents and supplies.

Sweat poured down Kaysea's face, and her hands shook as she held the glamour in place. The sidhe in the camp moved around, completely unaware of the fiery web that hung less than a dozen feet over their heads. "I can't hold it much longer," Kaysea said, her words strained.

"Now!" Eddie snapped, dropping his hands quickly.

Mikhail vanished in the same instant the flames rained down across the camp, lighting the tents and supplies on fire. None of the sidhe themselves caught on fire, their own magic protecting them. We'd expected that, but the entire camp lighting on fire at once was a hell of a distraction.

If they'd taken a second to think about it, the sidhe would have known it was a trick, but being surrounded by fire that appeared out of nowhere had thrown them all into a panic. It wouldn't last long, but we didn't need it to. Mikhail appeared just outside the tent and swiped his sword across the chest of a sidhe warrior before vanishing and appearing in a different spot. He didn't stay in one place long enough to do mortal damage to any sidhe, but he definitely added to the panic and confusion.

Movement between us and the grey tent in the center of the camp caught my attention. The girl made it out and was darting quickly between the burning tents. She made it to the woods and broke out into a full-on sprint.

"Time to go!" I sprinted after her. Mikhail appeared at my side a moment later, heat pouring in our wake. Glancing over my shoulder, I saw a wide circle of flame around the camp. I could already feel the magic of the sidhe rising to put out the flames. We were running out of time. Eddie raced behind us and spread flames in our path and outward, erasing our scent trail. I had no idea how he was doing it, but none of the trees or plants were burning.

"You are so telling me what you are when we get out of this!" I shouted as we leapt through the underbrush of the forest. Eddie just grunted behind me. After a few miles, we slowed down to catch our breath and our bearings. Whoever this girl was, she definitely had stamina. Andrei had been in the lead the whole time following her scent, and he waited at the front of our party, staring intently into the woods.

I turned to Mikhail. "Can you make sure we're not followed and catch up to us?"

"Yes, but even if there is no one in our immediate wake, they'll catch up to us soon enough. We need to get out of this realm."

"I know." I looked at the grey werewolf, who was pacing anxiously, not happy about this delay in his hunt. "We'll continue following the girl. As soon as we have both her and the boy, I'll get us out of here. It's too dangerous for us to back-track to a gateway now."

"That could cause problems for us later," Kaysea warned from where she was currently leaning against a tree, panting.

"My contact made sure there weren't any questions of us traveling here, but she couldn't erase the record of us traveling through that gateway. If someone looks into it, they're going to have questions about how we got out of here."

I chewed my bottom lip. Kaysea wasn't wrong. If I used my magic to open a gateway and get us out, I was cementing my fate. A lot of powerful beings were looking for this boy, and the question of how we got him out of the realm would be asked. There would be no hiding my magic. Until I had some sort of agreement in place with the fae Queens or the daemon Assembly, I would be in danger if they learned about my abilities. Especially with these devourers running around the fae realm, I would likely get lumped in with them.

"It's only a matter of time before my secrets come out anyway," I told Kaysea. "Survival is what matters now. And after what we just did and them losing the girl, all of those sidhe devourers will be coming for us. Can you run some more? We can't keep the same breakneck pace, but we need to travel quickly." I looked Kaysea over, trying to gauge how she was doing. The magic she'd used to hide Eddie's fire magic had taken a lot out of her, and the flat-out run through the woods hadn't helped.

"Stop worrying," she replied and pushed off the tree. "I'll be fine. Let's go."

At her words, Andrei took off at a steady jog and we all followed him. Mikhail regrouped with us after confirming no one was following us. Hopefully, Andrei was right in his trust that the sidhe tracker from the village didn't regroup with the enemy to help them find us. Unless they had another tracker in their party, it would take them a while to find our trail after Eddie destroyed most of it.

Slowly the landscape shifted, the trees spread out more, and most of the undergrowth vanished. It made our travel easier, but I couldn't shake the feeling of unease the further we traveled. We'd slowed down to a walk not because of Kaysea being tired but because Eddie kept tripping. The third time he tripped and slammed into a tree, I told Andrei to slow down. Whatever the hell Eddie was, his night vision was shit. I was impressed he'd managed as well as he did earlier, with only the light of the moon illuminating the woods. But now that light was filtering in and out as clouds passed overhead.

"Stop!" I snapped, and everyone immediately froze in their tracks. Andrei moved aside, and I cautiously moved in front of him and took in what lay ahead of us. "It's a fucking swamp," I said warily, as my eyes roamed the landscape, pausing on areas where water looked the deepest. The path we'd been on continued through the swamp, but I couldn't tell if it led the entire way through.

"What is it, Nemain?" Mikhail asked as he looked over the harsh landscape.

Boggarts, Jinx growled as he leapt down from the trees. The few trees in the swamp were spread out. He'd have to travel on the ground with the rest of us. *I haven't spotted any yet, but I can see traces of their magic. There are a good number of them.*

"This is unfortunate," I said mildly and looked at Andrei. "I take it the girl went into that?" The werewolf let out a low whine and jerked his head in a nod. "We can't go around then." I pulled both swords free as I continued to scan the swamp, looking for any signs of life. Wandering through fae swamps was high on my list of Things I Never Wanted To Do Again. I let out a bone weary sigh. This was going to suck.

"Care to fill the rest of us in?" Eddie asked.

"The girl made a run through boggart territory, which means *we* have to make a run through boggart territory. Which means we're about to get covered in mud and shit and get attacked by tiny creatures with nasty claws and teeth who are going to try and pull us into the swamp to drown us." I didn't bother to keep the disgust out of my voice. Last time I had tangled with boggarts, my hair smelled like swamp for weeks, no matter how many showers I took. The scent carried over even when I shifted into feline form. And on top of that, I'd lost a pair of my favorite daggers. "Let's just hope the girl made it through and isn't at the bottom of the swamp right now."

Mikhail pulled his sword free. "What should we expect?"

"They're short and usually walk upright, but sometimes they'll scuttle around on all fours. They won't come up past your knees, but they have long arms that end in wicked claws and their teeth are just as sharp. Their preferred method of attack is to swarm you to get you to panic and lose your footing. This swamp is their home, and they have power over it. The water is deep and the plants in it will try to pull you under if you fall into it. Once you drown, the plants will allow your body to resurface so the boggarts can feast on your flesh as the plants drink your blood."

"Fantastic," Eddie said flatly.

"Weaknesses?" Mikhail asked.

I shrugged. "Boggarts are pretty easy to kill. Their magic influences the environment and encourages the swamp to kill you, but they can't do any magic directly on you. It's just their teeth and claws you gotta watch out for. Their bites contain bacteria fueled by magic; it results in fast-acting infections. It won't kill us, but it means their bites hurt like hell and take longer to heal. They're fast and they coordinate their attacks, so expect at least a dozen to launch themselves at you."

We should travel in pairs. Jinx moved to stand next to me. *Nemain and me, Mikhail and Andrei, Eddie and Kaysea. Enough space between the pairs that we don't get in each other's way fighting, but not so far apart that any pair become an obvious target.*

"Agreed. We'll take up the rear. Eddie and Kaysea in the middle. We'll move carefully but quickly. If we don't see her anywhere in the swamp, we'll continue to the other side and see if we can pick up her trail there. Maybe she made it through unscathed." At everyone's nod, we started proceeding through the swamp when a scream of pain came from ahead. My blood ran cold. It was the girl. The goddamn boggarts got the girl.

"Fuck!" I yelled and took off running, shouting at the others as we moved in the general direction of where the scream had come from. "Eddie and Andrei, cover Kaysea! Keep anything nasty off her. Kaysea, do whatever you can to keep the stuff in the water, in the freaking water, and away from us. Jinx and Mikhail, cover me while I go for the girl!"

Another scream pierced through the night, and I veered off to the right, keeping an eye on the ground. We were off the main path now, and the few scraps of ground were water-logged and slippery. We needed to avoid the water as much as we could. Kaysea could handle whatever beasties were in there, but it would slow us down and we couldn't afford that.

A large tree rose out of the swamp directly ahead of us, long since dead, its bone white branches stretched eerily towards the stars. At the end of one of those branches was the girl. She'd got away from the boggarts after their initial attack, but now she was cornered with them climbing the tree after her, the swamp directly below her branch. I pushed myself to run faster as I saw a dark green vine rise out of the water towards the girl.

"Kaysea!" I wouldn't make it in time, and if the girl fell in the water, we might not get her out. I trusted Kaysea to take care of the plant and headed towards the boggarts climbing up the tree and attacking the girl from multiple angles, trying to get her to lose her balance and fall. I was closing in on the tree when the vine that had been stretching out of the swamp jerked violently to the side as a current appeared in the water. A second earlier, the swamp had been completely still. Now it rotated like a whirlpool, slowly picking up speed. The vine whipped around madly, unable to break free. Something dark and scaly leapt from the water only for a wave to slam it back down.

The boggarts still at the base of the tree turned to face us. Dozens of bright red eyes focused on me, trying to figure out if I was a potential meal or a threat. The one closest to me leapt with its talons outstretched. I didn't even bother dodging. One quick swipe of my sword and the small body split in half, falling on either side of me. I slowed, stopping a dozen feet from the base of the tree, Mikhail on my left and Jinx on my right. There had to be at least fifty boggarts there. Clearly, they'd been finding enough food to grow to a population this large.

The ones at the base of the tree crouched slightly. Their dark green skin was covered in mud, which allowed them to blend into the swamp. The ones in the tree shifted their focus away from the girl onto us. We had seconds before they attacked, and we needed to get the girl out of that tree. I wouldn't be able to climb it fast enough without the boggarts swarming me. Mikhail could mist up there, but the girl didn't know who we were and would be unlikely to trust him. A few of the boggarts climbed down the trunk of the tree headfirst, their claws sinking into the bark as they made their descent.

Jinx, get the girl. Mikhail and I will deal with the boggarts. Get her out of the swamp, and we'll cover your exit. I didn't wait for his agreement but launched into an attack. Reversing one blade so it was flat against my arm, I batted away any boggarts that came at my side as I slashed out with my other blade. The boggarts were fast, but if we could kill enough of them, the swarm would retreat to lick their wounds.

Mikhail fell in beside me and took out two boggarts that dove directly towards me. Two more leapt from the base of the tree, and I spun to cut them down, only to feel a sharp pain in my thigh as another set of boggarts launched an attack. One of them bit down hard on my thigh and tore a chunk out as another jammed its claws into my ribs. Dropping one of my swords, I yanked the one off my ribs before it could make its way to my face and claw out my eyes. It snarled and swiped at my arm as I threw it against the tree and sliced off its head. Blood poured from the wound down my leg. A quick glance at Mikhail told me he wasn't doing much better. I swiped my sword off the ground and kept slicing through the bodies. Still more came.

The girl gathered herself in a crouch and jumped off the branch, slamming to her knees in front of the trunk and taking off running. Jinx leapt down nimbly from the tree and tore off after her.

"Kaysea!" I yelled in between slashing my sword. "Follow Jinx and the girl! Try to keep everything in the water off us! We'll follow you!" I swore as a boggart landed on my back, sinking its talons into the space between my neck and shoulder. Before I could pull it off, Mikhail pierced it with his blade and flung it away. I grunted in thanks and slammed my sword into a boggart that had been aiming for his side. Kaysea and Eddie flew past us, Andrei following them, snapping boggarts out of the air as they tried to follow. "Let's go!" I yelled at Mikhail and we took off after the others.

Despite how many we killed, the boggarts kept up the chase through the swamp. My earlier estimate of fifty was definitely on the low side. They didn't back off until they reached the edge of the swamp. Even with their numbers, they wouldn't leave their territory. We kept running for another mile, just in case. And because I didn't want to smell the swamp for one second longer. Muck and unidentifiable filth covered our clothes, but at least none of us had fallen into the water. We stopped when we reached the edge of a meadow, and all of us collapsed onto the ground, panting.

"All in agreement that we never do that again?" Eddie asked and raised his hand.

All of us raised our hands except the girl, who was staring at us with a wary expression etched into her features. Andrei whined and looked at Kaysea, who shrugged her backpack off and tossed it to him. He snatched it out of the air and trotted off behind some weeds. Apparently, changing in front of us was fine, but he didn't want to do so in front of the girl.

She stared at the werewolf wide-eyed, as if just noticing his size. Her eyes were a startling silvery grey that contrasted sharply against her dark brown hair. I let my magic reach out towards her, and it gently touched her magic before withdrawing. Something about it seemed vaguely familiar, but I couldn't place it and she gave no reaction to my magic touching hers. Either she was an excellent actor or she hadn't felt it. I suspected it was the latter. She definitely had magic of some sort, but I didn't think she knew how to use it. Or maybe she didn't feel it at all. Something tickled in the back of my mind, but she spoke before I could continue pondering her odd magic.

"Who are you?" the girl asked as she slowly rose to her feet. She tried to hide it, but based on the way she was standing, she had a wound on her left side.

I glanced at Kaysea, who nodded and rose to her feet but didn't approach the girl yet.

"I'm Nemain. These are my friends. It's a bit of a long story, but we're not here to hurt you. We're not working with the sidhe who are looking for you." I left out the devourer part because I didn't know what this girl knew and didn't want to launch into explanations of what exactly the bad guys were at the moment. "A friend of mine asked me to look for you and the boy, to find both of you and get you somewhere safe while we figure out what the hell is going on. I promise you we mean you no harm."

"In my experience, people don't do things out of the kindness of their heart. Definitely not something this dangerous. What's in it for you?"

A small smile played across my face. I would have asked the same question if our positions were reversed. "I don't disagree with your assessment. I tend to feel the same. It's true that my friend asked me to look for both of you as a favor for her. She's rather involved in fae and daemon politics, and whatever is going on reeks of politics. The reason she asked this particular favor of me is complicated, and in the same way you don't trust us, we don't fully trust you either. The short and simple version is that the sidhe, who are after you, are working with warlocks and vampires who are after me."

The girl studied me with her serious grey eyes. "So this is an enemy of my enemy is a friend situation?" I had to give it to the girl. She kept her expression and tone completely even, and I didn't know if she believed us or would run at the first opportunity. I doubted she was past twenty years old, and she was already so jaded. I liked her.

"That's an accurate assessment." I gestured towards Kaysea, who started walking slowly towards the girl. "This is Kaysea. She's merfolk and has some healing magic. You're wounded on your left side. Please let her take a look."

"May I?" Kaysea asked from where she had stopped a few feet from the girl.

After a few tense seconds, the girl nodded and lifted her shirt, revealing a few nasty deep cuts, probably courtesy of some boggart's claws. The girl's jaw clenched as Kaysea reached out with her hands and hovered over the wounds, letting her magic soak in. The blood gradually stopped oozing out, and the skin stitched itself back together, although it still looked red and puffy.

Kaysea dropped her hands and took a step back. "Sorry, my magic is close to being tapped out, but they're mostly healed now. Once my magic has had time to replenish a little more, I can finish and remove any traces of scarring."

The girl let her shirt drop and shrugged. "Just another scar for the collection."

Andrei joined us again in his human form, fully clothed with a deer balanced on his shoulders. "Scented this deer before changing and hunted it down. I figured we could all use a decent meal and a brief rest before continuing." He looked at me uncertainly. "Unless we don't have time. . ."

"Food is a good idea," I replied, and my stomach rumbled in agreement.

"Thank the gods," Eddie muttered. "The vampire is the only one who has had a decent meal lately." Andrei stiffened slightly.

I walked past Eddie and casually slapped him upside the head. "Instead of trying to start trouble, how about you get a fire going and I'll help Andrei carve up the deer?"

"Sure thing." Eddie cracked a grin and flicked his lighter open, flame leaping obediently to his waiting hand.

I turned to the girl, who hadn't moved. "Why don't you help gather firewood and then we'll cook dinner?" She nodded and was walking towards Eddie when I asked, "What's your name, by the way?"

She paused and looked over her shoulder at me. "Bryn. My name is Bryn." Before she turned, the light from the fire reflected off the girl's eyes with a reddish glow. I stared after her in disbelief. *What in all the realms is one of you doing here?*

Chapter Ten

Bryn was quiet while we all chatted around the campfire, but she ate her fair share of dinner and told us the boy's name was Finn. After we ate, I waited until it was just me, Jinx, Mikhail, and Eddie still awake. Kaysea had fallen asleep and I didn't want to wake her. I stood up from the dying fire and walked a short distance away, beckoning them to follow me. "That girl is a valkyrie," I whispered.

Are you sure? Jinx looked over to where Bryn lay sleeping. *I've seen valkyries, and their magic looks different from hers. Her magic is oddly muted.*

"I don't think she's awoken yet."

Jinx swung his head back towards me, golden eyes calculating. *How do we awaken her?*

"I'm not sure." I frowned. "The valkyries were tight-lipped before all that Ragnarök garbage happened. And now . . . now most of them have shunned their heritage. The few who haven't are mostly in Asgard."

"What makes you think she's a valkyrie?" Mikhail asked.

"Valkyrie eyes give off a red glow when reflecting light, particularly light from a fire. I'm surprised no one in the fae villages realized it, but the fae who live in these mountains value their privacy. They may have never encountered valkyries before, so they didn't know what it meant, or they kept their suspicions to themselves." I suspected it was the latter. Some of the older fae would have recognized signs of a valkyrie. "It would also explain why she has magic but isn't capable of using it yet. Until valkyries awaken, their magic is dormant. Even an untrained valkyrie is a hell of a thing on a battlefield. We don't know much about her yet, but we know she's loyal to the boy, which means she'll fight against the devourers."

Do we tell her? Jinx asked. *Whoever her mother was, she likely left her in this realm because she didn't want her daughter to awaken and walk the path of a valkyrie. Can't really fault her for that after Ragnarök.*

"What role did the valkyries play in Ragnarök?" Mikhail asked.

"They fought on both sides," I said grimly. "Valkyrie magic is unique, and they guard the process of awakening that magic fiercely. What is known is that it requires a bond with another magical being. Technically, it can be with any species, but usually it was with someone from one of the Yggdrasil realms, Asgard being the most common. When Odin and his followers were exiled, any bonded valkyries had to go with them back to Asgard even if they didn't agree with the path Odin was taking. They would never abandon their bonded."

"The valkyrie had to kill their own in that final battle," Eddie said with a seriousness he rarely showed. "After that, a lot of them started rejecting the bonding because they didn't want to be in that position again. It meant they would never awaken their magic. But they were willing to make that sacrifice."

"It's actually pretty similar to the werewolf situation," I said. "Werewolf parents who didn't want their children to grow up and fight in the war against vampires would give their children away and hide them with humans."

"What happened to the valkyries if the one they bonded with fell in battle and they didn't?" Mikhail wondered aloud.

I kept my expression blank and my tone even as I answered. "They died. When their bonded dies, they lose their magic, and the loss of that magic kills them." Mikhail frowned, but Eddie slid a glance my way. I ignored him.

"So finding out how to awaken the girl's power will be difficult," Mikhail said. "She was likely left in the fae realm by her mother on purpose because they didn't wish for her to become a valkyrie."

"And without being awakened, she's quite vulnerable. She's practically a human." I didn't know if awakening the girl's magic was the right answer. She probably had no idea, and once we told her, she might have no interest in becoming a valkyrie. But without her magic, she was the weakest in our group. It was a wonder she'd made it this far without being killed.

"Do we tell her?" Mikhail asked, and we all looked at the sleeping girl.

"If an opportunity arises on our way to find the boy, I'll tell her; otherwise, I'll tell her when we're out of this realm and safe somewhere," I said. "If she wants to awaken her magic and become a full-blown valkyrie, I know someone who might help us."

"All right, let's get the show on the road then," Eddie said way too cheerily for someone who still smelled like swamp and hadn't slept for quite some time. He wandered towards the others while whistling "Flight of the Valkyries." Jinx sighed in a fatalistic way only felines could truly manage and stalked after him to help get the others moving.

"How do you think Kaysea's vision of the girl plays into all of this?" Mikhail asked softly.

I gave him a side-eyed look and replied in an equally soft but dry tone, "You mean the one where I shove her off a cliff to her death? I have no idea. Having met her . . . I like her. She's tough, and she's a survivor. Her loyalty to that boy is unshakable. She's not working with the enemy to capture him, and she's only going along with us because she's a pragmatist and knows it's not currently worth the energy or time to escape us." My lips twisted down as I remembered Kaysea's vision. The girl bleeding out. The boy screaming hysterically while magic built up in the air. And me shoving the girl over the edge of the cliff. "It's possible whatever Kaysea saw in that vision has changed, but if that were the case, she likely would have had another vision with the new outcome, given that she's been in close contact with the girl now for several hours."

"So Kaysea's vision is still likely to come to pass?"

I rubbed my face in frustration. "I don't know. Possibly."

Mikhail reached out and pulled my hand away from my face. He held it for a few seconds and looked at me with a mix of concern and amusement that somehow only he managed. "Let's try to avoid any cliffs on our adventure, then."

"How DID you end up taking care of Finn?" I asked as we made our way across a vast plain. We'd left the forest behind almost an hour ago, and walking out in the open like this was setting my nerves on edge. True, we'd be able to see anyone coming, but we were also sitting ducks out here.

"I left the village I grew up in a couple years ago," Bryn said, her eyes scanning the grass fields looking for any hint of danger. "There was a fae girl in a nearby village that I liked. We were together for a while before things between us fizzled out. I didn't want to go back to my old village just yet, so I got a job doing supply runs for the tavern in town and a few other businesses. One of my regular treks was to the village Finn lived in." Bryn's features softened. "I knew what it was like to be abandoned as a child, and I felt bad for him. I'd always try to bring him something when I came to town."

"Were you there the day the village was attacked?"

She shook her head. "No, I just happened to arrive the next day. I found the village destroyed and the children who survived told me that Finn had run off. It took me a couple days, but I was able to find him."

"How?" Kaysea asked. "How were you able to find him when no one else could?"

"I–I don't know exactly. I was in a bit of a panic while I was searching for him and just trusted my instincts."

Kaysea and I shared a look. Bryn didn't know it, but her magic was likely trying to find someone to bond with; she was the right age for it. Bryn caught us looking at each other, and her eyes narrowed in suspicion.

"How much further?" I asked before she could ask what Kaysea and I were thinking. I still hadn't decided when I should tell her the truth about what she was. Last night I had assumed we had more time, but if she had already formed a bond with the boy . . . I didn't know exactly what else was required for her magic to awaken. She might be further along in the process than we thought.

"See those boulders piled up ahead?" Bryn pointed towards some large grey boulders that rose out of the ground less than a mile ahead of us. "There is a cave hidden beneath it. I discovered it with some other kids from the village when we were exploring one summer."

"We're quite a ways from the village you grew up in, right?" Kaysea asked. Her expression was curious, not suspicious. The girl might still not trust us, but as far as Kaysea was concerned, she was one of us.

Bryn looked at Kaysea and must have seen that Kaysea

was genuinely curious about what brought her out there as a child and so far from the village she called home. She plucked a stalk from a nearby plant and held it between her fingers. "Notice how most of these plants have these long stems that end in this bulb?" She flicked the dark brown bulb, causing it to sway back and forth. "In another month, this will double in size, and by late summer, it will split open into a bright orange flower. The nectar is very sweet, and the fairies love it. Especially the pixies. They come here by the thousands and light up the night sky with their magic. It's a well-known event, so many of the villages make the trek here to witness it."

"Sounds beautiful," Kaysea said in wonder.

"It was," Bryn replied and gave Kaysea a small smile.

The three of us were a little ahead of the others. Jinx was exploring the tall grass of the meadows; Eddie and Andrei were arguing about something. The laughs in between responses told me it wasn't anything serious. Mikhail was trailing the group, wary eyes scouring the open plains on either side of us. I debated if I should wait to bring this up, but I didn't know how Bryn's demeanor would change once we reunited her with the child, and she currently seemed at ease with both me and Kaysea.

"Do you know anything about your mother, Bryn?"

She shook her head. "Whoever my parents were, they left me in a village here and never came back."

Not parents. Mother, I thought. Valkyries had only mothers.

"Has anyone ever commented on your magic?"

Bryn stopped abruptly. "Why the questions?"

I slowed down before turning to face her and decided to just put it all out there. She deserved to know. "I think I know what you are." I glanced at Kaysea. "And I'm guessing you know what she is as well." Kaysea nodded slowly. Bryn looked back and forth between us, her solemn grey eyes completely unreadable. "I . . . we think you're a valkyrie."

"Why?" Bryn's voice cracked ever so slightly, but she recovered quickly. "Why do you think that?"

"I've met valkyries before," Kaysea said gently. "I know what their magic looks like. You haven't awakened yet, so your magic looks different, but I suspected. Nemain clearly saw other details that clued her in. It's relatively known that some valkyrie choose to leave their daughters in realms outside Yggdrasil so they can live peaceful lives."

"We'll tell you everything we know once we get the boy and go somewhere safe," I said quickly. "I know this is a lot to process. Once you know about the valkyries, you can decide if you want to awaken your magic."

Bryn looked at me, her gaze steady. "How is that done?"

"I don't know exactly," I admitted. "That knowledge was pretty closely guarded. I know you'll have to choose someone to bond with, and that person has to accept the bond in return. It's not a romantic bond or anything like that." I paused, trying to think of the right way to phrase it. "Valkyries had different reasons for choosing who to bond with; usually it was with someone who they thought was going to be a great warrior, but there were other reasons. Sometimes they would bond with someone they thought was marked by fate. I think your magic has been trying to bond with the boy. You're at the right age for it to happen. I know someone who can answer all your questions once we get out of here. You don't have to decide anything now. You'll have time to think it over and decide what you want to do. I just wanted you to know what you are because you have to have wondered about it over the years. Growing up in a fae realm but not being fae."

I braced myself for Bryn's reaction. That was a lot to take in, and she had every right to be upset. But Bryn just nodded once in acceptance and started walking again. Kaysea and I traded looks with each other. Bryn had to be the most level-headed person I'd ever met in my life. Bryn looked back over her shoulder. "Thank you for telling me."

Kaysea and I dropped back a bit to let Bryn walk alone with her thoughts. She might have seemingly taken all this well on the surface, but that didn't mean she wasn't a mess inside. We'd leave her alone to process this and then help her when she was ready. Unease swept through me, and I slowed my pace slightly and scanned the meadows. My magic stretched out from me as if it were searching for something. Nothing seemed out of place, and I didn't see anyone else in sight. After a few seconds, my magic coiled back up inside me as if ready to spring into action at any moment.

Something wrong? Eddie asked in my head.

I jumped slightly and scowled at him. *I wish you wouldn't do that.* I picked up my pace to catch up to the others.

Why? Eddie asked. *This is how you and Jinx communicate. And I've joined in on your conversations before.*

Your voice freaks me out, I admitted.

Eddie smirked at me. *I'm talking in your head. Is that really considered a voice?*

You know what I mean; don't be a prat. Your voice is deeper and practically rumbles when you speak this way. I gave him an appraising look. *Almost like your true self is something much larger than what you currently appear as.* His smirk slipped a little, but he didn't say anything. My suspicions about what Eddie was grew, but I let it drop. It was a hell of an accusation to make and even if it were true, I wasn't sure what I'd do about it. *Something feels off. I don't see anything though, and my magic senses nothing specific. But something isn't right about this.*

Should we turn back?

I chewed my bottom lip as I thought about our options. We'd be at the cave in a few minutes. There was no way Bryn would turn back now. We'd have to drag her away. And if this was a trap, that would provide an excellent opportunity for someone to attack us. *We keep going. As soon as we have the boy, I'll open a gateway and get us the hell out of here.*

Eddie nodded, and we walked the remaining distance to the cave in silence, both of us scanning the surrounding area, looking for any hint of a threat. Mikhail and Jinx were doing the same. Jinx had probably overheard the conversation between me and Eddie. I was pretty sure Mikhail just always assumed there was a threat and didn't see why this situation would be any different. Kaysea and Andrei were still chatting with Bryn at the front of our group when we reached the cave entrance.

"Nice hideout," Eddie said.

I nodded. I'd only spotted the cave entrance because Bryn had specifically led us to this spot. Several large grey boulders shot up out of the earth at odd angles. Once upon a time they'd probably reached much higher, but over the years pieces of them had crumbled and fallen. Some fell to the ground, expanding the footprint of this rocky hill while others simply fell on top of each other. Beneath them there was a small opening where several large rocks overlapped. As I studied the rock formation I saw other small holes scattered further up.

"This must have been all kinds of fun to explore as kids," I said in appreciation. My brother and I certainly would have had fun climbing up the rocks and finding all the good hiding spots. "We should hurry, though. This realm isn't safe."

Bryn crouched by the opening and looked into the dark tunnel that burrowed into the ground beneath the stones. "Finn? It's safe to come out. There are some people with me, but they're not with the ones hunting us. You can trust me."

I didn't miss the fact that she didn't say he could trust us or that we were friends. But I couldn't fault her for that because I wouldn't have said such a thing either. She hadn't known us long enough to have that kind of trust yet.

The sound of boots scraping against stone and earth floated up from the tunnel, and we waited for the boy to come out. A moment later, a head with long tangled chestnut hair popped out of the cave entrance. Bryn held her hand out, and the boy grabbed it, moving quickly to stand next to her. He was young, probably a year or two older than Isabeau. I was now up to two young children with the mysterious magic that I was responsible for. How the hell did I get myself into this?

"His eyes," Kaysea breathed. I didn't move closer to the boy since he seemed quite wary of all of us, but instead crouched down so I could get a better look and froze. The inner circle of his iris was a bright gold that bled into an outer ring that was a deep green. The colors reminded me of the changing seasons, spring bringing forth life before fading into fall.

"Eyes of change," I murmured. "Guess we know we have the right kid."

Kaysea moved and crouched next to me, giving the boy a warm smile. "Hi, Finn. It's nice to finally meet you. We're going to get you and Bryn out of here and take you to some place safe, okay?"

The boy didn't respond, but he gripped Bryn's hand a little harder. Kaysea and I both stood slowly and took a couple of steps to give him more space. His magic was practically humming. He was at least a decade away from settling and getting full use of his magic. I'd never met a fae child that already had this much magic at such a young age.

My magic was curious about the boy, but it didn't try to reach out. Not that long ago it would have been raging within me, trying to get free and get a taste of the magic. I was still getting used to the fact that I no longer had to keep a stranglehold on my magic to keep it under control. It was an incredible feeling, and I hated that it had taken me centuries to come to an understanding with it.

131

Now I just had to figure out how the hell to use it more efficiently. The sidhe devourers had magic similar to mine, and they used it to devastating effect. I was nowhere near their level yet. I could wield my magic fairly well against one combatant, but it took a lot of concentration. Anything more than that and I basically had to let it run wild, which had the risk of injuring my allies or causing other unforeseen problems.

"I'm going to open a gateway that will take us to my home. It's heavily warded, so we'll be well protected there," I said.

The boy's eyes widened slightly at my words, and he looked ready to bolt until he spotted Jinx standing next to Mikhail. Hesitation flickered through his eyes, and he relaxed slightly. Interesting. Jinx was in his fae form and while not as intimidating as Andrei in his werewolf form, he was still a hundred pound predator with sharp fangs and long claws. My mentioning of the gateway had freaked the kid out, but the sight of a grimalkin had comforted him. We had suspected Luna was connected to the child, but this confirmed it. Maybe when she saw him, it would jog her memories and she could help fill in the gaps of what had happened.

As I stretched my hand out and started to open a gateway, I felt magic that wasn't mine rise. I spun around and saw dozens of gateways open in a half circle around us.

Before I could push my magic to open a gateway faster and get us out of there, the boy took off running. Damn it! We all rushed after him as he ran around the boulders and veered to the left. Andrei had closed the distance the fastest and was reaching out to grab him when more gateways opened in front of the boy. Magic shot out of two of them and slammed into Andrei and Mikhail, who had been hot on Andrei's heels.

They both flew back and hit the ground hard. The boy backpedaled but not fast enough. A hand shot out of the gateway and gripped him as a young sidhe male stepped through the portal. I let my magic reach out so it could sense the sidhe's magic. No trace of devourer. Just a sidhe then. Two more sidhe stepped out of the gateways and stood beside the one still holding the boy. The gateways snapped shut behind them.

I glanced behind us and saw the rest of the sidhe closing in on us. My magic informed me that the ones behind us were tainted with devourer magic. Lir was at the front of at least two dozen of them, a satisfied smile on his face. We were outnumbered and completely surrounded. The stone outcropping blocked us on one side; the only way out was to fight through the sidhe, and there was no way we'd be winning that. Maybe a couple of us would get through, but definitely not all of us. Not that it mattered. They had the boy, and we wouldn't leave him.

"Lovely to see you again, Nemain," Lir said smoothly.

"Nice trick with gateways," I replied and eyed him coldly.

He held up a small glass sphere and tossed it casually in the air. "Why thank you. I'm actually the one who came up with the design. They can only open gateways within the realm, so their use is somewhat limited. But they do recharge themselves in a matter of hours."

"Huh. That's pretty cool," Eddie said, and I gave him a look over my shoulder. He just shrugged. "What? That's a really useful design. The ones the daemons make are only good for one use."

I glared at him one last time before scanning for the others. Kaysea and Bryn were behind Eddie. He'd subtly put himself between them and the sidhe who surrounded us. Bryn was completely focused on Finn who was still being held by the young sidhe, two more sidhe around them. Andrei and Mikhail had both recovered from the hit they'd taken and were slowly getting to their feet in front of Eddie. None of us were close enough to Finn to make a grab for him before the rest of the sidhe were on us.

"Tell you what," Lir continued. "Not only will I extend my

previous offer of you coming home with me, but you can bring your friends. No harm will come to them, I promise you. I'll tell you everything and you can decide on what you want to do after that. I think once you hear our side of things, you'll understand why we do what we do, though."

I didn't want to be tempted by his offer, but I was. There was some wisdom in living to fight another day. They might be limited in opening gateways to other realms, but I wasn't. *Anyone have any amazing ideas?* I asked Jinx and Eddie.

Not any good ones, Eddie grumbled.

We could go with them and escape later, Jinx said.

Not a huge fan of that plan, Eddie replied. *They're not stupid. They'll separate us immediately once we get to their realm. Nemain might be able to escape at any time, but the rest of us wouldn't. And she'd have to fight her way through to get to us. There will be more of them there and our odds of surviving would be even worse.*

I mulled over Eddie's words. He wasn't wrong. We might live a little longer if we went with them, but it didn't mean we'd be any more successful in escaping. But trying to fight through now meant almost certain death for most of us. This had gotten out of hand fast.

"You promised!" the boy screamed from where he struggled once again to get free of the sidhe holding him. His vibrant, two-toned eyes locked with mine, full of desperation and fear. "You promised you would help us and keep us safe!"

I let out a slow breath. "You're right, kid. And I do try to keep my promises." I pulled both of my blades free and heard Mikhail and Eddie do the same. "Sorry, asshole. Going to have to pass on your offer."

Lir looked at me with a disappointed expression. "I really was hoping we could do this the easy way. I can't let you go, I'm afraid. We came here to retrieve the boy, but your presence will be useful as well. Last chance, before I have to do something to change your mind."

In response, I raised my swords a little higher. *Jinx, tell Mikhail to get the boy free. Tell Bryn to grab Finn and run. We'll do everything we can to buy them time to get away.* It was unlikely they'd make it far, but it was the only option now, I thought to myself with a grimace.

"Very well. Don't say I didn't warn you," Lir said calmly and snapped his fingers. Half a dozen sidhe warriors threw blades at us in a blink. Jinx and Kaysea threw up shields to block the daggers. At the same moment, the devourer magic wrapped around the blades and I screamed, "Down!" Both Eddie and Mikhail dove for Kaysea and Bryn, but they weren't fast enough. My blood ran cold as the blades passed through the magic shields like they weren't even there and sank into the chests of Kaysea and Bryn.

Chapter Eleven

"No!" Finn and I both yelled at the same time. I heard him fighting to get free but didn't look as I dove towards Kaysea. Andrei and Mikhail joined Jinx and formed a line between us and the sidhe, although Lir and the others made no move to take us. I knelt in front of Kaysea, Eddie appearing at my side, and I looked at the dagger that had sunk into her shoulder. It reeked of devourer magic. That's why they'd been able to pass through the shields. Before I could stop her, Kaysea tore the blade out. Blood poured out, and I ripped off the lower part of my shirt and stuffed it over the wound. She hissed in pain.

"I'll live," she pushed out. "Check . . . the girl."

I looked Kaysea over, not trusting her word that she'd be okay. Not only had the magic of the blade passed through the shield, but it had also started nullifying Kaysea's magic. Kaysea was a powerful healer, but I could barely feel a whisper of her magic. We needed to get her to someone else with healing magic until her magic came back.

"I've got her," Eddie said and nudged my hand out of the way to continue pressing on the wound.

I couldn't do anything else for her now. I moved to check

on Bryn. She'd tried to push herself up but had only made it halfway. One knee was still on the ground, and her other leg was bent with the foot on the ground as she leaned on her thigh, panting. One dagger had taken her in the stomach. The other was in her heart. I swallowed as I took in her injuries.

The only reason she was still alive was because she hadn't pulled the blades out and I could feel just the barest whisper of Kaysea's magic trying to heal her. But Kaysea was too weak to save her. If we pulled the blades out, Bryn would bleed out in less than a minute. As it was, she still only had minutes to live.

"Bryn! Are you okay? You have to be okay!" Finn screamed. "You have to be okay, Bryn!"

My eyes burned as I heard the pain in the boy's voice. My magic raged around me, but it couldn't help with this.

Bryn raised her head, eyes brimming with pain. "Thank you. For not leaving us."

Something inside me broke at her words. "I'm so sorry," I told her. The tears I'd been fighting back broke free and poured down my face.

"Nemain," Kaysea called out sharply.

I glanced at her, and she pointed behind us. I looked at what she was pointing at but didn't understand. Nothing there would help us. The meadow ended less than a dozen yards away on a cliff. We couldn't climb down it. There was no escape there.

All the thoughts in my head skidded to a stop.

A cliff.

Bryn was an unawakened valkyrie with a mortal wound. "Some must fall in order to rise," I whispered.

"What?" Bryn asked, the word somewhat slurred.

My mind kicked into high gear again. "Kaysea, do you see a bond between them? Is their magic joined?"

A pause, then a weak, "Yes."

I gently lifted Bryn's chin so she could look at me. "You've trusted me this far. Will you trust me a little bit further?"

Solemn grey eyes studied me. Bryn jerked her head in a nod, as if she no longer had the energy to speak. I had mere seconds to pull this off. I helped Bryn to her feet, and we stumbled to the edge of the cliff.

"I don't know what you're doing, Nemain, but I'm losing my patience. The wolf and the vampire are next. Say your goodbyes and come with me," Lir called out.

I ignored him and moved so Bryn was standing with her back to the cliff, clutching her stomach as she struggled to remain standing. I blocked out the frightened screams of Finn and my friends shouting at me. Nothing existed except me and Bryn.

"You're a valkyrie, Bryn. And valkyries must fall in order to rise. Death is how you claim your true power. You must accept the bond. Do you understand?"

"Yes," she breathed, and her entire body shook in pain.

Before she could fall to her knees, I shoved her over the cliff. The boy's piercing scream threatened to tear apart my soul, but I whirled and faced him. "Accept the bond, Finn! You have to accept it!"

The boy finally tore free from his captor and ran towards the cliff. The sidhe chased after him. I let Finn run past me and lunged forward to sink a vicious punch to the sidhe's face. His head snapped back, and he hit the ground.

"Retrieve the boy and Nemain!" Lir commanded. "Kill the rest!"

The sidhe warriors started forward with their weapons drawn but paused as a rush of magic exploded from beyond the cliff. I grabbed Finn and ran towards where the others had gathered around Kaysea to protect her.

Shield, Jinx! Whatever you can do, do it! I crashed next to Kaysea with the boy still in my grip. He struggled to get free.

"She's alive!" I told him, and he froze in my arms. "She's alive. Just wait."

I felt the moment Bryn's magic crashed into the shield Jinx had thrown up. Her magic battered against it, but Finn's magic interlaced with Jinx's shield. Bryn's magic retreated, as if it sensed Finn. Lir's warriors rushed towards us. Their swords with their devourer magic would go right through Jinx's shield. I looked at Lir's face and saw the exact moment his expression went from one of victory to dread.

That's right, asshole.

"Well played," he yelled and pulled a glass sphere from his pocket. It flashed a bright purple light, and a gateway opened next to him. Lir looked at me one last time before stepping through it and letting it shut behind him. His warriors continued their charge, unaware their commander had abandoned them. As they were closing in on us, a scream filled with endless rage came from the cliff. The warriors froze and stared at the cliff in uncertainty.

I turned in time to see the brilliant golden wings break above the cliff. Bryn had awakened. The daggers were gone and blood coated the front of her shirt, but her golden wings beat powerfully. Her eyes glowed red, filled with rage and insanity.

"Brace yourselves!" I yelled and pulled Finn tighter to me. Mikhail and Jinx had moved to either side of me. Eddie and Andrei were both covering Kaysea the best they could. Finn reached out and gripped Jinx's fur.

Bryn shot forward, her wings beating powerfully. Some of the sidhe warriors had clearly encountered valkyries before because they knew what was coming. They turned tail and ran. The others that weren't sure didn't move fast enough. Bryn screamed, and magic ripped out of her. The sidhe that hadn't run dropped their weapons and gripped their heads as they fell to their knees. Magic continued to pour out of Bryn as she screamed, and the sidhe warriors screamed with her as they writhed on the ground in agony. Jinx's shield, bolstered by Finn's magic, shook but didn't break. Even so, I gritted my teeth against the battering of Bryn's magic.

Finally, her scream cut out and the warriors who had fallen stopped moving. The few who had run at the sight of the valkyrie were almost to the tree line. Bryn dove towards the ground and swiped a sword off a fallen sidhe and went after the others. She cut them down from the air one by one, burying the sword deeply in the back of the last one and ripping his head off. Her rage spent, she flew back to us and landed gracefully. Blood coated every part of her, and her eyes were still glowing red.

Finn pulled against me, and I let the boy go. He launched himself at Bryn without hesitation, and she swept her wings back as he slammed into her. She hugged him tightly to her and cried. I decided it was best to give them a moment and turned my attention to the sidhe who had held the boy. He was regaining consciousness and rolled over to his side and shoved himself up on his knees. He froze as he took in the carnage around him, and his eyes fell on Bryn, who was still clutching Finn to her and crying softly. His eyes widened at her golden wings.

It took a few seconds for the shock to pass, but then the sidhe realized how much deep shit he was in and spun around to run. Only to slam into Mikhail, who gave him a solid shove, sending the young sidhe sprawling on the ground.

"Going somewhere?" Mikhail said smoothly as he cocked his head at the sidhe, who scrambled up and found Eddie boxing him in from the other side. The two of them circled around the sidhe slowly. He froze and the color leached from his face.

"You?" Andrei said in disbelief. "I let you go! You said they were forcing you to help them before!"

I looked at Jinx. "I take it this is the scout you caught that Andrei let go?"

Yes. Jinx growled, his golden eyes glowing as he stared at the scout. *He must have joined up with them after the idiot wolf set him free. He led them right to us.*

Andrei flinched at Jinx's words but remained quiet. I wanted to scream "I told you so!" at him, but the look of defeat on his face cut through me. Andrei truly had believed the scout was a good person put in a bad situation earlier. He hadn't wanted another innocent to die and thought he was saving a life. I was still furious at him.

We could have died because of that damn scout. And Bryn had been forced into the life of a valkyrie. She might have chosen it anyway, but I'd wanted to give her a choice in the matter. The scout's actions had led to that being taken away. And I held Andrei partly responsible for that. Based on the look on his face, he held himself responsible too.

"Beck?" Bryn asked in confusion. She carefully untangled herself from the boy and wiped the tears and blood off her face as she stepped forward. "What are you doing here?"

"You know him?" I looked over the young sidhe. Jinx said he had recognized him from the bar we'd stopped at, but I hadn't been paying close enough attention to recognize him.

"He's from my old village. He was one of the kids who used to play with me in this meadow." She spoke slowly as she started piecing together the events and why her old friend would be here. Her expression snapped into one of coldness and rage as she stared at Beck. "You led them here. They didn't track us. You speculated this was one of the places I would have hidden Finn, and they sent you here to confirm it. Then you worked with them to lay a trap for us!"

If Bryn hadn't just depleted her magic, she probably would have killed Beck right there. As it was, we could all feel the rage rolling off her in waves. Beck tried to take a step back, but Mikhail just shoved him forward again.

Seeing that running wasn't an option, he tried a different approach. "Please, Bryn! After they destroyed your village, they came to mine asking about you. We'd all heard what happened. I bargained with them to leave our village alone in exchange for helping them. They wanted to capture the boy, not kill him. I thought I could persuade them to not kill you either! I didn't have a choice!"

The red glow from Bryn's eyes faded, and they returned to their usual grey. Her expression was still hard, but I could tell she was wavering about what to do. "Why did you go back to them after Andrei set you free? You could have explained all that to us. Or you could have tried to find Bryn and warn her," I said calmly as I scrutinized him further. He looked like a typical young sidhe. Lovely light brown eyes, sharp features, and curly brown hair that he had pulled back in a braid. My magic crept forward and took a swipe at his magic. He jerked but didn't try to run.

"Ah," I said knowingly. "You're close to settling, probably going to happen any day now. But your magic"—I gave him a sharp smile—"your magic is nothing. The sidhe don't care about looks, bloodlines, or wealth. They care about magic. And your lack of it marks you as a nobody."

Beck's eyes darkened at my words, and he clenched his jaw.

"I never cared about your magic, Beck," Bryn said quietly, her expression somewhat lost. "You were my friend."

"You left!" Beck shouted. "Every day I had to see the disappointment in my parents' eyes! Listen to the whispers around the village about how I would settle with a sad little drop of magic! Lir promised to give me more magic in exchange for helping them. And then I wouldn't have to listen to anyone sneer at me anymore."

"So you sold out the one person who never gave a shit about your magic," Bryn said.

"I'm sorry, Bryn. I really am," Beck said softly. "But you always had magic even if you didn't know how to use it. You could never understand what it was like. I did what I had to."

"Yeah," Bryn said bitterly. "I'll do what I have to as well." Steely grey eyes looked at me, and I drew one of my swords and tossed it to her. She snatched it out of the air and stalked towards Beck, who tried to back away, but Mikhail kicked him in the back of the knees, causing him to crash to the ground.

"Wait!" Andrei called out, but Bryn didn't pause as she swung the sword, and Beck's head tumbled to the ground. Eddie reached out with a foot and gently nudged the body so it followed suit. I raised an eyebrow at him.

"What? It's funny when headless bodies topple over."

I sighed. "There's something wrong with you."

Kaysea and Mikhail grunted in agreement.

Bryn stared at the body of her former friend for another moment and tossed the sword back to me. "Can we get out of here?" Her expression was tired and pained as she went back to Finn and scooped him up in her arms. He wrapped his arms around her neck and she let her wings wrap around the front, covering the boy.

My response died in my throat as I felt the magic pulse in front of us. It wasn't the same as the magic Lir had used to open the gateways. This magic was achingly familiar, and I knew only one other being who had magic like mine. I moved quickly to stand between the source of the magic and my friends.

Eddie and Mikhail immediately drew their swords and stared in the direction I was looking, even though they couldn't see or sense the gateway. A single ripple in the air formed, and a gateway snapped open. My heart hammered in my chest, and I waited for Badb to step through the gateway. Instead, a sidhe male stepped through, and the gateway shut behind him.

"Ah, good. I caught you before you left." His voice was deep and calm as he spoke. He didn't seem the least bit concerned about being surrounded by people pointing swords in his direction.

I barely processed his words as my magic reached out and hesitated around him before retreating. I gritted my teeth and pushed it out again, forcing it to find out what type of magic he had. The stranger continued speaking calmly. "Nyx was worried I'd be late."

Jinx stiffened at my side at the casual mention of his mother. *Who are you?* He asked, not bothering to hide the hostility in his tone.

I pushed my magic harder, trying to crack through his shields. My heart beat wildly, as it had the moment I'd felt that familiar magic opening the gateway. The denial I'd felt at Badb being my biological mother had faded every day since Eddie had told me about her existence. And if Badb was who I'd inherited my ability to open gateways from, then I must have gotten the devourer magic from whoever my father was. I didn't know this stranger, but he had stepped through a gateway opened by Badb. That couldn't be a coincidence.

Finally, a small crack in his shield appeared and my magic dove in, only to be immediately thrust out. But it was enough. He had devourer magic.

"That was very rude, daughter," he said chidingly.

My heart froze mid-beat.

"Daughter?" I was vaguely aware of someone asking the question but I wasn't paying attention to what any of my friends were doing. Someone could have walked up behind me and slid a knife into my back and I wouldn't have noticed.

Daughter.

The word bounced around in my head, and I couldn't

form any other thoughts. I'd been slowly coming to terms with the fact that the shifters who'd raised me weren't my biological parents. I thought I would be prepared for this moment, but I was wrong. Sensing my distress, Jinx moved until he stood between me and the sidhe claiming to be my father. The others moved in so they were closer to me as well.

"We have a lot to discuss. But we shouldn't do it here," he said, deep blue eyes looking calmly at me. "Your mother opened the gateway so I could speak to you and explain. She wanted to come too, but a lot is at play right now. Only one of us could come, and we decided I was better suited for this task."

Task. I was a task.

It was enough to snap me out of my stupor. Rage replaced disbelief. After all this time, this was how he chose to greet me?

Fine.

If he wanted to pretend this wasn't life-changing news, I could do that. We needed information from him anyway. And once we were done with him, I could kick him out of my apartment and never see him again. He hadn't bothered to find me in all these years. I didn't need him or Badb in my life.

"We need to get out of this realm," I said evenly and stretched my hand out to open a gateway.

Mikhail sidled up next to me as a gateway opened into my apartment. "Is this wise? We don't know him. He could be lying."

"He's not," I said quietly. "At least not about being my father. We have questions, and he likely has answers." Mikhail didn't look convinced. "Trust me?"

Mikhail's twilight eyes bore into me. "Always."

He stepped back and ushered Bryn and Finn through the gateway and followed after them. Andrei gently picked Kaysea up and carried her through. I waited for Jinx and Eddie to pass before looking at the sidhe devourer who was my father.

He walked towards the gateway, pausing next to me. "You can call me Kalen."

———

ONCE WE WERE all in my apartment, I closed the gateway and allowed myself a brief moment to come to terms with everything. We'd survived. We'd found the boy. And soon we'd have our answers. I closed my eyes, and some of the tension I'd been carrying the past few days eased away, but not all of it. We had some victories to celebrate, but this was far from over. At least we had some time to breathe and collect ourselves. I smelled Andrei and opened my eyes to find him standing in front of me. He brushed a loose strand of hair behind my ear and let his fingers linger there. I leaned into his touch and inhaled his scent, and a little more tension bled out of me.

He grinned at me, and his hazel eyes lit up. "Would you like some coffee?"

"Sometimes I truly adore you, wolf."

His lips brushed mine. "I know," he said and headed into the kitchen.

I glanced at Kalen, who stood near the kitchen counter, subtly looking around the apartment. When he saw the brick wall full of weapons, he smiled slightly. I wondered if he would still smile if I grabbed a sword off the wall and stabbed him with it. Feeling my attention on him, he looked back at me.

"I need to check on my friend," I said flatly. "And then you will tell us everything."

"Of course." He nodded deeply.

Mikhail had posted up on the other side of the kitchen counter, a casual but short distance from Kalen. Trusting Mikhail to keep an eye on him, I checked in quickly on the others. Jinx and Eddie were with Bryn and Finn, getting them settled in the apartment. Both were looking wide-eyed at everything. I was assuming this was Finn's first time in the human realm; I'd have to ask Bryn later if it was hers as well. I turned my attention to Kaysea, crouching next to the couch where Andrei had carefully laid her.

"How you doing, Kaysea?" I pulled the cloth away from the wound. Blood gushed out, and I quickly put the cloth back in place. "Shit. It should have at least clotted by now. I should have brought that damn knife with us to see what exactly they spelled it with." I cursed inwardly at myself.

"You had a few things on your mind," Kaysea said wryly, pain still etched in her voice. "I can feel my magic coming back, but it's slow. A healer would be appreciated."

"Really? I was thinking about letting you bleed on my couch a little longer."

"No, you weren't. Jinx loves this couch and would give you bad luck for a month if you allowed my blood to stain it." Kaysea chuckled and quickly winced.

I squeezed her hand and walked over to the mirror in the living room, quickly tapping the glyph for Pele. The glyph glowed a light blue as it tried to connect to Pele's mirror. I tapped my fingers against the wood frame waiting for her to pick up. Pele would be the quickest way to get a healer, but she might be busy. I really didn't want to reach out to Kaysea's brother because I didn't have the patience for him right then, but if Pele didn't answer soon, I'd deal with it. As I was about to give up, the surface of the mirror shimmered and a familiar daemon face greeted me. Just not the daemon I was expecting.

"Uh, hi, Zareen," I said. "I take it Pele isn't around?"

"She's finishing up a meeting upstairs. I heard the mirror chiming and came to check who it was. When I saw it was you, I figured it was best to answer," she said hastily and took in my appearance. A worried frown spread across her face. "You've got blood on you. Is Kaysea okay?" she asked in alarm and looked over my shoulder, trying to see the room behind me. I huffed in amusement. Apparently, Kaysea had left quite an impression on Zareen.

"Actually, that's why I'm calling. I have a lot to catch Pele up on, but first I need a healer for Kaysea." The concern etched on Zareen's face erupted into full-on panic, and I quickly added, "She's fine. Or at least she will be fine. She got stabbed pretty good in the shoulder with a blade that had some nasty magic. She can't heal herself, and no one here is a healer. I figured Pele could send a healer she trusted over here."

"I'll be right there," Zareen said firmly and ended the call before I could agree one way or another. Alrighty then.

In case Kaysea hadn't heard the conversation, I let her know Zareen would be there soon to heal her. She smiled softly at the news, and then her eyes widened and the hand not attached to the injured shoulder shot to her hair and pulled some of the tangles.

She looked at me in a panic. "I need a brush! And someone needs to get the blood and dirt off my face!" She raised her arm and sniffed herself. "Oh, gods! I still smell like that damn swamp!"

I covered my mouth and tried to hide my laughter. "Priorities, Kaysea."

"Fuck you and your priorities!"

"I'll help Kaysea get cleaned up a bit," Eddie volunteered, and he whistled as he walked down the hallway to gather supplies from the bathroom.

I shook my head and moved on to the next problem. Kalen had settled at the kitchen bar and was watching Andrei make coffee and some sandwiches. It was perhaps cowardice on my part, but I wasn't ready to speak with him yet; instead, I walked over to where Bryn and Finn were standing by the window. Bryn looked like a light breeze would blow her over. We needed to get her cleaned up and in bed to rest, but she wouldn't do that until she knew Finn felt safe. The young sidhe boy was sitting cross-legged on the floor. Jinx had put his glamour back in place and was curled up in the boy's lap.

"Mikhail, I'm guessing Magos and Luna are with the kids downstairs. Would you mind going down there and asking them to come up?" I thought about how that conversation would go and added, "Elisa and the others will probably ask to come, but tell them to stay in their apartment while we get everything sorted. We'll do full introductions later." I really didn't want to get Elisa and the other vampire kids mixed up in this. They had enough to deal with on their own.

But as Elisa had pointed out to me on more than one occasion, they weren't going anywhere and were part of our group. It didn't matter if I wanted them involved or not. The rest of the magical community would see them as involved because of their association with me. We lived in the same building, and everyone knew they were under my protection. Trying to keep them out of this was a losing battle, and keeping information away from them would only put them in danger. They had a right to know.

Besides, Elisa was good at keeping the others in check. If there was a way they could help, then they would. Otherwise, they would stay out of the way. I glanced at Finn as he stroked Jinx's fur. They were used to taking care of young children because of Isabeau, so if anything we could use them as babysitters. Finn might enjoy having another kid his age to play with.

"Sure. I'll be right back," Mikhail said and left for the downstairs apartment.

I eyed Bryn's wings. The sun coming through the window lit up the golden feathers. I'd forgotten how magnificent the wings of a valkyrie were. And also how cumbersome. None of my furniture was designed for someone with wings. The best I could offer her was a stool. I didn't even know if she'd fit in the shower.

"Can you help me drag these curtains closed?" I gestured to the long black drapes on either side of the living room. "My friend, who is coming up, is a vampire. Isabeau must have been playing with the curtains and forgot to close them."

Bryn looked at me in confusion. "Isn't Mikhail a vampire? I'd never met a vampire before him. I heard they were sensitive to sunlight, but he seemed to handle it just fine, so I thought I was misinformed."

"Mikhail is a special case," I said. "Most vampires can't handle sunlight. It causes their skin to blister, and they're practically blind in direct sunlight."

"Oh," Bryn responded. "I'll close this side."

"Thank you," I said. "I'll grab a stool for you to sit on once they're closed. Sorry, I don't have anything more comfortable to offer you."

As I tugged the curtain closed, the apartment door opened and Magos and Mikhail walked in. Relief shone on Magos's face as he saw I was there and unharmed. When he saw Andrei in the kitchen using his coffee maker, his expression changed to one of annoyance. Luna trotted in behind them and moved towards Jinx, but she froze mid-step when she saw the lap Jinx was curled up in.

Finn's eyes widened at Luna. Jinx moved out of his lap a second before the boy sprung up and ran towards Luna. He crashed down in front of her and pulled her close to him. "Luna! I thought I'd never see you again!"

Luna nestled into the boy's arms and purred. Her magic flowed out of her and wrapped around them as if hugging the boy as well.

Fionn, Luna said with a relieved sigh. *I've missed you.*

Chapter Twelve

Finn carried Luna over to the large recliner chair in the living room that she and Jinx normally shared. He climbed onto the chair carefully, curled up with Luna, and was asleep in seconds. Bryn looked at Finn with a bemused expression as she stood next to the recliner, hip leaning against the side. "I know the kid is packing a lot of magic, but I'm pretty sure his ability to fall asleep in ten seconds, no matter the situation or environment, is one of his superpowers."

He's always had that ability, Luna agreed.

"Do you remember, Luna? Are your memories back?" I asked. Luna's violet eyes grew distant for a moment, and she shook her head. *Not exactly. I can remember people and some events, but not the context or history around them. I think they're coming back, though. Seeing Fionn again must have sparked something.*

"Fionn is his real name?" I looked at the sleeping boy. His shaggy chestnut hair was covering most of his face. He still had dirt all over him and blood from hugging Bryn. We'd have to get him cleaned up when he woke from his nap.

"Fionn," Kalen said from where he still sat in the kitchen. "Son of Balor and Siofra."

Everyone turned to look at Kalen, who graciously accepted a cup of coffee from Andrei. He took a sip, and a look of pure pleasure spread across his face. "Thank you, wolf. It's been a while since I've had coffee. It's one of the few things I truly enjoy in this realm."

"That's nice," I said sweetly. "Now tell us what the fuck you know."

"Starting with who you are," Magos said in a calm, polite voice and walked over to the kitchen and started pouring more coffee.

Andrei smoothly slid out of his way and grabbed the plate with stacked sandwiches. He brought it over to Bryn first, who grabbed half a sandwich. Andrei continued holding the plate in front of her, looking at her expectantly. She sheepishly grabbed another half. He smiled and continued bringing the plate around until everyone had grabbed some.

I strode over to the kitchen and sat on the stool next to Kalen, letting my magic out to wrap around me in a not-so-subtle threat. "Yes, Kalen. Why don't you introduce yourself properly?" I arched an eyebrow in challenge.

Kalen studied me, his blue eyes calculating. Something wasn't right about them, but I couldn't figure out what. I could see through most glamours, at least I thought I could, but I would bet my favorite pair of swords the eyes I was seeing weren't his true eyes. A smile spread across his handsome face, drawing attention to his strong features. Unlike most sidhe who leaned towards androgyny, Kalen's features were more rough and masculine. I tried to find similarities in our appearance but couldn't see any resemblance. It seemed the only thing I'd gotten from him was his devourer magic.

"Of course," he said smoothly, his posture relaxed. I didn't understand how he could be so unaffected by meeting me for the first time. Did he truly not care or was he just better than me at hiding his true emotions? My magic wrapped tighter around me. "Please forgive my rudeness. I am Kalen. I serve the Unseelie Queen and I am good friends with Nyx."

The tension in the room shot up at the mention of the Unseelie Queen. We knew the fae Queens were looking for the boy and they were major players in whatever was going on. But I'd been hoping we'd be able to keep our interaction with the fae Queens limited. I didn't want to be on their radar, at least not yet. If Kalen served the Unseelie Queen and he was here to provide us with information, did that mean the fae Queens knew we had Finn? Did they send Kalen here, hoping to knock me off my game? Or had Kalen come here without their knowledge?

Kalen said nothing and simply gave me a knowing smile and sipped his coffee as I thought of question after question, as if he knew every thought that had passed through my head. I forced myself to relax and picked up the coffee Magos had made for me and sipped it. Mmm . . . delicious.

"I do hope the Unseelie Queen allows us some time to get cleaned up before gracing us with her presence. I'd hate to look like this for my first encounter with her majesty." I gestured at my torn and bloodstained clothes.

"You have no cause to concern yourself about your first encounter," Kalen replied. "And neither do the others. The Queen trusts me to handle this and keep things quiet for now."

"Does she now?" Pure venom laced my words. The calmer Kalen was, the more pissed off I got. If he gave me one more pleasant smile, I was going to throw my coffee in his face.

"It's uncanny." Kalen's eyebrows rose slightly.

"What is?"

"You've never met your mother, yet she uses that same exact tone when I've done something to anger her. Usually she tries to stab me shortly thereafter. It's likely the reason my reflexes are so fast."

"Maybe you could try to not annoy her?" Eddie suggested.

Kalen grinned, and it was nothing like that pleasant smile he'd given earlier. This felt real and gave him a mischievous appearance. "Where would the fun in that be?"

"What did you mean by 'your mother'?" Magos asked, undeterred by the humorous turn in conversation. Magos and Mikhail were both studying Kalen with the same neutral expression. In Magos's case, that meant he was dissecting every word that had been spoken, analyzing them, and coming up with multiple scenarios. In Mikhail's case, it meant he was thinking about where to dump Kalen's body after killing him. I was team Mikhail at the moment.

"Badb is Macha's twin sister and Nemain's real mother. I am her father."

"She's not my real mother," I said icily. "And you're not my father. Macha was my mother, and Nevin was my father. They raised me after you and Badb abandoned me."

"We had our reasons," Kalen said evenly.

"I'm sure you did." I matched his even tone, and he briefly narrowed his eyes in annoyance. Score one for me. "Tell us what you know about Finn and why you're involved in this. And who the fuck these sidhe devourers are."

"Of course, it'll likely be a long conversation. Perhaps we can get more comfortable?" Without waiting for a response, Kalen took a seat in the remaining recliner chair, putting him across from Finn, Luna, and Bryn. Kaysea and Eddie were on the sofa next to him.

With Kaysea laid out, there wasn't much space, so Andrei perched on the shoulder and leaned across the back. I was too tired to sit on the kitchen stool, so I grabbed some of the floor pillows that Isabeau liked to lounge on and plopped down on the living room floor across from everyone. Mikhail and Magos moved to stand behind me, leaning against the wall and not taking their eyes off Kalen. Jinx leapt onto the coffee table and sat, tail swishing, as he also stared at Kalen. If Kalen was uncomfortable being stared at by two well-known vampire warriors and a clearly pissed off grimalkin, he didn't show it.

"All right, we're all comfortable." I gestured at everyone. "Talk."

"As I said earlier, Fionn is the son of Balor and Siofra," Kalen said calmly.

"How do you know that?" I asked. "I thought no one knew who Finn was? Everyone just knew a sidhe child had turned up in a village packing a crapton of magic."

"My Queen traveled to the village that was attacked and studied the magic Finn used to break through the ward around the basement. She recognized the elements of both Balor and Siofra in it; therefore, we assumed he was their child."

Annoyance shot through me. "And who, pray tell, are Balor and Siofra?"

"Balor is the brother of the fae Queens. He is the exiled fae King and the most powerful sidhe to have ever existed. Siofra is his bonded mate." Kalen took another sip of coffee with a completely relaxed look on his face, as if he hadn't just dropped a bit of knowledge that changed everything we knew about the fae.

"That's not possible," Kaysea said softly from the couch. "There's no way the fae Queens could have hidden the fact that they had a brother this entire time." I agreed with her. Pele would have a conniption when she found out.

"Balor ruled thousands of years ago. Few alive today were alive when he ruled. He was the one who led the fae as they explored the other realms. Taught other species how to use magic." Kalen glanced at me. "How to shift into other forms."

Andrei perked up. "Wait. The fae taught the shifters how to shift into their animal forms?"

"No," I murmured. "They taught my ancestors how to shift into their fae forms."

"Fae form? I thought this was your human form." He

waved in my direction. "And that you were human to begin with."

I pointed at my tapered ears, which looked exactly like Kalen's. "This look human to you? Most of the specifics have been lost over the course of history, but it's well known that the fae were the first to travel across realms. My ancestors were felines who were not only intelligent but had vast amounts of magic. The fae were able to teach them and other species how to shift into fae-like forms. We added our own flare of course because the sidhe are rather boring to look at." I held out my arm and ran my fingers across the exposed skin, the medium golden brown with lighter rosette markings, just like my feline coat. "We were feline first and then learned to shift. Now we commonly refer to this form as our 'human form' because most of us live in the human realm. But in truth it started out as a mimic of the sidhe form."

"We know the fae traveled across the different realms," Eddie said and glanced at Andrei. "Most of us, anyway. But who those fae were and what exactly happened is unknown. I'm going to go out on a limb and say Balor wasn't just spreading knowledge and goodwill wherever he went."

"That was how it started," Kalen said, "but not how it ended. Balor came across realms where war was rampant. He stepped in to end the war. In other realms, he found species he felt weren't living up to their potential and encouraged them to do so. If they pushed back . . . he pushed back harder." Kalen's expression was grim as he continued. "It didn't happen all at once, but gradually, Balor became a conqueror and then a tyrant. His sisters tried to pull him back, but he refused. The more realms he explored and species he encountered, the greater his magic became."

"What is his magic, exactly?" I asked.

"Balor's magic is unique, even among the sidhe, whose magic is often undefinable and vast," Kalen explained. "When he encounters new magic, he can absorb and learn how to reproduce it. Because he already has a vast magic well, the new magic becomes more powerful in his hands. And he's able to combine it with all the other magic he has."

"That sounds an awful lot like a devourer," I said as suspicion about where this story was going started to take root.

No one knew where the devourers had come from. Pele and her father suspected the Queens knew more than they ever let on. But what if the fae had been responsible for the creation of the devourers in the first place? They'd crafted their realm-protecting spell with the help of the daemons but only granted protection to a few select realms. Everyone else had been left to fend for themselves, which resulted in dozens of realms falling to devourers while the fae said nothing. *Did nothing*, I thought darkly.

"I see you can tell where this is headed," Kalen said. "When his sisters realized they could never convince him to stop, they devised another plan. They may not be as strong in magic as their brother, but they're every bit as smart. Perhaps even more so. It took them decades to lay their trap, but eventually they were able to lure him and most of his army to a realm that held several unique species that Balor had never encountered before. Most of them weren't as intelligent as other species, but their magic was interesting and they knew Balor would find it fascinating. The realm itself was quite beautiful, and Balor had been looking for a new realm for his most loyal followers to settle down.

"Once Balor and his army arrived in the realm, the sisters sprung their trap. Inspired by their brother's magic, they had devised a ward that absorbed any magic thrown at it and healed itself if it was damaged. They cut off any gateways that led to the realm. In all his travels, the one form of magic Balor had never come across was a being who could open gateways directly. He was reliant on the specific magic the fae used to

157

create gateways. The ward his sisters placed around his realm simply absorbed any gateways they tried to build."

"The sidhe live a long time, but they don't live forever," Eddie said. "If Balor and his army were trapped thousands of years ago, they should be dead by now."

"The Queens were crafty in their plan, but they overlooked one thing—the creatures that inhabited the realm. The ones they knew Balor would find fascinating. That particular realm was chosen because there wasn't much magic there. In most realms, the plants and animals generate magic. The human realm generates an obscene amount of magic because of how much magic the humans emit. Few creatures emitted magic in the realm Balor was trapped in, but a few did. And several predators in that realm evolved to hunt them. These predators could not only sense magic, but when they ate the flesh of magical creatures, they absorbed their magic and it nourished them. And extended their lifespan."

"Fuck me," Eddie said, a mix of awe and horror in his expression. "He made the fucking devourers, didn't he?"

"He made all sorts of things." Something dark flickered in Kalen's eyes, and he took another sip of coffee. "He absorbed the magic from those creatures and then began tinkering. First, he experimented with the various species in the realm. Once he got the process down, he started changing his army. The first few rounds had some issues, but he eventually worked out the problems."

"What type of issues?" I asked. Maybe Kalen knew of some weaknesses we could exploit in our next fight with Lir and his devourer buddies, because I had no doubt there would be another fight. They weren't going to give up on getting Finn back.

"The sidhe in his army had considerably more magic than the creatures he originally changed. The first few sidhe who were changed required a near constant intake of magic to sustain themselves; otherwise, their magic would cannibalize itself. Balor lost about a fifth of his army before he perfected the process."

"How do you know all this?" Eddie asked.

A savage smile spread across Kalen's face. His polite and calm mask cracked slightly, and I saw the real Kalen for a few seconds before that mask slipped back on. "It took several centuries, but eventually they figured out how to get past the ward. The more magic a creature or sidhe has, the longer it takes, which is why those who come through are usually not the strongest among them. Balor himself could never pass through that way. I've had the pleasure of speaking with a few who made it through."

"Not much loyalty among his people if you were able to get so much information from them," Eddie commented.

"Everyone has a lever you can pull," Mikhail murmured. "You simply have to know where to look."

"You would know," Andrei said coldly.

Kalen looked between the two of them with interest, no doubt storing all this information for later. He might be here to help us and answer some of our questions, but he was also here to learn all he could about us. I needed to keep us on track and limit the information he was gathering.

"So Balor is responsible for the Cataclysms," I said, getting the conversation back on track.

"He'll never be able to slip through the ward the way others can. He has far too much magic. As does most of his army. He needs another way out." Kalen shrugged casually. "This is where my information runs out on his plans, however. Despite finding the right levers"—he gave Mikhail a small smile—"the fae I've spoken with didn't know the details of his plans. I don't know what role the Cataclysms play in them or what he's currently plotting."

"What about his mother?" Bryn asked. She'd been so quiet

I'd almost thought she'd passed out while sitting up. But she was staring at Finn, who was still curled up fast asleep in the chair with Luna. She looked back at Kalen with an expression of sadness no one so young should ever have. "What role did his mother play in all this?"

"Siofra," Kalen said in obvious distaste, as if he'd bitten something rotten. "Siofra was several centuries younger than Balor and was adored by his sisters. They thought she was sweet and kind, if a little gullible. They made sure Siofra was not with Balor when they sprung their trap. Afterwards, they explained what they had done. Siofra was devastated and felt betrayed by them. But over the centuries, she seemed to come around and support what the sisters had done. She even became an advisor to them and played a vital role in a lot of highly political agreements with other species. The sisters had complete trust in her and hid almost nothing from her."

"Sounds like an excellent spy," I remarked.

"I thought the same." Kalen's eyes lit up, and he gave me a look of approval. "Alas, my warnings about Siofra were not taken seriously. Almost a century ago, she disappeared. There were speculations about where she went, but we didn't know for sure. Until now."

We all looked at the sleeping boy. "Are you sure?" Bryn asked.

"As sure as we can be based on his magic," Kalen replied. "Luna would know." He gave the silver grimalkin a curious look. "Perhaps we can jog her memory."

A growl rumbled through the living room as Jinx dropped his glamour and stood on the coffee table. Only a couple of feet separated him from Kalen's throat. *You won't be finding any levers to pull with her.*

"On the contrary, I think I already found it," Kalen said.

"Back off, Kalen," I said. "You are a guest in our house, so act like it. Unless you want to find out how we treat those who we don't consider guests."

Kalen didn't even flinch as Magos's sword touched his throat, the mist still clinging to the slightly curved blade.

"I overstepped. Please forgive my rudeness."

After a few tense seconds, Magos pulled the sword away, and it vanished, leaving mist curling in the air.

Kalen studied the mist as it slowly dissipated and glanced at Magos. "I never thought I'd meet such a warrior in person. I've heard of your kind before and always wanted to study the magic and training tactics you use to hone your skills. I assumed I'd never get the opportunity because I thought all had fallen off the path and lost access to the blade. It delights me to see at least one of you has remained strong over the years."

Out of the corner of my eye, I saw Mikhail stiffen, and anger swelled in me. Kalen seemed to know an awful lot about us. And he was using that information to get a rise out of us. Given that everyone in the room was currently staring daggers at him, it was working.

As I opened my mouth to threaten him with acts of violence, Magos cut in. "There is always more than one path to walk, many of which require different types of strength. Perhaps you should worry about which path you will choose rather than commenting on the paths of others."

Kalen just smiled politely, and the tension in the room continued to rise. My magic was practically vibrating around me in annoyance while at the same time trying to get close to Kalen. It seemed more curious than aggressive, which only annoyed me further. A familiar warmth spread across my skin for a second and vanished. Someone had just crossed the ward and entered the building.

I let out a deep breath and said to Kaysea, "Hope you

consider yourself presentable enough. Pele is here, and I'm pretty sure Zareen came with her."

Kaysea stuck her tongue out at me but smoothed her hair down a little bit. Eddie quickly grabbed the brush and towels he'd brought out and took them back to the bathroom down the hallway. Two sets of footsteps echoed up the stairs, and moments later, Pele opened the door. And was practically shoved aside by Zareen, who barreled into the living room and zeroed in on Kaysea. She stopped her mad dash and stared at Kaysea almost shyly and said, "Hi."

I snickered but cut it off after receiving a glare from Kaysea.

Pele snorted and shut the door. "Well, don't let the mermaid bleed to death while you stand there gawking."

"Right," Zareen squeaked and moved to kneel by Kaysea. "I'll have you healed up in a jiff."

Kaysea smiled warmly at Zareen and touched her hand. "Thank you, Zareen."

It was hard to tell with Zareen's red complexion, but I was fairly certain she was blushing. I also suspected Kaysea was happy about having an injury that required the attention of the pretty daemon before her. I felt the steady hum of Zareen's magic as she got to work healing Kaysea.

That escalated quickly, I thought to both Jinx and Eddie.

They are pretty adorable, Kalen chimed in.

I glared at him. Of course, he was also telepathic. Argh.

Pele still stood by the apartment door as she looked around the room, taking in the newcomers. Her eyes widened slightly when she saw Bryn's golden wings and then narrowed at Kalen. Pele's father ruled the daemon Assembly, and he was usually the one who dealt directly with the fae Queens. But Pele often dealt with those who served them. It was entirely possible she'd encountered Kalen before. I'd have to ask her about it later when we had some privacy.

Pele glanced at Magos. "Coffee."

Magos continued sipping his coffee as if he hadn't heard her. My lips twitched as I fought a smile. Finally, Pele added, "Please." Magos nodded and set about making her a cup. I thought I was high maintenance with my cream and sugar, but Pele was on another level. Six months ago, she'd discovered this caramel latte contraption and became obsessed with it. I was pretty sure Magos had learned how to make it just so Pele would be forced to be polite to him to get a cup.

Pele strode over to the couch, propped a hip against it, and studied the sleeping boy. Bryn moved slightly, clearly not comfortable with someone she didn't know so close to Finn. Pele slid her a glance. "Peace, valkyrie. I mean him no harm. I'm the one who asked Nemain to find you."

"Ah, the favor," Bryn replied. "Hell of a favor to ask a friend."

I snorted in agreement.

"Tell me everything," Pele said as Magos handed her a cup full of sugar and caffeine. It did smell pretty good, though.

I gave Pele the rundown of everything that had happened since we'd entered the fae realm. The others chimed in occasionally to add things I missed. Pele tapped a finger against the couch cushion as she processed the information we'd given her and twisted around so she could better face Bryn.

"You've been with Finn for months. How much does he know about his parents? About where he came from?" Pele asked.

"He's only eight years old," Bryn said. "Based on what he told me about his life, his parents were around, but it was mostly Luna and another sidhe who raised him. He was largely sheltered from everything, so he doesn't know much."

"What happened to the sidhe? Did they come across with Finn and Luna?" Pele asked.

"No." Bryn shook her head. "Based on what Finn told me,

I think the plan was for all three to escape, but something went wrong and the sidhe stayed behind so Luna and Finn could make it."

"So Luna is the only one who might be able to give us more information, but she has no memories from then," Pele said in frustration.

Jinx rumbled in warning at her. "Oh, calm yourself, grimalkin," Pele snapped. "I'm not threatening or blaming Luna in any way."

"Luna, you said earlier that you think some of your memories are coming back?" I asked.

Yes. But I'm missing large enough chunks that they still make little sense to me. I think they'll gradually come back the same way my magic returned to me, but that took months. We can't afford to wait that long.

"I know someone who might be able to help," Pele said. "I'll reach out to them and see if they're willing to meet with us. Before I do that, we need to discuss one more thing." Pele's cunning eyes fell on Kalen. "I take it you know the whole prophecy?"

Kalen went completely still.

"Thought so. Nemain deserves to know." The edge to her voice made it clear this was a command, not a suggestion.

"Know what?" I asked. My magic shifted uneasily.

"Why your birth parents left you to be raised by others. And how your fate and Finn's are intertwined."

Kalen stared at Pele. Something shifted in his eyes, and for a second they appeared solid black. I blinked, and they were back to blue. He sat there, predatory still, all his attention on Pele. She smiled at him, and there was nothing friendly about it.

"Enough," I said. Kalen's attention snapped to me. "Either tell me now or get out."

After a few tense seconds Kalen asked stiffly, "I take it all of you have heard part of the prophecy regarding Finn?"

"Kaysea has been receiving it in pieces. What we have so far is 'A change is coming carried on wings of gold, because some must fall in order to rise. A child of both worlds with eyes of change, born in darkness but pulled to the light,'" I recited.

"I've been getting visions about the first part for a while now," Kaysea explained, her voice already stronger. Whatever magic Zareen had used to help speed up Kaysea's healing had clearly worked. Zareen sat on the floor with her back against the couch, subtly sneaking glances at everyone. All her attention had been focused on Kaysea when she'd first arrived, but now she was trying hard not to stare at the valkyrie standing guard over Finn.

"Obviously that was referring to Bryn." Kaysea smiled softly at the valkyrie. "I didn't get the second part about Finn until a couple days ago, when we were in the village that the devourers attacked while looking for him. I haven't received any more visions since then."

"The prophecy in its entirety was heard centuries ago," Kalen said.

> *A change is coming carried on wings of gold,*
> *because some must fall in order to rise.*
> *A child of both worlds with eyes of change.*
> *Born in darkness but pulled to the light,*
> *Fated to descend to the dark, no matter the light.*
> *The realms will fall unless fate is shifted*
> *by one born of the love between Death's harbingers.'*

We sat in silence, processing this new information. I glanced at Pele, curious if she'd known the prophecy in its entirety or if she'd merely known of its existence and used this as an opportunity to get Kalen to say it. In either case, she must have gone to some great lengths to learn of it considering how long the fae Queens had kept it a secret. I repeated the verses to myself but didn't see how I was involved in this.

"I've never heard this prophecy before," Kaysea frowned. "I regularly check in with the other active fae seers. We help each other the best we can. No one ever mentioned this vision."

"It wasn't a fae seer who originally had the vision. It was a grimalkin. Jinx's mother, to be precise."

Jinx froze and slowly sat down before looking at me. *It's you. The second part of that prophecy is about you. You're the one who can shift fate. It's why my mother brought me to you so we could bond. Such a thing is so rarely done, and she never gave me an explanation for why she chose you.*

"Bullshit," I breathed, denial instantly on my tongue. "How do we know for sure it's about me?"

"The use of the word 'shifted' in the vision can't be a coincidence for one," Kalen said patiently. "What do you know about Badb and me?"

"I don't know anything about you. My mother—Macha—told Cian and me that her sisters died long before we were born. She rarely spoke of them. It obviously pained her, so we never asked. I didn't learn the truth until recently." I glanced at Eddie and continued. "A friend learned about my family history while looking into something else. I know all three sisters came to the human realm when the shifter realm fell. Badb was furious at the fae Queens for not doing more to help the shifter realm, and a war started between them. During the final battle, the older sister fell. After that, the Seelie Queen sent the Erlking after Badb. She killed him and shortly after that joined the court of the Unseelie Queen, making herself untouchable to the Seelie Queen. I have no idea where you fit into this."

"Your *friend*," Kalen pointedly looked at Eddie, "got one detail wrong. Badb didn't kill the Erlking. The Erlking never died. He simply became something else." Magic rippled off Kalen, and between one blink and the next, he became something *more*. Power practically radiated off him, and he looked at me with bottomless black eyes. "When I served the Seelie Queen, I was known as the Erlking. I left a trail of terror, blood, and death in my wake. Now that I serve the Unseelie Queen, I still leave death in my wake. But I do it with Badb the Great Battle Crow at my side. She goes by The Morrigan in the Unseelie court to honor her sisters. We are Death's harbingers, and you were born of our love."

Silence reigned across the living room. Mikhail might have a reputation as the vampire assassin, but that was child's play compared to the tales told of the Erlking. Even though he'd disappeared from the world centuries ago, fae and daemons alike still told scary tales of him to their children. And he was here. Drinking coffee and eating sandwiches with us. Tendrils of my magic stretched out, and I didn't stop it as it intertwined with his, not afraid in the least. Eddie made a choking sound, and the turquoise of Pele's eyes swirled and changed to a glowing red as she studied our magic.

Kalen pulled his magic back until it was once again hidden deep within him, and my own magic reluctantly came back to me. His eyes remained black. I wasn't sure if it was because he hadn't used whatever magic he had previously used to hide them or if I could see through it now that I knew the truth.

"Yeah . . . so we're all in agreement then that our favorite kitty cat is part of the prophecy?" Eddie asked lightly, his voice still a little rattled.

I nodded numbly, unable to say anything else. Dealing with the knowledge of Kalen and Badb being my birth parents was already more than enough; I could have done without the prophecy. Was it possible to opt out of a prophecy? I huffed a laugh, and everyone turned to look at me.

"Don't mind me," I said. "Just having a slight mental breakdown."

"You'll have to wait on that," Pele replied. "Finn is destined to destroy the realms unless Nemain changes his fate? Any thoughts on how he would do such a thing? And how Nemain is supposed to change it?"

"Finn has power, no doubt about that," I murmured and thought of him naturally using his magic to stabilize Jinx's shield back in the fae realm. A sidhe child shouldn't have been able to do such a thing, not until they were decades older and had settled. "But he's just a kid. I've been around some truly evil beings. Finn's not one of them."

"Not yet," Kalen agreed. "But there is a darkness in him. You've only seen a glimpse of Finn's power. Nyx was shaken to her soul when she had that vision, and she doesn't frighten easily. The boy has tremendous power, even more than his father did. We don't know how or why he's fated to bring about the destruction of the realms, only that you are the only one who can change his fate. And save the realms in the process."

"And how exactly am I supposed to do that?"

"No idea." Kalen shrugged.

I shot him an incredulous look. "Fantastic," I grumbled. "I take it the Queens know of this prophecy?"

"Only one of them," Kalen said steadily. "Nyx had the vision when Badb was pregnant with you. We knew immediately it was about you and the fae Queens would believe it as well. They would have taken you from us. But they didn't know yet about your mother being pregnant, so we hid it from them. Nyx helped us, and we hatched our plan. Macha and Nevin were already living off the beaten path. Badb claimed she needed to help her sister in the last few months of her pregnancy and the months afterward. You were born one week before Cian."

"At least the part about me being his older sister is still

accurate," I said wryly. Cian and I had always thought we were twins, but I had gloated over the fact that I was the older twin. Of course, I thought I'd been older by minutes, not a week. "Is it the Unseelie Queen who knows?"

"Yes." Kalen nodded, a troubled expression appearing on his face. "We don't know how she found out exactly. She came to us a few years after you were born and told us we had to be careful about giving away the ruse."

"And you really think she didn't tell her sister?" Pele asked, skepticism clear in her tone.

"No, I trust her on this. The Unseelie Queen loves her sister. I don't doubt that. But she's also aware of what her sister is . . . and what she's capable of. The Seelie Queen isn't always the most stable. She still wants revenge against Badb and me. She might very well have killed Nemain and risked damning the realms just so she could hurt us."

"And what does the Unseelie Queen want?" I asked. "The fae are always scheming. I can't imagine what kind of schemes a fae Queen has."

Kalen looked at me with those unreadable black eyes. "I wish I knew."

Chapter Thirteen

"So to recap," Eddie started. "The kid is the son of two evil fae and is destined to destroy the realms. Our lovely murderous Nemain, who herself is the daughter of two psychotic beings, is supposed to change the kid's fate. And on top of all this we have two fae Queens to contend with, one with a revenge hard-on and one with plans none of us are privy to. Did I get all that right?" he finished cheerfully.

I gave up, stretched across the floor, and put a pillow over my face. Eddie had left out the part where we didn't know what was going to happen when the fae and daemons found out about me. Kalen had survived all these years because he belonged to a fae court. He previously was under the protection of the Seelie Queen and now served the Unseelie Queen. I had no such protection and no interest in belonging to a fae court. That protection came with a leash I refused to wear. What I needed to do was come up with a plan so when it became known I had devourer magic and the ability to open gateways into any realm, the daemon Assembly and fae Queens didn't order my death. Or my servitude. There had to be a way to keep my freedom and my life. I just needed to figure that out while also keeping Finn safe from his evil parents and saving him from his prophesied dark fate. No big deal.

I pulled the pillow tighter against my face.

Someone nudged me with their foot, and I slid the pillow off my face and looked up at Pele.

"All of you should clean up and rest. I have a contact I can reach out to about the possibility of Luna's memories coming back faster. Assuming she's willing to help, it'll take at least a few hours to get everything set up."

"All right. I'll call you in a few hours after I get some sleep."

Pele nodded and left.

I pushed myself into a sitting position. "Zareen, once Kaysea is healed up, would you mind taking her back to the beach so she can check in with her family? Her magic will replenish faster in the water as well."

"Umm, sure," Zareen said. "Her wounds are healed, so we can do that now." She stood up and held out a hand to Kaysea, who accepted and rose from the couch.

Kaysea's concerned gaze fell on me. "Are you sure you want me to leave now? I'm already feeling much better. I could stay and rest here."

"Your brother is probably worried about you, and if you don't go back soon, he's going to track me down. Which will inevitably lead to a fight, and I know how much you hate that." I gave her a reassuring smile. "Besides, you should check in with your family and see how they're doing with all the changes and recent developments." I slid a glance to the side at Kalen and then back at Kaysea. Translation, ask your family about Kalen and find out what they know.

Kaysea didn't miss a beat. "You're right. I wouldn't be surprised if Connor was on his way here now." She smiled. "It was lovely meeting you, Bryn. I'm sure I'll see you again soon."

With one last look at the still-sleeping boy, Kaysea left with

Zareen escorting her. The two of them would probably enjoy some time together, I thought with a smile. With Pele and Kaysea gone, I looked around at everyone remaining. We had only two bedrooms and the couch on this floor. The apartment on the middle floor was empty, but I didn't want to leave Kalen unattended there. Finn was still fast asleep in the chair. The kid really could sleep anywhere. He needed a bath, but I didn't want to wake him up, and I knew Bryn wouldn't leave this apartment without him.

I looked at Mikhail and Magos. "Why don't the two of you show Kalen to the apartment on the second floor? He can rest there, and Mikhail can get cleaned up. The curtains should still be drawn on that floor."

"A shower sounds amazing," Mikhail replied and grabbed a bag that contained his clothes and belongings from where it rested behind the chair. As he walked past me, he murmured, "This makes the second-floor apartment mine by the way."

"You're back on the couch once this is over," I replied smoothly.

He raised an eyebrow in challenge and headed towards the door. Magos walked around the kitchen bar and stood in front of Kalen, gesturing to the door. "After you."

Kalen rose from where he'd been sitting. "Thank you. I could use a nap." He followed Mikhail and Magos, closing the door behind them. I looked at Eddie. "You're welcome to stay here or in one of the other apartments."

"I'm going to head back to my place. Got a few things I need to take care of at the shop. After that, I'll sync up with Pele at the bar." Eddie grabbed his backpack and headed out. Three down. Just a valkyrie and a werewolf left.

"I should go check on my sister and the other wolves," Andrei said. "You're not going anywhere for the next few hours, right?"

"Hopefully not," I said. "I need some sleep. We all do. And

we need to give Pele and Kaysea time to get some information on their ends."

Andrei strode over to me and cupped my face in his hands. "I'll see you later then." He kissed me, and I leaned into him. The fatigue that had been creeping up on me fell by the wayside. Maybe we could both get cleaned up in the shower?

There are children present, Nemain, Jinx said dryly.

Andrei pulled back and chuckled. I just shot a glare at Jinx and then an apologetic look at Bryn, who looked slightly embarrassed at our public display of affection. I gave Andrei one more quick kiss. "I'll see you later, wolf." His hazel eyes lit up at my words, and he gave me a playful grin and headed out.

I looked at Bryn, her golden wings drooping behind her. I sighed. Time to get the valkyrie cleaned up and then crashed out somewhere. Then I could do the same.

"It might be a bit of a tight squeeze, but I think you can fit in our shower. Come on, I'll show you."

Bryn grimaced as she stood, as if that had taken all her willpower, and followed me down the hallway. I showed her how to work the knobs for the shower and where the soap and shampoo were. They had indoor plumbing in the fae realms, but it operated differently. Luckily, we had a shower curtain and not a door so she'd be able to fit.

"There's a towel on the sink you can use. I'll find you some clothes."

"Thanks."

Leaving Bryn to figure out how the hell to wash the blood out of her wings, I went into my room and froze. My mouth hung open as I stared at the fae plant that sat on my dresser. Well, it had sat on my dresser. Now it sat next to the dresser in a wooden cask that looked suspiciously like the ones Pele had at the bar. When I'd left, the plant had been a little over a foot tall, its electric blue flower sitting on top of its thick stem, narrower vines wrapped around it. Now the damn thing was three feet tall at least, and its stem was considerably thicker.

"What. The. Hell." I growled. The blue petals shook and the flower slowly turned away from the window until it was facing my direction. I don't know how something with no face managed to look smug, but the damn flower did. Some pieces of plastic around the base of the makeshift flower pot got my attention. I snatched one of them up and looked at the label. Rotisserie whole chicken.

"How many damn chickens did those vampire brats feed you while I was gone?" I shook the wrapper at the flower, and it shook its petals rapidly in response. "I don't have the energy to deal with you right now. I'm getting some clothes and then I'm coming back here to sleep. If you annoy me with your vines, I'm going to grab my sword and cut you back until you're barely the size of a seedling again. You got me?" The vines tightened around the stem, and the flower rotated until it was once again facing the window. I shook my head and grabbed a pair of comfy pants and one of my baggier shirts.

I carried the clothes into the kitchen, grabbed the scissors from the drawer, and laid the shirt out. After a few seconds of deliberation, I cut two long slits down the back of the shirt. I'd probably have to help her get the shirt on, but it'd do for now. We could figure out how to get her more clothes that would work with her wings later. I cleaned up around the kitchen until I heard the water turn off in the bathroom and padded down the hallway and knocked on the bathroom door. "Bryn? I have some clothes you can wear. I can help you get the shirt on over your wings."

A moment later, the door opened, revealing a damp but clean valkyrie. "I'm not exactly sure how to dry my wings."

I huffed a laugh and thrust the clothes at her. "Pull the pants on, and then I'll help you get the shirt on. We'll towel dry your wings the best we can."

Bryn nodded and tossed the towel on the sink. She might not be a fae, but she'd grown up with them, and their casualness about nudity had clearly rubbed off on her. It was a bit of a struggle, but we got the shirt on her. It took three towels to get her wings mostly dry.

I frowned at the stack of wet towels. "I have no idea how you're going to be able to fly in the rain. Your wings just absorb water."

Bryn carefully folded the wings around herself and played with some of the feathers. "Aren't feathers supposed to be waterproof? Or water resistant?"

"I thought so, but I don't have a lot of experience with feathered wings." I shrugged. "We'll figure it out. Now that you're clean, you have two choices for sleeping arrangements. Magos is keeping our guest company downstairs, so you're welcome to use his bed. Or you can sleep on the couch next to Finn." I already knew which one she'd choose.

"I'll take the couch."

"Very well," I said and we headed back to the living room. "Jinx is going to stay out here. He's not spying on you or anything. He's just worried about Luna because he's a big softie, despite his grumpy demeanor." As I turned to head to my bedroom, I slammed my shin into the coffee table.

Call me a big softie again or something else equally insulting and I'll give you bad luck for a lot more than thirty seconds. Jinx growled.

I wisely bit back my sarcastic response. Grimalkins had all sorts of magic, but they were notorious for causing bad luck, and Jinx would absolutely make good on his threat.

"Nemain?" Bryn said tentatively, sleep mere seconds from claiming her. "Thank you."

"Sleep well, Bryn."

THE SOUND of the apartment door opening woke me up several hours later. The telltale sound of heels clicking on the hardwood floor told me it was Elisa. I silently got out of bed and waited just inside my bedroom. I left the door open so I could hear things better. Jinx would keep anything from getting out of hand, but I was genuinely curious about how this encounter would go.

"Oh. Hello," Elisa said. It sounded like she'd taken a few steps into the apartment and paused. Her deep, throaty voice didn't quite match with her tall willowy frame. I was used to it, but it seemed to catch Bryn off guard because she took a few seconds to respond, and I heard her heartbeat go up slightly. I could see why the sight of Elisa would do that to a young valkyrie.

Great. Love at first sight, Jinx grumbled in my head. *It's bad enough that Kaysea and that daemon were practically drooling over each other earlier. I'm not dealing with lovestruck teenagers.*

They're not teenagers. They're both young adults. Let this play out.

You are ridiculous, Jinx growled.

Oh, I'm sorry. Were you not making moon eyes at Luna earlier?

Jinx didn't respond, but I could practically feel his glare through the walls. He'd definitely be sending bad luck my way, but it was worth it.

Bryn finally recovered. "Hi. Umm, I'm Brynhild. Nobody calls me that though," she said quickly. "I mean everyone just calls me Bryn." I snickered but cut it off. Elisa had excellent hearing.

"Nice to meet you, Bryn." The sound of heels clicking against the floor resumed as Elisa moved further into the living room. "I'm Elisa. I live in the apartment on the bottom floor. Magos gave me a quick update a few hours ago. I just wanted to come up and check in on everyone and see if I could help with anything. I'm guessing this is Finn? He's adorable."

"He is certainly that," Bryn agreed. "You're a vampire, right?"

"I am. So are the others who live with me."

"Oh. You're only the third vampire I've met in my life," Bryn admitted. "I hadn't left the fae realms until recently, and I've only been to the human realms a handful of times before now." Cushions squeaked at Elisa joined Bryn on the couch.

"I can relate to that," Elisa said. "Less than a year ago, I'd never left the building I'd been born and raised in. Me and the others had lived in a space not much bigger than this apartment. I'd mostly been around other vampires my entire life, although some warlocks started showing up in recent years."

"Is that normal?" Bryn asked. "I mean, is that how vampires normally live?"

Elisa let out a humorless laugh. "No. Me and the others who live with me come from special bloodlines that give us more power than other vampires. The vampire Council, that's who rules all the vampires, kept us and others like us sequestered from the rest so they could study and control us."

"What about your parents? Where were they during all of this?"

"I don't know," Elisa said quietly. "None of us know who our parents are. We can speculate based on the powers we have, but that's it."

"I'm sorry," Bryn said in an equally quiet voice. "I don't know who my parents are, either. They left me in the fae realm when I was only a few weeks old. I didn't even know I was a valkyrie until a few hours ago." Bryn's golden feathers rubbed against the couch as she moved around. "Everything has happened so fast I feel like I'm still catching up. Nemain had to show me how to use the shower because I've never seen indoor plumbing like this," Bryn said with a laugh.

"Well, I may be a recent escapee, but I have more experience with this realm than you do." I could practically hear the smile in Elisa's voice. "Ask your questions, and I can help you catch up."

"Okay," Bryn said. "Let's start with an easy one. Where am I exactly?" There was a pause and then both of them laughed. Awww.

This is disgusting, Jinx complained.

Shush.

"You're in the town of Emerald Bay on the Washington coast. Which I know means nothing to you, and honestly, all the details about the country and geography don't really matter because that's all human business. What does matter is that this town is run by daemons."

"Is that what Pele is? A daemon?"

"Yeah," Elisa said. "Zareen is a daemon, too. I've only met a few of them, but they've all been really nice. Pele can be a little intense sometimes, but Zareen is awesome. She makes the most amazing pies and cupcakes you will ever eat."

"What's a cupcake?" Bryn asked.

"Dear gods," Elisa said in a horrified voice. "Okay, we'll address that problem at a later time. Daemons have towns like this all over the world. The fae also have a few, but they've mostly pulled out of the human realm. They're not fans of pollution or humans in general. Daemon-run towns like Emerald Bay are typically small and out of the way. There are some humans who live in town who have no idea about daemons or anything magical. But most of the population consists of nonhumans and humans who are in the know."

"Witches and warlocks?"

"Actually . . . no. Most of the nonhumans don't like witches and warlocks. There's some bad blood there." Elisa paused. "And some general snobbery by the fae and daemons who have stronger magic. The point is that most of the humans who live in Emerald Bay are aware of magic, but not witches or warlocks. Most humans are completely unaware of how much magic they produce, but sometimes it manifests in weird ways. Being able to see magic, for example. Or ghosts. Those humans sort of naturally flock to towns like this."

"Why do the daemons even have towns like this?" Bryn asked. "The fae rarely have anything good to say about the human realm, and they seem loath to come here."

"Well, the fae are more than a little snobby," Elisa pointed out. "But also the daemons love to have their fingers in all the political pies, so to speak. The human realm is used as a neutral meeting ground for beings from different realms. Also, a lot of nonhumans call the human realm home because their home realms fell to the devourers. They often live in towns like this and open up various businesses or do other types of work."

"I would like to see more of the town," Bryn said. "I've met a few beings besides fae, but not many. I'd love to meet others. Maybe even other valkyries?"

I squeezed my eyes shut at her words. Sooner or later Bryn would learn about the history of valkyries, and she probably wouldn't like it. Few valkyries would have any interest in meeting her and the ones who would be interested would likely want to use Bryn for their own purposes.

You should reach out to Sigrun, Jinx chided. *You know it's the right thing to do.*

I pursed my lips at the suggestion. He was right. But I still didn't want to do it. She'd probably ignore me anyway. *Once we get through this I will,* I told him.

"Nemain and her friends. . ." Bryn trailed off, and Elisa didn't push her. Elisa was patient and easy to talk to. Pele didn't care much for vampires, but even she was impressed by the young vampire. Pele always appreciated someone who would be useful in getting others to spill secrets. Bryn let out a breath. "Are they really good people? They put their lives at risk to save me and Finn. And they don't seem to be stopping anytime soon. What will they ask for in return?"

"Loyalty," Elisa said simply.

"That's it?"

"You ask that as if true loyalty isn't hard to give. It's one thing to say you're loyal to another, it's another thing to prove it," Elisa responded, and I could hear the steel in her voice.

"You speak true," Bryn agreed. "I'm just used to dealing with the fae where everything is a bargain. I can't help but worry that I'm running up a tab with all the help they've given me so far. Free food. A place to sleep. Even these clothes."

Elisa snorted. "We've been living rent free in the bottom floor apartment for months. Magos often helps babysit little Isabeau. Although I'm pretty sure he started doing that to get away from the verbal and occasional physical sparring matches between Nemain and Mikhail."

"Isabeau is one of the vampires who lives with you?"

"Yes. She's actually the reason we enacted our plan to escape when we did. She's much younger than us, six years old, which I'm guessing is only a couple years younger than Finn. We'll have to introduce them soon."

"That'd be nice," Bryn said, and then added, "I don't even know if he's ever met other kids his own age before."

I heard Elisa move across the couch. "We'll figure this out. Nemain's smart and vicious. She'll keep you protected. Isn't that right, Nemain?"

Busted.

"How long did you know I was eavesdropping?" I asked as I joined them in the living room.

"I thought I heard you when I first came in, but I wasn't sure." Elisa twisted on the couch to look at Jinx. "When Jinx didn't say anything or do anything to interrupt our conversation, I assumed you'd told him to keep his mouth shut." Elisa raised a dark eyebrow at me. "Was I wrong?"

"I'm pretty sure Pele is going to look past her centuries-long hatred of vampires to offer you a job at her bar." I gave

Elisa an amused look, and a delighted expression spread across her face. I snorted.

"How are you feeling, Bryn?" I scanned the valkyrie, trying to gauge how much she'd recovered after her nap. Her magic hummed around her, but it definitely hadn't come back all the way yet. I had no idea how fast valkyries recovered their magic after depleting it the way she had earlier.

"Much better." Bryn rose from the couch and stretched. Her wings snapped out, and Elisa barely leaned back enough to avoid being smacked in the face with the wings. Just as quickly, Bryn pulled the wings back around herself and looked at Elisa. "Sorry. I'm still getting used to them," she said, her tone a mix of apology and embarrassment.

"You've been a valkyrie less than a day," Elisa said with a grin. "An adjustment period is more than warranted."

"It's weird." Bryn stretched out her wings more carefully this time. "In some ways, they feel completely natural and as if I've had them all my life. It's only when I really focus on them that I become hyper aware of what they're doing, and then I overthink my movements."

"It was the same for me when I started shifting into a wolf," Elisa responded. "I had to learn the balance of letting the instincts take over but also keeping just enough of myself to think rationally."

"You can turn into a wolf?" Bryn looked at Elisa curiously.

Elisa grinned and stood up from the couch, taking a few steps back. A pulse of magic shot from her, and in a blink, a large black wolf stood in my living room. She wasn't as large as Andrei in his wolf form, but I suspected she was faster.

"Damn," Bryn whispered and looked around the floor surrounding the wolf. "Where do your clothes go though?"

Magic. Elisa's voice sounded in my head. It had a slight raspy quality to it now. Bryn's eyes widened as she no doubt had also heard Elisa's voice. Another pulse of magic and Elisa returned to her vampire form, fully clothed. "I don't know how it works exactly. I don't shift the way Nemain and Andrei do. It's more similar to how Jinx drops his glamour. It's just an instant thing. I'm telepathic only in wolf form as well."

"Some other species shift like that," I added. "Lokis, for example."

Finn stirred on the couch, and Luna jumped onto the coffee table as the boy sat up. He rubbed his eyes sleepily and blinked at all of us. Elisa didn't comment on his freaky eye colors.

"Enjoy your nap?" Bryn asked. Finn nodded. Kid definitely didn't talk much. Isabeau had been like that at first, but now she would talk your ear off if you let her. Finn probably just needed some time to adjust. Gods knew the kid had been through a lot.

"Why don't you help Finn get cleaned up, Bryn?" I suggested. "Elisa, could we borrow some of Isabeau's clothes until we get some for Finn? They're close enough in size that her clothes should fit him."

"Sure thing. I'll be right back." Elisa started to move towards the door but spun back around. "Isabeau is nosy. She's going to ask what I'm doing with her clothes and then she's going to want to meet Finn. I can tell her she has to wait but . . . well, you know how she can get, Nemain."

Sulky didn't even begin to cover it. Isabeau had really come out of her shell the past few months. Which was great, but it also meant dealing with some pretty epic temper tantrums. Every time she threw one, we all freaked out because so far we had no idea what her magic was.

Like all the other kids, Isabeau was from an Apex bloodline, so she would likely have some sort of special magic other vampires didn't have. It was possible that despite her bloodline, she didn't inherit anything, but we wouldn't know for sure for another few years. Anytime she experienced intense emotions, her magic had a chance of erupting into existence. It would be good to know what her magic was, but now wasn't the time to deal with it. If she turned out to be a pyrokinetic, I really didn't want to deal with her setting the first-floor apartment on fire today.

"Finn, are you up for meeting another kid for a few minutes? She has some clothes you can wear after you get cleaned up."

Finn had been petting Luna absently, but he looked up to meet my eyes. He held my stare for a minute as if searching for something, and then he nodded once and went back to petting Luna. Him encountering Isabeau would certainly be interesting.

"All right," Elisa said slowly. "I'll, umm, be right back with Isabeau and some clothes."

The water shut off in the bathroom a few seconds before the apartment door swung open and Isabeau came bounding in, Elisa right behind her with a pile of clothes in her hands. She dumped the clothes on the couch. "I grabbed a few different pants and plain T-shirts. No underwear, but I brought socks. I'm assuming whatever shoes he was wearing are still fine?"

"His shoes are still good." I grabbed some of the clothes and passed them off to Bryn in the bathroom.

A minute later, she walked back into the living room with Finn gripping her hand. Even wet, his hair still curled slightly. Now that he was clean, his bright green and yellow eyes seemed to stand out even more on his face.

"Finn, this is Isabeau. She lives downstairs with Elisa and a few others."

Isabeau practically skipped over to Finn, her unruly brown curls bouncing with every step. She crashed to a halt in front of him, her light brown eyes brightening as she took in his appearance. I expected her to start talking a mile a minute, but she was uncharacteristically silent. She cocked her head to the side as she continued to study Finn, who was staring at her with complete fascination. I waited for one of them to say something, but neither spoke or broke eye contact. I raised my eyebrows at Elisa, and she looked back at me, clearly equally confused by whatever was going on.

I looked back at the two kids suspiciously. *Jinx? Are they talking to each other?* I could push out my thoughts telepathically, but that was the extent of my powers in that department. Jinx could pick up thoughts from others if they weren't guarding their thoughts. Eddie seemed to be even more skilled at doing that than Jinx. Instead of responding, Jinx leapt up from where he'd been lying on the back of the chair, his back arched and hair standing on end. *What the hell?*

Isabeau glared at Jinx. "Don't be rude, Jinx!" Elisa, Bryn, and I looked back and forth between Jinx and Isabeau. *What the hell happened, Jinx?*

She and the boy are talking. I didn't even get a chance to hear what they were saying before she threw me out of their minds. Rudely, I might add! he growled and Isabeau snickered.

"What's going on?" Elisa asked.

"Well, we may not know the full extent of Isabeau's magic, but she definitely has strong telepathic abilities. She and Finn are chatting away, and she completely blocked Jinx from listening in," I explained.

Vampires came into their magic at a much younger age than most other species; even then, their magic was usually unpredictable and not as strong as it would be once they made it past puberty. For Isabeau to have this much magic and control over it at a young age was unusual. We'd have to talk to Mikhail and see if he had any ideas about which Apex bloodline she could be from.

The shock on Elisa's face quickly faded to horror. "Isabeau, have you been listening in on conversations I have with the others? When we talk about, umm, adult things?" Isabeau just gave her an innocent smile, and Elisa groaned. "You and I are going to have a conversation about this later."

A chime came from the mirror in the living room, and one of the glyphs on the side slowly flashed a light blue. Pele was calling. I bent down and picked Isabeau up and flicked her nose. "Elisa, can you take this little terror downstairs? We'll probably be heading over to Pele's soon, but I'll let you know if we need anything. Probably a good idea if y'all stay in tonight."

"Sure thing." Elisa took Isabeau from my arms. "We'll do a movie night."

"Jurassic Park!" Isabeau loudly declared and waved at Finn as they left. The fae child waved back but definitely looked a little shell shocked.

I huffed a laugh and tapped the glowing glyph on the mirror. The large centerpiece rippled and revealed Pele sitting at her desk.

"I know someone who can help Luna's memories come back faster," Pele said without preamble.

"Great." I let out a sigh of relief. "Should we head to the bar, or are we meeting them somewhere else?"

"She'll meet you in one of the meeting rooms here." Pele pursed her lips.

"What is it?" I asked.

"You should know before meeting her. She's a witch," Pele said calmly. "She knows you're coming, and I promised her safe passage. And I will keep that promise, Nemain. Do you understand?"

Pele's turquoise eyes bore into me. Tension and anger ran through me at hearing the word "witch". It was a gut reaction. My magic vibrated around me, picking up on my emotions. I took a few steadying breaths, and it calmed down.

"Best behavior," I said tightly. "Promise."

"Good," Pele said. "Eddie is already here. The witch will be here soon."

"About the other thing I asked you about before we left. Can it be done?"

Pele sighed. "The problem was never whether or not it could be done. It was finding a daemon who was willing to work on vampires. No doubt he only agreed to do it because I was asking."

"So you did find someone?" I asked.

"Yes," Pele said, her lips turning down in distaste. "Mikhail will need to be present, so bring them both with you."

"You promise not to set them on fire for entering your bar?" I asked dryly.

"Best behavior. Promise," Pele parroted my words back to me.

"We'll head over in a few minutes. Kalen will be coming with us," I warned.

"I figured." Pele looked away, and a troubled expression came over her face. "I've encountered him a few times while dealing with the fae. Obviously I didn't know who he was to you. He's always bothered me."

"He bothers me, too," I replied. "Also, in case you weren't aware, he's telepathic. Probably a strong one. So guard your thoughts while you're around him."

"Always do around the fae. Or sometimes I think things just to mislead them," Pele said with a sly smile. "I'll see you soon."

Chapter Fourteen

"Are you ready to do this, Luna?" I looked at the grey grimalkin. *I am.* She trotted towards the front door, Jinx following her. "You two ready?" Bryn looked at Finn, and he nodded. I loaded up on weapons, and we went down the stairs to the second-floor landing. I entered the apartment without knocking. I wasn't exactly sure what I'd find, but it definitely wasn't the three of them sitting on a couch staring at the large flat screen TV with fascination. Gunfire barked from the speakers, and I looked to see what they were watching. A man with dark hair was meticulously shooting his way through bad guys while stylized music blared in the background.

"Are you guys watching *John Wick*?" I asked incredulously. Mikhail held up a finger to me in response, asking me to hold on, and my jaw dropped open a little more. A minute later, the gunfire ended and Mikhail grabbed the remote and hit pause.

"We'll have to finish it later," he said. "Where are we heading, Nemain?"

I narrowed my eyes at him. "We're going to Pele's. She promised not to set you on fire, but honestly, after you shushed me with a finger *and* watched *John Wick* without me, I don't really care if she does."

"It was Magos's suggestion," Mikhail said in defense.

Magos flicked a glance at him. "We needed something to pass the time, and our guest hasn't seen very many movies. This was one of the better ones."

"It was very enjoyable," Kalen agreed.

I glared once more at all of them. "We're going to The Inferno. All of us." Magos looked at the windows, which had blackout curtains drawn to block out the sun and looked back at me, a question in his eyes. "We're going to take care of your little sunlight problem once and for all, my friend," I told him with a grin.

"How fascinating," Kalen commented. A thoughtful expression appeared on his face as he studied Mikhail. "I'm guessing your friend found another daemon who would be willing to try it, and they're going to use Mikhail's blood for the spell?"

"Yes," I said, somewhat surprised Kalen had guessed that so quickly. "Space will be tight in the car," I said to Mikhail and Magos. "You both can travel over there on your own and wait for us. When I get there, I'll hold the door open so you can enter, Magos."

Plan in place, everyone but me headed downstairs. I wanted to check in with Andrei before we left to let him know where we were going in case he came back to the apartment. The glyph glowed a few times, but no one answered. Tension crept into my muscles as I watched the glyph repeatedly glow and fade. It was possible they were all out for a run or they were somewhere in the house where they couldn't hear the chime. After another minute, I tapped the glyph, cutting the connection.

It was unlikely Lir or any of his lot had already found us. They'd track us to Emerald Bay eventually, but we probably had another day or two. I should have asked Pele to set up wards around the lodge, I thought in frustration. My magic wrapped around in comfort, and I sank into it a little. I'd try again from Pele's, and if they still didn't answer, I'd go there next. I headed down the stairs to catch up with the others, and my magic sank back into me so no one at The Inferno would be able to see it.

Everyone was waiting at the bottom landing. Mikhail and Magos both vanished into mist at my presence, and I held the door open, letting them and everyone else out of the apartment. It was taxing for Magos to travel in his mist form during the day but it would be a short trip.

With Magos and Mikhail on their way, the rest of us walked around to the small parking lot on the side of the building. My bike was still parked behind the bar, but it was the car we needed anyway. A fully restored 1971 blue Chevelle shone from its parking spot. Eddie had helped me acquire it when it became clear we needed some sort of transportation besides my bike. He had initially suggested a minivan, but once he woke up from the punch I'd landed to the side of his head, he came up with a different option.

"Jinx and Luna, you're welcome to make your own way to the bar or you can ride in the backseat with Kalen. Bryn will have to ride in the front seat on account of her wings. Finn can sit in her lap. It's a short ride."

I unlocked the car and pulled the front driver's seat forward so Kalen could get in. Luna hopped in after him, and Jinx grumbled as he did the same. I bit my tongue to keep from teasing him about it. He no doubt would have preferred to make his own way to the bar. Jinx hated riding in cars. But for some reason Luna enjoyed it, so Jinx went along. I'd be sure to tease him about it mercilessly once I was prepared to deal with a bad luck streak.

Bryn kept her wings tightly tucked around her as she slid

into the passenger seat and shifted to get comfortable. Finn looked around in the car and cautiously reached out and opened the glove compartment and started poking through the contents as I turned the key and the engine rumbled to life. Five minutes later, we parked on the street outside the bar. I pulled my seat forward once more to let the others out while Bryn stretched her wings wide in obvious relief.

I walked up to the dark wood door of The Inferno and held it open. I'd been around Mikhail and Magos often enough when they were in this form that I felt their presence pass by me and into the bar. Everyone else walked in, and I let the door shut behind me. I caught the attention of the person working the bar, and they jerked their head towards the stairs.

Mikhail and Magos followed me upstairs to where Pele was waiting in front of one of the many meeting rooms on this floor. She opened the ornate dark wood door at our arrival, and we all filed in after her. It was a large room with a round stone table at its center that could easily seat ten people. A few side tables were set up against the wall where assistants or bodyguards could sit while their employers worked on whatever business deals they were trying to arrange.

A short human woman was standing on the other side of the stone table, studying each of us as we wandered in. I studied her back. Only a few inches over five feet, dusky brown skin with large dark eyes and black hair that fell in a wave around her shoulders. She appeared to be in her early thirties, but that didn't mean anything. Witches had all kinds of ways to extend their lifespan.

"This is Lestari," Pele said. "I've worked with her in the past for some jobs that required delicate work with memory spells. She's good at what she does." Pele's words were casual, but I had never once in the centuries I'd known her heard her say anything good about a witch or warlock. They were usually dismissed by everyone else because their magic was far weaker than that of daemons or fae.

My eyebrows crept up a little as I surveyed the witch again, trying to ignore the tension building within me. The last time I'd been in a room with a witch, I'd killed her.

"I'm the best at what I do and you know it," Lestari said. She had a light accent. My travel around the human realm was limited and my interaction with humans even more so, but I was pretty sure she was from somewhere in Southeast Asia. Mmm . . . good food there. My musings over food ended abruptly at her next words. "And you must be the witch killer."

"Must I be?" I kept my voice flat and gave her a bored look.

"Your reputation precedes you, Nemain," Lestari replied. "Or do you deny cutting a bloody path across the human realm on your own and then later on with that warlock lover of yours? What was his name? Something annoyingly French?" She tapped a finger against her lips as she thought about it.

"Sebastian. His name was Sebastian," I answered, and it took me a moment to realize I was rubbing my arms where the blue flower tattoos had once been. They'd been part of a spell Sebastian had cast on me. Every year a new one appeared to mark the death of my lover, Kaysea's sister, Myrna. Sebastian had been a fan of using beautiful things as tragic reminders. My magic rippled under my skin, wanting to come out, but I pushed it back. I'd promised Pele I would behave and I would. Besides . . . I didn't want to just blindly kill witches and warlocks anymore. Mostly. This one was starting to piss me off.

"That's right. Sebastian." She practically spat his name and then gave me a calculating look. "I heard you killed him. And a few members of the warlock Circle. Sent them running with their tails between their legs."

"Sebastian had it coming. So did the Circle."

"No doubt," Lestari murmured. "And here you are.

Needing the services of a witch. Tell me, Nemain, why should I help someone who has spent a good amount of her life murdering my kind?"

My temper flared, and I barely held my magic in check. "You know exactly what sent me on that path. Don't act like I didn't have a reason to hate the warlocks and witches. My parents are dead because of your kind. Thousands of others died after *your kind* stirred up the hatred of the humans and left us to burn."

"Not all witches helped the warlocks! My grandmother fought back!" Lestari snarled. "She got burned along with the rest for her troubles!"

"So a handful of witches fought back and died. The ones who survived did so by allying with the warlocks," I snapped back. "That made them fair game to me."

"Not all the witches who survived were allied with the warlocks," Lestari scoffed. "Plenty of us were working against them. You never bothered to find out if any of the blood you were spilling was innocent. You fed your rage and never questioned it. It's what made you so easy for Sebastian to use."

My control snapped and my magic surged. I knew I wouldn't be able to contain it. I spun away from the witch and slammed my fists down on the stone table. Crystal blue flames shot out from me, and the table exploded. Frozen shrapnel flew outward. Jinx threw up a shield around everyone in the room, including the witch, and the stone chunks slammed harmlessly into it and fell to the floor.

I stood in the center of the room with my magic raging around me and flames still covering my arms. The room was littered with frozen chunks of the table and ashes. Lestari had taken a step back when the table had exploded, but otherwise she stood her ground. She was doing her best to keep her expression neutral, but fear was peeking through.

Still, she held my gaze when I looked at her and didn't

back down. Guilt nipped at me. I'd promised Pele I would behave, but instead I'd made a mess of her room and probably blew our chance of getting the witch to help us. Pele had overcome her dislike of vampires to not only allow Mikhail and Magos into her bar, but she had also found a daemon willing to help Magos.

"You're right," I said calmly and pulled my magic back, but not all the way. Instead, I let it wrap around me the way I usually did when I was home. It meant it was still visible to the witch, assuming she was capable of seeing magic, which I was pretty sure she was based on the way she was studying me. "I was so lost in rage and grief that I didn't see I was being used. I hurt and I wanted to hurt others."

Lestari studied me with an unreadable expression. Anger and disappointment rose in me. Not at her but at myself. I had really screwed this up. I gave Lestari a tight smile and turned to apologize to Pele for fucking this up and destroying her table.

"I'll help your friend," Lestari said before I got the words out. "Perhaps there is another room we can use?"

Kalen toed a frozen chunk of the table, and I clenched my jaw in an attempt to keep my face from turning bright red in embarrassment. Now that I no longer kept my magic tightly chained up, episodes like this were rarer, but they still happened when my temper snapped. I didn't know why, but it bothered me that I'd lost control like this in front of Kalen.

"I'm so sorry, Pele," I said. "Is there somewhere else we can meet for now? I'll help clean up this room later and replace the. . ."

I trailed off as Finn pulled away from Bryn and bent down to pick up a piece of the table. It was a pretty big chunk, and he needed to use both hands to pick it up. He peered at the frozen stone and carefully looked over all the other pieces.

Magic pulsed from him. He bit his bottom lip as he continued looking at the chunk of stone in his hands. I felt another pulse of magic, and Finn held the stone out straight in front of him and let go. It didn't fall. Instead, it spun slowly in the air and moved towards the center of the room. The other pieces on the floor vibrated and slowly lifted off the ground.

A little more magic pushed out of Finn, and the pieces snapped into the resemblance of a table, but the pieces didn't fit together since part of the table had turned to ash in my magic explosion. Finn's eyebrows bunched together in concentration, and more magic flowed out of him. A loud pop echoed through the room, causing everyone to flinch, and the table slammed to the ground.

It was whole again. Perfect. Not a scratch or crack on its smooth surface.

We all stood around it and stared at it in shock. Even Pele's mouth hung slightly ajar. Which for Pele was the equivalent of her jaw being on the floor. I slowly turned my head to look at Finn.

He looked around at all of us and back at the table in confusion. Finally, he looked at Bryn. "Did I do good?" he asked, his voice unsure.

"Yeah, kid," Bryn said firmly. "You did great." She emphasized her words towards the end and gave all of us a sharp look.

Pele recovered first. "Thank you, Finn," she said and took a seat at the table, running her fingers along the surface. "This is wonderful."

Finn looked at her for a few seconds as if he didn't quite believe her, but Pele just held his stare and gave him a small smile. He returned her small smile and scooped up Luna, who had been sitting by his feet and carried her over to Lestari.

"Can you help my friend?" Finn asked and carefully placed Luna on the table.

If I'd tried to pick you up like that when I was a kid, you would have scratched my eyes out, I thought dryly at Jinx.

194

Your hands were always dirty and gross.

"I'll try," Lestari said, cutting into my private argument with Jinx. "Luna, I'll need to take a look at your mind to evaluate the current state. Are you okay with me doing that?"

Yes, Luna replied.

Lestari nodded and took a seat in front of Luna, a look of concentration on her face. The rest of us sat at the table and said nothing. Minutes ticked by as Lestari continued to poke around in Luna's mind. If this didn't work, I wasn't sure what our next move would be.

"Okay, I can fix this," Lestari said. "It's going to take some time though, and I'll have to prepare a few things." Relief flooded me. Finally, something was going our way.

"How much time?" I asked.

"Mending the mind is delicate work," Lestari said. "Luna's memories are already coming back, which is good. All I'm going to be doing is encouraging that to happen faster. It will take several hours."

"Okay." I looked around the room. "Pele, is there someone who can guide Magos in the daemon realm? I'm guessing that will take some time, and we might as well get it done now."

Magos looked at me, a question in his eyes.

I smiled. "How would you like to walk in the sun again, my friend?"

He blinked and seemed taken aback before a wide smile spread across his face. "I would like that very much."

"Mikhail must go as well. Asmodeus will serve as a guide," Pele said. "I already filled them in on what was going on, and they were more than happy to assist."

I bit back whatever smartass comment I was going to make. Pele was hiding it well, but I knew she'd have words with me later over losing control of my magic. Teasing her at the moment over the centuries-long crush Asmodeus had on her wasn't a good idea for my health, so instead I just said, "Perfect."

The three of us headed downstairs and to the bar. Asmodeus was working along with two others when they saw us. "Asmodeus," I said in greeting and gave them a wide smile. "This is Magos and his nephew, Mikhail. I assume Pele filled you in?"

"She did." Asmodeus nodded, the overhead lights from the bar gleaming off their dark mahogany skin. They had the same bright turquoise eyes as Pele, but their skin was several shades darker, creating a beautiful contrast with their eyes. "Are you all ready to go?" At my nod, they moved towards Pele's office and pulled the curtain aside. "After you."

We walked into Pele's office and waited by the dark wooden arch that took up most of one side. The sound from the bar cut off as soon as Asmodeus let the curtain fall back into place. I looked over their appearance as they walked across the office.

Black pants that were high-waisted but loosely cut in the legs. Their top was also black but fit tightly against their skin and cut off at the midriff, giving us a delightful view of the hard muscles across their abdomen. The sleeves were long and loose but had a slit cut out across the upper arms, giving us a glimpse of more well-toned muscles. It was a beautiful outfit that was neither masculine nor feminine, reflecting Asmodeus's nonbinary nature.

I narrowed my eyes in speculation. "Is this outfit one of your sister's designs?"

"Yes," they said casually. "Just something new they're working on."

I moved slowly around Asmodeus as I scrutinized the outfit more. The pants fit loosely around the legs, but they were pretty tight on the top, doing wonders for their ass.

"So now your sister, who has a thriving fashion business, is also spending some time trying to move along your relationship with Pele." I grinned wickedly.

"I don't know what you mean," they replied and tapped some of the glyphs on the side of the arch.

I snorted. "It's been almost a century, Asmodeus. That's a hell of a long time to be carrying this torch."

Asmodeus ignored me like they usually did when I brought up this topic and stepped back from the gateway as it finished opening. "Asmodeus will stay with you and guide you back."

Mikhail nodded and strode through the gateway. Magos paused before me, his copper eyes gleaming. "Thank you, Nemain."

I shook my head. "This is all Pele's doing."

"I will give Pele my thanks as well," Magos said. "But this is only happening because of you, so thank you."

"I'm only doing it because having Mikhail as my only option during daylight hours doesn't work for me. You've made it pretty clear you'll be sorely put out if I kill him."

Magos shook his head as amusement lit up his features, and he followed the others into the daemon realm.

THE MEETING ROOM was still completely silent when I returned to it minutes later. Everyone was completely focused on Luna and Lestari. The silver grimalkin in her fae form was perched on the table like a sphinx. Jinx sat on the table as well, not touching Luna but still close. Lestari was sitting on a chair directly in front of her and staring directly into Luna's unfocused lavender eyes.

Neither was moving a muscle. I grimaced slightly. Mind magic was fragile and intense. Finn was positioned equally still next to Luna and holding onto her paw lightly. I'd never encountered a young kid who was so serious and calm all the time. Bryn stood directly behind him, a worried expression on her face. I had no doubt that were Finn to turn around and look at her, she'd drop that expression for one of confidence.

Pele, Eddie, and Kalen were drinking what smelled like tea at the other end of the table. I quietly joined them.

"It will probably be at least another hour here," Pele said and glanced at Kalen. "Any idea when the Queens are going to demand Finn's presence?"

Kalen studied his teacup with a thoughtful expression. "Most likely within the next twenty-four hours. Both Queens are aware he is in Nemain's care. They will want to meet him in person."

Bryn's eyes bore into me as I thought about our options. If the fae Queens made a direct request to bring Finn to them, we couldn't deny it. The fae Queens did not accept no as a response, and we couldn't afford to go to war with them. But we also couldn't just waltz into their domain without having precautions in place and an escape route planned.

"We'll decide our next course of action once Luna has her memories back and can help us fill in Finn's history. And maybe shed some light on what Balor is planning." I looked at Kalen, and he met my eyes. "Finn, Bryn, and Luna have my protection for as long as they want it."

"And if the Queens want the boy to stay in the fae realm?" Kalen asked in that polite tone of his.

I shrugged. "It's not the first time they'll be denied what they truly want now, is it?" I matched his polite tone, but I let the challenge show in my eyes.

Kalen's polite mask slipped slightly, showing a glimpse once again of that cunning predator I was sure was the real Kalen. "Easy to make such a declaration. Another thing entirely to follow through. Just how much are you willing to sacrifice to protect that child? You barely know him."

"I know enough." My voice was hard, and I let my magic

out a bit to wrap around me. "He will not pay the price for the actions of his parents. And he will not be used as a political pawn."

Kalen leaned forward slightly, his mask slipping even more, but his magic stayed hidden. "If you continue on this path, you will be known to the fae Queens. You might be able to shelter the boy while he grows up, but your time in the shadows will officially be over. You will be sought after by the fae Queens." Kalen glanced at Pele. "And the daemons. Your magic will not be ignored, and everyone will seek to use you. Or kill you. Most likely both."

"I know the price."

Kalen leaned back and slipped the polite mask back on. "I suppose we'll find out."

Of that I had no doubt. I was on a collision course with the fae Queens. There was no avoiding it at this point. The best I could do was try to steer the outcome so me and mine received the least amount of damage as possible. But I had no false hopes of coming out of this unscathed. Dealing with the fae always came with a cost.

I looked back at Finn as he sat patiently by Luna's side, waiting for his friend to be whole again. His parents might be the bad guys, but that didn't mean he was one. He deserved a chance to grow up without being influenced by his parents or the fae Queens. I didn't know how yet, but I was determined to make that happen.

"Is there an empty room here with a mirror I can use?" I asked Pele. "I want to check in with Andrei. If he doesn't answer, I'll make a run out to the wolf lodge to make sure everything is okay."

"Use the room next door." Pele gestured to the left. "If you end up going out there, take Kalen with you. If there's trouble, you should have backup."

I rubbed my face to cover the small smile that played across my lips. Kalen likely would have come with me anyway, but Pele's suggestion would make sure he did. If Lestari finished with Luna before we got back, Pele would determine whether any information should be hidden from Kalen and the fae Queens. Kalen was clearly thinking the same thing, but he didn't seem the least bit upset about possibly missing out on important information. If anything, he looked amused.

"Pele, I know it's a lot to ask, but would it be possible to set up a ward around the wolf lodge? I should have asked you to do it before. I don't think the werewolves are going anywhere." Even if Andrei is, I thought sadly. I'd been so happy to have him back in town, even with everything going on, but it hadn't taken long for things between us to get off course. "They're defenseless out there. Part of the trouble that may come their way is my fault. The least I can do is make sure their home is protected."

Pele frowned at me. "First you have me help a vampire, now the werewolves. I'm not liking this pattern, Nemain."

"You know I'm good for it." I winked at her, and she rolled her eyes.

"I'll send Asmodeus out when they get back. They're quite good with wards."

"I'm sure they're quite good at a lot of things." I gave Pele an innocent look.

She gave me a blank stare and sipped her tea. I might have been imagining it, but I was pretty sure she was fighting back a smile. Hmm . . . maybe things were progressing on that front. I'd have to gossip with Kaysea about it later.

"Give me a moment. I'll try one more time on the mirror before we head out." I left the room and entered the empty one next door. Once again, no one answered and the worry I'd been trying to ignore surged up. I took a few deep breaths and pulled my magic back in so it wouldn't be on display as we walked across the bar. A few minutes later, we piled into my Chevelle and sped out of town with the engine roaring.

Chapter Fifteen

"I DON'T SENSE ANYTHING," Kalen announced from where I'd pulled over about a mile from Andrei's place. We'd talked on the short drive about how to approach this. While haste was important, we couldn't just drive up to the lodge in case it was a trap. Kalen said he would be able to sense any major magical workings from a mile away, so we'd pulled over.

"Would you be able to sense them if they were not actively using magic?" I asked.

"No." He shook his head. "I can tell you that no one has set up any type of ward or magical trap in the area. No nasty spells are waiting for us. But if fae or other creatures are lying in wait for us and simply hiding their magic, I wouldn't be able to sense that. Not from this distance."

I studied the dense forest that lay before us. The road that led to the old lodge the werewolves called home went up another half mile and curved back around. If we walked, it was less than a mile as the crow flies.

"Let's go on foot from here," I said. "We'll move quickly but carefully. If this is a trap, I might be able to smell them before we get close."

We set off through the woods at a jog. Once we got within a quarter mile of the lodge, I slowed to a walk. The only scents I picked up were old ones left by the wolves. Unfortunately, the wind was blowing away from us, so I couldn't depend on it to alert us of anyone in the area. All I knew was that nothing had passed in this particular area except the wolves. Kalen didn't say anything, so I guessed he hadn't picked up on anything either. Maybe I was being paranoid about all of this and the damn wolves just hadn't answered the mirror.

Slowly, we walked past the tree line and onto the paved driveway in front of the lodge. The large three-story building stood peacefully in the clearing with a few cars parked out front, including Andrei's old Bronco. Nothing looked out of place as we walked up to the front door. I opened it, knowing it would squeak, but it no longer felt necessary to sneak about and I didn't want to startle the werewolves. We walked into the lodge, and I looked into the living room on the right. Two heads popped up from the couch.

"Hey, Nathaniel. Hi, Clint." I waved at the brothers. "Andrei around?"

Clint, the younger brother, flopped back down on the couch. He tolerated me but was still upset over Magos kicking his ass a few months ago. Nathaniel gave me a friendly smile. "Yeah, him and Stela are chatting upstairs. Who are your friends?" His expression remained friendly, but I knew from experience he'd keep that expression up until he went for your throat.

Nathaniel had also gotten his butt kicked by Magos, but unlike his younger brother, he wasn't upset about it. Instead, he liked to spar with me and Magos to better his fighting skills. He had no interest in getting involved in werewolf politics or fighting for dominance within the pack, but he enjoyed sparring and liked learning new techniques. Of all the werewolves who lived in the lodge, Nathaniel was my favorite. Aside from Andrei, of course.

A low groan from upstairs announced one of the doors opening. The lodge was well over a hundred years old and had once been a boarding house for trappers and huntsmen moving through the area. It'd been abandoned for some time before the werewolves had bought it and fixed it up. Andrei and Stela had been working on additions to the lodge to allow for more werewolves to live there. Nathaniel had continued that work in their stead, and almost two dozen werewolves lived in it now. The stairs squeaked as two wolves made their way down, chatting quietly with each other. Andrei and Stela.

Andrei looked at me in surprise when he reached the bottom of the stairs. Stela surveyed all of us warily. When I'd first met Stela, she tended to dress with a pinup style to further show off her curves. Her hair would often be styled in soft curls, and she was a fan of bright red lipstick. Now her hair was pulled back in a tight bun and she wore loose-fitting pants with cargo pockets and a long-sleeve thermal. I noticed the luggage stacked by the door that I'd missed on the way in. Looked like Andrei's hopes of Stela sticking around and staying out of werewolf politics were for naught.

"I was just about to head back to your place," Andrei said. "Something wrong?"

"Did you not hear me call you on the mirror?" I asked. "I tried twice and no one picked up."

The wolves looked at the tall mirror I'd set up in the living room. The chime was loud enough to be heard throughout the lodge. Nathaniel and Clint wouldn't have been able to miss hearing it from where they were lounging on the couch, five feet away from the mirror.

Nathaniel looked at me. "We've been here almost all day and didn't hear anything. Could it be broken?"

I walked over to the mirror and tried the vampire kids'

apartment. The glyph lit up, but the main surface of the mirror didn't change. Odd. I tried again using Kaysea's glyph. Same response. I looked at Kalen. "This mirror definitely worked before."

"The magic the mirrors use is pretty simple, and it's the same for all of them." He looked at the mirror thoughtfully. "I imagine it wouldn't be that hard to use magic to alter the mirror and thus make it useless. I've never tried it, but if someone figured out how to do it, it would probably take only a few seconds. They could have done it earlier, and with such a minor push of magic, we wouldn't feel any echo from it."

"So they could still be here," I finished. All the werewolves in the living room were immediately on alert. "Andrei, is everyone inside?"

"Yes." He nodded. "The pack was out late last night. Most of them are still sleeping."

"Good," I said. "Keep everyone inside. We're going to head out front and see if we can get our mystery guests to reveal themselves."

I went outside with Kalen at my back. Unsurprisingly, Andrei followed us. Unfortunately, so did his sister. I knew enough about Andrei's capabilities to know he could mostly keep himself out of trouble. I'd never seen Stela in a fight, so she was a complete wild card. If I had my way, they'd both be inside the house, but based on the stubborn looks on their faces, they weren't going anywhere. Frustrated, I looked away from them and stepped further out into the driveway.

"All right, I'm here!" I called out. "What are you waiting for?" My head snapped to the right as a surge of power came from that direction. Kalen had called it earlier. Fae were here. They'd simply kept their magic under wraps so we couldn't feel them and had stayed downwind so we couldn't smell them either. I wondered why they hadn't attacked us right away when they had the element of surprise. I let out a fatalistic sigh. This reeked of fae political bullshit.

As if on cue, two sidhe walked out of the wood and onto the driveway. Both wore long tunics and had their hair pulled back in a braid. Bands around their heads made of green vines with a gold wire twisted in marked them as representatives of the Seelie Queen. Shit. I hated being right sometimes. I kept my eyes on the sidhe in front of me but felt Kalen step forward to stand at my side. Thankfully, the werewolves remained where they were behind us.

"Meriol," Kalen said in greeting to the darker-haired fae on the left. "Odette. How fascinating to meet Queen Áine's emissaries in the human realm. Nice workings on that mirror by the way."

Odette smiled sweetly at Kalen, but Meriol couldn't hide the downward twitch of her lips. Neither had expected Kalen to be there, and they weren't happy about it.

"We've come to deliver a message to the shifter." Odette gave me a dazzling smile. "Might we have a word? It's Nemain, right?"

"Sure," I said, not bothering to return the smile. "What do you want?"

Both Odette and Meriol narrowed their eyes at me. The fae were all about manners. They'd stab you in the back, but they'd do it politely. The daemons would also stab you in the back, but they didn't care about being polite about it. I much preferred dealing with daemons.

"It would be best if we spoke in private." Odette directed a pointed look at Kalen.

"It would be best if you came back in a week," I said. "Or better yet, you can just stop beating around the bush and tell me what you want. I'll tell you to go fuck yourself. You'll threaten me. My friends. My family. That'll really piss me off, and then I'll kill the lot of you."

I don't know if it was my words or the promise of violence that edged my voice, but another two dozen fae poured out of the woods, wearing armor stamped with the Seelie Queen's seal. Great. Sidhe warriors. I knew Meriol and Odette wouldn't have come alone, but I was hoping they hadn't come with this much backup. More were likely waiting in the woods as well.

"We request that you come with us," Meriol said. "Our Queen would like to speak with you."

"Interesting," Kalen said. "*My* Queen hasn't mentioned such a thing."

"It's not our responsibility to keep you informed," Meriol snapped. "Come with us, Nemain. One cannot refuse a direct summons from the Queen. We will leave your"—Mariol looked at the werewolves behind me in distaste—"pets unharmed."

I glanced at Kalen, and he shook his head once. *You must not go to Queen Áine. You will not come back from that meeting.* His words were faint in my head. He was likely trying to keep the other fae from hearing them.

"Just what does your Queen want with me, anyway?" I let my magic build up within me. I'd never tried this before. Usually, I just let it out and tried to wield it in a general direction. But if I did that now, the sidhe would panic and likely injure the werewolves. The palms of my hand felt colder as the magic built up. "I'm planning on speaking with both of the Queens soon anyway. Why is she going through all this trouble to speak with me before I get a chance to talk to anyone else?"

"I do believe my Queen would like the answer to that as well," Kalen added.

"All your questions will be answered if you come with us," Odette replied.

"I'm going to have to decline," I said.

Odette looked over her shoulder, and the sidhe warriors

took one loud step forward. She looked back at me. "Are you quite certain that's your answer? The two of you are no match for us." The wolves behind me bristled at the slight of being left out.

I smiled wickedly, pulling both of my swords free. "This doesn't really feel like an official request. Sure, she might be annoyed that none of you make it back alive, but she won't be able to do anything about it. If I'm wrong, by all means, let me know. We can wait for Kalen to reach out to the Unseelie Queen to verify that she's aware of what her sister is up to." I gave Mariol and Odette a knowing smile.

"Retrieve Nemain," Odette ordered, and I felt her magic gather, posed to strike. "Kill the rest. We leave no witnesses."

More sidhe warriors rushed out of the woods to surround us. Apparently, they were taking no chances in bringing me back to the Queen. Odette snapped her hand up, and her magic shot out like a whip. I jerked my arm up to block it with my silver bracer, but a wall of blue flame spread in front of me and absorbed the magic.

Kalen stepped out, blue flames slighter darker than mine trailing behind him like a cape. "Come on, Knight. Let's see what you've got."

He shot a hand forward, and a narrow stream of flames crashed into Odette. She grunted and slid back a few feet but slammed a shield in place. Kalen and Odette circled each other, Kalen sending out wave after wave of flames powered by his devourer magic against Odette's shield. In return, Odette alternated between slamming concentrated beams of magic against Kalen's shield of flames and using earth magic to create sharpened stakes of stones and hurling them at him.

I wanted to know how the hell Kalen was using his devourer magic to create a shield. I'd only used mine for offense. But Mariol was on me in an instant. I barely had time to snap my arm up to block her attack. The silver bracer on my arm grew a little warmer as Mariol's magic crashed into me. The bracers could absorb several direct hits of magic, but Mariol packed quite a punch. I'd be lucky if I could take one more direct hit from her.

Not for the first time, I wished I had better control over my magic. It hummed underneath my skin, but I didn't dare let it out. With this many people around, I was worried it would attack the wrong person. I'd convince Kalen to give me some lessons once we made it out of this. For now, I needed to move fast and cut through the fae before they could overwhelm me with magic.

Mariol advanced on me, the other sidhe warriors spreading out until they surrounded me on all sides. I sensed familiar magic and a vicious smile spread across my face, causing Mariol's grin to falter.

"A couple of my friends have decided to join the party."

The mist that had been spread out and barely visible in the sunlight snapped together, revealing Mikhail and Magos. Mikhail rammed a dagger into the gap between the helmet and armor of one of the sidhe warriors, severing the spine. The warrior collapsed, and Mikhail tore into another before dancing back. Several of the sidhe surrounding me pivoted to take on this new enemy.

Magos easily parried a blow and smashed his palm into a sidhe's solar plexus. Even with the armor, the sidhe stumbled back from the blow. Another sidhe warrior moved in to strike at Magos, and he ducked under the blade, his own sword sliding into the gap on the underside of the arm, tearing through flesh and muscle. More sidhe peeled away and focused on Magos.

The remaining ones launched themselves at me. I dodged a sword thrust, spinning my blade low as I aimed for the opening behind the knee. The sidhe warrior screamed as my blade slipped between the armor gap, and he dropped to one knee. I thrust my sword through his neck, and his screams died as I kicked him off my blade.

I cut my way through the remaining sidhe warriors, trying to fight back to where Andrei and Stela had been. Hopefully, they had remained there or, better yet, gone back inside, but that seemed unlikely. Mikhail struck down a sidhe, and I got a clear glimpse of the werewolves.

Andrei had found a crowbar that he was wielding rather well, considering his lack of weapons' training. His eyes were glowing yellow, announcing the wolf was in charge and improving his speed and strength. Stela stood behind him, waiting to tackle anyone who made it past her brother, but she had no weapon. I needed to get over there and quickly, before the fae zeroed in on the weakest members of our party.

Three more warriors converged on me, and the heat increased in my bracers. The warmer they got, the closer they were to using up all their defensive magic. At best, I could take one more solid hit before the magic being flung at me would make it through. Two of the warriors swung their swords at me while the other thrust their spear. I had no room to maneuver, and in that instant I knew I couldn't avoid all three. I blocked the swords aimed for my arm and my side and prepared for the sharp thrust of the spear, but it never came.

Magos's sword slammed onto the spear, making it strike the ground instead. His fist smashed into the warrior's head, and the sidhe's neck snapped to the side as it dropped to the ground. Another sidhe stepped in to replace the fallen fae and focused on Magos while the other two continued attacking me. Block. Dodge. Thrust. Block. I wasn't making any solid hits, but they weren't making it past my defenses, either. The training I'd been doing with Mikhail and Magos was definitely paying off.

The warrior on my left executed a fast strike aimed at my chest. I parried and struck at their exposed sword arm, aiming for the inside of the elbow. The warrior pulled back but not fast enough, and my strike cut through the tendon. They dropped their sword and stepped back, rallying their magic while another sidhe slashed at me. I leaned back, the blade grazing my chest.

The stone and dirt trembled around the fae whose tendon I had cut, but before they could unleash their magic on me, blue flames crashed into both sidhe warriors. They screamed as they were flung backward, slamming into trees. Bone snapped, and they collapsed. The remaining sidhe warriors moved on me, but they were clearly tiring and their blocks were getting sloppy. I slid to the side after blocking one strike and thrust my sword into a gap in their armor. It cut deep, and the sidhe snarled in pain as they fell to the ground.

"Enough!" Odette bellowed.

I stepped away from the fallen sidhe, who was still clinging to life and looked to where Odette was standing with Mariol. My heart beat faster as I took in Andrei and Stela standing rigidly next to the sidhe, magic wrapped around them.

"Surrender yourself, Nemain, and we'll take your friends with us as well instead of leaving their remains behind," Odette offered. "That's a better deal than you deserve."

"You're offering to take my friends because you believe it will be a good way to control me," I replied as I thought through my options and ignored my frustration towards the werewolves. They should have gone back inside when they saw how far out of their depth they were. My magic fluttered under my skin as if trying to get my attention, and an idea came to me. I hadn't been able to use it before because I was concerned about injuring my friends. But now I had two targets in front of me, and they were holding Andrei and Stela off to the side because they were confident in their shield. Kalen hadn't been able to break through Odette's shield when they'd been fighting. But maybe both of us could.

211

How close were you to breaking through Odette's shield? I asked Kalen.

Close.

Get ready. He didn't answer, but I felt his magic rise.

"You shouldn't have come here," I told Odette, my expression hard.

Mariol just sneered at me, and Stela yelped as the magic binding her in place squeezed her tighter. Andrei growled, but he had zero chance of breaking free.

"And you definitely shouldn't have threatened my friends." I thrust my hands out in front of me, palms out. Twin blue flames burst out of my palms, the narrow streams aimed directly at the two sidhe. Neither moved as they were completely confident in their magic blocking my flames. Odette's eyes widened as my magic slammed into her shield, immediately followed by Kalen's. The shield held for a second before shattering.

Kalen pulled back his flames, but mine kept going and slammed into Mariol and Odette. Both screamed as they were slammed into the lodge behind them. Andrei and Stela fell to their knees, released from the magic holding them. Some of the sidhe warriors behind me rose as their wounds had healed enough for them to attack once more. I trusted the others to deal with them as I let my magic pour out of me. The blue flames coated Odette and Mariol, and their magic flooded back into me. I closed my eyes and ignored their screams as I devoured their magic. I'd never wielded my magic against the fae before, and it was exhilarating. The boost I'd gotten from devouring the magic of the warlocks six months earlier had been decent, but nothing like this. Finally, the incoming magic dwindled until it was completely gone. I didn't know when they had stopped screaming.

Opening my eyes, I cracked my neck from side to side. My magic pulled back within me and was practically vibrating after that meal. I glanced at Kalen. He was looking at the remains of Odette and Mariol, but I couldn't read anything in his expression. I looked at the two piles of ash, each with a perfect ring of frost around them.

"Ash and frost," Stela whispered.

I frowned and looked at her. Yellow eyes stared back at me, full of rage.

"When I was searching for Jolie, I found the cabin she'd been staying in. All that remained was a pile of ash with a ring of frost around it."

Oh shit.

"You killed Jolie!" Stela snarled.

"Jolie was working for the warlocks," I explained. "She was the niece of the warlock who had me kidnapped and tortured. The same warlock who tried to kill Andrei." Technically he *had* killed Andrei; I was just lucky that my brother was in a relationship with Hades and I had been able to call on the latter to bring back Andrei's soul. "Jolie was using you, Stela. She never loved you and would have left when Sebastian was done in this town."

"You don't know that!" Stela screamed and stalked towards me. Andrei grabbed her arm, but she pulled it out of his grasp and growled at him. "You knew, didn't you! You were protecting her! I'm your fucking sister and you didn't tell me!"

"Stela, please!" Andrei pleaded. "Nemain didn't have a choice!"

"I'm going to fucking kill you!" Stela's eyes glowed yellow as she lunged at me. Unlike her brother, Stela had little fighting experience. Her wolf nature was in charge, which made her fast and strong, but she had no actual fighting skill to go along with it. I easily dodged her lunge and slipped behind her. My fist connected with the back of her head, and she dropped like a stone. Andrei rushed over and cradled his sister.

I looked at Andrei as he held his sister close, brushing her hair out of her face, and felt a heaviness settle in my chest. Kalen and Mikhail waited a short distance away, but Magos came to stand by my side.

"She meant to kill you," he said softly.

"I know."

"Love and grief can make a person do irrational things. She might calm down enough to listen to reason. Or she might continue coming after you." Magos turned to look at me, sadness etched in his features. "She might come after those you care about if she decides she can't get to you. Just to cause you pain."

"I know," I repeated. My words were barely more than a whisper.

"I'm not worried about you being in any danger. We both know you can kill her in a blink. I won't let her harm anyone else, either." Magos glanced over his shoulder at his nephew. "And if she were to threaten anyone else, say Isabeau, for example, Mikhail would likely take her out. It's just the way he is. If there is a genuine threat to those he cares about, he will eliminate that threat."

"She's the only family Andrei has left," I said numbly. "Her death would destroy him."

Magos gently rested his hand on my shoulder. "I'm sorry, Nemain." He left, joining Mikhail and Kalen.

Andrei looked up at me, his usual bright eyes were dull and pained. The heaviness I'd been feeling became sharp as I accepted what I needed to do. Slowly, I walked over to the others.

"I need a minute with Andrei. Any thoughts on what we should do with them?" I gestured to some of the sidhe warriors who were stirring. Some of them had been dealt fatal wounds, but most were still alive.

"They were following the orders of Odette. With her and Mariol dead, they won't attack us anymore. Most of them probably want us dead, but they'll wait until they have better odds of defeating us. They should be capable of walking in a few minutes. We can make sure they get to the fae gateway in the woods. It's not far from here," Kalen offered.

"All right," I said. "Meet me back at the car when you're done."

Kalen nodded and walked over to one of the fallen warriors. Magos followed him, kicking a sword out of reach of another sidhe who was rising to his feet.

Mikhail looked at me for a long second, reading whatever was in my expression, and quietly said. "I'm sorry."

"Me, too." I turned away and walked back to the werewolf.

Chapter Sixteen

THE DOOR to the lodge creaked open, and Nathaniel cautiously stuck his head out. His eyes widened when he saw Stela on the ground, and he rushed out. "What happened?" He knelt in front of Andrei and the still unconscious Stela. Clint came out and stood next to his brother, shooting me a wary look.

"I'll explain later," Andrei said, shifting his hold on Stela. "Can you carry her inside? And keep the others in for now. I'll be there in a few minutes."

Nathaniel nodded and gently picked up Stela, carrying her inside. Clint looked at me.

"A friend of mine, Asmodeus, is going to be stopping by later," I told him. "They're a daemon, but they mean you no harm. They're going to set a ward around the lodge to protect all of you in case the fae return. Or anyone else, for that matter. I should have done it sooner, but it'll be done now. Asmodeus will explain how it works."

Clint jerked his head in a nod and headed inside, shutting the door behind him. I wouldn't be surprised if he or some of the other wolves were trying to eavesdrop on me and Andrei.

"Let's take a walk," I said. "Kalen and the others will deal with the remaining fae. We need to talk."

Andrei nodded and fell into step beside me. We walked in silence as I meandered through the woods until I came across a fallen tree. We were far enough from the lodge that none of the werewolves would overhear us. I sat down stiffly, Andrei next to me. Neither of us said anything, as if we both knew where this conversation was going and neither wanted to be the one to voice the words.

"This isn't going to work, is it?" he asked tonelessly as he stared straight ahead.

I wanted to disagree with him and tell him we could make this work. It wouldn't be easy, but that didn't mean it wouldn't be worth it. We made each other happy and there was definitely love there. Maybe not the epic love of my parents, but that didn't mean it couldn't turn into that.

"No, it's not." I pushed the words out and ignored the pain that radiated through me. Ignored my magic vibrating underneath my skin as it felt my pain, but didn't know what to do about it. "I always knew we saw things differently. You're kind, Andrei. Usually, people who are kind and sweet annoy the hell out of me, but you're so genuine about it that I can't help but love that about you. I was so worried that being around me would change you. Make you into someone you didn't want to be. I don't think it would have. I think you are who you are, and me being who I am isn't going to change that."

Andrei turned to look at me with hazel eyes that slowly turned a bright yellow. "I love you."

"I know," I said sadly. "I love you, too, wolf. But there are others in my life that I love. Others I'm responsible for. I didn't think about that before. I might be willing to risk myself, but I will not risk them. Your kindness and generosity puts them at risk. If anything were to happen to them because of your actions, or inactions, it would tear us apart. You understand

217

what I mean because I'm sure similar thoughts have crossed your mind regarding your sister. She will never forgive me for killing Jolie. Even if she does come to accept why I did it, forgiveness is something else entirely."

"You had no choice," Andrei argued. "She would understand that, eventually."

I shook my head. "I did have a choice, though. I could have held her captive and made her confess everything in front of Stela. That would have provided your sister closure. I could have turned her over to some witches who aren't loyal to the warlock Circle for trial. But to be honest, none of those things even crossed my mind. She had knowingly hurt me. She'd set events in action that led to your death, and she felt no remorse about it. So I felt no remorse about killing her. I still don't."

Andrei looked away.

"When you and I first became involved I had no intention of getting involved in fae or daemon politics. I just wanted to be left alone. That's not possible anymore."

"Why can't it be?" Andrei argued. "I know you want to make sure Finn is safe and I do too, but after that...we could go back to how things were."

"There is no going back. Finn is the son of an exiled fae King and the nephew of the current fae Queens," I said bitterly. "He's dripping in fae politics and our fates are intertwined."

"It doesn't have to be you." Andrei reached out and gripped my hand.

"It does though." I thought about the look of anger and fear that Lestari had given me when we met. "When my parents died I became a monster because it was easier to give in to the rage I was feeling then process my grief. Sebastian saw that hate and anger within me. If it wasn't for Pele, Kaysea, and Cian I don't know if I ever would have seen the truth about him, that he was using me. I didn't want to." I slipped my hand out of Andrei's hand and ran my fingers across his jawline, enjoying the warmth of his skin. He leaned into my touch and the pain in my chest grew to the point where it felt like I couldn't breathe. "I don't know how I'm supposed to stop Finn from his dark fate. But I know the first step is to protect him now and make sure he has good people in his life."

I lowered my hand and Andrei moved until he was kneeling in front of me. My claws dug into the bark to keep from reaching out to him as I met his stare full of longing. In a blink his eyes turned yellow. "I could stay," he said, his voice hoarse.

"No, you can't." The wood bit into my skin as my fingers pushed in deeper. "And I can't go with you. Go with your sister and protect her. I would strongly advise both of you to not get caught up in the war between the werewolves and vampires, but if you can't dissuade your sister from that path, at least tell them what we know so far. The wolves are no longer just going up against the vampires. They're going up against the warlocks and some incredibly fucked up fae too."

"We can't win."

"Not directly," I agreed. "But things are going to start heating up. Cat's out of the bag, so to speak. If I were someone who could influence the werewolves, I would advise them to be patient. Gather information. Train the younger generation. A war is coming, and it's going to be a hell of a lot bigger than vampires versus werewolves. Let the vampires think you're defeated. At some point, the fae and the daemons are going to hit them hard. If the wolves are smart, they can wait and hit them after their numbers have been depleted."

"Kick them when they're down?" He let out a flat, raspy laugh.

"Always kick them when they're down, wolf." I gave him a sad smile. "Never forget that."

Andrei rose and stood in front of me, running his fingers

down my cheek and under my jaw. I allowed myself to breathe in his scent and enjoy his touch one last time.

"Don't think I'll ever be able to forget anything about you, kitty cat." He looked at me for a few more seconds and slowly stepped away.

I watched him go and didn't say a word. A few minutes later, I pulled my claws out of the fallen log where I'd buried them to keep myself rooted to that spot. I shook the dirt and pieces of bark off my hand and headed back to the car, not looking back once.

———

The others were waiting for me at the car. Nobody commented on my red-rimmed eyes. I'd used the jog back to the car to piece myself back together. Ending things with Andrei was the right call, but it hurt. Even my magic was oddly subdued, as if it didn't know what to do with this heartache. But I couldn't allow myself to dwell on that. Too many people were depending on me to allow myself to fall apart now, no matter how much I wanted to.

"Head back to the bar and we'll meet you there." I told Mikhail and Magos. They both looked at me with stony expressions. "Please," I said, unable to make myself explain that I didn't have the energy to ride back in the car with all three of them. I would have sent Kalen off on his own if it had been an option. I don't know if it was the 'please' or what they saw in my expression but both of them vanished into mist.

"I'm sorry," Kalen said gently. "The wolf seemed like—"

"Don't," I cut him off. "You don't know anything about me and you sure as shit don't have the right to try and comfort me now. You didn't even meet me until a day ago, so just keep your condolences to yourself." I shoved Kalen aside and opened the driver's side door.

"We have met." The moment he said the words, I could tell he hadn't meant to. His mask snapped back into place, and his mouth formed a hard line. *Oh no you don't.*

"When?" I growled and slammed the door shut. I walked back to Kalen, only an inch separating us. "When?" I repeated, temper flaring. When he didn't answer, I shoved him hard. He took a step back and looked away from me. "When did you fucking meet me?" I shoved him again, and my magic snapped out around me. Blue fire ran down my arms as I shoved him once more.

His magic finally erupted out of him, and a slightly darker blue fire shot down his arms to clash into mine. He dropped the glamour he'd been holding and once again became something more. Something predatory. Obsidian eyes glared at me in frustration and annoyance.

"You were eight years old," he said stiffly. "The magic you'd inherited from Badb had already manifested and you'd been opening gateways for years. But no signs of my magic had made an appearance yet. It was a few days after your birthday, and I wanted to see you."

"The wood shack," I said tonelessly as the memory resurfaced. That was the moment my life had truly changed, even if I didn't understand it at the time. A few days after my eighth birthday, the rest of my magic had fully awakened. Cian and I had been playing in a wood shack behind our house that our parents used to store extra food. We were pretending it was a fort and having fun until Cian annoyed me. It was a normal enough occurrence, growing up we'd be as thick as thieves one minute and then at each others throats the next. But that day when I lost my temper, my devourer magic had erupted.

I swallowed as I remembered the look on my brother's face. He'd never admit it, but I'd scared the hell out of him that day. When the blue flames had spread down my arms, hungry and chaotic, I'd panicked. At the time I hadn't known what it was

221

or how to control it, I just knew I didn't want to hurt Cian. I'd managed to throw the fire at the wood shack and it exploded across our yard causing me to panic and run. I hadn't even thought about what I was doing, I'd just run blindly away from Cian and the destruction I'd caused. I'd felt so lost in that mad dash through the woods, thinking my parents would be furious at me for almost hurting my brother and destroying all the food they had stored. The forest had blurred as I'd run for miles and miles while sobbing before eventually stopping at a lake.

I'd scrubbed the tears off my face and was sitting there feeling completely lost when a traveling merchant had found me. He'd offered me some spare dried fruit and listened to me sob about how I'd gotten into a fight with my brother and had destroyed all our food for the winter.

By the end of it, he'd suggested I return home and explain what had happened. He was sure my parents cared more about my safety than some wooden shack and would be grateful to see me okay. He'd been right. My parents had been searching the woods trying to find me and were relieved when I came home. They were concerned about my magic, but they hadn't been angry with me at all.

"You were the merchant." I stared at him in disbelief.

Kalen nodded slowly. "You were so upset and frightened. No one was around to comfort you and I couldn't stay away, so I took the chance. I told your mother, Badb, I mean, what I had done, but no one else knew."

"Did she ever. . ."

He swallowed and gazed off into the distance. "She used to run with you when you were younger. Her scent was different, but she appeared the same as her sister in feline form. You never noticed the difference."

"Why?" My voice cracked, and I forced myself to take a few measured breaths. "Why the deception?"

Kalen looked back at me with those impenetrable black

eyes. I refused to look away despite how unsettling they were. I was used to all-black daemon eyes, like Zareen's. But hers were different somehow, more expressive. I understood why when people spoke of the Erlking, they did it with hushed whispers, as if saying his name were enough to make him appear. He stared at me now with the full force of his power, and I raised my chin and stared back.

"How much do you know about how Badb and I met?"

"I know about her," I said. "I know about the shifter realm falling and her tearing open that gateway into the fae realm as revenge. About how that kicked off the war between the surviving shifters and the fae Queens. I know you were sent to kill her but apparently fell in love with her instead."

Kalen's expression softened slightly. "Your mother held my heart from the moment I saw her."

I didn't know how to react to his words or the love in his voice. This all felt so surreal and I didn't know how to process it, so I did what I always did and shut down my emotions as best I could. "I don't know anything about you. Aside from what I've heard about the Erlking. The loyal assassin of the fae Queens."

"It took some time and many experiments before Balor figured out how to warp the magic of the sidhe warriors and taint them with devourer magic. And then came the problem of getting them out of the realm they were trapped in. It was easier to get the creatures he experimented on out of the realm because the spell had been specifically crafted to contain fae. Getting out any sidhe took a lot of time and effort, and few made it through in the beginning. My father was one of the few."

"What was his mission?" I asked. "What was his purpose for being sent out of the realm?"

"To gather information and figure out a way to communicate back," Kalen replied. "Six of them were sent out, but two died in the process. The remaining four split up with an agreement to meet again in two months with whatever information they'd found. My father, however, had no interest in continuing with the plan. He'd served Balor because he was young and foolish, and then he'd been trapped with the rest of the army. Once he made it back to the fae realm, he simply wanted to live a normal life."

"Don't we all."

"He did for a while," Kalen said softly. "Even fell in love with a beautiful sidhe with ice magic named Shayla. They were both surprised when she became pregnant in less than a year. It usually takes years for a strong enough bond to form before pregnancy is possible."

"None of the other sidhe who had crossed over with him came looking for their wayward companion?"

"They did." Kalen gave me a feral grin. "My father had strong fire magic. Unusual among the fae, it was made even stronger with the devourer magic. He killed two of them, and my mother killed the other."

"Given how most of our family history has gone, I'm going to go out on a limb here and say there was no happy ending?" Most likely blood and ashes, I thought grimly.

"As I said before, the early experiments Balor did on the sidhe didn't work out well. My father and the others were the first to survive, but it wasn't perfect. He had to absorb the magic from others every few months to survive; otherwise, his devourer magic would attack his own fae magic. Balor seems to have corrected this in his later experiments. My father learned to deal with it, but what neither he nor my mother knew was that I would also have that problem."

I squeezed my eyes shut as I realized where this was going. "You started to absorb your mother's magic when you were still in the womb."

"Yes," Kalen confirmed. His tone was so even and calm,

like we weren't discussing him draining the life from his mother. "Neither of them realized it at first. They thought she was simply tired. But then her magic faded. My father was terrified at the idea of losing his love, so he convinced my mother to end the pregnancy. When they tried magical means of doing so . . . my magic simply absorbed it. They tried other means, but my magic was strong enough at that point to thwart their efforts. Not even halfway through the pregnancy, my mother was wasting away. It was clear she wouldn't survive, so they sought help from Shayla's cousin who was quite powerful, and one of the Queen's advisors. She was able to use the bond the two already had and adjust it so that my father's magic could support my mother, but she also told the Queens about his strange magic. My father was forced to tell the Queens about his history. By that point, both of my parents knew they weren't going to survive this. They bargained for the life of their child. My father would tell the Queens everything he knew about what their brother had been up to while in exile. And they would care for me."

A lingering sense of dread ran through me. For the longest time, I'd feared my magic because it felt so out of control. I'd been terrified I would lose it one day and kill someone I loved. It had been the reason I'd been so scared that day I destroyed the wood shack behind our house. At the time, I thought I had almost killed my brother. Now that I had a better under-standing of my magic, I was fairly certain it would never attack anyone I truly loved. But Kalen's father didn't have that luxury, and he'd had to live with the knowledge that the magic that made him powerful was the same magic that threatened those he loved most.

"What happened?" I asked softly, even though there was only one outcome.

"With the bond in place, I was able to feed not only on my mother's magic but also my father's," Kalen said, still managing to keep that even tone. "They both clung to life until Shayla gave birth. I took my first breath at the same moment my parents took their last."

"Our family history just gets more depressing the more I learn about it," I muttered.

"The Queens raised me. Or rather, those who served them raised me. The Seelie Queen, Áine, took the most interest in me, though. She made sure I was trained as I grew older, and I served her for centuries until I met your mother." Kalen paused for a moment. "I don't know who Áine hates more. Your mother for opening those gateways into the fae realm and surviving all of Áine's attacks or me for choosing your mother over the Queen I had served so loyally my entire life."

"This is the part where you tell me you abandoned me and lied to me my entire life to protect me, right?" I asked. Part of me understood this reasoning, but I was still pissed off about it. Especially given how things had played out.

"Your mother and I swore a blood oath to Queen Elvinia that we would never act against the interest of the Queens. And that we would never directly act in violence towards either of them. Áine wasn't happy with this agreement, but she couldn't do anything to stop it. She lost a lot of political points in the war she waged against your mother, and we were seen as an asset to have in the fae court. We made sure Badb's sister and her mate were protected in our agreement, and everything was fine for some time. Áine did her best to make our lives difficult, but she couldn't act directly against us. Then Badb became pregnant and we panicked. At first we panicked because we didn't know if it would be the same as when my mother was pregnant with me, and you would absorb Badb's magic. But you didn't. I kept waiting for Badb to grow weaker but your magic seemed to be dormant. But we still had the problem of hiding the pregnancy from the Queens. We were trying to figure that out when Macha sent news that she was also pregnant."

My heart stumbled at the mention of my mother's name. Macha might not have given birth to me, but she was my mother all the same. It had been centuries since her and my father's death, but I still missed them all the same. "Everyone always commented on how interesting it was for a shifter to have twins like me and Cian," I remarked.

"We took advantage of how little is known about the shifters," Kalen admitted. "No one could really question how rare or common it was for a shifter to have twins since there are so few left. We still don't know how or why Macha became pregnant so closely after Badb. If it was just luck or something more at play. But we used it to our advantage."

My magic remained wrapped around me, small patches of blue flame occasionally flickered across my skin. I was trying to keep my emotions under control but I was still wheeling from ending things with Andrei and even breathing felt difficult. Once we made it past the next few days, I'd get a bottle of whiskey, probably several bottles, and talk it out with Kaysea. I'd found out what I wanted to know. I'd have more questions later, but this was enough for now. Except for one final question.

"Why didn't you save them?" I barely said the words above a whisper, but he heard them and understood all the same.

"We didn't know." Kalen looked at me, and I realized I was wrong before about his eyes. They might be black and endless, but pain and regret were reflected there. He didn't try to hide it from me. I suspected I was one of the few people in the world he wouldn't hide this from. "By the time we found out, you and Cian were in the wind. Macha and Nevin were dead."

"How could you not know?" I asked, my voice hoarse.

"We don't know," Kalen said. "Macha and Nevin had ways

of contacting us if they ever needed to. They never did. We don't know why."

"Maybe if you'd been around more, you would have known something was wrong!" I snapped, and my magic flared around me in blue flames. Bits of the leaves in the trees above us burned and fell to the ground as ashes.

"We had to stay away!" Kalen growled, his magic erupting from him in dark blue flames. "Áine sent some of the Tuatha Dé Danann who were loyal to her sniffing around. We couldn't let them figure out the deception, so we had to keep our distance. I realize you are hurt by this and you have every right to be. But don't think for a second it didn't cost us. We loved you the moment you were born, and having to stay away from you felt like dying a little every day."

His words punched me in the gut, and my magic pulled itself back and sank inside me once more. "You might have felt like you were dying. But Macha and Nevin, my *real* parents, did die. And part of me wishes it had been you." I regretted the words the moment they slipped out. The mask of indifference Kalen usually wore once again slipped back into place. "We should head back," I said hoarsely and headed to the car, not waiting for a response.

I slid into the driver's seat. Kalen slowly walked to the car and we drove back to the bar in silence as I tried hard not to think of the flash of pain I'd seen in Kalen's eyes at my words. Or about the memory of the traveling merchant who had given me dried fruit and listened to every word I'd spoken, as if my voice were the most beautiful thing he'd ever heard.

Chapter Seventeen

W HEN WE SHUFFLED BACK into the meeting room at The Inferno, it was clear not much had changed while we'd been gone. The witch was still staring into Luna's eyes, neither of them moving, and Finn was still perched in his chair, holding onto Luna's paw. Bryn glanced at me as I walked in, and I waved at her in greeting before focusing on Pele. "How's it going?"

"Lestari should finish up any second now. She's carefully pulling her magic out of Luna's mind," Pele replied.

As if on cue, Lestari slammed back in her chair and let out a long jagged breath before sagging. Luna remained where she was, but turned her head to look at Finn. Whatever he saw in her eyes caused him to start crying quietly, and she immediately leapt onto his chest. He clutched her to him as silent tears continued to fall. Lestari watched both of them for a few seconds, her expression tired but showing hints of softness as she watched the sidhe child and grimalkin comfort each other. Slowly she stood and headed towards the door.

"You're leaving?" I asked in surprise.

"Even if I wanted to stay, I have about ten minutes before I pass out, and I likely won't wake up for a day or two. Pele already prepared a room for me." Lestari's dark eyes bore into me. "To be honest, I don't really want to stay. I'm glad I was able to help the grimalkin, but I saw bits of her memories as I worked my magic. All of you are wading into some dangerous waters, and I don't want any part of it. There's enough going on between witches and warlocks without me getting mixed up in fae nonsense."

"Thank you for your help in this," I said, bowing my head in appreciation. "When you are rested, there are some things you should know that involve the warlocks, specifically the Circle. Perhaps you can warn other witches who may be acting against them. I understand if you don't want to see me again. Pele can pass on the information to you."

"I'll speak with you again, Nemain," Lestari said, surprising me. "Do try to not kill any more witches between now and then." Message and warning delivered, Lestari left the room.

The corner of my lips tugged up in a small smile. It hadn't escaped my notice that she'd said nothing about killing warlocks.

Low murmured greetings sounded from outside the hallway, followed by a familiar soft laugh. The door swung open, revealing Kaysea. I scanned the mermaid up and down as she entered the room, looking for any signs of her previous injury, but she moved with her usual fae grace. Between Zareen's healing and her return trip to the water, she seemed to be completely healed. Some tension I didn't realize I'd been carrying eased out of me.

Kaysea smiled. "I'm fine, Nemain. My magic isn't fully back yet, but it will be in a few days." She looked at where Finn was still holding Luna tightly to him. "I ran into the witch on my way in. Did it work? Does Luna have her memories back?"

"Yes. We're giving Finn and Luna a moment to process

everything." Lowering my voice, I asked, "Did you find anything else out when you were back in your realm?"

Kaysea's eyes darkened. "Yes. Bryn should hear this. We can decide how much to tell Finn after he and Luna catch up."

I caught Bryn's attention and waved her over. Reluctantly, she left Finn's side and walked over to us, keeping her wings carefully tucked in.

"What is it?" Bryn asked as she joined our group.

"Kaysea has something she wants to share with us," I said. Mikhail, Magos, and Eddie remained where they were, leaning against the wall next to the door. They'd be able to hear everything we said, even if whispered. Pele moved closer to us, but Jinx remained on the table, all of his focus on Luna. Only his ears twitching to the side told me he was also monitoring our conversation. Kalen stood slightly behind me. I could feel his attention on me, but I continued to ignore him because I was mature like that.

"I learned two things actually," Kaysea said, her delicate features tightening in concern. "As soon as I returned home, Connor found me. The new ruler of Tír fo Thuinn, Queen Ashling, already knows about you, Bryn. She knows you're a valkyrie and bonded to Finn. She knows the prophecy as well."

"How?" Pele cut in. "All of you came straight home from the fae realm after retrieving Finn. Unless Ashling is working with the enemy, how did she learn this so fast?"

"I don't know," Kaysea replied. "But knowing stuff like this before anyone else has basically been her job for the past several decades. She investigated and handled all potential and existing security threats to our realm. She must have an inner circle she relies on, but I don't know who they are. I don't even think my parents know. Ashling is a strong believer in keeping all her cards close to her chest."

"What did she say exactly? Do we need to worry about her?" I asked.

"Anyone would be a fool not to worry about Ashling," Kaysea said. "But I don't think she's working with Balor or any of his allies. In true Ashling form, her words were vague, but I think she was trying to give me both a warning and some advice."

"A warning about what?" Bryn asked, glancing over her shoulder at Finn.

"About you actually, well, specifically your bonding with Finn." Bryn's golden wings rustled as she turned sharply back to Kaysea. "I know you don't know much about the valkyries and we haven't had much time to fully explain everything to you, but valkyries have their own form of magic. They also get magic from whatever being they're bonded with. The stronger the being, the stronger a valkyrie will be." Kaysea swallowed. "According to Ashling, there is no record of a valkyrie ever bonding with a fae. Finn is likely the most powerful sidhe to ever exist, which likely means Bryn is the most powerful valkyrie to ever exist. Ashling didn't seem concerned about this, but she could have simply been hiding any misgivings about the situation. But this could cause problems with the rest of the fae. And we have no idea how the realms of Yggdrasil will react when they learn of this."

"What about the daemons?" I asked Pele.

She stared at the wall as she thought through her answer. "No one from the Assembly will outwardly voice any serious concerns. But there are some I'll need to monitor and see what they try to do when they think no one is watching."

"Will the other valkyries come after me?" Bryn frowned. "Or Finn?"

I sighed. "The valkyries are . . . complicated. I know of one who can help us navigate this. Her name is Sigrun. She's lived outside of the Yggdrasil realms and apart from the rest of the valkyries for a long time. She has her own history with them, but that's hers to tell. I'll reach out to her once we make it through our immediate problems." Sigrun and I weren't friends exactly, but we had a good working relationship, and she'd be willing to help Bryn once I explained the situation. "What was the advice Ashling gave you?"

"It was more of a gentle suggestion," Kaysea said. "There is a cavern underneath the royal castle with some mystical qualities. No one really understands how it works, but miles and miles of tunnels run through it. It's not a nice place." Kaysea shivered. "Its magic seeps into you, and the longer you're in it, the more it feels like claws tearing your mind apart. But in the process, sometimes it will give you glances of what you seek. I concentrated hard on Finn as I swam through it and opened myself to its magic." The color from Kaysea's face drained and she wrapped her arms around herself.

"What did you see?" I asked.

"I saw a world in which you fail to change Finn's fate." A distressed look spread across Kaysea's delicate features. "I saw what he can do with his magic and where that dark path leads." None of us spoke as we waited for Kaysea to finish. "Finn can merge realms together. Not just open gateways between them, but literally merge them together. I saw him merge the devourer realms with the human, fae, and daemon realms. It was the end of the realms as we know them."

All of us stood there in shocked silence. In the past, every time a Cataclysm had occurred, a gateway had opened between a devourer realm and another realm. The loss of life had been horrific. Entire realms had fallen to the devourers, and that was from only a few gateways opening. If Finn could merge realms together . . . no one would survive.

Luna is ready to talk, Jinx said. I nodded and said to the others, "Let's hear what Luna has to say. Then we'll figure out what to do next." I looked at Bryn, who appeared shaken from Kaysea's news. "We will not fail Finn," I said firmly. "What

Kaysea saw isn't set in stone. I won't let Finn go down that path."

She nodded gravely, and we all took our seats at the table, Bryn returning to her position standing by Finn's side.

Once we were settled, Luna gracefully leapt off Finn and back onto the table. Jinx immediately went to her side, and I could see the uncertainty in his movements. My friend was deeply in love with Luna, and he was probably not sure where they stood now that she had all of her memories back. Luna gently bumped her head against his. *I still love you, you grumpy fool.*

Relief flashed in Jinx's golden eyes as he bumped his head against Luna.

"Jinx and Luna sitting in a tree. . ." I sang softly. Eddie and Mikhail chuckled quietly. Jinx glared at me, and Luna just gave me an exasperated look.

"All right, Luna," Pele said, getting straight to business. "What can you tell us?"

While the Queens and most of the Tuatha Dé Danann trusted Siofra, a few remained suspicious of her. Among those were my mother and a sidhe friend of hers, Lyra. Luna's voice softened at the mention of the fae's name. *Lyra was a sidhe, but her magic wasn't particularly strong, so she was often overlooked. Siofra was always good at manipulating others. She saw Lyra at court one day and befriended her, no doubt thinking she could use Lyra for her own purposes. But Lyra and my mother had planned this out, hoping it would play out like that. Lyra pretended to be upset over constantly being dismissed by others in the fae court and thus thankful for Siofra paying attention to her.*

At the time, I was young, barely entering my third decade. I wanted to help, and after some convincing, my mother finally agreed to let me be involved. We orchestrated several public fights, and I spent more time with Lyra, loudly complaining about my mother and others at the court. This went on for several decades, but eventually Lyra and I were part of Siofra's circle. She never fully trusted us. I don't think she trusts anyone except

Balor and some of his closest friends. But when the time came for Siofra to rejoin her mate in the exiled realm, we went with her.

Your mother agreed to let you go? Jinx asked. He had been younger than Luna when his own mother had sent him to stay with me. While Luna had pushed her mother to let her do this, it had been Jinx's mother who had decided his fate. Jinx had agreed to do what his mother had asked of him, but part of me always wondered if he would have been so agreeable if he'd been a little older and more aware of what his mother had truly been asking.

She didn't know, Luna replied. *Siofra didn't give us any warning. She just asked us to come with her and said to bring anything we cared about. Lyra and I both suspected where she was taking us, and Lyra told me she'd understand if I didn't want to go. But by then . . . Lyra was my friend, and she was still committed to this path. I couldn't let her face it alone.*

"What did the two of you think to accomplish by going to an exiled realm?" Kalen arched an eyebrow at Luna. "No offense, but you had to have known you'd be cut off once you were there, so it's not like you could have sent back any useful information."

We thought it was worth the risk. It seemed unlikely Siofra would go to join her mate in exile without some sort of plan in place to return to the fae realms. So we went with Siofra, and I left a message for my mother, letting her know what was happening. Lyra and I had been keeping her informed of the small bits of information we'd gleaned over the years, so we had a system in place for message drop-offs. I wish I could have seen her one last time before I left. I don't know if she's still alive.

What was her name? Jinx asked gently.

Carina.

As soon as we can, I'll ask my mother about her. Given my mother's level of plotting, she likely knew your mother.

Thank you. Luna leaned against Jinx, and he rubbed his head against her.

"What was it like there?" I asked.

Harsh, Luna said with a humorless laugh. *Both the environment and the fae who were trapped there. Lyra and I did our best to be useful to Siofra without seeming too interested in what she and Balor were planning. Balor himself, well, he's terrifying. I practically grew up around the Tuatha Dé Danann, and they're considered the most powerful of the sidhe aside from the Queens themselves. They're nothing compared to Balor. He has a presence about him. When he looks at you, it's like he can see right through to your soul. It's unsettling. His second-in-command, Lir, is also quite frightening.*

I wrinkled my nose at the mention of Lir. Our lives would have been so much easier if we'd killed him back in the fae realm.

We were able to gather information about what Balor and Siofra were plotting. In addition to the experimentations they were conducting to create different kinds of devourers, they were also trying to figure out how to break the ward around the realm. The Queens knew they had to focus the power of the ward, so besides being self-healing and having the ability to absorb any magic thrown at it, the ward is more sensitive to the magic of some individuals. Balor is at the top of that list, followed by the most powerful in his inner circle and then trickling down from there. That's why it's easier for Balor to send out the creatures he makes from other realms and those who aren't in the top tier of his soldiers. Being tainted with devourer magic is also necessary to slip through the ward.

"How did Lir get out, then? He's basically Balor's right-hand guy." I frowned. Lir had clearly been changed with devourer magic, but he was still dripping with some serious fae magic, and as part of Balor's inner circle, the ward should have kept him locked in that realm.

Balor was always crafty. Even before he was exiled, he was suspicious of his sisters. Lir only held the position of a common foot soldier in his army. Nobody knew he was, in fact, the general, so he was never specifically targeted by the ward. It likely took them a long time to get him through the realm, though, because of how much magic he has. I don't think anyone else with his level of magic has successfully made it through.

I grimaced. It was bad enough Balor had powerful magic, but he was clearly smart and cunning as well. The Queens might have been able to outsmart him enough to get him trapped in a realm, but who knew what other surprises he had in store. I would have preferred to be dealing with a dumb brute, but that was clearly asking too much. I looked at Finn to see how he was taking all of this and found him wearing what I was starting to assume was his default expression, solemn and touched with sadness. He seemed so lost and alone. Anger surged in me, and blue flames flickered briefly across my fingers. It wasn't fair that Finn had been born into this. I would do everything I could to protect him going forward, but I could do only so much against the legacy that would follow him.

Luna saw the expression on my face and followed my gaze to Finn. Magic sparked from her, as she no doubt felt the same as me. *Everyone was surprised when Siofra announced she was pregnant. No one doubted the love and devotion between Balor and Siofra. They might be twisted and cruel, but their love is real. It was just strange that centuries went by without any hints of there being a child. Siofra did delay the pregnancy for years, and when Finn was born. . .* Luna's bright lavender eyes darkened. *I'll never forget the way they looked at Finn the night he was born. It wasn't love I saw in their eyes. It was satisfaction and victory.*

"How much magic did he have the night he was born?" Pele asked.

I wasn't sure where she was going with that, but whatever she was thinking, I could tell she didn't like it based on her tight expression. Kalen's face held a similar expression. My eyebrows bunched together as I tried to figure out what was disturbing them so much. We all knew Finn's parents wanted to use him to break free of the realm.

Finn had more magic the night he was born than many sidhe will have in their entire life. I have no proof, but I suspect Siofra and Balor did something to make Finn as powerful as he is.

Finn shifted uncomfortably, and Bryn moved closer and wrapped one of her wings slightly around the boy.

At first, Lyra and I thought they wanted to use Finn to eventually undo the ward as he truly came into his power. Given how much power he had at birth, it seemed likely Finn would surpass even his father in terms of power. Siofra studied the magic of the ward constantly, and Balor tested out several spells to unravel the ward. He didn't have enough power to make it work, but Finn probably would. It would take a decade or more for Finn's power to truly settle and for him to have control over it. But we thought given how long Balor had been trapped, they were more than willing to wait. We were fools. And we'd forgotten about the ability that made Balor so dangerous.

I was racking my brain trying to remember what Kalen had told us about Balor's abilities when Finn spoke, his voice completely calm. "He was going to absorb my magic."

Emotions raged in the room, shifting between anger, disgust, and disbelief. It was one thing to be told an enemy was cruel and without mercy. It was another to find out they would act that way against their own child. Luna squeezed her eyes shut at Finn's words. *How long have you known?*

Finn reached out and gently stroked her back as he gave her a small smile. "I overheard you and Lyra discussing it a year ago when you were trying to figure out how long we had. You thought they'd wait until I was at least in my third decade. Lyra thought we couldn't afford to take the chance."

Lyra was right. It became clear they didn't plan on waiting long. In truth, neither Balor nor Siofra spent much time with Finn. They left me and Lyra to raise him and would only check in on him every few weeks to see how his magic was developing.

"That's all kinds of fucked up," Eddie said with a shake of his head.

"Language!" Bryn barked and glared at him.

Eddie just stared at her in disbelief, and I couldn't help but laugh. Given the grim topic we were on, it seemed a little ridiculous to be worried about profanity. But the normalcy of it helped bring down the tension in the room.

We'd been studying how Balor was able to break through the ward in small bursts to send out the creatures he'd made or the devourer sidhe hybrids. Neither of us was powerful enough to do it, but we were confident we could instruct Finn on how to make a tear. We were still deciding when to do it when Lir came for Finn. We'd run out of time. Lyra attacked Lir and managed to beat him only because he hadn't been expecting it.

Still, all she'd managed to do was wound him. We only had minutes before he recovered or other guards came at the sound of the commotion, so we instructed Finn on what to do. A sacrifice is needed to make a tear in the ward; otherwise, it will simply absorb the magic of whoever is making the tear. I fed the ward my magic while Finn ripped open a hole. Lir woke as we were almost done and tried to stop us.

Lyra tried to fight him off, and he wounded her. I thought I saw her lunge for the hole in the realm that Finn had made, but I lost consciousness at that point. When I woke in the forest in that fae realm, I was alone without any magic or memories about who I was or how I'd gotten there. I just knew a part of me was missing.

Finn continued to stroke Luna's back in comfort. "I tried to hold on to you when we stepped through the tear, but I lost my grip. I don't know if Lyra made it through or not. She might still be trapped there."

Gods willing, she was dead and they hadn't been torturing her this entire time, I thought darkly. "We'll try to find out what happened to Lyra," I told Finn.

"What's our next move?" Bryn asked.

"It's time for us to meet the fae Queens," I replied.

Chapter Eighteen

"ALL RIGHT, FEARLESS LEADER," Eddie said around a mouthful of leftover pizza he'd found in our fridge. "What's our plan?"

I leaned both of my elbows on the kitchen counter as Kaysea reached across Eddie to snag a piece of pizza. We'd reconvened at my apartment to plan our next steps. Luna was exhausted and needed to rest, and the apartment with all its wards made the most sense to use as our home base. "We need to meet with the fae Queens. They are not only an immediate threat, but we'll need them on our side in the long run."

"I'm surprised we haven't heard anything from them yet," Pele said, nibbling on some leftover crust. "Aside from sending him, I mean." She jerked her head towards Kalen.

"Funny you should say that," I started, and Pele narrowed her eyes at me. "Some sidhe warriors showed up when we went to check on Andrei. They blocked any calls from being received on the mirror to draw me out. Queen Áine sent them, unofficially of course, with orders to capture me and bring me to the Seelie court. We were able to take all of them out, but Áine isn't going to stop. She's going to continue coming after me and Finn. Dealing with the unofficial attempts will be hard enough, but sooner or later they'll make some official requests. And those we won't be able to ignore."

"You can't bring Finn to them!" Bryn said quickly in alarm. "We can't trust them. And I won't be parted from him."

"You're right," I said calmly and held my hands out to her, palms outstretched. "You, Finn, and Luna are staying here."

Bryn nodded in obvious relief before her eyebrows bunched together in concern. "What about you, though? Is it safe for you to meet with them?"

"Kalen is arranging safe passage for me now. By tradition, I'm allowed to bring two beings with me for support." I avoided looking at Magos and Mikhail even as I felt their frustrated glares. "Eddie and Jinx will come with me. While Jinx has spent most of his time in the human realm with me, he still knows quite a bit about the fae realms, and he's good at sneaking around unseen in case we need to do some spying. And Eddie has proven himself useful at working around fae magic."

"We'll stay here with you," Magos told Bryn. "The wards around this building are strong, and Mikhail and I can deal with most things that may come our way. If we need to, I can reach out to Nemain's brother, Cian, and we can retreat to the death realm where he lives with Dante."

Mikhail fumed silently beside his uncle, a storm flaring in his dark eyes. We'd had an epic fight about this earlier while we waited for Eddie, Kaysea, and Pele to arrive from the bar.

"Finn will be safe here with all of you," I said. "Kaysea and Pele are both going home to their realms. If anything goes wrong, if the Queens try to hold us prisoner, Kaysea and Pele will use whatever political power they need to get us out."

The apartment door slammed open, and Isabeau marched in holding several DVDs. "We're going to do a movie night, Finn! We can watch all the Jurassic Park movies!" She stopped abruptly and looked at the TV in our living room. Isabeau wrinkled her nose and spun around to march back out the door. "Our TV is bigger downstairs, so you all should come down there."

Elisa crashed through the front door in time to move out of the way of Isabeau as she bulldozed her way out of the apartment. Elisa let out a long breath. "You'll probably want to make your way downstairs soon. She doesn't like it when people are late for movie night, and I don't want to listen to it."

"Go downstairs." I waved towards the door. "We're going to leave in a few minutes."

Finn looked at the front door where Isabeau had passed through only seconds before and trailed after her.

Bryn looked at me worriedly. "Please be careful and let us know as soon as you have any updates."

I nodded at her, and she and Elisa headed downstairs. Luna walked over to Jinx. I couldn't hear whatever they were saying to each other, but I didn't tease them this time. I was happy my friend had found someone, and I would do everything I could to get Jinx back here safely to Luna. While I was talking to the Queens, Jinx was going to try and find his mother. She owed us some answers, and she might know something about Luna's mother as well.

"I'm going to head back to the bar," Pele said. "Contact me immediately once you have an update. I'll give you a few hours to get settled once you're there, but if I don't have an update, I'll start putting my plans in motion."

I nodded. At the moment, the daemons weren't involved in this, but they would be if they learned the true history of the devourers and who Finn really was. Ideally, we wanted to avoid that for as long as possible. It was hard to predict what the daemons would do once they learned of Balor's and Finn's existence. I needed to bargain for Finn's freedom and safety with the fae Queens first and then do something similar with the daemons. Sooner or later they would know the full history.

Kaysea rose from where she'd been lounging on the sofa. "I'm going to head back as well. I'll reach out to Pele if I over-hear anything related to your presence in the fae Queens' courts." Luna followed after Pele and Kaysea, heading to the downstairs apartment.

Magos strode over, studying the weapons I'd strapped to myself. "I'll be fine," I told him with a grin. "I'm going to talk to the Queens, not declare war on them."

The concern on Magos's face blossomed into all-out worry.

Mikhail slung an arm around his uncle's shoulder. "Don't worry, Uncle. Eddie and Jinx can smooth over anything sharp our lovely Nemain says."

Magos let out a long breath. "Add some throwing daggers into your boots, just in case." He left, leaving me with Mikhail, Eddie, and Jinx.

Mikhail walked over to our storage chest against the weapons wall and pulled out two slender daggers. I held still as he knelt in front of me, suddenly very aware of my own heart-beat. He ran a hand down the back of my leg. Even through the fabric, I felt the heat of his touch. He carefully slid the dagger into the built-in sheath inside my boot and repeated the gesture with my other leg before rising to stand in front of me. Mere inches separated us. Something sparked in Mikhail's twilight eyes, and I swallowed.

"There's something you should know, Nemain." The way he said my name should be illegal because every thought emptied out of my head. "If you don't come back, I'm not going to bother taking over the second-floor apartment. I will, however, take over your room. And all your weapons."

What?

Eddie choked on a laugh as Mikhail took a step back.

"You go near my room, and I will cut you into pieces and feed you to my plant," I ground out.

"Are you sure you don't want me in your room?" Mikhail gave me a wicked smile.

"We're leaving," I snapped and stretched out my hand to open a gateway. I'd never opened one in this particular area before, but Kalen had been able to project the image into my mind, so I found it easily enough. We strode through the gateway, and I slammed it closed behind us before Mikhail could add any more commentary.

"Welcome to the castle of the fae Queens, everyone," I announced. "Let's try not to die."

"It will probably take me a few hours to finish getting everything arranged, but you'll be safe in these rooms," Kalen said as we all took in our surroundings. The palace of the fae Queens was a far cry from the small towns and wilderness we'd been traveling in.

We were currently in the sitting room, and I could see two bedrooms on one side of the room and double doors, likely leading to another room on the other side. Elegant but comfortable looking chairs were in the center of the room around a glass table. Beneath the table was a large potted box that held orchids and some other plants I didn't recognize; some of the flowers were closed up now, but I suspected they would open during the day when the sunlight filtered in through the large skylight. Dainty vines grew up the walls of the room. Overall, this room was much more enclosed than the buildings we'd been in previously, which wasn't surprising considering the size of the castle. But even here, nature was an important part of the overall design.

"There's another room through here." Kalen walked over to the double doors and slid them open.

Out of curiosity, I went in to take a look. "These are guest rooms?" I asked in disbelief. A large canopy bed was placed in one corner of the room. A few chairs were arranged in front of an ornate stone fireplace. But what really caught my attention was the large freaking swimming pool taking up a third of the room. The water was crystal clear, and flowering lilies glided across the top, giving off a pleasant scent. Stone steps led down to the water, and several seats had been carefully carved out of the stone. I knelt and dipped my fingers in the water, not surprised to find it warm.

"It's the palace of the Queens. What were you expecting?" Kalen asked dryly.

"Are you sure we're safe in these rooms?"

Kalen's jaw hardened slightly. "You're not safe anywhere in the Queens' castle. Or the fae realms, for that matter. Never forget that."

I rolled my eyes. "Okay, let me rephrase that. How long will it take for the Seelie Queen to learn we're in these exact rooms?"

"You've officially been granted safe passage here in this realm, but there is no reason to tempt fate. As long as you don't leave these rooms, she shouldn't learn of your presence here. No one has a reason to be in these rooms, so no servants will come here to clean or anything. You'll have to make do without food for a few hours." Kalen gave me a sly look. "And cheap whiskey."

"Okay, Judgy McJudgy Pants."

"Don't cause any trouble. I'll be back as soon as I can."

I scrutinized the room a little more and checked the stone walls for any obvious hidden passages. I didn't find any, but that didn't mean there weren't some here. They were likely hidden behind a glamour I just wasn't sensing.

Once I was satisfied with my initial security check, I walked over to the pool and pulled my boots off and rolled my pants up. I plopped down and dangled my feet into the water and sighed. I wished I had the space for a large swimming pool in my apartment. I was a short drive from the beach, but the water along the Washington coast was cold and the waves were rough. Emerald Bay was a convenient place for us to stay, but I missed having a nice river or warm ocean to swim in. I didn't even have a tub in the apartment, only a shower.

"Think the Queens will let me visit once this is over just so I can use this room?" I asked Eddie and Jinx as they took a seat on either side of me. Like me, Eddie had removed his shoes and rolled up his pants so he could splash his feet in the water. Jinx just glared at the water with distaste.

I'm going to set out to find my mother. You stay here and splash around in the dirty water with your stinky feet.

It's not dirty! I lifted my feet out of the water and watched the clear water drip off them.

You really think your gross feet are the first feet to splash around in it? Jinx turned and held his tail up high as he sauntered out of the room.

Be careful! I told him. He just flicked his tail in response. I sighed and gently pushed a lily away with my toes.

Eddie grunted. "We should have brought the whiskey. Might take a nap for a bit or see if there's anything in these rooms worth stealing. Have you seen any—"

Eddie stopped abruptly as a section of the pool darkened. We both stared at it, and a flicker of something moving underwater caught my eye. I jerked my feet out of the water but wasn't fast enough. A thick vine lashed out, wrapping around my ankle, and yanked me into the water. Eddie grabbed onto my outstretched arms, but whatever had a hold of me was too strong and he got pulled in as well. I tried to kick my way free, but we were pulled in deeper, which didn't seem possible because the pool simply wasn't this deep.

The water turned an inky black around us. Eddie's amber eyes glowed, and something jerked me hard around the waist.

If I'd been thinking clearly, I would have let go of Eddie so at least he had a chance to get away, but we both remained clamped onto each other and he came along for the ride.

A few seconds later, both of us were flung out of the water. I landed hard on a stone floor and coughed up a bunch of water while listening to Eddie do the same. Once I no longer felt like my lungs were flooded, I looked around to figure out where the hell we were. It was a circular room with nothing in it except the small pool of water in the center that we'd been thrown out of. Unlike the inviting pool in my room, this water was black and foreboding. If I stared at it long enough, I could see the tendrils of something moving underneath the surface.

I walked over to the stone wall and laid my hand against it, jerking it back quickly. Pulling some of my magic out, I threw a ball of blue flame at the wall. Instead of making a chunk of the wall explode, the flame splashed harmlessly across the stone, and my magic soaked into it. As if to mock us, the room had no roof. The night sky was clear above us, but there would be no climbing up these walls or breaking through them with magic. Who had brought us here?

The stone scraped behind me as Eddie rose to his feet. "You know Jinx is going to say I told you so about the swimming pool, right?"

"My vote is we make it back before he does and we just don't mention this to him."

A section of the stone wall slid away, and a sidhe strolled in. "Oh, you won't be going anywhere anytime soon, I'm afraid," the sidhe said in a rich musical voice. She wore a dark red tunic that played off her rich brown skin beautifully. Her hair spilled over her shoulders and down to her waist. Between the loose hair and the lack of weapons, she clearly wasn't a warrior.

She gave me a small smile and let some of her magic out. I gritted my teeth at the sudden onslaught, and she pulled it back. I'd bet my life she was Tuatha Dé Danann. Which meant she served one of the Queens directly.

"Seelie or Unseelie?" I asked. I didn't bother to pull either of my swords out. If she moved to attack us, I'd use my magic. With only Eddie with me, I could let it loose and direct it at her. It pulsed under my skin, eager to come out and play.

"Seelie." She smiled brightly. "I had originally asked for the task of bringing you here, but Queen Áine wanted to give those two sycophants a chance. I didn't push it because I knew they'd fail. And even better, you took them out for me. I do love it when things work out my way without even having to work for it."

"So happy to oblige. What do you want from me?"

"Me?" She placed a hand against her heart and gave me a surprised look. "Oh, I don't want anything from you. We just need you out of the way so we can get to the boy."

"Does Elvinia know what her sister is up to? Methinks she's not going to be too happy about Áine going behind her back like this. Kalen is in the process of arranging a meeting with them as we speak."

"There's no proof that the Seelie Queen had anything to do with your disappearance. In fact, it seems more likely that Balor's followers got to you first. All the more reason for the boy to be brought to the Queens. For his own safety, of course." A smug smile spread across the sidhe's face. "Both of you will remain our guests here for now until we decide what to do with you. Maybe you'll turn out to be useful down the line. Do enjoy your stay."

She waved at us and turned to head back to the opening in the wall. Blue fire burst from my hand, and I hurled my magic at her. The flame went right through her and splashed across the wall before being absorbed. Her image faded from sight, but her musical laugh echoed through the room. She had projected an illusion of herself. I'd heard some of the Tuatha

Dé Danann could do that. I just had no idea it'd be so real. Even her magic had felt real. If the Tuatha Dé Danann had power like that, I couldn't imagine what the Queens were like. Or Balor.

"Well, that's just fantastic." Eddie walked over to study the wall.

I went back to the water and knelt down beside it. I swiped my hand across the water and waited. A head with smooth, rubbery skin rose from the black water. A bright orange eye focused on me, blinked once, and sank back under the water. Yep. Not going in the water. I glanced up at the night sky and didn't see anything blocking access to the outside. No rocks appeared to be loose, so I let my magic stretch out towards where a roof would be. Nothing. No magic traces at all. Finally, I flung some fire up at it and watched it shoot well past the upper walls of the room and into the inky black night before disappearing.

"Looks like up is the only way out," I said.

"Great, want me to throw you?" Eddie asked as he stared up at the sky in frustration. I was pretty sure his frustration went beyond our current circumstances. It held a longing in it.

I took a deep breath. Here's hoping my suspicions were right. "Sure would be nice if one of us could fly out of here," I said and looked down from the sky that promised freedom to Eddie.

His amber eyes glowed, and I caught the faint smell of smoke.

I flashed a toothy grin at him. "Why don't you tell me about your performance issues, dragon?"

"I was wondering when you'd figure it out," he said flatly as he let his usual friendly, easygoing mask drop, and the predator came out. "Does Pele suspect as well?"

"Not that I'm aware of." I shrugged. "Haven't shared my suspicions with anyone else. It's Pele though. She won't care. I mean, she doesn't care that I'm part devourer. She was more upset with me for not telling her a long time ago."

"Slight difference here, cat. Dragons preyed on daemons for thousands of years before daemons were finally able to turn the tables."

"About that." I tapped a finger on my bottom lip. "Aren't y'all supposed to be extinct? Thought the daemons wiped all of you out?"

"Like daemons ever make anything that easy." Eddie let out a low laugh that set my instincts on edge. "They trapped most of the dragons in the original realm both of our species were born in. The dragons caught in other realms were publicly hunted down and executed. They let everyone believe the dragons were dead, and it immediately made the daemons one of the major players with magic. Put them on par with the fae."

"So why were you exiled?" The image of blazing green eyes and fiery red hair surfaced in my mind. "The painting of the woman in your office. This has to do with her?"

"Cerridwyn." He spoke the name with so much love and longing it pained me even before the echo of those emotions appeared in his eyes. "She's the daughter of the most powerful dragon of the older generation. We fell in love ages ago and kept it a secret because we knew he wouldn't approve. To break us apart, he convinced the other elder dragons to exile me from the realm. In a bid to protect me, Cerridwyn put a spell on me that bound my dragon nature so I wouldn't immediately be detected and captured by the daemons. Unfortunately, I haven't been able to figure out how to break it, and it blocks me from not only shifting but accessing most of my magic."

I moved towards him and let my magic out a bit. "It was a binding spell?"

He nodded and narrowed his eyes at me, no doubt seeing my magic flickering around me.

"May I?" I asked and hovered my hand in front of his chest.

Those burnt amber eyes studied me for a moment, and he gave me another slow nod. Carefully, I let my magic seep inside him. I'd only done this a few times before, and it took a lot of concentration. Letting my magic go to town and devour any magic it encountered was easy. But making it leave most of the magic alone and only target one aspect of it was something else altogether.

I squeezed my eyes shut as I concentrated. Instead of pushing my magic, I let it continue to slowly spread. Eddie's magic felt like coals that were still smoldering but were so close to being put out completely. Muscles shifted underneath my hand, but Eddie didn't say anything as I continued to search. Finally, I came across a foreign bit of magic.

"There you are," I murmured and let my magic poke at it a little more. Eddie's sharp intake of breath made me pull my magic back a bit. "Sorry. I think I found the binding, though."

"Can you remove it?"

"Yes. . ." I said, my voice unsure. "But you should know I've never actually done this before. I've been practicing letting my magic wrap around magical objects, and then pulling back without absorbing their magic. But I've never tried to let my magic devour a small amount of magic while leaving the rest of the magic alone."

Eddie's warm hand covered mine, and I opened my eyes to meet his stare. "I trust you," he said seriously, and his eyes held no doubt. "Besides, the fae Queen might find a use for you, but it's unlikely she'll find a use for me. Other than torturing me to get to you. Rather die horribly by your hand than horribly by that bitch's hand."

"Thanks," I said with a wry smile. "Here we go."

I pushed my intention towards my magic. I'd been working on this with Kaysea. Once we'd figured out that in addition to being part shifter and devourer, I was also likely part fae, Kaysea had been working with me on how to interact with my magic. Most beings interacted with magic as if it were a tool, but to the fae, magic was sentient. Or at least close enough to being sentient that it didn't matter calling it anything else.

It was why the fae had to be careful about the words they spoke. It wasn't that the fae couldn't lie; their words were laced with magic, and if they promised one thing but did another, their magic could backfire on them. It was why my magic had been so out of control for most of my life. I'd been keeping it wrapped in chains and treating it like a monster, so that's what it had acted like. I was learning how to interact with it respectfully and without making it feel trapped. I was making progress, but this was still far beyond anything I'd attempted before. I really hoped I didn't turn my friend into a pile of ashes ringed with frost.

Only the binding, I whispered to my magic. *Nothing more.* I repeated those words over and over while nudging the magic towards the cold band within Eddie. Slowly and gently, my magic wrapped around the band and took a nibble. It was such a small amount of magic that I barely felt it. Part of me instantly missed the influx of magic I usually got when I let my magic devour that of others, and blue flames shot from my arms and covered Eddie.

"Nemain. . ." He growled but held still as the flames licked across his skin but didn't burn him or take any of his magic.

"Sorry! Sorry!" I yelped and repeated my chant. *Only the binding. Nothing more.*

The flames slowly flowed off Eddie and back onto my arms and across my shoulders. I let out a sigh of relief and felt the binding crumble away. Instead of pushing more magic towards it, I waited patiently for the small amount of magic I'd directed towards the binding to finish devouring it. Sweat dripped down my face, and I shook it out of my eyes. A minute later, the binding vanished and the small embers of Eddie's magic erupted.

I stumbled back, and my magic wrapped around me as Eddie exploded into bright yellow and orange flames. A deep laugh spilled out of him as the flames grew brighter. I took a few more steps back and raised my hand to block my eyes from the brightness. I felt another wave of heat and slowly lowered my arm. And looked up . . . and up . . . and up. . .

"Damn, Eddie," I said with a whistle.

Told you I was amazing. Eddie's voice rumbled through my head.

"Now I understand why your telepathic voice sounds so much deeper and larger than your normal voice. Your dragon form is just a tad bit bigger than I expected." I took another step back to get a better view of Eddie's dragon form.

Standing on all fours, he was easily over twenty feet tall and probably close to sixty feet long once you included his long tail, which had to curl around his body due to the limited space.

"Not as bulky as I thought you'd be, though," I said thoughtfully. His body was pretty sleek and resembled a feline build. Despite his size, I could see how he would be agile on both the ground and in the air. His black scales had an iridescent quality to them that I suspected would be quite beautiful in the sunlight. His amber eyes looked even brighter in this form, as if they were lit from a fire within, and two black horns stretched out and back from the top of his head. "I admit it. You're very pretty in this form. Definitely an improvement in the looks department."

Hilarious. Ready to get out of here?

"Do you even remember how to fly?"

In response, Eddie lashed out with his right paw and snatched me up before I could dive out of the way. He casually tossed me in the air towards his back, and I had to turn at the last second to avoid impaling myself on one of the spikes that ran down his back.

"It was a valid question!" I snapped and immediately latched onto the spike in front of me as Eddie sank to the ground and then leapt straight up into the air. The walls of the tower were too narrow for Eddie to stretch out his wings, but his leap carried us to just above the tower walls and his wings snapped open immediately. With only a couple beats of his wings, he carried us above the tower and off into the night sky.

Hold on, Eddie warned, and I gripped the spike in front of me tighter as he shot higher into the sky. A deep rumbling came from him, and I realized he was laughing. I couldn't help but laugh along with him. I'd been on a lot of crazy adventures in my life, but even I never thought I'd be riding a dragon across the starlit night.

Chapter Nineteen

I SHIVERED SLIGHTLY as we glided through the chilly night air. Eddie had flown up high enough that we'd be hard to see from the ground, but that also meant the temperature had dropped and I was having a hard time figuring out where we were. The circular room we'd been trapped in had definitely not been part of the castle. I had no idea what the creature in the water had been, but I suspected it had pulled us through a portal underwater that had brought us to that room. If it'd been a gateway to another realm, I would have felt it, which meant we were still in the same fae realm, but I didn't know how close we were to the castle. It could take us days to fly back, if not longer. Some lights flickered in the distance beneath us, and I squinted at them.

Can you fly north a little more? That might be the castle up ahead. Maybe we lucked out and didn't go that far after all.

All right, Eddie agreed reluctantly. He clearly was enjoying having this form back.

I was about to assure him that he'd have plenty of opportunities to fly again when a flash of movement came from the clouds to our right. *I think we're about to have company,* I warned him. Luckily, I still had a death grip around the spike on his back because Eddie immediately dove towards the ground in a spin.

My stomach lurched, and I thought for a second I would throw up, but I managed to hold it in. The wind ripped tears from my eyes so I squeezed them shut and blinked hard a few times trying to clear them. We were flying too fast, and the clouds were too dense for me to count how many were following us. I glimpsed enough to recognize the feathered reptilian creatures from before. The sidhe devourers had found us.

Get us to the ground! You can't see well enough to fight them in the air, not to mention I'll fall off in the process!

In response, Eddie picked up speed, pulling his massive wings in tight as we streaked towards the ground.

Eddie? You can see the ground, right? I asked. When he didn't respond and I glimpsed the ground beneath us, I screamed at him, "Pull up, Eddie!"

His wings snapped open, and I slammed into the spike behind me hard enough for my head to swim for a moment. Dirt flew up from either side of him as his claws dragged across the ground. Finally, he slowed to a stop, and I practically ran down his back to reach the precious ground. Riding a dragon was not nearly as fun as I thought it would be. If we weren't about to be surrounded by the enemy, I would have stopped to kiss the glorious ground beneath my feet. Instead, I pulled my swords free and let my magic flow out of me.

Eddie moved away from me to give himself room to work. *I'm not that blind at night, you know,* he grumbled.

I shot him an incredulous look. "I watched you walk into a tree branch a couple of days ago. And it wasn't a small branch. You are most definitely that blind at night!"

Whatever.

I shook my head at him and returned to concentrating on

the sky. Six flying beasts landed around us, bearing sidhe riders. My magic snapped at them, only to get slapped back with the devourer magic they all had. Looked like this would be a sword fight after all. Three of them drew swords and focused on me, while the remaining three looked at Eddie and smiled.

"Fortune has smiled upon us and we'll have a feast tonight! I've never had a dragon before," a tall white-haired sidhe said as she started towards Eddie.

Shit. I spun back as one of the sidhe who'd stayed behind took a swipe at my midsection. "Get out of here, Eddie!" I screamed and dodged another strike. Bastards were fast. "Go!"

I'm not leaving you. Eddie roared, and flame shot towards the three sidhe advancing on him.

Their magic rose and solidified into a wall in front of them, light from the full moon causing it to shimmer slightly. The flames slammed into the wall and were quickly absorbed into it. Eddie's fire was driven by his magic. These fae had devourer magic. They would absorb any magic we threw at them and grow more powerful. Dragons were beings loaded with power, and they would indeed love to feast on Eddie's magic.

"I've got this!" I ducked under another sword swipe. "Get the fuck out of here now!"

Eddie roared one last time in frustration and launched into the sky. Several concentrated beams of magic shot after Eddie like spears. I had no idea if their hits landed, but he didn't come crashing back to the ground, so I took it for a win. The white-haired sidhe grunted and turned back to join her companions in taking me out, so she didn't see the shadow barreling down on her on silent wings.

One of her companions started to call out a warning, but I slammed the pommel of my sword into his throat after blocking a thrust from another. Eddie's jaws closed around the sidhe before she even had a chance to scream, and he took off once more. The feathered reptilians screeched in rage and flew after him.

I let out a chuckle as I wiped away some blood dripping down my forehead. "You should probably think twice about referring to a dragon as a feast, considering all of you are bite size to them."

"Lir wants you back in one piece, but he's a fool," a dark-haired sidhe sneered. The remaining warriors fell into step behind him. He must be the leader of this group. "With you out of the way, it will be much easier to snag the child later. Lir has been slipping in his old age. It's time for someone new to take over."

"I'm going to take a wild guess and say you're that someone?"

In response, he thrust his sword at me in a move too fast for me to track. Only centuries of experience and training allowed me to move fast enough to keep the sword from spearing my liver. I spun away and blocked strike after strike from the other fae who had fanned out around me after their leader had made his first move.

I'd fought with worse odds before and come out on top. But these fae were probably the best sword fighters I'd ever gone up against other than Magos. They couldn't all come at me at once without getting in each other's way. But they had worked together long enough as a unit that they knew each other's moves well. One would slide in for a thrust which I would block, and then they would gracefully move out of the way for their companion to move in.

I was already bleeding from a dozen wounds. My shifter magic was healing me, but it was slower than it was a few minutes ago. They weren't scoring surface wounds; they were scoring hits that would be fatal on anyone who didn't have magical healing abilities, and it was taxing my magic. I couldn't keep this up forever. They knew it and were just having fun with me.

I growled in rage but couldn't figure out a way out of this. The dark-haired sidhe spun towards me and slashed at my throat. I leaned back and thrust towards his ribs. My blade was blocked by another, and the lead fae grinned at me before slamming a dagger into my thigh. I screamed, ripping the dagger out as fire burned down my leg, and I threw the dagger into the ground. It sank hilt deep into the soil. I'd gotten it out of me fast, but it wouldn't matter. I could smell the poison.

A numbness followed in the wake of the fire, and I suspected I had minutes at best before I lost control of my leg and collapsed. I stepped back and let myself limp a little more than I actually needed to. The dark-haired sidhe cocked his head at me but didn't take the bait. Another sidhe was a little overzealous and moved in to swipe at my other leg. I sidestepped his attack and slammed one of my swords onto his, driving it into the ground. I snapped my other sword up underneath his jaw and through his head. His magic sputtered around him, and I yanked my other sword up and through the back of his neck until it joined the first sword. A feral smile spread across my lips as I twisted the swords away and the head came with them. The body thumped to the ground, and I used one sword to slide the head off the other.

The remaining four sidhe bared their teeth at me. They'd been enjoying this fight and thought they had it in the bag. In truth, they still did. My right leg was almost completely numb, and soon it wouldn't be able to bear my weight any longer. But I'd still make them pay for it.

"We're going to cut you to pieces," the leader growled.

He stepped forward but stopped when a black feathered cloak fell to the ground. Everyone moved back and glanced up to where a gateway hovered ten feet above us. I'd been so focused on the fight, I hadn't even noticed it opening. The sidhe looked at each other uncertainly, but I recognized the magic that had opened that gateway, so I wasn't surprised when a tall, ashen-haired shifter with impossibly bright green eyes dropped out of it.

She hit the ground and rolled, and then threw an axe straight at a sidhe's head. He slid out of the way on liquid joints only to be cut down as Badb appeared behind him, snatching the same axe she'd thrown out of the air and slamming it into the back of his head. It took my mind a few seconds to make sense of what I was seeing, but then I felt the gateway slam shut behind her as she opened another and dove through, only to appear at my side a second later.

"Kill her!" the dark-haired sidhe bellowed as he launched himself at her. "Kill The Morrigan!"

Badb whirled forward with her axes and cut into the sidhe in front of her, sliding out of the way of the fae leader's strike. The two remaining fae split up, one joining their leader in the fight against The Morrigan and one staring at me.

Sharp blue eyes looked me over, taking my injuries into account. "Shame you're so wounded. This fight won't be much fun." His tone was light, and he didn't seem all that upset over the death of the others.

"If I wasn't wounded, this wouldn't be a fair fight. This way, you at least have a chance." I gave him a cocky grin as adrenaline coursed through me, fighting back some of the fatigue.

He feigned a strike at my right side and whirled to the other side, striking at my face. I snapped my sword up to parry, leaning to the side slightly as the blade slid within an inch of my face. With the other two sidhe occupied with Badb, it was just me and him. We bared our teeth at each other and broke apart. Excitement raced through me as I matched him, strike for strike. It wasn't often I got to go up against a swordsman just as good as me, if not better.

Magos still beat me in most fights, but at this point, I knew most of his moves. I simply wasn't good enough to block them. But this sidhe had a completely different fighting style. He was fast and vicious, and I found myself laughing as we traded blows. With every step, I could feel the wariness and numbness creep back in as the adrenaline faded. It was time to end this dance.

The sidhe made an impossibly fast diagonal slash across my chest, which I barely managed to parry. His blade slid off mine and I immediately dropped my sword and fell to my knee at the exact moment my leg gave out. Off balance from the resistance to his sword suddenly evaporating, the sidhe stumbled forward, and I thrust my remaining sword between his ribs, stopping short of his heart.

The sidhe slowly dropped to his knees in front of me, and I looked into his crystal blue eyes. "Appears this fight was too much fun for you after all."

"Appears so," he said as blood dripped from his mouth.

I took in a deep breath as I was about to shove the blade through his heart when his scent played across my tongue, reminding me of some of the barren deserts I'd come across in my travels. Endearing. Brutal. And often hopeless. I studied the sidhe in front of me. One hand was braced around my sword that was less than an inch from his heart, but he made no move to pull it out. His other hand had fallen to his thigh. I spied another knife holstered there, but he didn't even attempt to grab it. His expression was one of pain, but relief was also there.

"Goddamn it," I growled and yanked my sword out. The sidhe hissed in pain but stayed on his knees.

Badb strode over to me, blood dripping from her axes. "What's wrong?"

My breath caught at her words. I'd been preparing myself for seeing Badb in person, knowing she would look exactly like

Macha. But I hadn't thought about what it would feel like to hear Macha's voice again. An old ache tore through me. It had been centuries since I'd heard that voice. I swallowed and shoved everything I was feeling deep inside.

"What's wrong is the stupid, annoying magic I inherited from you to sense other being's souls!" I growled at her, the words just pouring out as I struggled to deal with Badb's presence and how casual she was treating this whole situation. Just like Kalen, she was acting like us finally meeting wasn't a big deal. I clenched my swords tighter as I continued yelling at her. "Macha at least got a much better understanding when she read souls! I only get vague impressions and feelings that I have to somehow interpret! I thought I just hadn't inherited much of her gifts, but really you just suck at it and you passed on your crappy soul-reading skills to me!"

I half limped, half hopped over to another fallen sidhe and swiped my blades clean on their shirt before thrusting them into the sheathes on my back. I knew I was acting completely irrational but I couldn't stop myself. The mental and physical exhaustion of the last few days was too much and I was done. I was fucking done.

Badb leaned in and smelled the sidhe, who looked confused and wary about what was going on. She pulled back with a grimace. "His heart's not in it. He's following commands because he's a soldier and that's what soldiers do, but he doesn't give a shit about Balor's cause." She shrugged. "Doesn't mean you can't kill him. Probably should, in fact."

"He's a really good swordsman, and I enjoyed that fight." I hobbled back over to the sidhe, who was looking at me with a bewildered expression. "What's your name?"

"Niall."

"Here's the deal, Niall. I'm going to ask my dragon friend to make a flyover here and burn all these bodies to a crisp. I'm sure I'll run into Lir at some point, and I'm going to say every one of you died here. This is your chance to get out. I'm not asking you to join me and my merry band of misfits. Despite you being a hell of a swordsman, there's no way we would trust you." I stretched my hand out and opened a gateway into a realm that technically belonged to the fae but was only lightly populated. "You have no reason to go back to that shitty realm. There's not much going on in this realm, so it'll give you time to heal and figure out what you want to do."

Niall glanced at the gateway and then back at me. "Is this a trick?"

"No," I said. "It's probably a dumb move on my part. But I'm making it, regardless."

Doubt still shone in Niall's eyes as he looked at the gateway.

"We don't have time for this." Badb grabbed the back of Niall's jacket and threw him through the gateway. "I understand why my daughter is doing this, and it's possible I would have come to the same decision myself. But know this. If you ever make a move against my daughter again, I will skin you alive and break every bone in your body. Then I'll wait for you to heal and do it again. And that will be a goddamn delight compared to what her father will do to you."

"Understood." Niall grunted as he coughed up more blood.

Badb waved her hand, and the gateway slammed shut. Emerald green eyes that were at once familiar and different looked at me. "We need to purge that poison out of you."

"Sounds great," I mumbled as the world spun around me and I blacked out.

WHEN I OPENED MY EYES, I had to blink a few times to adjust to the light. Finally, I was able to focus and understand what I was seeing: the massive skylight in the common area of the rooms Kalen had originally left us in. I rubbed at my face, trying to remove the last of the drowsiness, and swung my legs over to move into a seated position. Or at least I tried to. It was more of a dragging motion than swinging. I winced as a muscle spasm ran up my back but still managed to get myself upright. Ugh. I hated being poisoned.

A steaming cup appeared in front of me, and I grabbed it and took a sip then looked at the cup in distaste and set it down on the table. Mikhail shrugged and sat in the chair next to me. "It was the best I could come up with. Apparently, the fae are more into tea than coffee."

"What are you doing here?" I blinked at him in confusion.

"Badb opened a gateway into the middle of the downstairs apartment, pointed at me, and said, 'I need you to watch over my daughter while I go hunting.'" Mikhail gave me an amused smile. "That didn't go over well. Everyone had questions. Isabeau was upset over movie night being interrupted. Bryn wanted to know if you were okay. And of course, Magos wanted to come right away. Badb, being the wonderful communicator she is, told everyone to shut up and then stepped back into the gateway. We thought she was leaving, but she opened up another gateway directly behind me, yanked me through, and slammed it closed before anyone could follow."

"Magos is going to be so pissed."

"Your mother is definitely not his favorite person right now."

"She's not my mother," I said automatically.

Mikhail gave me a look but didn't comment. "I sent word to Magos once I confirmed you were okay and he didn't need to call on Pele and Kaysea for reinforcements."

"Good." I glanced around. "Where is everyone?"

"Eddie is passed out on one of the beds. We tried to wake him up a few hours ago, and he literally breathed fire at us, so we chose to let him sleep some more. Jinx is still out on whatever mission you sent him on. Badb is searching the nearby area to see if any more of Balor's people are around. Eddie told her about the fae who arranged for you to be transported out of this castle before he passed out.

"What's unclear is how Balor's people knew where you would be. It seems unlikely Queen Áine's people are working with them, at least not the one who kidnapped you from the castle. Clearly there's a rat somewhere though." Mikhail sipped his cup of tea, which, unlike me, he seemed to enjoy. "Kalen is working on expediting your meeting with the Queens so that we can get out of this realm as soon as possible."

"Wonderful," I muttered and pushed myself off the couch. My legs really didn't want to respond to me, but I managed to march into the room Eddie wasn't sleeping in and started going through the drawers. Sure enough, a variety of clothes were available for guests in different sizes. I preferred daemon clothes because they tended to be less showy and more functional, but I'd take whatever clean clothes were available right then.

I settled on the clothes that would annoy me the least and went to the attached bathroom. No beautiful swimming pool in this room but given my experience with the last one, I was okay with that. Half of this bathroom was cleared out and had a large skylight above it. Dark green and grey stones made up the floor and walls, with two copper showerheads sticking out from the wall. I stepped under one of them and tapped a stone next to the showerhead with a water droplet glyph. The water came on, and I tapped another glyph to raise the temperature slightly.

Bloody water swirled around my feet as the hot water ran through my hair. I reached into a small cubby that blended in with the stone wall and pulled out some soap. By the time I was done scrubbing my hair and skin, the muscles in my legs felt normal again. It'd be nice if I could go a few more hours before having to face off against six sidhe warriors, but at least I wouldn't be limping around the castle. I turned off the water and dried myself. Once I was dressed, I walked back out to the living room but stopped when I saw Mikhail's expression. He looked genuinely alarmed.

"What's wrong?" I scanned the room looking for threats but didn't see anything.

"Nothing. Nothing's wrong," Mikhail said quickly. "I just wasn't expecting to see you dressed like . . . like that. It's not your normal look, is all."

I frowned at him and glanced down at what I was wearing. Realization dawned on me, and I quirked a smile at Mikhail. "Does my showing so much skin make you uncomfortable?" I teased him.

"Not at all," Mikhail said. "Just doesn't seem that practical for fighting is all."

I huffed a laugh. "Trust me. It was the most practical option of what I had available." I pulled on the shirt, but it didn't help much. It was a midriff shirt and meant to leave the lower abs exposed. Thanks to me having more in the chest department than most sidhe, the shirt basically ended a couple of inches below my boobs. The fabric was stretchy enough that it still worked with the overall look. The shirt had no sleeves and instead had a high collar that went around the back of my neck, opening to a scooped front. The pants were long and flowy and hung low on my hips. I hated them, but there wasn't any alternative. I'd thought about trying to wash the blood out of my pants, but they were also torn up pretty badly, so they truly were a lost cause.

"The sidhe do make clothes for fighting, but this is considered normal fashion among the sidhe. These rooms are stocked with casual clothes which means tunics with flowy sleeves and dresses that leave far more skin exposed than this shirt. This is the only shirt that wouldn't get in the way of my swords."

"Right. Well, it doesn't look bad. I prefer your usual look, though." Mikhail gestured to where my swords were laid out on a table against the wall.

I checked them over. I'd wiped them off quickly earlier with the intention of cleaning them later. But they were shiny and clean now. "Did someone clean my gear?" I asked as I started strapping things on.

"I did," Mikhail replied casually. "Didn't have anything else to do while you and Eddie were passed out."

"Thanks." I glanced at him once I had everything back on and found him staring at me with an expression I couldn't begin to decipher. My heart skipped a couple of beats as we stared at each other. I opened my mouth to say something, what I didn't know, but the door to the rooms opened, revealing Kalen and Badb. I looked back at Mikhail, but the expression was gone.

"Good, you're awake," Kalen said in greeting. "It's time to meet the Queens."

Chapter Twenty

We followed Kalen through several halls until we passed through a large archway into a garden one could find only in the fae realms. "Wow," I breathed as I took in the mesmerizing chaos around me. I had known the throne room of the Queens was an outdoor garden, and I'd suspected it would be grandiose. But this went beyond even what I imagined.

Several pathways were laid out, and some trees were strategically planted where they would provide shade. But in true fae fashion, the plants had been allowed to grow however they wanted. I couldn't even see the other castle walls. As we walked further down the main path, the archway we had passed through disappeared behind towering walls of greenery. Ahead of us, a vine stretched over the walkway, delicate pink blossoms hanging down.

"Don't touch anything," I murmured to Mikhail and Eddie. "Those pink flowers ahead of us will release a puff of pollen if they're disturbed. It'll cause hallucinations for days if it's inhaled."

"I know," Eddie replied, keeping his voice low. "I'm going

to try and snag a couple on the way out. The daemon youth will pay a lot for those flowers."

I snickered as we continued on the path, pointing out other plants of note to Mikhail and Eddie. Eventually, we reached a small clearing with a raised platform in the center. Roots from the nearby trees had grown up onto the platform and intertwined to make two thrones.

Flowering vines wound their way around the thrones, their bright green stems and blossoms providing splashes of color against the dark roots. The flowers on the right throne were a purple so dark they were almost black; it gave the throne a foreboding appearance, especially in comparison to the throne on the left, which had bright red flowers.

Most beings probably would have found the throne on the left more cheerful. But to me, the flowers just looked like splashes of blood against the roots.

Both thrones were empty. I glanced around the clearing and didn't see anyone. "Did you bring us to the wrong garden, Kalen?"

Before he could respond, a voice called out from somewhere in the garden. "It's the right garden." A few seconds later, someone who could only be one of the fae Queens walked into the clearing from a small path behind the thrones. The plants twisted and swayed as she walked by, trying to be as close to her as possible. She dragged her fingers gently along the sides of the path, touching them as she went. Her rich chestnut brown skin practically glowed in the early morning sunlight and her dark brown hair was gathered back away from her face, allowing the curls to fall down her back. She wore no crown, but flowers adorned her hair. The Queen walked around the thrones and paused in front of us, looking each of us over, her gaze lingering on Mikhail. Interest sparked in her eyes as she admired him.

I stepped in front of Mikhail, blocking her view. "Hi." I

gave her a smile that was really more a baring of teeth. "I do believe we're supposed to meet two Queens. Will your sister be joining us?"

The Queen focused on me with green eyes that reminded me of grassy fields in spring. They were the same green Finn had in his eyes. The more I studied her, the more I could see other small pieces of family resemblance. "My sister is attending to matters outside the castle. She'll be joining us shortly. I am Queen Áine of the Seelie courts."

I forced my expression into a neutral one and kept my voice pleasant. "Pleasure to meet you, Queen Áine. Thank you for seeing me and my friends. And for sharing your hospitality and allowing us to stay at the castle. It's been a wonderful stay so far. The swimming pool in our room was to die for."

Áine gave me a sweet smile in return and took a seat at the throne with bright red blossoms. "So glad you liked it. I went to some trouble arranging that for you. Now that I know how much you enjoyed it, I'll be sure to keep that in mind for the future."

Footsteps coming down the main pathway prevented my retort. Probably for the best because I wasn't great at word games and was about to drop the fake pleasantries altogether. A sidhe with the same chestnut brown skin as Áine walked down the pathway towards us. Her glossy black hair was cut short and barely reached her shoulders. She wore a simple black tunic with black pants similar to mine.

All of her clothing was dirty and covered with ashes. No flowers wound through her hair, and the plants didn't sway towards her the way they did to Áine, but I had no doubt this was the Unseelie Queen. Badb trailed behind her, expression completely blank as she surveyed all of us until she met Kalen's eyes. For just a second, her expression softened and her eyes sparked as she looked at him, then she slipped back into her mask of indifference.

The new Queen walked straight up to me, ignoring all my friends. I met her stare and was slightly surprised to find her eyes to be gold. The same exact gold as the inside part of Finn's two-toned eyes. "Only a few miles away from this castle is a charred section of meadow. Everything was burnt to ashes. It wasn't like that yesterday. It must have happened during the night. Do you know anything about that?" I wasn't surprised that the Unseelie Queen skipped pleasantries and went straight for the jugular.

"Why would I know anything about that?" I asked. "My friends and I were shown to our rooms immediately upon our arrival and we didn't leave through the main doors until this morning. Not sure what they did for most of the night, but I enjoyed the swimming pool. Queen Áine was kind enough to arrange for me."

"Fine." She turned away from me and took a seat on the throne with the dark flowers. A long serpent with bright yellow scales slid down a nearby tree and up the throne, winding its body through the roots until it rested a large triangular head on the Queen's shoulder. Light green eyes that shone with intelligence focused on me as the Queen absently stroked it. "As you have no doubt already figured out. I'm Queen Elvinia of the Unseelie court. Kalen informed us that you were successful in locating the lost fae child, but you had concerns you wanted to address before bringing him to us."

"I'm not going to stand here and pretend to be good at the political games typically played in your court. While you would probably find my failings to be amusing, I don't have the patience for it, so I'll be rather direct if that works for you." Áine frowned, but a flicker of amusement danced in Elvinia's eyes and she waved me on, so I continued. "Finn isn't just some random lost sidhe child with unusual amounts of power. He's the son of the exiled fae King. Which makes him your nephew.

271

And the focus of an old prophecy about the falling of the realms."

"The boy is no doubt scared," Áine said, her face taking on a concerned appearance. Only Kalen's glare kept me from rolling my eyes. "He should be with his family. We can protect him and figure out this prophecy."

"No," I said simply.

"No?" A musical laugh spilled forth from Áine. "I don't think you understand your place here, which is no place. You have no place or standing in this court. You were hired to find the boy and bring him to us. The first part of that is done. Now do the rest."

"Technically, I wasn't hired for anything. I was doing a favor for my dear friend, Pele. You know, the daughter of the leader of the daemon Assembly. I'm sure you've met before." I gave Áine a toothy grin. "I never agreed to bring the boy to you. I did, however, promise the boy and his guardian I would keep them safe. And that means keeping them far away from you."

"He's our family!" Áine snapped. "You have no right!"

I snorted. "You didn't even know he existed until recently, so don't pretend like the family ties really mean that much to you. You want him here so you can use him for your own purposes. Aside from destroying any resemblance of a decent childhood, you also can't keep him safe. I can."

"There is no safer place than here with us," Áine argued.

I looked at Elvinia, who returned my look with a thoughtful expression. "Queen Elvinia, didn't you say upon your arrival that you were investigating a large section of land that had been burned to ash mere miles from this castle?"

"I did," she said. "We're not sure what caused it, but a significant echo of magic was left behind. A being of considerable power was involved."

I didn't have to turn around to know Eddie had a wide grin on his face. As if he needed anything else to inflate his ego.

"Your realm doesn't seem all that safe." I shrugged at Áine, who glared at her sister in annoyance.

"Besides, I'm the one referred to in the prophecy, 'The realms will fall unless fate is shifted by one born of the love between Death's harbingers,'" I recited. "I'm the only one capable of keeping him from his dark fate of destroying the realms."

"I know the prophecy and I know who you are!" Áine said. "Others fit that description. You might be a shifter and your mother, Macha, might have qualified as a harbinger of death. But your father certainly didn't." I didn't bother correcting her about my true parentage as she continued. "Besides, if they truly were Death's harbingers, I doubt they would have let themselves be burned at the stake while their children watched."

A cruel smile spread across her face as every part of me stilled. I was vaguely aware of Mikhail stepping forward and resting a hand on my shoulder as my magic unfurled. Áine's smile grew wider as Elvinia leaned forward slightly, her golden eyes darkening in warning. A memory of smoke and burnt flesh came back to me as my magic pushed a little more. It wanted a bite of the Seelie Queen, and I wasn't sure I really wanted to stop it.

Don't. Badb's word echoed in my head. *It's what she wants. Guards are hidden throughout this garden, and the magic of the Queens is deadly. We won't walk away from this.*

We. The word clanged through me. If I made a move against the fae Queens, Mikhail and Eddie would fight by my side. Die by my side. I glanced at Kalen and Badb and saw the truth in their eyes. They would fight for me as well. Even knowing they would likely die.

I trembled as I pulled my magic back, giving myself a

moment to steady my emotions before raising my chin and meeting the unflinching stare of the Seelie Queen. She had relaxed back on her throne, disappointment etched in her features. She had purposely baited me, hoping I would do something rash so she would have an excuse to kill me. Kalen had arranged for our safe passage, but if we raised a hand against either Queen, they would have been within their rights to strike me down.

And I'd come so close to giving her what she wanted. I took another breath, centering myself. I could be patient.

"As far as the prophecy. Maybe you're right, and others exist who would have fit the bill of the one who could have changed Finn's fate. But I'm the one who found him," I said, letting my tone take on an edge as I said each word slowly and clearly. "I found him. I saved him. I saved his guardian, too. He's mine. I will not give him to you."

"None of this matters," Áine snapped, waving a hand at me in dismissal. "You have no standing in this court. I am ordering you to bring the boy to us!"

I clenched my jaw until it ached. There was no going back after this next part. I let out a deep breath. Kalen's and Badb's stares weighed on me, but I didn't look away from the Seelie Queen. "Actually, I do have standing in the fae court. Just not in yours."

"Just because your aunt and uncle belong to a fae court doesn't give you any claim to one," the Queen replied. Her words were steady, but a flicker of doubt passed through her eyes. "Macha and Nevin never belonged to a fae court."

"Macha and Nevin aren't my real parents," I said, even as the words felt like a betrayal. In my heart, they would always be my real parents. "I am the daughter of Badb the Great Battle Crow. Known in the fae courts as The Morrigan. My father is the one who once served you as the Erlking. They now both serve in the Unseelie court, and thus I belong to the

Unseelie court as well. Only Queen Elvinia could give me the order to bring the boy in." And if she gave that order, we were all screwed. Kalen trusted her not to give it, but I didn't know her at all, and I hated hinging our entire plan on this.

Áine's head snapped to the side to glare at her sister. "You knew all along that they had a child! You knew of this ruse and helped them make a fool of me!"

"I knew nothing until recently," Elvinia said with a shrug. "She's right though. Nemain belongs to me."

Every part of me tensed at her words and the way her golden eyes focused on me. *Nemain belongs to me.* Not *Nemain belongs to my court.* I couldn't take back the words now, and even if I could, I wouldn't because it was our best play. Kalen had warned me that this path would require sacrifice on my part. This was only the beginning.

"Tell her to bring the boy to us," Áine commanded her sister.

Elvinia gave her a cool look. "No, I don't think I will."

Áine stared at her sister for a few more moments. I'd seen that look before, many times, from Cian. This wasn't over between them, and their sibling fight would be epic. Magic poured out of Áine as she stood from the throne, and it nearly took me to my knees. Eddie grunted behind me, but everyone managed to stay standing as magic rolled off Áine in waves. Just as suddenly as she unleashed it, she pulled her magic back in.

"See you around, Nemain," Áine said coldly and walked off down the main path leading out of the garden.

I turned my attention back to the remaining Queen, who had cocked her head to the side as she studied me. I really hated being stared at and I hated it even more when it was done by these Queens.

"I understand why you don't want to bring my nephew to the court now, but you can't keep him away forever," Elvinia commented. I noticed how she referred to Finn as her nephew and not as "the boy" like Áine. "His magic is only going to increase as he gets older. He'll need to be taught how to use it."

"I have friends who can help him for now, and if he needs additional teachers in the future, we'll ask for your guidance," I said. "We can't keep him away from the fae courts forever, and I have no intention of doing so. I only want to make sure he gets a chance to grow up without the poison of the courts whispering in his ear. Or that he doesn't not get to grow up at all because someone decides the prophecy is too chancy and buries a dagger in his heart."

"What are you proposing?"

"Fifty years," I said. "He gets fifty years free of the influence of the fae courts."

"Five decades is a long time," she pointed out.

"You are thousands of years old." I laughed. "Five decades is nothing to you. But it will be everything to him."

She studied me for a few moments and nodded. "He will get his five decades of freedom," she agreed, and I almost sighed in relief. "You, however, will not."

I froze as I stared at her. Badb's expression was still completely blank, but Kalen gave me a pitying glance. "What do you mean?"

"Your parents have served me well over the past few centuries." Elvinia grinned wickedly at me. "You will do the same. I have much to discuss with you. But for now, return home with your friends. I will send for you later."

Without another word, I turned and left the garden where I had bargained for the freedom of a child by giving up my own.

WE RECONVENED in the rooms we'd been staying in. Eddie had loudly stated, "Well, that went great!" and then went to investigate the food that had been brought to our rooms while we'd been meeting with the Queens.

While Eddie was stuffing his face, the rest of us checked in with Jinx, who had returned to the rooms with his mother, Nyx. Both of the grimalkins had dropped their glamours and were lounging in the sunny spots of the room. Based on how Jinx was pointedly ignoring his mother and flicking his tail in annoyance, I gathered their conversation regarding just how much she had known and not told us hadn't gone well.

I plopped down next to Nyx and crossed my legs in front of me. *Nice to see you again, Nyx.*

Hello, child. Enjoy your meeting with the fae Queens?

I'm fairly certain the only one who enjoyed that meeting was Elvinia. I get the impression that somehow everything went the way she wanted it to.

It often does, but not always. Elvinia is very good at playing the long game. We're just not exactly sure what her long game is.

How reassuring, I added dryly. *Care to tell me why your son is lying over there stewing in frustration?*

He was rather upset about me not telling him some things earlier. I told him he learned about them at the exact time he was supposed to know about them and not a moment before. Apparently, that answer was not satisfactory to him.

Jinx leapt onto the table where Eddie was picking at the food. "Hey!" Eddie exclaimed and tried to snatch the plate loaded with meat away from Jinx. The grimalkin slammed his paw down on the plate, claws outstretched, and glared at Eddie. *Mine.*

Eddie grumbled something about how he could swallow Jinx in one bite if he wanted to and grabbed the plate of dried fruits to snack on instead. I rolled my eyes at them and turned back to Nyx.

Not going to lie. I'm on Jinx's side here. It's fucked up that none of you told us anything. Just because we know everything now doesn't mean we're going to forgive you for withholding this information from us.

Nyx looked away from her son and met my eyes. *We always knew you would be upset with us when you found out the truth. We did what was necessary. If we'd told you the truth earlier, you would have become involved with the fae courts that much earlier. We wanted to give you as much freedom as we could.*

Jinx stiffened from where he was lying on the table next to the plate of meat he'd defended but had no actual interest in eating. He deliberately turned his head even further away from the direction of Nyx.

She huffed a laugh. *I'll see you both soon.*

I rose and reluctantly headed over to the others. "You guys ready to go?"

"Yup!" Eddie announced as he swiped something off the table against the wall. Gods knew how much shit he'd stolen in our short stay here.

I reached out with my power and opened a gateway back to our apartment. "You guys go," I said. "I'll meet you there."

Eddie and Jinx strolled through the gateway. Mikhail paused, looking at me suspiciously. "I just need a few minutes. I'll be right there, promise."

"Don't do anything stupid," Mikhail replied unhappily and headed towards the gateway. Before stepping through, he gave my parents a warning look, and much to my surprise, they gave him a shallow nod, as if they understood his concern. Mikhail stepped through the gateway and gave me another warning look. "Stay out of any swimming pools."

I flipped him off and let the gateway close, turning to face Kalen and Badb.

"You were listening to my conversation with Nyx." I narrowed my eyes at Kalen.

"Can you really blame me for trying to know my daughter?" He shrugged, not even attempting to deny my accusation.

"Spying on me isn't a good way of going about it!" I growled.

I felt Badb's heated glare on me. She hadn't said anything yet, but I was fairly certain she was seconds away from tearing into me if I kept laying into Kalen. After all these centuries, there was definitely no question about how much my parents still loved each other.

I sighed and chewed on my bottom lip. "Look, I'm sorry. I realize I haven't been entirely fair to the both of you. I understand why you did what you did. I just need more time to process it and some space to do that."

"We'll give you as much space as we can," Badb said as she slipped her hand into Kalen's. "But be warned, Elvinia will call for you soon. We should meet a few times before then so we can prepare you for navigating the fae court."

I nodded. "I agree. I'd also like both of you to train me with my magic. You're the only two people in existence who can help me learn how to fully control it. Pretty sure I'm going to need it." I glanced at Badb and ignored the pang in my heart at how much she looked like Macha. "In fact, before I leave, I'd like you to teach me how to open a gateway within the same realm."

Her green eyes narrowed in suspicion. "Why?"

"There's one last thing I need to do before leaving. Something I wager you would have loved to have done ages ago but couldn't because of your agreement to the Unseelie Queen." A wicked grin spread across my face, and a second later, a matching one spread across Badb's.

Kalen permitted himself a small smile as he said, "You really are our daughter."

Less than an hour later, I slipped through a gateway into the Seelie Queen's private chambers. It had taken a lot of practice and concentration for me to open a gateway there. Apparently, the trick to opening gateways within the same realm was to not push too much with the magic as you opened it. In hindsight, it sounded remarkably simple, and I couldn't believe I'd never figured it out before.

However, actually doing it was far from simple. It required a fraction of the magic I usually used to open gateways, so I kept blowing past the level I needed. It'd taken me ten minutes to open this gateway because I'd had to increase the magic I was using so slowly. Badb assured me I'd get better with practice. After seeing her use gateways to fight, I was highly motivated to do so.

I silently moved through the common area of the Queen's chambers to where I heard water splashing. Easing open the door, I made my way to the pool of water where the Queen was lounging surrounded by water lilies with delicate pink flowers. "Does this swimming pool also come with a creepy tentacle monster?" I asked and felt a rush of satisfaction at the Queen jumping at the sound of my voice.

She whirled around in the water, her magic already pouring off her. My magic ripped out of me, and I wagged a finger at her. "Ah, ah, ah, ah." Her magic pulsed around her, but she made no move to attack me. "I just want to talk," I told her.

"You surprised me in my chambers to talk?" she asked, the expression on her face stating she clearly didn't believe this. "Even with your magic, you won't be able to kill me. My magic will overwhelm you, and I'll rip your heart out for daring to even try to take me on."

"I really did come here to talk." I circled around the pool, my magic trailing behind me in ghostly blue flames. "Well, to ask you a couple of questions, really."

"Like what?"

"Why did you go after my mother and her sisters in the first place? I know Badb ripped a gateway open in your realm, but you survived."

"When your mother ripped open those gateways into the

fae realms, she opened one in my home," the Queen hissed. "I survived, but my lover died. We'd been together for centuries. Do you know what it's like to lose a piece of your soul?"

I looked at her coldly. "As a matter of fact, I've lost several pieces of my soul over the years. If you're looking for sympathy from me, you won't find any. It was your decision to cut off the shifter realm. Thousands of shifters had to watch their loved ones die in front of them. How many lives have been lost over the centuries from the Cataclysms? And you never thought to warn anyone about the true cause behind them? Where the devourers actually came from?"

"So your reasoning is that I had it coming?" Áine's lips twisted in derision. "One act of violence always leads to another. I suggest you remember that."

"I have several kindhearted people in my life. They would urge me to consider that revenge is never ending until someone breaks the cycle. Until someone is the better person." The flames that had been trailing behind me exploded until they completely encircled the bathing pool and the Queen; her magic pushed against it only to pull back instantly.

I bared my teeth. "I'm not the better person. Nothing would make me happier than to see you rotting in the ground. I won't make a move against you now. But if I find out you played a direct role in the death of Macha and Nevin, all bets are off."

The Queen's magic raged, and I could feel it building. The air felt thicker, and the hair on the back of my neck stood up. I stepped back through the gateway and slammed it shut. I took a couple of deep breaths and opened another gateway, this time to my apartment. It was time to get the hell out of the fae realm.

Chapter Twenty One

THE APARTMENT WAS silent when I arrived. Everyone was probably still in the downstairs apartment. I stood in the center of our sparring mat in the living room, unsure what to do next. A couple of weeks ago I'd been plotting with Kaysea and Pele on how to create some political alliances so when the truth of my magic came out, the daemons and fae wouldn't kill me on sight. I huffed out a laugh and rubbed my face.

Well, I'd managed to secure one hell of an alliance. I was an official member of the Unseelie court. The daemons wouldn't be happy when they learned about my existence and that my allegiance belonged to the fae, but they wouldn't be able to do anything about it. I wasn't my own person anymore. Not really. I belonged to the Unseelie Queen now.

The reality of it hit me, and my legs gave out. I slumped to the floor and sat cross-legged on the mat. Hot tears ran down my face. I'd allow myself this time when no one was around to lose my shit, but I couldn't let the others see me like this. Elisa would start plotting how to murder the fae Queens with Misha and Damon throwing out wild ideas.

Apparently Isabeau could read everyone's minds, so who knew what she would pick up. Bryn would understand why I'd done what I'd done, but she would still feel guilty over it. And Finn already carried too much on his shoulders for one so young. I wouldn't add to it.

I wasn't sure how long I sat there. I'd stopped crying but still felt numb. My magic hovered around me like a guard. The apartment door creaked open, and I didn't bother looking up. Even if I hadn't caught his scent, I recognized those soft, careful footsteps. Mikhail sat in front of me, his knees almost touching mine.

"Eddie's gone back to his place. He got some news that had him practically running out of here," Mikhail said calmly. "I let Pele and Kaysea know everything was okay and you'd reach out to them soon with more information. The vampire kids and the valkyrie are passed out in the downstairs apartment. I filled Magos in, and he's resting as well. I'm pretty sure the kids wore him out, but he won't admit it."

"Okay," I said, my voice hoarse.

A warm hand reached out and brushed my cheek, tilting my chin up. Fierce dark blue eyes flecked with purple met mine. "This was the best move," he said firmly. "I know it hurts and you feel like you've lost part of yourself. But you're still you. Finn has a chance now because of you. We'll figure out the rest as we go."

"We?"

"You're stuck with me on the couch for a while longer. It makes sense for Bryn and Finn to have the second-floor apartment."

"That's mighty generous of you," I said, feeling a little more like myself. "I might start charging you rent for the couch."

Mikhail rolled to his feet in one smooth motion, holding

out a hand to me. "Nobody in this building pays rent. I'm sure Pele is going to ask us all for something ridiculous one day in return."

"Probably." I laughed and slid my hand into his. He pulled me to my feet and brushed some loose strands of hair back behind my ear. I breathed in his scent and felt steadier. "I'm going to call Pele and Kaysea and fill them in on everything. We need to get some clothes for Finn." I frowned. "And we need to figure out where to get clothes that will work with a valkyrie's wings—furniture, too. Daemons are our best bet. Some of them have wings, although they're not exactly the same as Bryn's."

"I'll go scope out the furniture in the second-floor apartment to get a better idea of what we need to get." Mikhail headed for the door as I moved to the mirror. I stopped abruptly, and Mikhail paused with his hand on the door. "What's wrong?"

"There's someone here," I said, striding over to the weapons wall and swiping one of my spare swords. "I'm not sure who, but they're waiting just outside the ward. If Pele or Kaysea had sent someone, they would have called ahead first. And if this was fae related, Kalen or Badb likely would have delivered the message to us."

"You greet our guest," Mikhail replied. "I'll scout the area to see if they have any surprises in store for us."

I nodded, and we headed downstairs, keeping our movement quiet. No sound came from the first-floor apartment, so everyone was probably sleeping. Mikhail disappeared into mist, and I walked out to greet our surprise visitor.

A tall sidhe with broad shoulders stood just outside the ward, wearing a long, hooded cloak. At my approach, he pulled back the hood, revealing blue eyes and silver hair that looked even paler in the bright daylight. He trailed his hand across the ward boundary, and I felt the magic from it spark.

The wards around the building had been laid by Pele herself, and they were strong. Anyone with devourer magic would eventually be able to get through them, but it would take time. As long as I stayed on this side of the ward, I was safe from any magic. If our visitor decided to throw a knife, I'd have to be fast enough to dodge.

"Hello, Lir." I smiled, flashing my fangs.

"Hello, Nemain. I'm glad to see you survived that unfortunate encounter with some of my colleagues in the fae realm."

"Are you?" I arched an eyebrow at him. "Really?"

He let out a low laugh. "You did me a favor, actually. Conley had been eyeing my position for quite some time and was becoming a thorn in my side. I knew he would make his move eventually. I'll admit I didn't anticipate this. It was short-sighted, even for him. You're of far more value alive than you are dead."

"What do you want from me?" I asked, stepping closer to the ward boundary. "Your interest in me feels personal, but I never met you before that day in the forest."

"I have a history with your family," he replied vaguely, holding up his right hand and studying his fingers.

I peered at them. Something was off. At first I thought it was the paleness of his skin, but now I saw that they were slowly becoming more translucent, as if they were fading away.

Lir sighed. "Emir and his warlocks are useful, but they are human at the end of the day, and their magic has limitations. I'm afraid our little chat has come to an end. I'll see you again soon. Tell Finn his parents say hello."

Within seconds, Lir completely faded away until no trace of him remained. Mikhail snapped into existence at my side. "There's no one else in the area. He came here by himself."

I stared at the spot where Lir had stood. "Technically, he didn't come here at all. That was a projection."

Mikhail frowned. "He can do that?"

"Not by himself, no. It's a rare ability among the fae," I said, thinking of my encounter with the sidhe who served the Seelie Queen. "The fae can project an illusion of themselves that is quite powerful. They can even cast magic with their projected self. The warlocks helped Lir do this. It doesn't seem to be nearly as powerful as what the fae can do since they managed to hold it for only a few minutes."

"Why did he bother coming at all?" Mikhail asked. "We knew they would figure out where we lived eventually. Why reveal that information to us? He could have waited for us to let our guard down and snatch you or Finn when the opportunity presented itself."

"I have no idea," I said, shaking my head. "We've killed a lot of his soldiers over the past few days if you include the group that attacked us in the fae realm. We know it takes a lot of time and effort to get the fae devourers out of the realm they're exiled in. Maybe he knows he won't have the backup he needs to capture me or Finn anytime soon but wanted me to know he's still around." I let out a long sigh, feeling incredibly tired. "I'm sure he had a reason for coming here, but I don't know what it is. I'll talk to Kalen and Badb about it next time I see them. Lir said he has a history with my family. Maybe they'll know what the hell he's talking about."

I turned back to the apartment, Mikhail at my side. "I really wanted to like the fae," Mikhail said lightly as we walked inside. "Mostly to annoy you because you dislike them so much." I snorted and trudged up the stairs. "But you were right. They're even more devious than the vampires, and dealing with them is goddamn exhausting."

Laughing softly, I glanced over my shoulder at him. "Told you so."

SEVERAL HOURS LATER, I was awoken from my nap by Isabeau prancing through our apartment announcing it was movie time. I groaned into my pillow and hoped that maybe if I didn't come out of my room, she'd take the hint and head back downstairs. Or better yet, she'd focus her attention on Mikhail. A high-pitched giggle ran through my head, and I winced.

I'm going to give the plant all the food in the fridge if you don't come out of your room in the next thirty seconds, she said cheerfully.

Don't you dare, I growled back at her.

That giggle ran through my head in response, followed by her counting down. *Thirty. Twenty-nine. Twenty-eight.*

Fine. I rolled out of bed and walked over to my dresser to find some clothes, pausing when I saw my reflection in the mirror atop my dresser. Even after getting some sleep, I still looked tired, and my expression held a grimness I wouldn't be able to hide. I didn't want to deal with questions tonight; I wouldn't be able to put it off for much longer, but we needed a night with no talk of fae plotting, speculation on what the various bad guys were up to, or what the prophecy about Finn meant long term. We'd earned a night off.

I closed the dresser drawer and took a step back. My shifter magic ran through me, and I changed to my feline form. Shaking out my fur a couple of times, I pawed open my bedroom door and padded into the living room. Isabeau squealed in delight and threw her arms around my neck.

Not so loud, I scolded her and flicked my ears back. She laughed and ran downstairs. I trotted after her. *Come on, vampire.*

Mikhail let out a long-suffering sigh and followed me downstairs. Everyone was gathered in the living room of the downstairs apartment. Magos was lounging in one of the comfy reclining chairs next to the couch, taking in the chaos. Jinx and Luna were perched on the back of the chair. Mikhail sank down in the opposite chair. Apparently, it was an unspoken rule that the vampires got the chairs.

"What are we watching again?" Bryn asked from where she was sitting on the floor in front of the couch.

We'd have to get some furniture for her that would work with the wings, but for now the floor was the best option. I noticed with amusement that she'd chosen to sit where she could lean back against Elisa's legs if she wanted to. This little fact wasn't missed by Damon and Misha, who treated Elisa like their sister. I could tell by the way they kept exchanging glances with each other that they would be teasing the hell out of Elisa about this in the near future.

"We are continuing the dinosaur theme and watching the new Jurassic Park movies," Isabeau announced from where she was currently lying across the three teenage vampires. Isabeau never just sat anywhere. She either lounged on top of other people or would climb up onto the top of the couch and lie across the back. Misha groaned at her announcement. "But the new ones are terrible!"

"Nothing with dinosaurs is terrible!" Isabeau growled.

Elisa started to laugh but quickly cut it off when Isabeau glared at her. She was such a tiny little tyrant. Her eyes narrowed on me, and I remembered that she could probably hear everything I was thinking. *Dinosaurs it is*, I thought. A huge smile spread across her face, and she turned her attention to Finn, who was also sitting on the floor, but closer to Magos. Finn was still getting used to the chaos that was Isabeau and the rest of the vampire brats. Magos was always calm, so Finn naturally gravitated towards him.

"Don't listen to them, Finn. You'll love the movies! Maybe after we watch this, we can get Eddie to shift into his dragon form! Dragons are basically dinosaurs," Isabeau chirped, and I squeezed my eyes shut.

"Isabeau," Elisa warned.

Isabeau just shot her an innocent look and pantomimed

zipping her lips shut. I let out a sigh. Keeping secrets from Isabeau was going to be a whole new level of challenging now that we knew she could not only read minds but seemed to be exceptionally good at it. Pele would probably want to park her on a stool in her bar, I thought with a snort.

Misha hit play, and the thematic music started playing. I looked over to where everyone was sitting, trying to decide where to squeeze in. There wasn't a lot of space with the coffee table in front of the couch and chairs, and I was too big in this form to lie across the back of the couch.

Finn saw my dilemma and the coffee table lifted a few inches off the ground and slid forward and then to the side, out of the way. It gently lowered to the floor. Nobody said anything as they glanced at Finn.

"Let's hope he and Isabeau never team up. Gods know what kind of trouble they'll get up to," Damon muttered.

Isabeau stuck her tongue out at him, and he ruffled her curly hair. I padded over and flopped down on the floor where the coffee table had been, stretching out with my head directly in front of Finn. He reached out and stroked the back of my head a few times, and I leaned back a little more until my head was resting against his legs. I relaxed against him as dinosaurs made their way across the screen.

They do sort of look like dragons, I thought. Isabeau really would be thrilled if Eddie let her ride him in his dragon form. Probably best to wait until Bryn was confident in her flying skills so she could catch the kid if she fell off.

This definitely wasn't the life I thought I'd have, but as I listened to Isabeau lecture everyone about the different types of dinosaurs, the vampire kids teasing her back, and the vampires occasionally adding commentary to keep the argument going, I realized I was happy with where I was. This felt right. I didn't know what the future would bring with me belonging to the Unseelie court and the Unseelie Queen herself. Or how exactly I was supposed to save Finn from his prophesied dark fate. But my circle of friends who were rapidly becoming my family would help me along the way. Some of the tension I'd been carrying eased out of me, and I settled in closer to Finn and let myself enjoy the night.

Epilogue

HE STARED at the painting that hung on his office wall, still processing the information his contact had given him. Piercing green eyes looked back at him from a face he remembered perfectly even though he hadn't seen it in a very long time. He'd painted her portrait a few years after he'd been exiled to this realm. At first, he'd been convinced he'd find a way back to their home realm to rescue her in no time, so he hadn't bothered setting roots anywhere. But soon, it had become clear he wouldn't be finding a way back to his home realm on his own. He'd need help to get back home. Back to her.

"I'm close," he told her. He often talked to the painting as if it was really her. It might make him crazy, but he couldn't help it. Every fiber of his being missed her.

Some days he couldn't bear to talk to anyone. To see anyone that wasn't her. On those days, he'd hole up in this office and tear through every document, map, and artifact he'd found over the years, looking for something maybe he had missed. He never found anything. Nothing he or his contacts had found had turned into anything useful.

Until now.

"It's not exactly what I was hoping for." He ran his fingers through his loose dirty blond hair. "But the information is good, I'm sure of it. I'm going to give Nemain a few days before bringing this information to her. It'll give me some time to get more information together anyway, because pulling this off is going to be complicated, and Nemain's life is already complicated enough. Honestly, I feel bad asking her to do this. I know she will. Not because she swore to help me in exchange for keeping her secret but because she's my friend, and Nemain will do anything to help her friends." He smiled. "And we'll do anything to help her."

He poured himself another shot of whiskey and tossed it back. "I think you'll like her. She can be a bit rough around the edges, but her loyalty is unquestionable. You will definitely like Pele and Elisa." He chuckled. "Pele is always scheming and plotting, and Elisa is observant and calculating. Pele hasn't asked her yet, but I know she's going to ask Elisa if she'd like a job. It'll be good for the young vampire. She needs something to do, and she'll be good as Pele's protégé. You'll like all of them. I promise."

Sleep pulled at him. His body was still tired after shifting to his dragon form for the first time in so long. He rose from where he'd been leaning against the desk and stepped closer to the painting, hand reaching out to delicately trace her jawline.

"I'm coming back for you, my love. Just hold on a little longer."

Want to Read More?

The next book in the series, A Shift in Fortune is out now! Signed paperbacks with character artwork are available on the Greymalkin Press Shop at www.greymalkinpress.com.

Want to Read a Free Short Story?

Curious about how Nemain and Kaysea met? Want to read other short stories set within the Lost Legacies world? Sign-up for the newsletter at <u>maddoxgreyauthor.com</u> to get free short stories and stay informed of upcoming releases and events!

Acknowledgments

Thank you so much for reading *A Shift in Fate*! Nemain's life is going to change pretty drastically after this book. While there are a lot of tropes I'm a fan of, looking at you rivals to lovers, found family will always be my favorite. I'm glad that Nemain has found hers. Now she just has to protect it.

Huge thanks to my editing team, Sara LaPolla and Karen Robinson, and my beta readers! Always a pleasure working with you all and I can't thank you enough for your feedback and suggestions.

To everyone who took a chance on an unknown author and picked up A Shift in Shadows and kept reading, you are absolutely amazing and I hope you enjoy the ride.

This will be a twelve book series, okay thirteen if you count the prequel, so we got a ways to go and some more quirky characters to meet!

Lost Legacies Guide

<u>CHARACTERS:</u>

Andrei - local werewolf, in a casual relationship with Nemain

Bryn - young woman living in fae realm where she was abandoned as a baby, knows Finn and has become protective of him

Cian - feline shifter with necromantic magic; twin brother of Nemain; has a strained relationship with her but still loves her fiercely

Damon - teenage vampire on the run from the Vampire Council

Dante - necromancer, incredibly powerful and in a long-term relationship with Nemain's brother Cian

Eddie - local who owns and runs a shop of magical oddities and supplies, nobody knows what he is

Elisa - oldest of the teenage vampire runaways

Finn - mysterious fae child with powerful magic

Isabeau - child vampire that the teenage vampires take care of and treat as a younger sister

Jinx - a fae cat known as a grimalkin, him and Nemain have been together since she was born; he's grumpy and has the ability to inflict bad luck on others

Kaysea - mermaid princess and bestie of Nemain; Myrna was her twin sister; older brother Connor is very protective of her

Luna - another grimalkin (because the only thing better than one cat is two cats); unlike Jinx she is sweet and cuddly; has no memories of her life prior to a year ago

Magos - old vampire warrior, his past is a bit of a mystery but he's loyal to Nemain and their relationship is similar to that of a an uncle/niece despite not being related

Mikhail - vampire assassin of the Vampire Council; nephew of Magos

Misha - part of the teenage vampire group, looks very similar to Elisa but they don't know for sure if they're actually related, either way they consider each other brother & sister

Myrna - Nemain's mermaid lover who was killed by Sebastian, twin sister of Kaysea and younger sister of Connor

Nemain - feline shifter and fae hybrid with devourer magic; all around freak of nature; raised by Macha and Nevin who she only learned recently were actually her aunt and uncle; biological parents are Badb and Kalen

Pele - daemon who runs the local tavern, The Inferno; close friends with Nemain who she has been in an ongoing casual poly relationship with for centuries

REALMS:

*Note, this is not an extensive list of all the realms because there are many. Only those relevant to the story are mentioned.

Human Realm - the modern world that humans are familiar with; most humans are completely unaware that their realm is one of many or that magical beings walk amongst them

Fae Realms

Mag Ildathach - belongs to the Seelie Court; name means multi-colored plains

Mag Mell - belongs to neither the Seelie or the Unseelie; like all death realms it is difficult to fully comprehend or travel in without necromantic magic; currently where Dante & Cian call home

Tír fo Thuinn - despite being referred to as a realm, this is actually a territory that stretches across all the fae realms, it is the dominion of the sea fae, all the oceans and seas belong to them

Tír na mBeo - only realm shared by the Unseelie & Seelie Queens

Fallen Realms

Kanima - former realm of the feline shifters; this is where Nemain's parents were born; it fell to devourers and the survivors fled to the human realm

Cerulle - former realm of Magos and Mikhail; also fell to devourers; survivors fled to the human realm and were later killed during the vampire and werewolf war

About the Author

After earning a degree in history and political science, Maddox was pulled kicking and screaming from the world of academia and thrust into the tech industry. Because they had bills to pay and nerd muscles to flex.

Whenever possible, they leave reality behind to build fantasy worlds filled with snarky morally grey characters and hot but devious love interests. Maddox currently resides in the northeast, but they'll always consider themselves Californian at heart. They live with their partner and faithful, but often stinky, furry companions.

To get regular email updates about new releases and other announcements, be sure to sign up for the newsletter on maddoxgreyauthor.com

facebook.com/maddoxgrey.author

instagram.com/maddoxgrey.author

tiktok.com/@greymalkinpress

Made in United States
Troutdale, OR
09/23/2024

23057715R00190